REDSHIRTS

REDSHIRTS

····· *John Scalzi*

TOR®

A TOM DOHERTY ASSOCIATES BOOK · NEW YORK

REDSHIRTS

Copyright © 2012 by John Scalzi

Edited by Patrick Nielsen Hayden

A Tor Book
Published by Tom Doherty Associates, LLC
175 Fifth Avenue
New York, NY 10010

www.tor-forge.com

ISBN 978-0-7653-3479-4

First Edition: June 2012
First Trade Paperback Edition: January 2013

Printed in the United States of America

20 19 18 17 16 15 14 13 12 11

Redshirts *is dedicated to the following:*

To Wil Wheaton, whom I heart with all the hearty heartness a heart can heart;

To Mykal Burns, my friend since the TRS-80 days at the Glendora Public Library;

And to Joe Mallozzi and Brad Wright, who took me to space with them.

REDSHIRTS

From the top of the large boulder he sat on, Ensign Tom Davis looked across the expanse of the cave toward Captain Lucius Abernathy, Science Officer Q'eeng and Chief Engineer Paul West perched on a second, larger boulder, and thought, *Well, this sucks.*

"Borgovian Land Worms!" Captain Abernathy said, and smacked his boulder with an open palm. "I should have known."

You should *have known? How the hell could you* not *have known?* thought Ensign Davis, and looked at the vast dirt floor of the cave, its powdery surface moving here and there with the shadowy humps that marked the movement of the massive, carnivorous worms.

"I don't think we should just be waltzing in there," Davis had said to Chen, the other crew member on the away team, upon encountering the cave. Abernathy, Q'eeng and West had already entered, despite the fact that Davis and Chen were technically their security detail.

Chen, who was new, snorted. "Oh, come on," he said. "It's just a cave. What could possibly be in there?"

"Bears?" Davis had suggested. "Wolves? Any number of large predators who see a cave as shelter from the elements? Have you never been camping?"

"There are no bears on this planet," Chen had said, willfully missing Davis' point. "And anyway we have pulse guns. Now come on. This is my first away mission. I don't want the captain wondering where I am." He ran in after the officers.

From his boulder, Davis looked down at the dusty smear on the cave floor that was all that remained of Chen. The land worms, called by the sound of the humans walking in the cave, had tunneled up under him and dragged him down, leaving nothing but echoing screams and the smear.

Well, that's not quite true, Davis thought, peering farther into the cave and seeing the hand that lay there, still clutching the pulse gun Chen had carried, and which as it turned out had done him absolutely no good whatsoever.

The ground stirred and the hand suddenly disappeared.

Okay, now *it's true,* Davis thought.

"Davis!" Captain Abernathy called. "Stay where you are! Any movement across that ground will call to the worms! You'll be eaten instantly!"

Thanks for the useless and obvious update, you jackass, Davis thought, but did not say, because he was an ensign, and Abernathy was the captain. Instead, what he said was, "Aye, Captain."

"Good," Abernathy said. "I don't want you trying to make a break for it and getting caught by those worms. Your father would never forgive me."

What? Davis thought, and suddenly he remembered that Captain Abernathy had served under his father on the *Benjamin Franklin.* The ill-fated *Benjamin Franklin.* And in fact, Davis' father had saved the then-Ensign Abernathy by tossing his unconscious body into the escape pod before diving in himself and launching the pod just as the *Franklin* blew up spectacularly around them. They had drifted in space for three days and had almost run out of breathable air in that pod before they were rescued.

Davis shook his head. It was very odd that all that detail about Abernathy popped into his head, especially considering the circumstances.

As if on cue, Abernathy said, "Your father once saved my life, you know."

"I know—" Davis began, and then nearly toppled off the top of his boulder as the land worms suddenly launched themselves into it, making it wobble.

"Davis!" Abernathy said.

Davis hunched down, flattening himself toward the boulder to keep his center of gravity low. He glanced over to Abernathy, who was now conferring with Q'eeng and West. Without being able to hear them, Davis knew that they were reviewing what they knew about Borgovian Land Worms and trying to devise a plan to neutralize the creatures, so they could cross the cave in safety and reach the chamber that housed the ancient Central Computer of the Borgovians, which could give them a clue about the disappearance of that wise and mysterious race.

You really need to start focusing on your current situation, some part of Davis' brain said to him, and he shook his head again. Davis couldn't disagree with this assessment; his brain had picked a funny time to start spouting a whole bunch of extraneous information that served him no purpose at this time.

The worms rocked his boulder again. Davis gripped it as hard as he could and saw Abernathy, Q'eeng and West become more animated in their attempted problem solving.

A thought suddenly came to Davis. *You're part of the security detail,* it said. *You have a pulse gun. You could just vaporize these things.*

Davis would have smacked his head if the worms weren't already doing that by driving it into the boulder. Of course! The pulse gun! He reached down to his belt to unclasp the gun from its holster. As he did so another part of his brain wondered why, if in fact the solution was as simple as just vaporizing the worms, Captain Abernathy or one of the other officers hadn't just ordered him to do it already.

I seem to have a lot of voices in my brain today, said a third part of Davis' brain. He ignored that particular voice in his brain and aimed at a moving hump of dirt coming toward his boulder.

Abernathy's cry of "Davis! No!" arrived at the exact instant Davis fired, sending a pulsed beam of coherent, disruptive particles into the dirt mound. A screech emanated from the mound, followed by violent thrashing, followed by a sinister rumbling, followed by the ground of the cave erupting as dozens of worms suddenly burst from the dirt.

"The pulse gun is ineffective against Borgovian Land Worms!" Davis heard Science Officer Q'eeng say over the unspeakable noise of the thrashing worms. "The frequency of the pulse sends them into a frenzy. Ensign Davis has just called every worm in the area!"

You couldn't have told me this before I fired? Davis wanted to scream. *You couldn't have said, Oh, by the way, don't fire a pulse gun at a Borgovian Land Worm at our mission briefing? On the ship? At which we discussed landing on Borgovia? Which has fucking land worms?*

Davis didn't scream this at Q'eeng because he knew there was no way Q'eeng would hear him, and besides it was already too late. He'd fired. The worms were in a frenzy. Somebody now was likely to die.

It was likely to be Ensign Davis.

Through the rumble and dust, Davis looked over at Abernathy, who was gazing back at him, concern furrowed into his brow. And then Davis was wondering when, if ever, Abernathy had ever spoken to him before this mission.

Oh, Abernathy must have—he and Davis' father had been tight ever since the destruction of the *Franklin*. They were friends. *Good* friends. It was even likely that Abernathy had known Davis himself as a boy, and may have even pulled a few strings to get his friend's son a choice berth on the *In-*

trepid, the flagship of the Universal Union. The captain wouldn't have been able to spend any real time with Davis—it wouldn't have done for the captain to show favoritism in the ranks—but surely they would have spoken. A few words here and there. Abernathy asking after Davis' father, perhaps. Or on other away missions.

Davis was coming up with a blank.

Suddenly, the rumbling stopped. The worms, as quickly as they had gone into a frenzy, appeared to sidle back under the dirt. The dust settled.

"They're gone!" Davis heard himself say.

"No," Abernathy said. "They're smarter than that."

"I can make it to the mouth of the cave!" Davis heard himself say.

"Stay where you are, Ensign!" Abernathy said. "That's an order!"

But Davis was already off his boulder and running toward the mouth of the cave. Some part of Davis' brain howled at the irrationality of the action, but the rest of Davis didn't care. He knew he *had* to move. It was almost a compulsion. As if he had no choice.

Abernathy screamed "No!" very nearly in slow motion, and Davis covered half of the distance he needed to go. Then the ground erupted as land worms, arrayed in a semicircle, launched themselves up and toward Davis.

And it was then, as he skidded backward, and while his face showed surprise, in fact, that Ensign Davis had an epiphany.

This was the defining moment of his life. The reason he existed. Everything he'd ever done before, everything he'd ever been, said or wanted, had led him to this exact moment, to be skidding backward while Borgovian Land Worms bored through dirt and air to get him. This was his fate. His destiny.

In a flash, and as he gazed upon the needle-sharp teeth spasming in the rather evolutionarily suspect rotating jaw of the land worm, Ensign Tom Davis saw the future. None of this was really about the mysterious disappearance of the Borgovians. After this moment, no one would ever speak of the Borgovians again.

It was about him—or rather, what his impending death would do to his father, now an admiral. Or even more to the point, what his death would do to the relationship between Admiral Davis and Captain Abernathy. Davis saw the scene in which Abernathy told Admiral Davis of his son's death. Saw the shock turn to anger, saw the friendship between the two men dissolve. He saw the scene where the Universal Union MPs placed the captain under arrest for trumped-up charges of murder by negligence, planted by the admiral.

He saw the court-martial and Science Officer Q'eeng, acting as Abernathy's counsel, dramatically breaking down the admiral on the witness stand, getting him to admit this was all about him losing his son. Davis saw his father dramatically reach out and ask forgiveness from the man he had falsely accused and had arrested, and saw Captain Abernathy give it in a heartrending reconciliation right there in the courtroom.

It was a great story. It was great drama.

And it all rested upon him. And this moment. And this fate. This destiny of Ensign Davis.

Ensign Davis thought, *Screw this, I want to live,* and swerved to avoid the land worms.

But then he tripped and one of the land worms ate his face and he died anyway.

From his vantage point next to Q'eeng and West, Captain Lucius Abernathy watched helplessly as Tom Davis fell prey to the land worms. He felt a hand on his shoulder. It was Chief Engineer West.

"I'm sorry, Lucius," he said. "I know he was a friend of yours."

"More than a friend," Abernathy said, choking back grief. "The son of a friend as well. I saw him grow up, Paul. Pulled strings to get him on the *Intrepid*. I promised his father that I would look after him. And I did. Checked in on him from time to time. Never showed favoritism, of course. But kept an eye out."

"The admiral will be heartbroken," Science Officer Q'eeng said. "Ensign Davis was the only child of the admiral and his late wife."

"Yes," Abernathy said. "It will be hard."

"It's not your fault, Lucius," West said. "You didn't tell him to fire his pulse gun. You didn't tell him to run."

"Not my fault," Abernathy agreed. "But my responsibility." He moved to the most distant point on the boulder to be alone.

"Jesus Christ," West muttered to Q'eeng, after the captain had removed himself and they were alone and finally free to speak. "What sort of moron shoots a pulse gun into a cave floor crawling with land worms? And then tries to run across it? He may have been an admiral's son, but he wasn't very smart."

"It's unfortunate indeed," Q'eeng said. "The dangers of the Borgovian Land Worms are well-known. Chen and Davis both should have known better."

"Standards are slipping," West said.

"That may be," Q'eeng said. "Be that as it may, this and other recent missions have seen a sad and remarkable loss of life. Whether they are up to our standards or not, the fact remains: We need more crew."

CHAPTER ONE

Ensign Andrew Dahl looked out the window of Earth Dock, the Universal Union's space station above the planet Earth, and gazed at his next ship.

He gazed at the *Intrepid*.

"Beautiful, isn't she?" said a voice.

Dahl turned to see a young woman, dressed in a starship ensign's uniform, also looking out toward the ship.

"She is," Dahl agreed.

"The Universal Union Capital Ship *Intrepid*," the young woman said. "Built in 2453 at the Mars Dock. Flagship of the Universal Union since 2456. First captain, Genevieve Shan. Lucius Abernathy, captain since 2462."

"Are you the *Intrepid*'s tour guide?" Dahl asked, smiling.

"Are you a tourist?" the young woman asked, smiling back.

"No," Dahl said, and held out his hand. "Andrew Dahl. I've been assigned to the *Intrepid*. I'm just waiting on the 1500 shuttle."

The young woman took his hand. "Maia Duvall," she said. "Also assigned to the *Intrepid*. Also waiting on the 1500 shuttle."

"What a coincidence," Dahl said.

"If you want to call two Dub U Space Fleet members waiting in a Dub U space station for a shuttle to the Dub U spaceship parked right outside the shuttle berth window a coincidence, sure," Duvall said.

"Well, when you put it that way," Dahl said.

"Why are you here so early?" Duvall asked. "It's only now noon. I thought I would be the first one waiting for the shuttle."

"I'm excited," Dahl said. "This will be my first posting." Duvall looked him over, a question in her eyes. "I went to the Academy a few years late," he said.

"Why was that?" Duvall asked.

"It's a long story," Dahl said.

"We have time," Duvall said. "How about we get some lunch and you tell me."

"Uh," Dahl said. "I'm kind of waiting for someone. A friend of mine. Who's also been assigned to the *Intrepid*."

"The food court is right over there," Duvall said, motioning to the bank of stalls across the walkway. "Just send him or her a text. And if he misses it, we can see him from there. Come on. I'll spring for the drinks."

"Oh, well, in *that* case," Dahl said. "If I turned down a free drink, they'd kick me out of Space Fleet."

· · · · ·

"I was promised a long story," Duvall said, after they had gotten their food and drinks.

"I made no such promise," Dahl said.

"The promise was implied," Duvall protested. "And besides, I bought you a drink. I *own* you. Entertain me, Ensign Dahl."

"All right, fine," Dahl said. "I entered the Academy late because for three years I was a seminary student."

"Okay, that's moderately interesting," Duvall said.

"On Forshan," Dahl said

"Okay, that's *intensely* interesting," Duvall said. "So you're a priest of the Forshan religion? Which schism?"

"The leftward schism, and no, not a priest."

"Couldn't handle the celibacy?"

"Leftward priests aren't required to be celibate," Dahl said, "but considering I was the only human at the seminary, I had celibacy thrust upon me, if you will."

"Some people wouldn't have let that stop them," Duvall said.

"You haven't seen a Forshan seminary student up close," Dahl said. "Also, I don't swing xeno."

"Maybe you just haven't found the right xeno," Duvall said.

"I prefer humans," Dahl said. "Call me boring."

"Boring," Duvall said, teasingly.

"And you've just pried into my personal preferences in land speed record time," Dahl said. "If you're this forward with someone you just met, I can only imagine what you're like with people you've known for a long time."

"Oh, I'm not like this with everyone," Duvall said. "But I can tell I like you already. Anyway. Not a priest."

"No. My technical status is 'Foreign Penitent,'" Dahl said. "I was allowed to do the full course of study and perform some rites, but there were some physical requirements I would not have been able to perform for full ordination."

"Like what?" Duvall asked.

"Self-impregnation, for one," Dahl said.

"A small but highly relevant detail," Duvall said.

"And here you were all concerned about celibacy," Dahl said, and swigged from his drink.

"If you were never going to become a priest, why did you go to the seminary?" Duvall asked.

"I found the Forshan religion very restful," Dahl said. "When I was younger that appealed to me. My parents died when I was young and I had a small inheritance, so I took it, paid tutors to learn the language and then traveled to Forshan and found a seminary that would take me. I planned to stay forever."

"But you didn't," Duvall said. "I mean, obviously."

Dahl smiled. "Well. I found the Forshan religion restful. I found the Forshan religious war less so."

"Ah," Duvall said. "But how does one get from Forshan seminary student to Academy graduate?"

"When the Dub U came to mediate between the religious factions on Forshan, they needed an interpreter, and I was on planet," Dahl said. "There aren't a lot of humans who speak more than one dialect of Forshan. I know all four of the major ones."

"Impressive," Duvall said.

"I'm good with my tongue," Dahl said.

"Now who's being forward?" Duvall asked.

"After the Dub U mission failed, it advised that all non-natives leave the planet," Dahl said. "The head Dub U negotiator said that the Space Fleet had need of linguists and scientists and recommended me for a slot at the Academy. By that time my seminary had been burned to the ground and I had nowhere to go, or any money to get there even if I had. The Academy seemed like the best exit strategy. Spent four years there studying xenobiology and linguistics. And here I am."

"That's a good story," Duvall said, and tipped her bottle toward Dahl.

He clinked it with his own. "Thanks," he said. "What about yours?"

"Far less interesting," Duvall said.

"I doubt that," Dahl said.

"No Academy for me," Duvall said. "I enlisted as a grunt for the Dub U peacekeepers. Did that for a couple of years and then transferred over to Space Fleet three years ago. Was on the *Nantes* up until this transfer."

"Promotion?" Dahl said.

Duvall smirked. "Not exactly," she said. "It's best to call it a transfer due to personnel conflicts."

Before Dahl could dig further his phone buzzed. He took it out and read the text on it. "Goof," he said, smiling.

"What is it?" Duvall asked.

"Hold on a second," Dahl said, and turned in his seat to wave at a young man standing in the middle of the station walkway. "We're over here, Jimmy," Dahl said. The young man grinned, waved back and headed over.

"The friend you're waiting on, I presume," Duvall said.

"That would be him," Dahl said. "Jimmy Hanson."

"Jimmy Hanson?" Duvall said. "Not related to James Hanson, CEO and chairman of Hanson Industries, surely."

"James Albert Hanson the Fourth," Dahl said. "His son."

"Must be nice," Duvall said.

"He could buy this space station with his allowance," Dahl said. "But he's not like that."

"What do you mean?" Duvall said.

"Hey, guys," Hanson said, finally making his way to the table. He looked at Duvall, and held out his hand. "Hi, I'm Jimmy."

"Maia," Duvall said, extending her hand. They shook.

"So, you're a friend of Andy's, right?" Hanson said.

"I am," Duvall said. "He and I go way back. All of a half hour."

"Great," Hanson said, and smiled. "He and I go back slightly farther."

"I would hope so," Duvall said.

"I'm going to get myself something to drink," Hanson said. "You guys want anything? Want me to get you another round?"

"I'm fine," Dahl said.

"I could go for another," Duvall said, waggling her nearly empty bottle.

"One of the same?" Hanson asked.

"Sure," Duvall said.

"Great," Hanson said, and clapped his hands together. "So, I'll be right back. Keep this chair for me?"

"You got it," Dahl said. Hanson wandered off in search of food and drink.

"He seems nice," Duvall said.

"He is," Dahl said.

"Not hugely full of personality," Duvall said.

"He has other qualities," Dahl said.

"Like paying for drinks," Duvall said.

"Well, yes, but that's not what I was thinking of," Dahl said.

"You mind if I ask you a personal question?" Duvall said.

"Seeing as we've already covered my sexual preferences in this conversation, no," Dahl said.

"Were you friends with Jimmy before you knew his dad could buy an entire planet or two?" Duvall asked.

Dahl paused a moment before answering. "Do you know how the rich are different than you or me?" he asked Duvall.

"You mean, besides having more money," Duvall said.

"Yeah," Dahl said.

"No," Duvall said.

"What makes them different—the smart ones, anyway—is that they have a very good sense of why people want to be near them. Whether it's because they want to be friends, which is not about proximity to money and access and power, or if they want to be part of an entourage, which is. Make sense?"

"Sure," Duvall said.

"Okay," Dahl said. "So, here's the thing. When Jimmy was young, he figured out that his father was one of the richest men in the Dub U. Then he figured out that one day, he would be too. Then he figured out that there were a lot of other people who would try to use the first two things to their own advantage. Then he figured out how to avoid those people."

"Got it," Duvall said. "Jimmy would know if you were just being nice to him because of who his daddy was."

"It was really interesting watching him our first few weeks at the Academy," Dahl said. "Some of the cadets—and some of our instructors—tried to make themselves his friend. I think they were surprised how quickly this rich kid had their number. He's had enough time to be extraordinarily good at reading people. He has to be."

"So how did you approach him?" Duvall said.

"I didn't," Dahl said. "He came over and started talking to me. I think he realized I didn't care who his dad was."

"Everybody loves you," Duvall said.

"Well, that, and I was getting an A in the biology course he was having trouble with," Dahl said. "Just because Jimmy's picky about his companions doesn't mean he's not self-interested."

"He seemed to be willing to consider me a friend," Duvall said.

"That's because he thinks we're friends, and he trusts my judgment," Dahl said.

"And are we?" Duvall said. "Friends, I mean."

"You're a little more hyper than I normally like," Dahl said.

"Yeah, I get that 'I like things restful' vibe from you," Duvall said.

"I take it you don't do restful," Dahl said.

"I sleep from time to time," Duvall said. "Otherwise, no."

"I suppose I'll have to adjust," Dahl said.

"I suppose you will," Duvall said.

"I have drinks," Hanson said, coming up behind Duvall.

"Why, Jimmy," Duvall said. "That makes you my new favorite person."

"Excellent," Hanson said, offered Duvall her drink, and sat down at the table. "So, what are we talking about?"

· · · · ·

Just before the shuttle arrived, two more people arrived at the waiting area. More accurately, five people arrived: two crewmen, accompanied by three members of the military police. Duvall nudged Dahl and Hanson, who looked over. One of the crewmen noticed and cocked an eyebrow. "Yes, I have an entourage," he said.

Duvall ignored him and addressed one of the MPs. "What's his story?"

The MP motioned to the one with a cocked eyebrow. "Various charges for this one, including smuggling, selling contraband and assaulting a superior officer." She then motioned to the other crewman, who was standing there sullenly, avoiding eye contact with everyone else. "That poor bastard is this one's friend. He's tainted by association."

"The assault charge is trumped up," said the first ensign. "The XO was high as a kite."

"On drugs *you* gave him," said the second crewman, still not looking at anyone else.

"No one can prove I gave them to him, and anyway they weren't drugs," said the first. "They were an offworld fungus. And it couldn't have been that. The fungus relaxes people, not makes them attack anyone in the room, requiring them to defend themselves."

"You gave him Xeno-pseudoagaricus, didn't you," Dahl said.

The first crewman looked at Dahl. "As I already said, no one can prove I gave the XO anything," he said. "And maybe."

"Xeno-pseudoagaricus naturally produces a chemical that

in most humans provides a relaxing effect," Dahl said. "But in about one-tenth of one percent of people, it does the opposite. The receptors in their brains are slightly different from everyone else's. And of those people, about one-tenth of one percent will go berserk under its influence. Sounds like your XO is one of those people."

"Who are you, who is so wise in the way of alien fungus?" said the crewman.

"Someone who knows that no matter what, you don't deal upward on the chain of command," Dahl said. The crewman grinned.

"So why aren't you in the brig?" Duvall asked.

The crewman motioned to Dahl. "Ask your friend, he's so smart," he said. Duvall looked to Dahl, who shrugged.

"Xeno-pseudoagaricus isn't illegal," Dahl said. "It's just not very smart to use it. You'd have to either study xenobiology or have an interest in off-brand not-technically-illegal alien mood enhancers, possibly for entrepreneurial purposes."

"Ah," Duvall said.

"If I had to guess," Dahl said, "I'm guessing our friend here—"

"Finn," said the crewman, and nodded to the other one. "And that's Hester."

"—our friend Finn had a reputation at his last posting for being the guy to go to for substances that would let you pass a urine test."

Hester snorted at this.

"I'm also guessing that his XO probably doesn't want it known that he was taking drugs—"

"Fungus," said Finn.

"—of any sort, and that in any event when the Xeno-pseudoagaricus made him go nuts, he attacked and Finn here was technically defending himself when he fought back. So rather than put Finn in the brig and open up an ugly can of worms, better to transfer him quietly."

"I can neither confirm nor deny this interpretation of events," Finn said.

"Then what's with the MPs?" Hanson asked.

"They're here to make sure we get on the *Intrepid* without any detours," said Hester. "They don't want him renewing his stash." Finn rolled his eyes at this.

Duvall looked at Hester. "I'm sensing bitterness here."

Hester finally made eye contact. "The bastard hid his stash in my foot locker," he said, to Duvall.

"And you didn't know?" Duvall asked.

"He told me they were candies, and that if the other crew knew he had them, they'd sneak into his foot locker to take them."

"They would have," Finn said. "And in my defense, every-thing *was* candied."

"You also said they were for your mother," Hester said.

"Yes, well," Finn said. "I *did* lie about that part."

"I tried to tell that to the captain and the XO, but they didn't care," Hester said. "As far as they were concerned I was an accomplice. I don't even *like* him."

"Then why did you agree to hold his . . . candies?" Duvall said. Hester mumbled something inaudible and broke eye contact.

"He did it because I was being nice to him, and he doesn't have friends," Finn said.

"So you took advantage of him," Hanson said.

"I don't *dislike* him," Finn said. "And it's not like I meant for him to get in trouble. He *shouldn't* have gotten in trouble. Nothing in the stash was illegal. But then our XO went nuts and tried to rearrange my bone structure."

"You probably should have known your product line better," Dahl said.

"The next time I get something, I'll run it by you first," Finn said sarcastically, and then motioned toward the window, where the shuttle could be seen approaching the berth. "But it's going to have to wait. Looks like our ride is here."

CHAPTER TWO

The *Intrepid*'s four other new crew members were met on the ship by a petty officer named Del Sol, who quickly marched them off to their stations. Dahl was met by the *Intrepid*'s chief science officer, Q'eeng.

"Sir," Dahl said, saluting.

Q'eeng returned the salute. "Ensign Junior Rank Dahl," he said. "A pleasure to meet you. I do not always greet my department's new arrivals in this manner, but I have just come off duty and I thought I would show you your station. Do you have any personal items you need to stow?"

"No, sir," Dahl said. His and the others' foot lockers were going through ship's security for inspection and would be delivered to their quarters, the locations of which would be uploaded to their phones.

"I understand you spent several years on Forshan, and that you speak the language," Q'eeng said. "All four dialects."

"Yes, sir," Dahl said.

"I studied it briefly at the Academy," Q'eeng said, and then cleared his throat. *"Aaachka faaachklalhach ghalall chkalalal."*

Dahl kept his face very still. Q'eeng had just attempted in the third dialect the traditional rightward schism greeting of "I offer you the bread of life," but his phrasing and accent had transmuted the statement into "Let us violate cakes together." Leaving aside the fact it would be highly unusual for a member of the rightward schism to voluntarily speak the third dialect, it being the native dialect of the founder of the leftward schism and therefore traditionally eschewed, mutual cake violating was not an accepted practice anywhere on Forshan.

"Aaachkla faaachklalhalu faadalalu chkalalal," Dahl sad, returning the correct traditional response of "I break the bread of life with you" in the third dialect.

"Did I say that correctly?" Q'eeng asked.

"Your accent is very unusual, sir," Dahl said.

"Indeed," Q'eeng said. "Then perhaps I will leave any necessary Forshan speaking to you."

"Yes, sir," Dahl said.

"Follow me, Ensign," Q'eeng said, and strode forward. Dahl raced to keep up.

Around Q'eeng the *Intrepid* was a hive of activity; crew members and officers moved purposefully through the halls, each appearing to have someplace very important to get to. Q'eeng strode through them as if he had his own bow wave; they would magically part for him as he came close and close behind him as he walked past.

"It's like rush hour in here," Dahl said, looking around.

"You'll find this crew to be quite efficient and effective," Q'eeng said. "As the flagship of the Universal Union, the *Intrepid* has its pick of crew."

"I don't doubt that, sir," Dahl said, and looked briefly behind him. The crew members behind him had slowed down considerably and were staring at him and Q'eeng. Dahl couldn't read their expressions.

"I understand you requested at the Academy to be stationed on the *Intrepid*," Q'eeng said.

"Yes, sir," Dahl said, returning his attention to his superior officer. "Your department is doing some real cutting-edge work. Some of the stuff you do on board is so out there we had a hard time re-creating it back at the Academy."

"I hope that's not a suggestion that we're doing sloppy work," Q'eeng said, with a slight, tense edge to his voice.

"Not at all, sir," Dahl said. "Your reputation as a scientist is unimpeachable. And we know that in the kind of work your department does, initial conditions are both significant and difficult to re-create."

Q'eeng seemed to relax at this. "Space is vast," he said. "The *Intrepid*'s mission is to explore. Much of the science we do is front line—identify, describe, posit initial hypotheses. Then we move on, leaving it to others to follow our work."

"Yes, sir," Dahl said. "It's that front line science that appeals to me. The exploration."

"So," Q'eeng said. "Do you see yourself participating in away team missions?"

Directly in front of them, a crew member seemed to stumble over his own feet. Dahl caught him. "Whoa," Dahl said, propping him back up. "Careful with those feet, now." The crew member pulled away, his mumbled "Thanks" very nearly dopplered as he hastened off.

"Agile *and* polite," Dahl said, grinning, then stopped grinning when he noticed Q'eeng, also stopped, staring at him very intently. "Sir," he said.

"Away teams," Q'eeng said again. "Do you see yourself participating in them?"

"At the Academy I was known more as a lab rat," Dahl said. Q'eeng seemed to frown at this. "But I realize that the *Intrepid* is a vessel of exploration. I'm looking forward to doing some of that exploration myself."

"Very good," Q'eeng said, and started moving forward again. "Being a 'lab rat' is fine at the Academy and may be fine on other ships. But the reason that the *Intrepid* has made so many of the discoveries that interested you in the first place is because of its crew's willingness to get into the field and get its hands dirty. I'd ask you to keep that in mind."

"Yes, sir," Dahl said.

"Good," Q'eeng said, and stopped at a door marked "Xenobiology." He opened it, showing the laboratory beyond, and stepped through. Dahl followed.

It was empty.

"Where is everybody, sir?" Dahl asked.

"The *Intrepid* crew does a lot of cross-consultation with crew members in other departments, and often have secondary or supernumerary postings," Q'eeng said. "You are supernumerary with the Linguistics Department for your facility in Forshan, for example. So people don't always stay chained to their workstations."

"Got it, sir," Dahl said.

"Nevertheless," Q'eeng said, pulled out his phone, and made a connection. "Lieutenant Collins. The newest member of your department is at your laboratory to present himself to you." A pause. "Good. That is all." Q'eeng put away his phone. "Lieutenant Collins will be along presently to welcome you."

"Thank you, sir," Dahl said, and saluted. Q'eeng nodded, saluted in return and walked off into the hallway. Dahl went to the door and watched him go. Q'eeng's bow wave preceded him until he turned a corner and went out of sight.

· · · · ·

"Hey," someone said behind Dahl. He turned. There was a crew member standing in the middle of the lab.

Dahl looked back out the door, to where Q'eeng had turned, and then back to the new crew member. "Hi," Dahl said. "You weren't here two seconds ago."

"Yeah, we do that," the crew member said, and walked over to Dahl and stretched out his hand. "Jake Cassaway."

"Andy Dahl." Dahl took his hand and shook it. "And how exactly *do* you do that?"

"Trade secret," Cassaway said.

A door opened from the other side of the lab and another crew member entered the room from it.

"There goes the trade secret," Cassaway said.

"What's in there?" Dahl asked, motioning to the door.

"It's a storage room," Cassaway said.

"You were hiding in the storage room?" Dahl said.

"We weren't hiding," said the other crew member. "We were doing inventory."

"Andy Dahl, this is Fiona Mbeke," Cassaway said.

"Hello," Dahl said.

"You should be glad that we were doing inventory," Mbeke said. "Because now that means that it won't be assigned to you as the new guy."

"Well, then, thanks," Dahl said.

"We'll still make you get coffee," Mbeke said.

"I would expect nothing less," Dahl said.

"And look, here is the rest of us," Cassaway said, and nodded as two new people came through the hallway door.

One of them immediately approached Dahl. He saw the lieutenant's pip on her shoulder and saluted.

"Relax," Collins said, and nevertheless returned the salute. "The only time we salute around here is when His Majesty comes through the door."

"You mean Commander Q'eeng," Dahl said.

"You see the pun there," Collins said. "With 'king,' which is what his name sounds like."

"Yes, ma'am," Dahl said.

"That's a little nerd humor for you," Collins said.

"I got it, ma'am," Dahl said, smiling.

"Good," Collins said. "Because the last thing we need is another humorless prick around here. You met Cassaway and Mbeke, I see."

"Yes, ma'am," Dahl said.

"You've figured out that I'm your boss," she said, then motioned to the other crew member. "And this is Ben Trin, who is second in command of the lab." Trin came forward to shake Dahl's hand. Dahl shook it. "And that's all of us."

"Except for Jenkins," Mbeke said.

"Well, he won't see Jenkins," Collins said.

"He might," Mbeke said.

"When was the last time you saw Jenkins?" Trin said to Mbeke.

"I thought I saw him once, but it turned out to be a yeti," Cassaway said.

"Enough about Jenkins," Collins said.

"Who's Jenkins?" Dahl asked.

"He's doing an independent project," Collins said. "Very intensive. Forget it, you'll never see him. Now . . ." She reached over to one of the tables in the lab, grabbed a tablet and fired it up. "You come to us with some very nice scores from the Academy, Mr. Dahl."

"Thank you, ma'am," Dahl said.

"Is Flaviu Antonescu still heading up the Xenobiology Department?" Collins asked.

"Yes, ma'am," Dahl said.

"Please stop appending 'ma'am' to every sentence, Dahl, it sounds like you have a vocal tic."

Dahl smiled again. "All right," he said.

Collins nodded and looked back at the tablet. "I'm surprised Flaviu recommended you for the *Intrepid*."

"He refused at first," Dahl said, remembering the discussion with his Academy department head. "He wanted me to take a post at a research facility on Europa."

"Why didn't you take it?" Collins asked.

"I wanted to see the universe, not be down a sixty-kilometer ice tunnel, looking at Europan microbes."

"You have something against Europan microbes?" Collins asked.

"I'm sure they're very nice as microbes go," Dahl said. "They deserve someone who really wants to study them."

"You must have been pretty insistent to get Flaviu to change his mind," Collins said.

"My scores were high enough to get Commander Q'eeng's attention," Dahl said. "And as luck would have it, a position opened up here."

"It wasn't luck," Mbeke said.

"It was a Longranian Ice Shark," Cassaway said.

"Which is the opposite of luck," Mbeke said.

"A what?" Dahl asked.

"The crew member you're replacing was Sid Black," Trin said. "He was part of an away team to Longran Seven, which is an ice planet. While exploring an abandoned ice city, the away team was attacked by ice sharks. They carried Sid off. He wasn't seen again."

"His leg was," Mbeke said. "The lower half, anyway."

"Quiet, Fiona," Collins said, irritated. She set down the tablet and looked back at Dahl. "You met Commander Q'eeng," she said.

"I did," Dahl said.

"Did he talk to you about away missions?" Collins asked.

"Yes," Dahl said. "He asked me if I was interested in them."

"What did you say?" Collins asked.

"I said I usually did lab work but I assumed I would participate on away missions as well," Dahl said. "Why?"

"He's on Q'eeng's radar now," Trin said to Collins.

Dahl looked at Trin and back at Collins. "Is there something I'm missing here, ma'am?" he asked.

"No," Collins said, and glanced over at Trin. "I just prefer to have the option to indoctrinate my crew before Q'eeng gets his hands on them. That's all."

"Is there some philosophical disagreement there?" Dahl asked.

"It's not important," Collins said. "Don't worry yourself about it. Now," she said. "First things first." She pointed over to the corner. "You get that workstation. Ben will issue you a work tablet and give you your orientation, and Jake and Fiona will catch you up on anything else you want to know. All you have to do is ask. Also, as the new guy you're on coffee duty."

"I was already told about that," Dahl said.

"Good," Collins said. "Because I could use a cup right about now. Ben, get him set up."

· · · · ·

"So, did you guys get asked about away teams?" Duvall asked, as she brought her mess tray to the table where Dahl and Hanson were already sitting.

"I did," Hanson said.

"So did I," Dahl said.

"Is it just me, or does everyone on this ship seem a little weird about them?" Duvall asked.

"Give me an example," Dahl said.

"I mean that within five minutes of getting to my new post I heard three different stories of crew buying the farm on an away mission. Death by falling rock. Death by toxic atmosphere. Death by pulse gun vaporization."

"Death by shuttle door malfunction," Hanson said.

"Death by ice shark," Dahl said.

"Death by *what*?" Duvall said, blinking. "What the hell is an ice shark?"

"You got me," Dahl said. "I had no idea there was such a thing."

"Is it a shark *made* of ice?" Hanson asked. "Or a shark that *lives* in ice?"

"It wasn't specified at the time," Dahl said, spearing a meat bit on his tray.

"I'm thinking you should have called bullshit on the ice shark story," Duvall said.

"Even if the details are sketchy, it fits your larger point," Dahl said. "People here have away missions on the brain."

"It's because someone always dies on them," Hanson said.

Duvall arched an eyebrow at this. "What makes you say that, Jimmy?"

"Well, we're all replacing former crew members," Hanson said, and then pointed at Duvall. "What happened to the one you replaced. Transferred out?"

"No," Duvall said. "He was the death by vaporization one."

"And mine got sucked out of the shuttle," Hanson said. "And Andy's got eaten by a shark. Maybe. You have to admit there's something going on there. I bet if we tracked down Finn and Hester, they'd tell us the same thing."

"Speaking of which," Dahl said, and motioned with his fork. Hanson and Duvall looked to where he pointed to see Hester standing by the end of the mess line, tray in hand, staring glumly around the mess hall.

"He's not the world's most cheerful person, is he," Duvall said.

"Oh, he's all right," Hanson said, and then called to Hester. Hester jumped slightly at his name, seemed to consider whether he should join the three of them, and then appeared to resign himself to it, walked over and sat down. He began to pick at his food.

"So," Duvall finally said, to Hester. "How's your day?"

Hester shrugged and picked at his food some more, then finally grimaced and set down his fork. He looked around the table.

"What is it?" Duvall asked.

"Is it just me," Hester said, "or is everyone on this ship *monumentally fucked up* about away missions?"

CHAPTER THREE

D ahl was at his workstation, classifying Theta Orionis XII spores, when Ben Trin's work tablet pinged. Trin glanced at it, said "I'm going to get some coffee," and headed out the door.

What's wrong with my *coffee?* Dahl wondered, as he went back to his work. In the week since his arrival on the *Intrepid,* Dahl had, as promised, been tasked with the role of coffee boy. This consisted of keeping the coffee pot in the storage room topped off and getting coffee for his lab mates whenever they rattled their mugs. They weren't obnoxious about it—they got their own coffee more often than not—but they enjoyed exercising their coffee boy privileges from time to time.

This reminded Dahl that he needed to check on the status of the coffee pot. Cassaway had been the last one to get a cup; Dahl looked up to ask him if it was time for him to start another pot.

He was alone in the lab.

"What the hell?" Dahl said, to himself.

The outside door to the lab slid open and Q'eeng and Captain Abernathy stepped through.

Dahl stood and saluted. "Captain, Commander," he said.

Q'eeng looked around the laboratory. "Where are your crewmates, Ensign Dahl?" he said.

"Errands," Dahl said, after a second.

"He'll do," Abernathy said, and strode forward purposefully toward Dahl. He held a small vial. "Do you know what this is?" he said.

A small vial, Dahl thought, but did not say. "A xenobiological sample," he said instead.

"Very good," Abernathy said, and handed it to him. "As you know, Ensign, we are currently above the planet Merovia, a planet rich with artistic wonders but whose people are superstitiously opposed to medical practices of any sort." He paused, as if waiting for acknowledgment.

"Of course, sir," Dahl said, giving what he hoped was the expected prompt.

"Unfortunately, they are also in the throes of a global plague, which is decimating their population," Q'eeng said. "The Universal Union is concerned that the damage caused by the plague will collapse their entire civilization, throwing the planet into a new dark age from which it will never recover."

"The government of Merovia has refused all Universal Union medical help," Abernathy said. "So the *Intrepid* was secretly assigned to collect samples of the plague and engineer a counter-bacterial which we could release into the wild, burning out the plague."

Counter-bacterial? Dahl thought. *Don't they mean a vaccine?* But before he could ask for clarification, Q'eeng was speaking again.

"We sent a covert two-man away team to collect samples, but in doing so they became infected themselves," Q'eeng said. "The Merovian Plague has already claimed the life of Ensign Lee."

"Damn plague liquefied the flesh right off her bones," Abernathy said, grimly.

"The other *Intrepid* crew member infected is Lieutenant Kerensky," Q'eeng said. At this, both Abernathy and Q'eeng looked at Dahl intensely, as if to stress the sheer, abject horror of this Lieutenant Kerensky being infected.

"Oh, no," Dahl ventured. "Not Kerensky."

Abernathy nodded. "So you understand the importance of that little vial you have in your hands," he said. "Use it to find the counter-bacterial. If you can do it, you'll save Kerensky."

"And the Merovians," Dahl said.

"Yes, them too," Abernathy said. "You have six hours."

Dahl blinked. "Six hours?"

Abernathy angered at this. "Is there a problem, mister?" he asked.

"It's not a lot of time," Dahl said.

"Damn it, man!" Abernathy said. "This is *Kerensky* we're talking about! If God could make the universe in six days, surely you can make a counter-bacterial in six hours."

"I'll try, sir," Dahl said.

"Try's not good enough," Abernathy said, and clapped Dahl hard on the shoulder. "I need to hear you say that you'll *do* it." He shook Dahl's shoulder vigorously.

"I'll do it," Dahl said.

"Thank you, Ensign Dill," Abernathy said.

"Dahl, sir," Dahl said.

"Dahl," Abernathy said, and then turned to Q'eeng, turning his attention away from Dahl so completely it was as if a switch had been thrown. "Come on, Q'eeng. We need to make a hyperwave call to Admiral Drezner. We're cutting things close here." Abernathy strode out into the hallway, purposefully. Q'eeng followed, nodding to Dahl absentmindedly as he followed the captain.

Dahl stood there for a moment, vial in his hand.

"I'm going to say it again," he said, again to himself. "What the hell?"

· · · · ·

The storage room door opened; Cassaway and Mbeke came out of it. "What did they want?" Cassaway asked.

"Checking inventory again?" Dahl asked, mockingly.

"We don't tell you how to do your job," Mbeke said.

"So what did they want?" Collins asked, as she briskly walked through the outside door, Trin following, cup of coffee in hand.

Dahl thought hard about yelling at all of them, then stopped and refocused. He held up the vial. "I'm supposed to find a counter-bacterial for this."

"Counter-bacterial?" Trin asked. "Don't you mean a vaccine?"

"I'm telling you what they told me," Dahl said. "And they gave me six hours."

"Six hours," Trin said, looking at Collins.

"Right," Dahl said. "Which, even if I knew what a 'counter-bacterial' was, is no time at all. It takes weeks to make a vaccine."

"Dahl, tell me," Collins said. "When Q'eeng and Abernathy were here, how were they talking to you?"

"What do you mean?" Dahl asked.

"Did they come in and quickly tell you what you needed?" Collins said. "Or did they go on and on about a bunch of crap you didn't need to know?"

"They went on a bit, yes," Dahl said.

"Was the captain particularly dramatic?" Cassaway asked.

"What is 'particularly dramatic' in this context?" Dahl asked.

"Like this," Mbeke said, and then grabbed both of Dahl's shoulders and shook them. "'Damn it, man! There is no *try*! Only *do*!'"

Dahl set down the vial so it was not accidentally shaken

out of his grip. "He said pretty much exactly those words," he said to Mbeke.

"Well, they're some of his favorite words," Mbeke said, letting go.

"I'm not understanding what any of this means," Dahl said, looking at his lab mates.

"One more question," Collins said, ignoring Dahl's complaint. "When they told you that you had to find this counterbacterial in six hours, did they give you a reason why?"

"Yes," Dahl said. "They said that was the amount of time they had to save a lieutenant."

"Which lieutenant?" Collins said.

"Why does it matter?" Dahl asked.

"Answer the question, Ensign," Collins said, uttering Dahl's rank for the first time in a week.

"A lieutenant named Kerensky," Dahl said.

There was a pause at the name.

"*That* poor bastard," Mbeke said. "He always gets screwed, doesn't he."

Cassaway snorted. "He gets *better,*" he said, and then looked over to Dahl. "Somebody else died, right?"

"An ensign named Lee was liquefied," Dahl said.

"See," Cassaway said, to Mbeke.

"Someone really needs to tell me what's going on," Dahl said.

"Time to break out the Box," Trin said, sipping his coffee again.

"Right," Collins said, and nodded to Cassaway. "Go get it, Jake." Cassaway rolled his eyes and went to the storage room.

"At least someone tell me who Lieutenant Kerensky is," Dahl said.

"He's part of the bridge crew," Trin said. "Technically, he's an astrogator."

"The captain and Q'eeng said he was part of an away team, collecting biological samples," Dahl said.

"I'm sure he was," Trin said.

"Why would they send an astrogator for that?" Dahl said.

"Now you know why I said 'technically,'" Trin said, and took another sip.

The storage room door slid open and Cassaway emerged with a small, boxy appliance in his hands. He walked it over to the closest free induction pad. The thing powered on.

"What is that?" Dahl asked.

"It's the Box," Cassaway said.

"Does it have a formal name?" Dahl asked.

"Probably," Cassaway said.

Dahl walked over and examined it, opening it and looking inside. "It looks like a microwave oven," he said.

"It's not," Collins said, taking the vial and bringing it to Dahl.

"What is it, then?" Dahl asked, looking at Collins.

"It's the Box," Collins said.

"That's it? 'The Box'?" Dahl said.

"If it makes you feel better to think it's an experimental quantum-based computer with advanced inductive artificial intelligence capacity, whose design comes to us from an advanced but extinct race of warrior-engineers, then you can think about it that way," Collins said.

"Is that actually what it is?" Dahl asked.

"Sure," Collins said, and handed the vial to Dahl. "Put this in the Box."

Dahl looked at the vial and took it. "Don't you want me to prepare the sample?" he asked.

"Normally, yes," Collins said. "But this is the Box, so you can just put it in there."

Dahl inserted the vial into the Box, placing it in the center of the ceramic disk at the bottom of the inside space. He closed the Box door and looked at the outside instrument panel, which featured three buttons, one green, one red, one white.

"The green button starts it," Collins said. "The red button stops it. The white button opens the door."

"It should be a little more complicated than that," Dahl said.

"Normally it is," Collins agreed. "But this is—"

"This is the Box," Dahl said. "I get that part."

"Then start it," Collins said.

Dahl pressed the green button. The Box sprang to life, making a humming sound. On the inside a light came on. Dahl peered inside to see the vial turning as the disk he placed it on was rotated by a carousel.

"You have got to be kidding me," Dahl said, to himself. He looked up at Collins again. "Now what?"

"You said Abernathy and Q'eeng said you had six hours," Collins said.

"Right," Dahl said.

"So in about five and a half hours the Box will let you know it has a solution," Collins said.

"How will it tell me that?" Dahl asked.

"It'll go *ding*," Collins said, and walked off.

· · · · ·

Roughly five and a half hours later there was a small, quiet *ding*, the humming sound emanating from the Box's carousel engine stopped and the light went off.

"Now what?" Dahl said, staring at the Box, to no one in particular.

"Check your work tablet," Trin said, not looking up from

his own work. He was the only one besides Dahl still in the lab.

Dahl grabbed his work tablet and powered up the screen. On it was a rotating picture of a complex organic molecule and beside that, a long scrolling column of data. Dahl tried to read it.

"It's giving me gibberish," he said, after a minute. "Long streaming columns of it."

"You're fine," Trin said. He set down his own work and walked over to Dahl. "Now, listen closely. Here's what you do next. First, you're going to take your work tablet to the bridge, where Q'eeng is."

"Why?" Dahl said. "I could just mail the data to him."

Trin shook his head. "It's not how this works."

"Wh—" Dahl began, but Trin held up his hand.

"Shut up for a minute and just listen, okay?" Trin said. "I know it doesn't make sense, and it's stupid, but this is the way it's got to be done. Take your tablet to Q'eeng. Show him the data on it. And then once he's looking at it, you say, 'We got most of it, but the protein coat is giving us a problem.' Then point to whatever data is scrolling by at the time."

" 'Protein coat'?" Dahl said.

"It doesn't have to be the protein coat," Trin said. "You can say whatever you like. Enzyme transcription errors. RNA replication is buggy. I personally go with protein coat because it's easy to say. The point is, you need to say everything is almost perfect but one thing still needs to be done. And that's when you gesture toward the data."

"What'll that do?" Dahl asked.

"It will give Q'eeng an excuse to furrow his brow, stare at the data for a minute and then tell you that you've overlooked some basic thing, which he will solve," Trin said. "At which point you have the option of saying something like 'Of course!' or 'Amazing!' or, if you really want to kiss his ass, 'We never would have solved that in a million years, Commander Q'eeng.' He likes that. He won't acknowledge that he likes it. But he likes it."

Dahl opened his mouth, but Trin held up his hand again. "Or you can do what the rest of us do, which is to get the hell off the bridge as soon as you possibly can," Trin said. "Give him the data, point out the one error, let him solve it, get your tablet back and get out of there. Don't call attention to yourself. Don't say or do anything clever. Show up, do your job, *get out of there*. It's the smartest thing you can do." Trin walked back over to his work.

"None of this makes the slightest bit of sense," Dahl said.

"No, it doesn't," Trin agreed. "I already told you it didn't."

"Are any of you going to bother to explain any of this to me?" Dahl asked.

"Maybe someday," Trin said, sitting down at his workstation. "But not right now. Right now, you have to race to get that data to the bridge and to Q'eeng. Your six hours is just about up. Hurry."

· · · · ·

Dahl burst out of the Xenobiology Laboratory door and immediately collided with someone else, falling to the ground and dropping his tablet. He picked himself up and looked around for his tablet. It was being held by the person with whom he collided, Finn.

"No one should ever be in that much of a rush," Finn said.

Dahl snatched back the tablet. "You don't have someone

about to liquefy if you don't get to the bridge in ten minutes," Dahl said, heading in the direction of the bridge.

"That's very dramatic," Finn said, matching Dahl's pace.

"Don't you have somewhere to be?" Dahl asked him.

"I do," Finn said. "The bridge. I'm delivering a manifest for my boss to Captain Abernathy."

"Doesn't anyone just send messages on this ship?" Dahl asked.

"Here on the *Intrepid,* they like the personal touch," Finn said.

"Do you think that's really it?" Dahl asked. He weaved past a clot of crewmen.

"Why do you ask?" Finn said.

Dahl shrugged. "It's not important," he said.

"I like this ship," Finn said. "This is my sixth posting. Every other ship I've been on the officers had a stick up their ass about procedure and protocol. This one is so relaxed it's like being on a cruise ship. Hell, my boss ducks the captain at every possible opportunity."

Dahl stopped suddenly, forcing Finn to sway to avoid colliding with him a second time. "He ducks the captain," he said.

"It's like he's psychic about it," Finn said. "One second, he's there telling a story about a night with a Gordusian ambisexual, and the next he's off getting coffee. As soon as he steps out of the room, there's the captain."

"You're serious about this," Dahl said.

"Why do you think I'm the one delivering messages?" Finn said.

Dahl shook his head and started off again. Finn followed.

The bridge was sleek and well-appointed and reminded Dahl of the lobby of some of the nicer skyscrapers he had been to.

"Ensign Dahl," Chief Science Officer Q'eeng said, spotting him from his workstation. "I see you like cutting it close with your assignments."

"We worked as fast as we could," Dahl said. He walked over to Q'eeng and presented the tablet with the scrolling data and the rotating molecule. Q'eeng took it and studied it silently. After a minute, he looked up at Dahl and cleared his throat.

"Sorry, sir," Dahl said, remembering his line. "We got ninety-nine percent there, but then we had a problem. With, uh, the protein coat." After a second he pointed to the screen, at the gibberish flying by.

"It's always the protein coat with your lab, isn't it," Q'eeng murmured, perusing the screen again.

"Yes, sir," Dahl said.

"Next time, remember to more closely examine the relationship between the peptide bonds," Q'eeng said, and punched his fingers at the tablet. "You'll find the solution to your problem is staring you right in the face." He turned the tablet toward Dahl. The rotating molecule had stopped rotating and several of its bonds were now highlighted in blinking red. Nothing had otherwise changed with the molecule.

"That's amazing, sir," Dahl said. "I don't know how we missed it."

"Yes, well," Q'eeng said, and then tapped at the screen again. The data flew off Dahl's tablet and onto Q'eeng's workstation. "Fortunately we may have just enough time to get this improved solution to the matter synthesizer to save Kerensky." Q'eeng jabbed the tablet back at Dahl. "Thank you, Ensign, that will be all."

Dahl opened his mouth, intending to say something more. Q'eeng looked up at him, quizzically. Then the image of Trin popped into Dahl's brain.

Show up, do your job, get out of there. It's the smartest thing you can do.

So Dahl nodded and got out of there.

Finn caught up with him outside the bridge a moment later. "Well, that was a complete waste of my time," Finn said. "I like that."

"There's something seriously wrong with this ship," Dahl said.

"Trust me, there isn't a damn thing wrong with this ship," Finn said. "This is your first posting. You lack perspective. Take it from an old pro. This is as good as it gets."

"I'm not sure you're a reliable—" Dahl said, and then stopped as a hairy wraith appeared before him and Finn. The wraith glared at them both and then jabbed a finger into Dahl's chest.

"You," the wraith said, jabbing the finger deeper. "You just got lucky in there. You don't know how lucky you were. Listen to me, Dahl. *Stay off the bridge.* Avoid the Narrative. The next time you're going to get sucked in for sure. And then it's all over for you." The wraith glanced over to Finn. "You too, goldbrick. You're fodder for sure."

"Who are you and what medications aren't you taking?" Finn said.

The wraith sneered at Finn. "Don't think I'm going to warn either of you again," he said. "Listen to me or don't. But if you don't, you'll be dead. And then where will you be? *Dead,* that's where. It's up to you now." The wraith stomped off and took an abrupt turn into a cargo tunnel.

"What the hell was that?" Finn asked. "A yeti?"

Dahl looked back at Finn but didn't answer. He ran down the corridor and slapped open the access panel to the cargo tunnel.

The corridor was empty.

Finn came up behind Dahl. "Remind me what you were saying about this place," he said.

"There's something seriously wrong with this ship," Dahl repeated.

"Yeah," Finn said. "I think you might be right."

CHAPTER FOUR

Come on! We're almost to the shuttles!" yelled Lieutenant Kerensky, and Dahl had one giggling, mad second to reflect on how *good* Kerensky looked for having been such a recent plague victim. Then he, like Hester and everyone else on the away team, sprinted crazily down the space station corridor, trying to outrun the mechanized death behind them.

The space station was not a Universal Union station; it was an independent commercial station that may or may not have been strictly legally licensed but that nonetheless sent out on the hyperwave an open, repeating distress signal, with a second, encoded signal hidden within it. The *Intrepid* responded to the first, sending two shuttles with away teams to the station. It had decoded the hidden signal while the away teams were there.

It said, *Stay away—the machines are out of control.*

Dahl's away team had figured out that one before the message was decoded, when one of the machines sliced Crewman Lopez into mulch. The distant screams in the halls suggested that the second away team was in the painful process of figuring it out, too.

The second away team, with Finn, Hanson and Duvall on it.

"What sort of assholes encode a message about *killer machines*?" Hester screamed. He had brought up the rear of his away team's running column. The distant vibrating *thuds* suggested one of the machines—a big one—was not too far behind them at the moment.

"Quiet," Dahl said. They knew the machines could see them; it was a good bet the machines could hear them too.

Dahl, Hester and the other two remaining crew members on the team hunkered down and waited for Kerensky to tell them where to go next.

Kerensky consulted his phone. "Dahl," he said, motioning him forward. Dahl sneaked up to his lieutenant, who showed him the phone with a map on it. "We're here," he said, pointing to one corridor. "The shuttle bay is here. I see two routes to it, one through the station's engineering core and the other through its mess hall area."

Less talk, more decision making, please, Dahl thought, and nodded.

"I think we stand a better chance if we split up," Kerensky said. "That way if the machines get one group, the other group might still get to the shuttles. Are you rated to fly one?"

"Hester is," Dahl heard himself say, and then wondered how he knew that. He didn't remember knowing that bit of information before.

Kerensky nodded. "Then you take him and Crewman McGregor and cut through the mess hall. I'll take Williams and go through Engineering. We'll meet at the shuttle, wait for Lieutenant Fischer's away team if we can, and then get the hell out of here."

"Yes, sir," Dahl said.

"Good luck," Kerensky said, and motioned to Williams to follow him.

He hardly looks liquefied at all, Dahl thought again, and then went back to Hester and McGregor. "He wants to split up and have the three of us go through the mess hall to the shuttle bay," he said to the two of them, as Kerensky and Williams skulked off down the corridor toward Engineering.

"What?" McGregor said, visibly upset. "Bullshit. I don't want to go with you. I want to go with Kerensky."

"We have our orders," Dahl said.

"Screw them," McGregor said. "You don't get it, do you? Kerensky's untouchable. You're not. You're just some ensign. We're in a space station filled with fucking killer robots. Do you really think *you're* going to make it out of here alive?"

"Calm down, McGregor," Dahl said, holding out his hands. Beneath his feet, the corridor floor vibrated. "We're wasting time here."

"No!" McGregor said. "You *don't get it*! Lopez already died in front of Kerensky! She was the sacrifice! Now anyone with Kerensky is safe!" He leaped up to chase after Kerensky, stepping into the corridor just as the killing machine that had been following them turned the corner. McGregor saw the machine and had time to make a surprised "O" with his mouth before the harpoon the machine launched pushed into him, spearing him through the liver.

There was an infinitesimal pause, in which everything was set in a tableau: Dahl and Hester crouched on the side of the corridor, killing machine at the corner, the harpooned McGregor in the middle, dripping.

McGregor turned his head toward the horrified Dahl. "See?" he said, through a mouthful of blood. Then there was a yank, and McGregor flew toward the killer machine, which had already spun up its slicing blades.

Dahl screamed McGregor's name, stood and unholstered his pulse gun, and fired into the center of the pulpy red haze where he knew the killer machine to be. The pulse beam glanced harmlessly off the machine's surface. Hester yelled and pushed Dahl down the corridor, away from the machine, which was already resetting its harpoon. They turned a corner and raced away into another corridor, which led to the mess hall. They burst through the doors and closed them behind them.

"These doors aren't going to keep that thing out," Hester said breathlessly.

Dahl examined the doorway. "There's another set of doors here," he said. "Fire doors or an airlock door, maybe. Look for a panel."

"Found it," Hester said. "Step back." He pressed a large red button. There was a squeak and a hiss. A pair of heavy doors slowly began to shut, and then stalled, halfway closed. "Oh, come on!" Hester said.

Through the glass on the already closed set of doors, the killer machine stepped into view.

"I have an idea," Dahl said.

"Does it involve running?" Hester asked.

"Move back from the panel," Dahl said. Hester stepped back, frowning. Dahl raised his pulse gun and fired into the door panel at the same time the machine's harpoon punctured the closed outer door and yanked it out of the doorway. The panel blew in a shower of sparks and the heavy fire doors moved, shutting with a vibrating *clang*.

"Shooting the panel?" Hester said, incredulous. "That was your big idea?"

"I had a hunch," Dahl said, putting his pulse gun away.

"That the space station was wired haphazardly?" Hester said. "That this whole place is one big fucking code violation?"

"The killer machines kind of gave that part away," Dahl said.

There was a violent *bang* as a harpoon struck against the fire door.

"If that door is built like the rest of this place, it won't be long before that thing's through it," Hester said.

"We're not staying anyway," Dahl said, and pulled out his phone for a station map. "Come on. There's a door in the kitchen that will get us closer to the shuttle bay. If we're lucky we won't run into anything else before we get there."

· · · · ·

Two corridors before the shuttle bay, Dahl and Hester ran into what was left of Lieutenant Fischer's party: Fischer, Duvall, Hanson and Finn.

"Well, aren't we the lucky bunch," Finn said, seeing Dahl and Hester. The words were sarcastic, but Finn's tone suggested he was close to losing it. Hanson put a hand on his shoulder.

"Where's Kerensky and the rest of your team?" Fischer asked Dahl.

"We split up," Dahl said. "Kerensky and Williams are alive as far as I know. We lost Lopez and McGregor."

Fischer nodded. "Payton and Webb from our team," he said.

"Harpoons and blades?" Dahl asked.

"Swarming bots," Duvall said.

"We missed those," Dahl said.

Fischer shook his head. "It's unbelievable," he said. "I just transferred to the *Intrepid*. This is my first away team. And I lose two of my people."

"I don't think it's you, sir," Dahl said.

"That's more than I know," Fischer said. He motioned them forward and they made their way cautiously to the shuttle bay.

"Anyone else here rated to fly one of these things?" Fischer asked, as they entered the bay.

"I am," Hester said.

"Good," Fischer said, and pointed to the shuttle Kerensky had piloted. "Warm her up. I'll get started on mine. I want all of you to get into that shuttle with him." He pointed at Hester. "If you see any of those machines coming, don't wait, take off. I'll have enough space for Kerensky and Williams. Got it?"

"Yes, sir," Hester said.

"Get to it, then," Fischer said, and ducked into his own shuttle.

"Everything about this mission sucks," Hester said in their own shuttle, as he banged through the shuttle's pre-flight sequence. Finn, Duvall and Hanson were strapping themselves in; Dahl kept watch by the hatch, looking for Kerensky and Williams.

"Hester, did you ever tell me that you knew how to fly a shuttle?" Dahl asked, turning to look at Hester.

"Kind of busy now," Hester said.

"I didn't know he was rated to fly a shuttle, either," Finn said, from his seat. His anxiousness was needing a release, and talking seemed like a better idea to him than wetting himself. "And I've known him for more than a year."

"Not something you'd think you'd miss," Dahl said.

"We weren't close," Finn said. "I was mostly just using him for his foot locker."

Dahl said nothing to this and turned back to the hatch.

"There," Hester said, and punched a button. The engines thrummed into life. He strapped himself in. "Close that hatch. We're getting out of here."

"Not yet," Dahl said.

"The hell with that," Hester said. He pressed a button on his control panel to seal the hatch.

Dahl slapped the override at the side of the hatch. "Not yet!" he yelled at Hester.

"What is wrong with you?" Hester yelled back. "Fischer's got more than enough space for Kerensky and Williams. My vote is for leaving, and since I'm the goddamn pilot, my vote's the only one that counts!"

"We're waiting!" Dahl said.

"For fuck's sake, *why*?" Hester said.

From his seat, Hanson pointed. "Here they come," he said.

Dahl looked out the hatch. Kerensky and Williams were hobbling slowly into the shuttle bay, propping each other up. Immediately behind them were the pounding of the machines.

Fischer popped his head out his shuttle hatch and saw Dahl. "Come on!" he said, and ran toward Kerensky and Williams. Dahl leaped out of his shuttle and followed.

"There's six of them behind us," Kerensky said, and they came up to the two of them. "We came as fast as we could. Swarming bots—" He collapsed. Dahl grabbed him before he could hit the floor.

"You got him?" Fischer said to Dahl. He nodded. "Get him on your shuttle. Tell your pilot to go. I've got Williams. Hurry." Fischer slung his arm around Williams and dragged him toward his shuttle. Williams turned back to look at Kerensky and Dahl, utterly terrified.

The first of the machines stomped into the shuttle bay.

"Come on, Andy!" Duvall yelled, from the shuttle hatch. Dahl put on a burst of speed and crossed the distance to the shuttle, fairly hurling Kerensky at Duvall and Hanson, who had unlatched himself from his seat as well. They grabbed the lieutenant and dragged him in, Dahl collapsing in afterward.

"*Now* can we go?" Hester said, rhetorically, because he slapped the hatch button without waiting for a response. The shuttle leaped up from the shuttle bay deck as something slammed into the side and clattered off.

"Harpoon," Finn said. He had unstrapped himself and was hovering over Hester, looking at a rearview monitor. "It didn't take."

The shuttle cleared the bay. "Good riddance," muttered Hester.

"How's Kerensky?" Dahl asked Duvall, who was examining Kerensky.

"He's nonresponsive, but he doesn't look too bad," she said, and then turned to Hanson. "Jimmy, get me the medkit, please. It's on the back of the pilot's seat." Hanson went to get it.

"Do you know what you're doing?" Dahl asked.

Duvall looked up briefly. "Told you I'd been ground forces, right? Got medic training then. Spent lots of time patching people up." She smiled. "Hester's not the only one with hidden skills." Hanson came back with the medkit; Duvall cracked it open and got to work.

"Oh, shit," Finn said, still looking at the monitor.

"What is it?" Dahl said, coming over to Finn.

"The other shuttle," Finn said. "I've got a feed from their cameras. Look."

Dahl looked. The cameras showed dozens of machines pouring into the shuttle bay, targeting their fire at the shuttle. Above them a dark, shifting cloud hovered.

"The swarm bots," Finn murmured.

The camera view wobbled and shook and then went blank.

Finn slipped into the co-pilot seat and punched the screen they had just been looking at. "Their shuttle's been compromised," he said. "The engines aren't firing, and it looks like the hull integrity has been breached."

"We need to go back for them," Dahl said.

"No," Hester said. Dahl flared, but Hester turned and looked at him. "Andy, no. If the shuttle's been breached even a little, those swarming bots are already inside of it. If they're already inside of it, then Fischer and Williams are already dead."

"He's right," Finn said. "There's no one to go back for. Even if we did, we couldn't do anything. The bay is swarming with those things. This shuttle doesn't have weapons. All we'd be doing is letting the machines get a second shot at us."

"We were lucky to get out at all," Hester said, returning to his controls.

Dahl looked back at Kerensky, who was now moaning softly while Duvall and Hanson tended to him.

"I don't think luck had much to do with it," he said.

CHAPTER FIVE

I think I'd like to dispense with the bullshit now," Dahl said to his lab mates.

The four of them were quiet and looked at each other. "All right, you don't have to fetch us all coffee anymore," said Mbeke, finally.

"It's not about the *coffee,* Fiona," Dahl said.

"I know," Mbeke said. "But I thought it was worth a shot."

"It's about your away team experience," Collins said.

"No," Dahl said. "It's about my away team experience, and it's about the fact all of you disappear whenever Q'eeng shows up, and it's about the way people move away from him whenever he walks down the corridors, and it's about that fucking *box,* and it's about the fact there's something very wrong with this ship."

"All right," Collins said. "Here's the deal. Some time ago, it was noticed that there was an extremely high correlation between away teams led by or including certain officers, and crewmen dying. The captain. Commander Q'eeng. Chief Engineer West. Medical Chief Hartnell. Lieutenant Kerensky."

"And not only about crewmen dying," Trin said.

"Right," Collins said. "And other things, too."

"Like if someone died with Kerensky around, everyone else would be safe if they stuck with him," Dahl said, remembering McGregor.

"Kerensky's actually only weakly associated with that effect," Cassaway said.

Dahl turned to Cassaway. "It's an *effect?* You have a *name* for it?"

"It's the Sacrificial Effect," Cassaway said. "It's strongest with Hartnell and Q'eeng. The captain and Kerensky, not so much. And it doesn't work at all with West. He's a goddamn death trap."

"Things are always exploding around him," Mbeke said. "Not a good sign for a chief engineer."

"The fact that people die around these officers is so clear and obvious that everyone naturally avoids them," Collins said. "If they're walking through the ship, crew members know to look like they're in the middle of some very important errand for the crew chief or section head. That's why everyone's rushing through the halls whenever they're around."

"It doesn't explain how you all know to get coffee or inspect that storage room whenever Q'eeng is on his way."

"There's a tracking system," Trin said.

"A tracking system?" Dahl said, incredulously.

"It's not that shocking," Collins said. "We all have phones that give away our locations to the *Intrepid*'s computer system. I could, as your superior officer, have the computer locate you anywhere on the ship."

"Q'eeng isn't your underling," Dahl said. "Neither is Captain Abernathy."

"The alert system isn't strictly legal," Collins allowed.

"But you all have access to it," Dahl said.

"*They* have access to it," Cassaway said, pointing to Collins and Trin.

"We give you warning when they're on their way," Trin said.

"'I'm going to get some coffee,'" Dahl said. Trin nodded.

"Yes, which only works as long as you two are actually here," Cassaway said. "If you're not around, we're screwed."

"We can't have the entire ship on the alert system," Trin said. "It would be too obvious."

Cassaway snorted. "As if *they'd* notice," he said.

"What does that mean?" Dahl asked.

"It means that the captain, Q'eeng and the others seem oblivious to the fact that most of the ship's crew go out of their way to avoid them," Mbeke said. "They're also oblivious to the fact that they kill off a lot of the crew."

"How can they be oblivious to that?" Dahl said. "Hasn't someone told them? Don't they know the stats?"

Dahl's four lab mates shared quick glances at each other. "It was pointed out to the captain once," Collins said. "It didn't take."

"What does that mean?" Dahl asked.

"It means that talking to them about the amount of crew they run through is like talking to a brick wall," Cassaway said.

"Then tell someone else," Dahl said. "Tell Admiral Comstock."

"You don't think that's been tried?" Cassaway said. "We've contacted Fleet. We've contacted the Dub U's Military Bureau of Investigation. We've even had people try to go to journalists. Nothing works."

"There's no actual evidence of malfeasance or command incompetence, is what we're told," Trin said. "Not us, specifically. But whoever complains about it."

"How many people do you have to lose before it becomes command incompetence?" Dahl asked.

"What we've been told," Collins said, "is that as the flagship of the Dub U, the *Intrepid* takes on a larger share of sensitive diplomatic, military and research missions than any other ship in the fleet. Because of that, there is commensurate increase of risk, and thus a statistically larger chance crew lives will be lost. It's part of the risk of such a high-profile posting."

"In other words, crew deaths are a feature, not a bug," Cassaway said, dryly.

"And now you know why we just try to avoid them," Mbeke said.

Dahl thought about this for a moment. "It still doesn't explain the Box."

"We don't have any good explanation for the Box," Collins said. "No one does. Officially speaking, the Box doesn't exist."

"It looks like a microwave, it *dings* when it's done and it outputs complete nonsense," Dahl said. "You have to present its results in person, and it doesn't matter what you say when you give the data to Q'eeng, just so long as you give him something to fix. I don't really have to point out all the ways that's so very fucked up, do I?"

"It's how it's been done since before we got here," Trin said. "It's what we were told to do by the people who had our jobs before us. We do it because it works."

Dahl threw up his hands. "Then why not use it for everything?" he asked. "It'd save us all a lot of time."

"It doesn't work with everything," Trin said. "It only works for things that are extraordinarily difficult."

"Like finding a so-called counter-bacterial in six hours," Dahl said.

"That's right," Trin said.

Dahl looked around the room. "It doesn't bother you that a science lab has a *magic box* in it?" he asked.

"Of course it bothers us!" Collins said sharply. "I hate the damn thing. But I have to believe it's not actually magic. We just somehow got hold of a piece of technology so incredibly advanced it looks that way to us. It's like showing a caveman your phone. He wouldn't have the first idea how it worked, but he could still use it to make a call."

"If the phone were like the Box, the only time it would let the caveman make a call would be if he were *on fire*," Dahl said.

"It is what it is," Collins said. "And for some reason we have to do the Kabuki dance of showing off gibberish to make it work. We do it because it *does* work. We don't know what to do with the data, but the *Intrepid*'s computer does. And at the time, in an emergency, that's enough. We hate it. But we don't have any choice but to use it."

"When I came to the *Intrepid*, I told Q'eeng that at the Academy we had trouble replicating some of the work you guys were doing on the ship," Dahl said. "Now I know why. It's because you weren't actually *doing* the work."

"Are you done, Ensign?" Collins said. She was clearly getting tired of the inquisition.

"Why didn't you just tell me all of this when I came on board?" Dahl said.

"What are we going to say, Andy?" Collins said. " 'Hi, welcome to the *Intrepid*, avoid the officers because it's likely you'll get killed if you're on an away team with them, and oh, by the way, here's a magic box we use for *impossible things*'? That would be a lovely first impression, wouldn't it?"

"You wouldn't have believed us," Cassaway said. "Not until you were here long enough to see some of this shit for yourself."

"This is nuts," Dahl said.

"That it is," Collins said.

"And you have no rational explanation for it?" Dahl asked. "No hypothesis?"

"The rational explanation is what the Dub U told us," Trin said. "The *Intrepid* takes on high-risk missions. More people die because of it. The crew has developed superstitions and avoidance strategies to compensate. And we use advanced technologies that we don't understand but which allow us to complete missions."

"But you don't believe it," Dahl said.

"I don't *like* it," Trin said. "I don't have any reason not to believe it."

"It's saner than what Jenkins thinks," Mbeke said.

Dahl turned to face Mbeke. "You've talked about him before," he said.

"He's doing an independent research project," Collins said.

"On this?" Dahl asked.

"Not exactly," Collins said. "He's the one who built the tracking system we use for the captain and the others. The computer system AI sees it as a hack and keeps trying to patch it. So he's got to keep updating if we want it to keep working."

Dahl glanced over at Cassaway. "You said he looked like a yeti."

"He does look like a yeti," Cassaway said. "Either a yeti or Rasputin. I've heard him described both ways. Both are accurate."

"I think I met him," Dahl said. "After I went to the bridge to give Q'eeng the Box data about Kerensky's plague. He came up to me in the corridor."

"What did he say to you?" Collins asked.

"He told me to stay off the bridge," Dahl said. "And he told me to 'avoid the narrative.' What the hell does that mean?"

Mbeke opened her mouth to speak but Collins got there first. "Jenkins is a brilliant programmer, but he's also a bit lost in his own world, and life on the *Intrepid* has hit him harder than most."

"By which she means that Jenkins' wife got killed on an away mission," Mbeke said.

"What happened?" Dahl asked.

"She was shot by a Cirquerian assassin," Collins said. "The assassin was aiming at the Dub U ambassador to Cirqueria. The captain pushed the ambassador down and Margaret was standing right behind him. Took the bullet in the neck. Dead before she hit the ground. Jenkins chose to at least partly disassociate from reality after that."

"So what does he think is happening?" Dahl asked.

"Why don't we save that for another time," Collins said. "You know what's going on now and why. I'm sorry we didn't tell you about this earlier, Andy. But now you know. And now you know what to do when either me or Ben suddenly say that we're going to get coffee."

"Hide," Dahl said.

" 'Hide' isn't a word we like to use," Cassaway said. " 'Perform alternative tasks' is the preferred term."

"Just not in the storage room," Mbeke said. "That's *our* alternative tasking place."

"I'll just alternatively task behind my work desk, then, shall I," Dahl said.

"That's the spirit," Mbeke said.

· · · · ·

At evening mess, Dahl caught up his four friends with what he learned in the lab, and then turned to Finn. "So, did you get the information I asked you for?" he said.

"I did indeed," Finn said.

"Good," Dahl said.

"I want to preface this by saying that normally I don't do this sort of work for free," Finn said, handing his phone over to Dahl. "Normally something like this would have been a week's pay. But this shit's been weirding me out since that away mission. I wanted to see it for myself."

"What are the two of you talking about?" Duvall said.

"I had Finn pull some records for me," Dahl said. "Medical records, mostly."

"Whose?" Duvall asked.

"Your boyfriend's," Finn said.

Dahl looked up at that. "What?"

"Duvall's dating Kerensky," Finn said.

"Shut up, Finn, I am not," Duvall said, and glanced over to Dahl. "After he recovered, Kerensky tracked me down to thank me for saving his life," she said. "He said that when he first came to in the shuttle, he thought he'd died because an angel was hovering over him."

"Oh, God," Hester said. "Tell me a line like that doesn't actually work. I might have to kill myself otherwise."

"It doesn't," Duvall assured him. "Anyway, he asked if he could buy me a drink the next time we had shore leave. I told him I'd think about it."

"Boyfriend," Finn said.

"I'm going to stab you through the eye now," Duvall said to Finn, pointing her fork at him.

"Why did you want Lieutenant Kerensky's medical records?" Hanson asked.

"Kerensky was the victim of a plague a week ago," Dahl said. "He recovered quickly enough to lead an away mission, where he lost consciousness because of a machine attack. He recovered quickly enough from that to hit on Maia sometime today."

"To be fair, he still looked like hell," Duvall said.

"To be fair, he should probably be dead," Dahl said. "The Merovian Plague melts people's flesh right off their bones. Kerensky was about fifteen minutes away from death before he got cured, and he's leading an away mission a week later? It takes that long to get over a bad cold, much less a flesh-eating bacteria."

"So he's got an awesome immune system," Duvall said.

Dahl fixed her with a look and flipped Finn's phone to her. "In the past three years, Kerensky's been shot three times, caught a deadly disease four times, has been crushed under a rock pile, injured in a shuttle crash, suffered burns when his bridge control panel blew up in his face, experienced partial atmospheric decompression, suffered from induced mental instability, been bitten by two venomous animals and had the control of his body taken over by an alien parasite. That's before the recent plague and this away mission."

"He's also contracted three STDs," Duvall said, scrolling through the file.

"Enjoy your drink with him," Finn said.

"I think I'll ask for penicillin on the rocks," Duvall said. She handed the phone back to Dahl. "So you're saying there's no way he could be walking around right now."

"Forget the fact that he should be dead," Dahl said. "There's no way he could be alive and *sane* after all this. The man should be a poster boy for post-traumatic stress disorder."

"They have therapies to compensate for that," Duvall said.

"Yeah, but not for this many times," Dahl said. "This is seventeen major injuries or trauma in three years. That's one every two months. He should be in a constant fetal position by now. As it is, it's like he has just enough time to recover before he gets the shit kicked out of him again. He's unreal."

"Is there a point to this," Duvall said, "or are you just jealous of his physical abilities?"

"The point is there's something weird about this ship," Dahl said, scrolling through more data. "My commanding officer and lab mates fed me a bunch of nonsense about it today, with the away teams and Kerensky and everything else. But I'm not buying it."

"Why not?" Duvall asked.

"Because I don't think they were buying it either," Dahl said. "And because it doesn't explain away something like this." He frowned and looked over at Finn. "You couldn't find anything on Jenkins?"

"You're talking about the yeti you and I encountered," Finn said.

"Yeah," Dahl said.

"There's nothing on him in the computer system," Finn said.

"We didn't imagine him," Dahl said.

"No, we didn't," Finn agreed. "He's just not in the system. But then if he's the programming god your lab mates suggest he is, and he's currently actively hacking into the computer system, I don't think it should be entirely surprising he's not in the system, do you?"

"I think we need to find him," Dahl said.

"Why?" Finn asked.

"Because I think he knows something that no one else wants to talk about," Dahl said.

"Your friends in your lab say he's crazy," Hester pointed out.

"I don't think they're actually his friends," said Hanson.

Everyone turned to him. "What do you mean?" said Hester.

Hanson shrugged. "They said the reason they didn't tell him about what was going on is that he wouldn't have believed it before he had experienced some of it himself. Maybe that's right. But it's also true that if he didn't know what was going on, he wouldn't be able to do what they do: avoid Commander Q'eeng and the other officers, and manage not to get on away team rosters. Think about it, guys: all five of us were on the same away team at one time, on a ship with thousands of crew. What do we all have in common?"

"We're the new guys," Duvall said.

Hanson nodded. "And none of us were told any of this by

our crewmates until now, when it couldn't be avoided any-more."

"You think the reason they didn't tell us wasn't because we didn't know enough to believe them," Dahl said. "You think it was because that way, if someone had to die, it would be us, not them."

"It's just a theory," Hanson said.

Hester looked at Hanson admiringly. "I didn't think you were that cynical," Hester said.

Hanson shrugged again. "When you're the heir to the third largest fortune in the history of the universe, you learn to question people's motivations," he said.

"We need to find Jenkins," Dahl said again. "We need to know what he knows."

"How do you suggest we do that?" Duvall asked.

"I think we start with the cargo tunnels," Dahl said.

CHAPTER SIX

Dahl, where are you going?" Duvall said. She and the others were standing in the middle of the Angeles V space station corridor, watching Dahl unexpectedly split off from the group. "Come on, we're on shore leave," she said. "Time to get smashed."

"And laid," Finn said.

"Smashed *and* laid," Duvall said. "Not necessarily in that order."

"Not that there's anything wrong with doing it in that order," Finn said.

"See, I bet that's why you don't get a lot of second dates," Duvall said.

"We're not talking about *me*," Finn reminded her. "We're talking about Andy. Who's ditching us."

"He is!" Duvall said. "Andy! Don't you want to get smashed and laid with us?"

"Oh, I do," Dahl assured her. "But I need to make a hyperwave first."

"You couldn't have done that on the *Intrepid*?" Hanson asked.

"Not this wave, no," Dahl said.

Duvall rolled her eyes. "This is about your current obsession, isn't it," she said. "I swear, Andy, ever since you got a bug in your ass about Jenkins you're no fun anymore. Ten whole days of brooding. Lighten up, you moody bastard."

Dahl smiled at this. "I'll be quick, I promise. Where will you guys be?"

"I've got us a suite at the station Hyatt," Hanson said. "Meet us there. We'll be the ones quickly losing our sobriety."

Finn pointed to Hester. "And in his case, his virginity."

"Nice," Hester said, but then actually grinned.

"Be there in a few," Dahl promised.

"Better be!" Hanson said, and then he and the rest wandered down the corridor, laughing and joking. Dahl watched them go and then headed to the shopping area of the station, looking for a wave station.

He found one wedged between a coffee shop and a tattoo parlor. It was barely larger than a kiosk and had only three wave terminals in it, one of which was out of service. A drunken crewman of another ship was loudly arguing into one of the others. Dahl took the third.

"Welcome to SurfPoint Hyperwave," the monitor read, and then listed the per-minute cost of opening a wave. A five-minute wave would eat most of his pay for the week, but this was not entirely surprising to Dahl. It took a large amount of energy to open up a tunnel in space/time and connect in real time with another terminal light-years away. Energy cost money.

Dahl took out the anonymous credit chit he kept on hand for things he didn't want traced directly to his own credit account and placed it on the payment square. The monitor registered the chit and opened up a "send" panel. Dahl spoke a phone address back at Academy and waited for the connection. He was pretty sure that the person he was calling would be awake and moving about. The Dub U kept all of its ships and stations on Universal Time because otherwise the sheer number of day lengths and time zones would make it impossible for anyone to do anything, but the Academy was in Boston. Dahl couldn't remember how many time zones behind that was.

The person on the other end of the line picked up, audio

only. "Whoever you are, you're interrupting my morning jog," she said.

Dahl grinned. "Morning, Casey," he said. "How's my favorite librarian?"

"Shit! Andy!" Casey said. A second later the video feed kicked in and Casey Zane popped up, smiling, the USS *Constitution* behind her.

"Jogging the Freedom Trail again, I see," Dahl said.

"The bricks make it easy to follow," Casey said. "Where are you?"

"About three hundred light-years away, and paying for every inch of it on this hyperwave," Dahl said.

"Got it," Casey said. "What do you need?"

"The Academy Archive would have blueprints of every ship in the fleet, right?" Dahl asked.

"Sure," Casey said. "All the ones that the Dub U wants to acknowledge exist, anyway."

"Any chance they'd be altered or tampered with?"

"From the outside? No," Casey said. "The archives don't connect to outside computer systems, partly to avoid hacking. All data has to go through a live librarian. That's job security for you."

"I suppose it is," Dahl said. "Is there any chance I can get you to send me a copy of the *Intrepid* blueprints?"

"I don't think they're classified, so it shouldn't be a problem," Casey said. "Although I might have to redact some information about the computer and weapons systems."

"That's fine," Dahl said. "I'm not interested in those anyway."

"That said, you're actually on the *Intrepid*," Casey said. "You should be able to get the blueprints out of the ship's database."

"I can," Dahl said. "There have been some changes to a

few systems on board and I think it'll be useful to have the original blueprints for compare and contrast."

"Okay," Casey said. "I'll do it when I get back to the archives. A couple of hours at least."

"That's fine," Dahl said. "Also, do me a favor and send it to this address, not my Dub U address." He recited an alternate address, which he had created anonymously on a public provider while he was at the Academy.

"You know I have to record the information request," Casey said. "That includes the address to which I'm sending the information."

"I'm not trying to hide from the Dub U," Dahl said. "No spy stuff, I swear."

"Says the man using an anonymous public hyperwave terminal to call one of his best friends, rather than routing it through his own phone," Casey said.

"I'm not asking you to commit treason," Dahl said. "Cross my heart."

"All right," Casey said. "We're pals and all, but espionage isn't in my job description."

"I owe you one," Dahl said.

"You owe me dinner," Casey said. "The next time you're in town. The life of an archive librarian isn't that horribly exciting, you know. I need to live vicariously."

"Trust me, at this point I'm seriously considering taking up the life of a librarian myself," Dahl said.

"Now you're just pandering," Casey said. "I'll wave you the stuff when I get in the office. Now get off the line before you don't have any money left."

Dahl grinned again. "Later, Casey," he said.

"Later, Andy," she said, and disconnected.

· · · · ·

There was a guest in the suite when Dahl got there.

"Andy, you know Lieutenant Kerensky," Duvall said, in a curiously neutral tone of voice. She and Hester were on either side of Kerensky, who had an arm around each of them. They seemed to be propping him up.

"Sir," Dahl said.

"Andy!" Kerensky said, slurringly. He disengaged from Duvall and Hester, took two stumbling steps and clapped Dahl on the shoulder with the hand that was not holding his drink. "We are on shore leave! We leave rank behind us. To you, right now, I am just Anatoly. Go on, say it."

"Anatoly," Dahl said.

"See, that wasn't so hard, was it?" Kerensky said. He drained his drink. "I appear to be out of a drink," he said, and wandered off. Dahl raised an eyebrow at Duvall and Hester.

"He spotted us just before we entered the hotel and attached himself like a leech," Duvall said.

"A drunken leech," Hester said. "He was blasted before we got here."

"A drunken horny leech," Duvall said. "The reason he has his arm around my shoulder is so he can grope my tit. Lieutenant or not, I'm about to kick his ass."

"Right now the plan is to get him drunk enough to pass out before he attempts to molest Duvall," Hester said. "Then we dump him down a laundry chute."

"Shit, here he comes again," Duvall said. Kerensky was indeed stumbling back toward the trio. His progress was more lateral than forward. He stopped to get his bearings.

"Why don't you leave him to me," Dahl said.

"Seriously?" Duvall said.

"Sure, I'll baby-sit him until he passes out," Dahl said.

"Man, I owe you a blowjob," Duvall said.

"What?" Dahl said.

"What?" Hester said.

"Sorry," Duvall said. "In ground forces, when someone does you a favor you tell them you owe them a sex act. If it's a little thing, it's a handjob. Medium, blowjob. Big favor, you owe them a fuck. Force of habit. It's just an expression."

"Got it," Dahl said.

"No actual blowjob forthcoming," Duvall said. "To be clear."

"It's the thought that counts," Dahl said, and turned to Hester. "What about you? You want to owe me a blowjob, too?"

"I'm thinking about it," Hester said.

"What's this I hear about *blowjobs*?" Kerensky said, finally wobbling up.

"Okay, yes, one owed," Hester said.

"Excellent," Dahl said. "See the two of you later, then." Hester and Duvall backed away precipitately.

"Where are they going?" Kerensky asked, blinking slowly.

"They're planning a birthday party," Dahl said. "Why don't you have a seat, sir." He motioned to one of the couches in the suite.

"Anatoly," Kerensky said. "God, I hate it when people use rank on shore leave." He fell heavily onto the couch, miraculously not spilling his drink. "We're all brothers in the service, you know? Well, except those of us who are sisters." He peered around, looking for Duvall. "I like your friend."

"I know," Dahl said, also sitting.

"She saved my life, you know," Kerensky said. "She's an angel. You think she likes me?"

"No," Dahl said.

"Why not?" Kerensky blithered, hurt. "Does she like women or something?"

"She's married to her job," Dahl said.

"Oh, well, *married*," Kerensky said, apparently not hearing the rest of what Dahl said. He drank some more.

"You mind if I ask you a question?" Dahl said.

With the hand not holding his drink, Kerensky made little waving motions as if to say, *Go ahead*.

"How do you heal so quickly?" Dahl asked.

"What do you mean?" Kerensky asked.

"Remember when you got the Merovian Plague?"

"Of course," Kerensky said. "I almost *died*."

"I know," Dahl said. "But then a week later you were leading the away team I was on."

"Well, I got *better,* you see," Kerensky said. "They found a cure."

"Yes," Dahl said. "I was the one who brought the cure to Commander Q'eeng."

"That was *you*?" Kerensky said, and then lunged at Dahl, enveloping him in a bear hug. Kerensky's drink slopped up the side of the glass and deposited itself down the back of Dahl's neck. "You saved my life too! This room is filled with people who saved my life. I love you all." Kerensky started weeping.

"You're welcome," Dahl said, prying the sobbing lieutenant off his body as delicately as he could. He was aware of everyone else in the room studiously ignoring what was happening on the couch. "My point was, even with a cure, you healed quickly. And then you were seriously injured on the away mission I was on. And yet a couple of days later you were fine."

"Oh, well, you know, modern medicine is *really good,*" Kerensky said. "Plus, I've always been a fast healer. It's a family thing. We've got stories about one of my ancestors, in the Great Patriotic War? He was in Stalingrad. Took, like, twenty shots from Nazi bullets and still kept coming at them. He was *unreal,* man. So I inherited that gene, maybe." He looked down at his drink. "I know I had more drink than this," he said.

"It's a good thing you heal so fast, considering how often you get hurt," Dahl ventured.

"I *know!*" Kerensky said, suddenly and forcefully. "*Thank* you! No one else notices! I mean, what the hell is up with that? I'm not stupid, or clumsy, or anything. But every time I go on an away mission I get all fucked up. Do you know how many times I've been, like, *shot?*"

"Three times in the last three years," Dahl said.

"Yes!" Kerensky said. "Plus all the *other* shit that happens to me. You know what it is. Fucking captain and Q'eeng have a voodoo doll of me, or something." He sat there, brooding, and then showed every sign of being about to drift into sleep.

"A voodoo doll," Dahl said, startling Kerensky back into consciousness. "You think so."

"Well, no, not literally," Kerensky said. "Because that's just *stupid,* isn't it. But it *feels* like it. It feels like whenever the captain and Q'eeng have an away mission they know is going to be all fucked up they say, 'Hey, Kerensky, this is a *perfect* away mission for you,' and then I go off and, like, get my *spleen* punctured. And half the time it's some stupid thing I have no idea about, right? I'm an astrogator, man. I am a fucking brilliant astrogator. I wanna just . . . *astrogate.* Right?"

"Why don't you point that out to the captain and Q'eeng?" Dahl asked.

Kerensky sneered, and his lip quivered at the effort. "Because what the hell am I going to say?" he said, and started making Humpty-Dumpty movements. "'Oh, I can't go on this mission, Captain, Commander Q'eeng. Let someone else get stabbed through the eyeball for a change.'" He stopped with the movements and was quiet for a second. "Besides, I don't know. It seems to make sense at the time, you know?"

"No, I don't know," Dahl said.

"When the captain tells me I'm going to be on an away mission, it's like some other part of my brain takes over," Kerensky said. He sounded like he was trying to puzzle through something. "I get all confident and it seems like there's a perfectly good reason for a goddamn astrogator to take medical samples, or fight killer machines or whatever. Then I get back on the *Intrepid* and I think to myself, 'What the *fuck* was I just doing?' Because it doesn't make sense, does it?"

"I don't know," Dahl said again.

Kerensky looked lost in thought for a second, and then waved it all away. "Anyway, fuck it, right?" he said, brightening up. "I lived another day, I'm on shore leave, and I'm with people who saved my life." He lunged at Dahl again, even more sloppily. "I love you, man. I do. Let's get another drink and then go find some hookers. I want a blowjob. You want a blowjob?"

"I've already got two on order," Dahl said. "I'm good."

"Oh, okay," Kerensky said. "That's good." And then he began to snore, his head nestled on Dahl's shoulder.

Dahl looked up and saw his four friends staring down at him.

"You *all* owe me blowjobs," he said.

"How about a drink instead," Finn said.

"Deal," Dahl said. He glanced down at Kerensky. "What do we do about Sleeping Beauty here?"

"There's a laundry chute outside," Hester said, hopefully.

CHAPTER SEVEN

Here are the blueprints to the *Intrepid* that I downloaded from the ship's database," Dahl said to Finn and Duvall at midday mess, showing them a printout. He laid down a second printout. "And here are the blueprints I received from the Academy Archive. Notice anything?"

"Nope," said Finn, after a minute.

"Nope," said Duvall, shortly thereafter.

Dahl sighed and pointed. "It's the cargo tunnels," he said. "We use them to transport cargo throughout the ship, but there's no reason a human couldn't go into them. The ship maintenance crew goes into them all the time to physically access ship systems. They're designed that way so ship maintenance doesn't get in the way of the rest of the crew."

"You think Jenkins is in there," Duvall said.

"Where else is he going to be?" Dahl said. "He only comes out when it suits him; no one ever sees him otherwise. Think how populated this ship is. The only way you can disappear is if you stay in a place other crew don't usually go."

"The flaw in this reasoning is that the cargo tunnels are *tunnels*," Finn said. "And even if people aren't there, they're still crawling with those autonomous delivery carts. If he stayed in any one place for long he'd be blocking their traffic or he'd get run over."

Dahl waggled a finger. "See, that's what you two aren't seeing. Look . . ." He pointed to a square inside the maze of cargo tunnels. "When the carts aren't delivering something, they have to go somewhere. They're not hanging out in the corridors. Where they go is to one of these distribution hubs. The hubs are more than large enough for a person to hole up in."

"As long as there's not a bunch of carts cluttering it up," Duvall said.

"Exactly," Dahl said. "And look. In the blueprints of the *Intrepid* we have on ship, there are six cart distribution areas. But in the ones from the archives, there are seven." He tapped the seventh distribution hub. "This distribution hub is away from major systems in the ship, which means that maintenance crews have no reason to get near it. It's as far away as you can be from anyone and still be on the ship. That's where Jenkins is. The ghost in the machine. That's where we find him."

"I don't see why you don't ask your boss to make an introduction," Duvall said. "You said that Jenkins was technically under her anyway."

"I tried that and got nowhere with it," Dahl said. "Collins finally told me that Jenkins only appears when he wants to appear and otherwise they leave him alone. He's helping them keep track of the captain, Q'eeng, and the others. They don't want to piss him off and leave themselves vulnerable."

"Speaking of which," Finn said, and motioned with his head.

Dahl turned around to see Science Officer Q'eeng coming up to him. He started to get up.

Q'eeng waved him back down. "At ease, Ensign." He noticed the blueprints. "Studying the ship?"

"Just looking for ways to do my job more efficiently," Dahl said.

"I admire that initiative," Q'eeng said. "Ensign, we're about to arrive at the Eskridge system to answer a distress call from a colony there. The reports from the colony are sketchy but I suspect a biological agent may be involved, so I'm assembling a team from your department to accompany me. You're on it. Meet me in the shuttle bay in half an hour."

"Yes, sir," Dahl said. Q'eeng nodded and headed off. He

turned back to Duvall and Finn. They were looking at him oddly. "What?" he said.

"An away team with Q'eeng," Duvall said.

"A sudden, oddly coincidental away team with Q'eeng," Finn said.

"Let's try not to be too paranoid," Dahl said.

"That's funny, considering," Finn said.

Dahl pushed the blueprints at Finn. "While I'm away, Finn, find a way for us to sneak up on Jenkins without him being aware of it. I want to talk to him, but aside from that warning I don't think he wants to talk to us. I don't want to give him that choice."

· · · · ·

"This is all *your* fault, you know," Cassaway hissed at Dahl. He, Cassaway and Mbeke constituted the away team with Q'eeng and a security team member named Taylor. Q'eeng was piloting the shuttle to the colony; Taylor took the co-pilot seat. The xenobiologists were in the back. The two other xenobiologists had been coldly silent to him during the mission briefing and for most of the shuttle ride down to the planet. These were the first words either of them had spoken to him the entire trip.

"How is this my fault?" Dahl said. "I didn't tell the captain to take the ship here."

"It's your fault for asking about Jenkins!" Cassaway said. "You're pissing him off with all your questions about him."

"I can't ask questions about him now?" Dahl said.

"Not questions that make him retaliate against us," Mbeke said.

"Shut up, Fiona," Cassaway said. "It's your fault too."

"My fault too?" said Mbeke, incredulous. "I'm not the one asking all these stupid questions!"

Cassaway jabbed a finger in Dahl's direction. "You're the one who brought up Jenkins in front of him! Twice!"

"It slipped," Mbeke said. "I was just making conversation the first time. The second time I didn't think it would matter. He already knew."

"Look where we are, Fiona." Cassaway waved to indicate the shuttle. "Tell me it doesn't matter. You never told Sid Black about Jenkins."

"Sid Black was an asshole," Mbeke said.

"And this one isn't?" Cassaway said, pointing at Dahl again.

"I'm right here, you know," Dahl said.

"Fuck you," Cassaway said, to Dahl. He looked at Mbeke again. "And fuck you too, Fiona. You should have known better."

"I was just making conversation," Mbeke said again, brokenly, her eyes on her hands, which were in her lap.

Dahl looked at the two of them for a moment. "You didn't know Q'eeng was coming to see you, did you," he said, finally. "No time for you or Collins and Trin to get coffee or for you to hide out in the storage room. Q'eeng just showed up at the lab and you were all caught flat-footed. And when he told Collins he needed an away team—"

"She volunteered us," Mbeke said.

"And you," Cassaway said, spitting out the words. "Q'eeng wanted her or Ben to come too, but she sold you out. Reminded him you had solved the Merovian Plague. Said you were one of the best xenobiologists she's ever had on staff. It's a lie, of course. You're not. But it worked because you're here and not her or Ben."

"I see," Dahl said. "I don't suppose that's unexpected, because I'm the new guy. The low man on the totem pole. The guy that's meant to be replaced every couple of months anyway, right? But you two," he said, nodding to the both of them. "You thought that you were protected. You survived long enough that you thought Collins wouldn't push you at Q'eeng if she had to. You thought she might even pick one of you over Ben Trin, didn't you."

Cassaway looked away from Dahl; Mbeke started crying quietly.

"It came as a surprise to find out just where you sat on the totem pole, didn't it?" Dahl said.

"Shut up, Dahl," Cassaway said, not looking at him.

They were quiet all the rest of the way down to the planet.

· · · · ·

They found no colonists, but they found parts of them. And a lot of blood.

"Pulse guns on full power," Q'eeng said. "Cassaway, Mbeke, Dahl, I want you to follow the blood trails into the woods. We still might find someone alive, or find a dead one of whatever it is that did this. I'm going to check out the administrative office and see if there's anything there that can explain this. Taylor, you're with me." Q'eeng strode off toward a large, blocky trailer with Taylor following.

"Come on," Cassaway said, and led Dahl and Mbeke toward the woods.

A couple hundred meters in, the three of them found a ruined corpse.

"Give me the sampler," Dahl said to Mbeke, who was carrying that piece of equipment. She unslung the device and gave it to Dahl, who knelt and pushed the sampling tool into what remained of the corpse's abdomen.

"It'll be a couple of minutes for this thing to give me a result," Dahl said, not looking up from the corpse. "The sampler's got to go through the DNA library of the entire colony.

Make sure that whatever got this guy doesn't get me while we're waiting."

"I'm on it," he heard Cassaway say. Dahl returned to his work.

"It's someone named Fouad Ali," Dahl said, a couple of minutes later. "Looks like he was the colony doctor." Dahl looked up and past Ali's corpse, into the woods. "The blood trail continues off that direction. Do we want to keep looking?"

"What are you doing?" Dahl heard Mbeke ask.

"What?" Dahl said, and turned around to see Cassaway pointing his pulse gun at him, and Mbeke staring at Cassaway, confused.

Cassaway grimaced. "Damn it, Fiona, can't you ever just shut up?"

"I'm with Fiona," Dahl said. "What are you doing?" He tried to stand up.

"Don't move," Cassaway said. "Don't move or I'm going to shoot you."

"It looks like you're going to shoot me anyway," Dahl said. "But I don't know why."

"Because one of us has to die," Cassaway said. "That's how it works on the away teams. If Q'eeng's leading the away team, someone is going to die. Someone always dies. But if someone dies, then whoever's left is safe. That's how it works."

"The last person who explained this idea to me got chopped up into little pieces even after someone else died," Dahl said. "I don't think it works the way you think it does."

"Shut up," Cassaway said. "If you die, Fiona and I don't have to. You'll be the sacrifice. Once the sacrifice is made, the rest are safe. We'll be safe."

"That's not the way it works," Dahl said. "When was the last time you were on an away team, Jake? I was on one a couple of weeks ago. It's not how it works. You're missing details. Killing me isn't going to mean you're safe. Fiona . . ." Dahl glanced over at Mbeke to try to reason with her. She was in the process of raising her own pulse gun.

"Come on, guys," Dahl said. "Two pulse gun blasts are going to be hard to miss."

"Put your gun on low power," Cassaway said to Mbeke. "Aim for the center mass. When he's down, we cut him up. That'll cover us. We can explain the blood by saying we were trying to save—" And that's as far as he got before the things dropped out of the tree above and onto him and Mbeke.

The two of them fell, screaming as they tried to fight off the things now tearing into their flesh. Dahl gaped for a second then ran in a burst toward the colony, sensing rather than seeing that his sudden movement had only barely saved him from being jumped on himself.

Dahl weaved through the trees, screaming for Q'eeng and Taylor. Some part of his brain wanted to know if he was running in the right direction; another part wanted to know why he wasn't using his phone to contact Q'eeng. A third part reminded him that he had a pulse gun of his own, which might be effective against whatever was currently eating Cassaway and Mbeke.

A fourth part of his brain was saying, *This is the part where you run and scream a lot.*

He was listening to the fourth part.

His eye caught a break in the woods, and in that break he could see the distant trailers of the colony and the forms of Q'eeng and Taylor. Dahl screamed at the top of his lungs and ran in a straight line toward them, waving his hands to get their attention. He saw their tiny forms jiggle, as if they heard him.

Then something tripped him and he went down.

The thing was on him instantly, biting and tearing at him.

Dahl screamed and pushed and in his panic saw something that looked like it could be an eye and jammed his thumb into it. The thing roared and reared back and Dahl pushed himself back from the thing, and it was on him again and Dahl could feel teeth on his shoulder and a burning sensation that let him know that whatever had just bit him was also venomous. Dahl looked for the eye again, jabbed it a second time and got the thing to reel back again, but this time Dahl was too dizzy and sick to move.

One sacrifice and whoever's left is safe, my ass, he thought, and the last thing he saw was the thing's very impressive set of teeth coming down around his head.

· · · · ·

Dahl woke up to see his friends surrounding him.

"Ack," he said.

"Finn, give him some water," Duvall said. Finn took a small container with a straw from the holder at the side of the medical bay cot and put it to Dahl's lips. He sipped gingerly.

"I'm not dead," he eventually whispered.

"No," Duvall said. "Not that you didn't make an effort. What was left of you should have been dead when they brought you back to the ship. Doc Hartnell says it's only luck that Q'eeng and Taylor got to you when they did, otherwise that thing would have eaten you alive."

The last phrase jogged something in Dahl's memory. "Cassaway," he said. "Mbeke."

"They're dead," Hanson said. "There wasn't much left of them to get back, either."

"You're the only one from the away team still alive," Hester said. "Besides Q'eeng."

"Taylor?" Dahl croaked.

"He got bit," Duvall said, correctly interpreting the

question. "The things have a venom. It doesn't kill people, it turns them psychotic. He went crazy and started shooting up the ship. He killed three of the crew before they brought him down."

"That's what they think happened at the colony," Finn said. "The doctor's record shows that a hunting party got bit by these things, went back to the colony and started shooting up the place. Then the creatures came in, took the dead and killed off the survivors."

"Q'eeng was bit too, but Captain Abernathy had him isolated until they could make an antivenom," Hanson said.

"From your blood," Hester said. "You were unconscious so you couldn't go crazy. That gave your body time to metabolize and neutralize the venom."

"He was lucky you survived," Duvall said.

"No," Dahl said, and lifted his arm to point at himself. "Lucky he needed me."

CHAPTER EIGHT

W hat are these?" Dahl asked from his bed, taking one of the buttonlike objects that Finn held in his hand.

"Our way to sneak up on Jenkins," Finn said, passing out the rest. "They're delivery cart ID transponders. I pried them off disabled carts in the refuse hold. The cargo tunnel doors register each time they're opened and closed and look for identification. If you're a crew member, your phone IDs you. If you're a cart, one of these do."

"Why not just leave our phones behind and have no ID?" Hanson asked, holding his button up to the light.

"Because then there's an unexplained door opening," Finn said. "If this Jenkins is as paranoid and careful as Andy here thinks he is, that's not going to escape his notice."

"So we leave our phones behind, take one of these, and go on after him," Dahl said.

"That's the plan I came up with," Finn said. "Unless you have a better one."

"I just spent two weeks doing nothing but healing," Dahl said. "This works for me."

"So when do we go find this guy?" Duvall asked.

"If he's tracking the captain and the senior officers, then he's going to be active when they are," Dahl said. "That means first shift. If we go in right after the start of third shift, we have a chance to catch him while he's asleep."

"So he's going to wake up with five people hovering over him and staring," Hester said. "*That's* not going to make him any more paranoid than he already is."

"He might not be asleep, and if he catches sight of us, he might try to run," Dahl said. "If just one of us goes, he might get past us. He's less likely to get past five of us, each coming in from a different corridor."

"Everybody be ready to take down a yeti," Finn said. "This guy is big and hairy."

"Besides that, whatever the hell is happening on this ship, I think we all want to know about it sooner than later," Dahl said.

"So, right after third shift," Duvall said. "Tonight?"

"Not tonight," Dahl said. "Give me a day or two to get used to walking again." He stretched and winced.

"When do you get off medical leave?" Hanson asked, watching his movements.

"Last day today," Dahl said. "They're going to do a final checkup after you all leave. I'm all healed, just stiff from lying around on my ass," he said. "A couple of days, I'll be ready to go. The only things I have to do between now and then is get discharged from here and go by the Xenobiology Lab to find out why neither of my superior officers has bothered to come see me since I've been in sick bay."

"It might have something to do with two of your colleagues getting eaten," Hester said. "That's just a guess."

"I don't doubt that," Dahl said. "But I need to find out what else it is, too."

. . . . .

"Don't bother," Lieutenant Collins said, as Dahl walked through the door of the Xenobiology Lab. "You don't work in this lab anymore. I've had you transferred."

Dahl paused and looked around. Collins was in front of him, antagonistic. Trin, at a workstation behind her, was resolutely focused on whatever was on his work tablet. From other workstations, two new faces gawked openly at him.

"The new Cassaway and Mbeke?" Dahl asked, turning his attention back to Collins.

"Jake and Fiona aren't *replaceable*," Collins said.

"No, just expendable," Dahl said. "At least when it came down to them being on an away team." He motioned with his head to the new crew members. "Told them yet about Q'eeng? Or the captain? Have you explained your sudden absences when one of them shows up? Hauled out the Box yet, Lieutenant?"

Collins was visibly making an effort to control herself. "None of that is your concern, Ensign," she said, finally. "You're not part of this lab anymore. Ensign Dee, the junior science officer on the bridge, fell to her death a week ago, on an away mission. I recommended you to Q'eeng as her replacement. He agreed. You start tomorrow. Technically, it's a promotion. Congratulations."

"Someone once told me to stay off the bridge," Dahl said, and then nodded over at Trin. "Two people did, actually. But one of them was more forceful about it."

"Nonsense," Collins said. "The bridge is the perfect place for someone like you. You'll be in contact with senior officers on a daily basis. They'll get to know you very well. And there will be lots of opportunities for adventure. You'll be going on away missions weekly. Sometimes even more often than that." She smiled thinly.

"Well," Dahl said. "You putting me in for this promotion certainly shows what you think of me, Lieutenant."

"Think nothing of it," Collins said. "It's no more than you deserve. And now, I think you better run along, Ensign. You'll need your rest for your first day on the bridge."

Dahl straightened and saluted crisply. Collins turned away without acknowledgment.

Dahl turned and headed for the door but then changed his mind and stalked up to the new crew. "How long have you been here?" he asked the closest one of them.

She looked at the other crewman and then back at Dahl. "Four days," she said. "We transferred in from the *Honsu*."

"No away teams yet," Dahl said.

"No, sir," she said.

Dahl nodded. "A piece of advice for you." He pointed back at Collins and Trin. "When they suddenly go for coffee, that's a very good time for you to do an inventory on the storage room. Both of you. I don't think those two were going to bother to tell you that. I don't think they're going to bother to tell that to anyone who works in this lab ever again. So I'm telling you. Watch them. Don't let them sell you out."

Dahl turned and walked out, leaving two very confused crewmen and two very pissed-off officers.

· · · · ·

"Slow down, Andy," Duvall said, moving faster herself to keep up. "You just got out of sick bay."

Dahl snorted and stomped down the corridor. Duvall came up even to him.

"You think she got you assigned to the bridge to get back at you for your lab mates," she said.

"No," Dahl said. "She got me assigned to the bridge because when she had to assign Jake and Fiona, it rubbed her face in it."

"In it?" Duvall said. "In what?"

Dahl glanced at Duvall. "That she's *afraid*," he said. "Everyone on this entire ship is afraid, Maia. They hide and they disappear and they find ways to *not think* about how much time they spend hiding. And then comes the moment when they can't hide and they have to face themselves. And they hate that. *That's* why Collins assigned me to the bridge. Because otherwise every time she looked at me she'd be reminded that she's a coward." He sped up again.

"Where are you going?" Duvall asked.

"Leave me alone, Maia," Dahl said. Duvall stopped in her tracks. Dahl left her behind.

In fact Dahl had no idea where he was going; he was burning off frustration and anger, and being on the move was the closest thing the jam-packed *Intrepid* offered to being alone.

This was why, when the crew presence finally thinned and Dahl felt the fatigue his disused muscles had been trying to alert him about, he was surprised to find himself outside the cargo tunnel door closest to Jenkins' secret hideaway.

He stood outside the door for a long minute, remembering the plan to sneak up on Jenkins as a team and find out what he knew.

"Fuck it," he said. He smacked the access panel to open the corridor door.

A yeti was standing directly on the other side. It grabbed him and pulled him into the corridor. Dahl yelled in surprise but was too weak to resist. He stumbled into the corridor. The yeti, whom Dahl now recognized as Jenkins, closed the door behind them.

"Stop yelling," Jenkins said, and stuck a finger in his ear, twisting it. "Jesus, that's annoying."

Dahl looked at the closed door and then back at Jenkins. "How did you *do* that?" he asked. "How did you know?"

"Because I am a student of the human condition," Jenkins said. "And as humans go, you're pretty predictable. And because I have you under constant surveillance through your phone, you dumbass."

"So you know—"

"About your overly complicated plan to sneak up on me, yes," Jenkins said. "Your friend Finn gets partial credit for the cart ID thing. What he doesn't know is that when decommissioned cart IDs get scanned, I get an immediate alert. He's not the first person to think of that to access these corridors. And you're not the first person to try to find me."

"I'm not," Dahl said.

Jenkins snapped his fingers, as if to focus Dahl's attention. "What did I just say? Redundant conversation isn't going to do us any good."

"Sorry," Dahl said. "Let me try again. Others have tried to find you and failed."

"That's right," Jenkins said. "I don't want to be found, and those who use my services don't want me to be found either. Between us we managed to avoid anyone I don't want to see."

"So you want to see me," Dahl said, carefully.

"It's more accurate to say *you* want to see *me,* and I'm willing to let myself be seen by you," Jenkins said.

"Why me?" Dahl asked.

"You just got assigned to the bridge," Jenkins said.

"I did," Dahl said. "And I remember you telling me very specifically to stay off the bridge."

"And that's why you came looking for me," Jenkins said. "Even though it would ruin the plan you made with your friends."

"Yes," Dahl said.

"Why?" Jenkins asked.

"I don't know," Dahl said. "I wasn't thinking clearly."

"Wrong," Jenkins said. "You *were* thinking clearly, but you weren't thinking consciously. Now think about it consciously, and tell me why. But hurry. I'm feeling exposed here."

"Because you know *why*," Dahl said. "Everyone else in the *Intrepid* knows something's fucked up about this ship. They've got their ways to avoid getting sucked into it. But they don't know *why*. You do."

"Maybe I do," Jenkins said. "But why would it matter?"

"Because if you don't know why something is the way it is, then you don't know anything about it at all," Dahl said. "All the tricks and superstitions aren't going to do a damn bit of good if you don't know the reason for them. The conditions could change and then you're screwed."

"That's all very blandly logical," Jenkins said. "It doesn't explain why you decided to track me down now."

"Because someone's actively trying to *kill* me now," Dahl said. "Collins got me assigned to the bridge because she's decided she wants me dead."

"Yes, death by away team. Very effective on this ship," Jenkins said.

"I'm on the bridge tomorrow," Dahl said. "After that, it's not a matter of *if* I get killed, it's when. I'm out of time. I need to know *now*."

"So you can avoid dying," Jenkins said.

"It would be nice," Dahl said.

"Collins wants to avoid death and you just called her a coward for it," Jenkins said.

"That's not why she's a coward," Dahl said.

"No, I suppose not," Jenkins said.

"If I can understand why, maybe I can keep myself from getting killed, and maybe I can keep others from being killed too," Dahl said. "I have people I care about here. I'd like to see them live."

"Well, then," Jenkins said. "Let me ask you one more question, Dahl. What if I tell you what I think, and it sounds insane to you?"

"Is that what happened?" Dahl asked. "Collins and Trin. You worked for them. You told them you had a theory. They heard it and they didn't believe it."

Jenkins chuckled at that. "I said insane, not unbelievable," he said. "And I think Collins, for one, believes it just fine."

"How do you know?" Dahl asked.

"Because it's what's made her a coward," Jenkins said, then looked at Dahl appraisingly. "But maybe not you. No, maybe not at all. And maybe not your friends. So gather them up, Ensign Dahl. Meet me in my hidey-hole tonight. Same time you were going to invade. I'll see you then." He turned to go.

"May I ask you a question?" Dahl asked.

"You mean, besides that one?" Jenkins asked.

"Two, actually," Dahl said. "Cassaway said they got on that away mission because you didn't tell them Q'eeng was coming to see them. He said it was retaliation for me trying to find out about you. Was it?"

"No," Jenkins said. "I didn't tell them Q'eeng was on the way because at the time I was taking a dump. I can't watch everything all the time. What's your second question?"

"You told me to stay off the bridge," Dahl said. "Me and Finn. Why did you do that?"

"Well, I told your friend Finn because he just happened to be there, and I didn't think it would hurt, even if he's a bit of an asshole," Jenkins said. "But as for you, well. Let's just say I have a special interest in the Xenobiology Lab. Call it a sentimental attachment. And let's also just say I guessed that your response to what happens here on the *Intrepid* would go beyond the usual fear response. So I figured offering you a warning and piece of advice in person couldn't hurt."

Jenkins moved his hand as if to say, *See.* "And look where we are now. At the very least you're still alive. So far." He reached over to the access panel and slapped open the door to return Dahl to the *Intrepid.* Then he walked off.

CHAPTER NINE

Come *on,*" Jenkins said, and pounded on the display table. Above the table, a holographic image flickered and then died. Jenkins pounded the table again. Dahl looked over to Duvall, who with Hanson, Finn and Hester was jammed into Jenkins' tiny living space. She rolled her eyes.

"Sorry," Jenkins muttered, ostensibly to the five crewmen jammed into his living space, but mostly to himself. "I get equipment when everyone else throws it out. The carts bring it to me. Then I have to repair it. It's a little buggy sometimes."

"It's all right," Dahl said. His eyes took a visual tour of his surroundings. Along with Jenkins and the five of them, the delivery cart storage area was jammed with Jenkins' possessions: the large holographic table, situated between him and the five crew members, a thin cot, a small wardrobe with boxes of hygienic wash wipes piled on it, a pallet of Universal Union away team rations and a portable toilet. Dahl wondered how the toilet was emptied and serviced. He wasn't sure that he really wanted to know.

"Is this going to start anytime soon?" asked Hester. "I thought we'd be done by now, and I kind of have to pee."

Jenkins motioned to the toilet. "Be my guest," he said.

"I'd rather *not,*" Hester said.

"You can just tell us what you want us to know," Dahl suggested. "We don't have to have a slide show presentation."

"Oh, but you *do,*" Jenkins said. "If I just *tell* you, it'll sound crazy. Graphs and images make it . . . well, *less* crazy, anyway."

"Swell," Finn said, and looked over at Dahl, as if to say *Thanks for getting us into this.* Dahl shrugged.

Another table pound by Jenkins, and the holographic image stabilized. "Ha!" Jenkins said. "Okay, I'm ready."

"Thank God," Hester said.

Jenkins fiddled his hands over the table, accessing a display of flat images parallel to the top of the display table. He found one he wanted and flipped it up into the view of the rest of them.

"This is the *Intrepid*," Jenkins said, motioning to the rotating graphic that now hovered atop the holographic table. "The flagship of the Universal Union Space Fleet, and one of the fleet's largest ships. But for all that, one of just thousands of ships in the fleet. For the first nine years of its existence, aside from being appointed the flagship, there was nothing particularly special about it, from a statistical point of view."

The *Intrepid* shrank and was replaced by a graph showing two closely conforming lines plotted across time, one representing the ship, the other representing the fleet as a whole.

"It had a general mission of exploration and from time to time engaged in military actions, and in both scenarios suffered crew losses consistent with Dub U average, if slightly lower, because the Dub U sees the flagship as a symbol, and generally gave it less strenuous missions. But then, five years ago, this."

The graph scrolled to include the last five years. The *Intrepid*'s line spiked violently and then plateaued at a substantially higher level than the rest of the fleet.

"Whoa," Hanson said.

"'Whoa' is right," Jenkins said.

"What happened?" Dahl asked.

"Captain Abernathy is what happened," Duvall said. "He took command of the *Intrepid* five years ago."

"Close but wrong," Jenkins said, and waved his hands over the table, rooting through visual elements to find the one he wanted. "Abernathy did take command of the *Intrepid* five years ago. Before that he was captain of the *Griffin* for four years, where he developed a reputation of being an unconventional and risk-taking but effective leader."

" 'Risk-taking' could be a euphemism for 'getting crew killed,' " Hester said.

"Could be but isn't," Jenkins said, and threw an image of a battle cruiser into the view. "Here's the *Griffin*," he said. A graph scrolled out behind it, like the one that scrolled out behind the *Intrepid* earlier. "And as you can see, despite Abernathy's 'risk-taking' reputation, the crew fatality rate is on average no worse than any other ship in the line. That's impressive considering the *Griffin* is a battle cruiser—a Dub U warship. It's not until Abernathy gets to the *Intrepid* that fatalities for crew under his command spike so massively."

"Maybe he's gone nuts," Finn said.

"His psychological reviews for the last five years are clean," Jenkins said.

"How do you know—" Finn stopped and held up his hand. "You know, never mind. Dumb question."

"He's not insane and he's not purposefully putting his crew at risk, is what you're saying," Dahl said. "But I remember Lieutenant Collins saying to me that when people complained about the high crew death rate on the *Intrepid*, they were told that as the flagship it engaged in riskier missions." He pointed at the screen. "You're telling us that it's not true."

"It's true that away missions result in higher deaths now," Jenkins said. "But it's not because the missions themselves are inherently more risky." He fiddled and threw several ship images up on the screen. "These are some of our combat and infiltration ships," he said. "They routinely take on high-risk missions. Here are their average crew fatalities over time." Graphs spewed out behind their images. "You can see their fatalities are higher than the Dub U baseline. But"—Jenkins dragged over the image of the *Intrepid*—"their crew fatalities are still *substantially* lower than the *Intrepid*'s, whose missions are generally classified as having far less risk."

"So why do people keep dying?" Duvall asked.

"The missions themselves are generally not risky," Jenkins said. "It's just that something always goes *wrong* on them."

"So it's a competence issue," Dahl said.

Jenkins tossed up a scrolling image featuring the *Intrepid*'s officers and section heads and their various citations and awards. "This is the flagship of the Dub U," he said. "You don't get to be on it if you're an incompetent."

"Then it's bad luck," Finn said. "The *Intrepid* has the worst karma in the known universe."

"That second part might be true," Jenkins said. "But I don't think luck has anything to do with it."

Dahl blinked and remembered saying the same thing, after he dragged Kerensky into the shuttle. "There's something going on with the officers here," he said.

"Five of them, yes," Jenkins said. "Abernathy, Q'eeng, Kerensky, West and Hartnell. Statistically speaking there's something highly aberrant about them. When they're on an away mission, the chance of the mission experiencing a critical failure increases. When two or more of them are on the same away mission, the chance of a critical failure increases exponentially. If three or more are on the mission, it's almost certain someone is going to die."

"But never any of *them*," Hanson said.

"That's right," Jenkins said. "Sure, Kerensky gets the shit kicked out of him on a regular basis. Even the other four are occasionally knocked around. But death? Not for them. Never for them."

"And none of this is normal," Dahl prompted.

"Of course not!" Jenkins said. He flipped up pictures of the five officers, with graphs behind them. "Each of them has experienced exponentially higher fatality rates on away missions than any other officers in the same positions on other ships. That's across the *entire* fleet, and across the *entire existence* of the fleet, back to the formation of the Dub U nearly two hundred years ago. You have to go back to the blue water fleets for the same types of fatalities, and even the officers themselves didn't escape mortality. Captains and senior officers were dropping dead all the time."

"That's what scurvy and plague will do," Hester said.

"It's not just *scurvy*," Jenkins said, and waved at the officers' pictures. "Officers die today too, you know. Having rank changes mortality patterns somewhat but doesn't eliminate them. Statistically speaking, all five of these guys should be dead two or three times over. *Maybe* one or two of them would have survived all the experiences they've had so far. But all five of them? The odds are better that one of them would get struck by lightning."

"Which they would survive," Finn said.

"But not the crewman next to him," Duvall said.

"Now you're getting it," Jenkins said.

"So what you're saying is all this is impossible," Dahl said.

Jenkins shook his head. "Nothing's impossible," he said. "But some things are pretty damned unlikely. This is one of them."

"How unlikely?" Dahl asked.

"In all my research there's only one spaceship I've found that has even remotely the same sort of statistical patterns for away missions," Jenkins said. He rummaged through the graphic elements again, and then threw one onto the screen. They all stared at it.

Duvall frowned. "I don't recognize this ship," she said.

"And I thought I knew every type of ship we had. Is this a Dub U ship?"

"Not exactly," Jenkins said. "It's from the United Federation of Planets."

Duvall blinked and focused her attention back at Jenkins. "Who are they?" she asked.

"They don't exist," Jenkins said, and pointed back at the ship. "And neither does this. This is the starship *Enterprise*. It's fictional. It was on a science fiction drama series. And so are we."

. . . . .

"Okay," Finn said, after a moment. "I don't know about anyone else here, but I'm ready to label this guy officially *completely fucking insane.*"

Jenkins looked over to Dahl. "I told you it would sound insane," he said. He waved at the display. "But here are the stats."

"The stats show that there's something screwed up with this ship," Finn said. "It doesn't suggest we're stars in a fucked-up science fiction show."

"I never said you were the *stars*," Jenkins said. He pointed at the floating images of Abernathy, Q'eeng, Kerensky, West and Hartnell. "*They're* the stars. You're extras."

"Perfect," Finn said, and stood up. "Thank you *so* much for wasting my time. I'm going to get some sleep now."

"Wait," Dahl said.

"'Wait'? Seriously, Andy?" Finn said. "I know you've been obsessed with this for a while now, but there's being on the edge and then there's going all the way *over* the edge, and our hairy friend here is so far over the edge that the edge doesn't even know him anymore."

"You know how I hate to agree with Finn," Hester said. "But I do. This isn't right. It's not even wrong."

Dahl looked at Duvall. "I'm voting for nuts, too, Andy," she said. "Sorry."

"Jimmy?" Dahl asked, looking at Hanson.

"Well, he's *definitely* nuts," Hanson said. "But he thinks he's telling the truth."

"Of course he does! That's why he's *nuts*," Finn said.

"That's not what I mean," Hanson said. "When you're nuts, your reasoning is consistent with your own internal logic, but it's *internal* logic, which doesn't make any sort of sense outside your own head." He pointed at Jenkins. "His logic is external and reasonable enough."

"Except the part where we're all fictional," Finn sneered.

"I never said that," Jenkins said.

"Gaaah," Finn said, and pointed to the *Enterprise*. "Fictional, you unmitigated asshole."

"*It's* fictional," Jenkins said. "*You're* real. But a fictional television show intrudes on our reality and warps it."

"Wait," Finn said, waving his hands in disbelief. "*Television?* Are you fucking kidding me? There hasn't been *television* in hundreds of years."

"Television got its start in 1928," Jenkins said. "The last use of the medium for entertainment purposes was in 2105. Sometime between those two dates there's a television series following the adventures of the crew of the *Intrepid*."

"I really want to know what you're smoking," Finn said. "Because whatever it is, I'm betting I can make a hell of a profit on it."

Jenkins looked back at Dahl again. "I can't work like this," he said.

"Everyone shut up for a minute," Dahl said. Finn and Jenkins calmed themselves. "Look. I agree it sounds crazy. Even *he* admits it sounds crazy." Dahl pointed at Jenkins. "But think about what we've seen go on in this ship. Think of how people act here. What's messed up here isn't that this guy thinks we're on a television show. What's messed up here is that as far as I can tell, at this point, it's the *most rational explanation* for what's going on. Tell me that I'm wrong."

Dahl looked around at his friends. Everyone was silent. Finn looked like he was barely holding his tongue.

"Right," Dahl said. "So at least let's hear the rest of what he has to say. Maybe it gets more nuts from here. Maybe it starts to make more sense. Either way, it's better than what we have now, which is nothing."

"Fine," Finn said, finally. "But you owe us all handjobs." He sat back down.

"Handjobs?" Jenkins asked Dahl.

"Long story," Dahl said.

"Well, anyway," Jenkins said. "You're right about one thing. It's messed up that the most rational explanation for what does go on in this ship is that a television show intrudes on our reality and warps it. But that's not the worst thing about it."

"Jesus Christ," Finn said. "If that's not the worst thing, what is?"

"That as far as I can tell," Jenkins said, "it's not actually a very good show."

CHAPTER TEN

R ed alert!" said Captain Abernathy, as the Calendrian rebel ship fired its torpedoes at the *Intrepid*. "Evasive maneuvers! Now!" Dahl, standing at his science post on the bridge, positioned his feet for stability as the ship yawed widely, moving its bulk to avoid the nimble guided projectiles headed for it.

You'll notice that the Intrepid's *inertial dampeners don't work as well in crisis situations,* Dahl remembered Jenkins telling them. *The ship could do hairpin turns and loop-de-loops any other time and you'd never notice. But whenever there's a dramatic event, there goes your footing.*

"They're still coming right at us!" yelled Ensign Jacobs, at the weapons station, tracking the torpedoes.

Abernathy pounded the button on his chair that opened a broadcast channel. "All hands! Brace for impact!"

Dahl and everyone else on the bridge grabbed on to their stations and braced themselves. *This would be a good time for a restraint system,* Dahl thought.

There was a far crump as the torpedoes hit the *Intrepid*. The bridge deck swayed from the impact.

"Damage report!" barked Abernathy.

Decks six through twelve will almost always sustain damages during an attack, Jenkins had said. *It's because these are the decks the show has sets for. They can cut away from the bridge for shots of explosions and crew being flung backward.*

"Decks six, seven and nine have sustained heavy damages," Q'eeng said. "Decks eight and ten have moderate damage."

"More torpedoes!" cried Jacobs. "Four of them!"

"Countermeasures!" yelled Abernathy. "Fire!"

Why didn't you use countermeasures in the first place? Dahl thought.

In his head, Jenkins answered. *Every battle is designed for maximum drama,* he said. *This is what happens when the Narrative takes over. Things quit making sense. The laws of physics take a coffee break. People stop thinking logically and start thinking dramatically.*

"The Narrative"—Jenkins' term for when the television show crept into their lives, swept away rationality and physical laws and made people know, do and say things they wouldn't otherwise. *You've had it happen to you already,* Jenkins had said. *A fact you didn't know before just pops into your head. You make a decision or take an action you wouldn't otherwise make. It's like an irresistible impulse because it* is *an irresistible impulse—your will isn't your own, you're just a pawn for a writer to move around.*

On the view screen, three orange blossoms burned brightly as the *Intrepid's* countermeasures took out torpedoes.

Three, not four, Dahl thought. *Because having one get through will be more dramatic.*

"One's still heading our way!" Jacobs said. "It's going to hit!"

There was a violent bang as the torpedo smacked against the hull several decks below the bridge. Jacobs screamed as his weapons station exploded in a shower of sparks, flinging him backward to the deck of the bridge.

Something will explode on the bridge, Jenkins said. *That's where the camera spends nearly all its time. There has to be damage there, whether it makes sense or not.*

"Reroute weapons controls!" yelled Abernathy.

"Rerouted!" said Kerensky. "I have them."

"Fire!" Abernathy said. "Full spread!"

Kerensky smashed his fingers into the buttons of his station.

The view screen lit up as pulse beams and neutrino missiles blasted toward the Calendrian rebel, exploding in a constellation of impacts seconds later.

"Direct hits!" Kerensky said, looking at his station for information. "It looks like we cracked their engine core, Captain. We've got about a minute before she blows."

"Get us out of here, Kerensky," Abernathy said, and then turned to Q'eeng. "Additional damages?"

"Deck twelve heavily damaged," Q'eeng said.

The door to the bridge opened and Chief Engineer West came through. "And our engines are banged up pretty good," he said, as though he would have been able to hear Abernathy and Q'eeng's conversation, through a door, while red alert sirens were blaring. "We're lucky we didn't crack our own core, Captain."

"How long until it's repaired?" Abernathy asked.

Just long enough to introduce a plot complication, Dahl thought.

"Ten hours would be pushing it," West said.

"Damn it!" Abernathy said, pounding his chair again. "We're supposed to be escorting the Calendrian pontifex's ship to the peace talks by then."

"Clearly there are those among the rebels still opposed to the talks," Q'eeng said, looking toward the view screen. In it, the rebel ship blew up impressively.

"Yes, clearly," Abernathy said. "But they were the ones who asked for the talks to begin with. Why jeopardize them *now*? And why attack *us*?" He looked off, grimly.

Every once in a while Abernathy or one of the other officers will say something dramatic, or rhetorical, or leading, and then he and everyone else will be quiet for a few seconds, Jenkins told them. *That's a lead-out to a commercial break. When that happens, the Narrative goes away. Watch what they do next.*

After several seconds Abernathy blinked, relaxed his posture and looked at West. "Well, you should probably have your people start fixing those engines, then." His voice was notably less tense and drama-filled.

"Right," West said, and went right back out of the door. As he did so he looked around, as if wondering why he felt it necessary to come all the way to the bridge to deliver a piece of information he could have easily offered by phone.

Abernathy turned to Q'eeng. "And, let's get repair crews to those damaged decks."

"Will do," Q'eeng said.

"And while you're at it, get someone up here to repair the weapons station," Abernathy said. "And see if we can't find some power spike dampeners or something. There's not a damn reason why everything on the bridge has to go up in sparks anytime we have a battle."

Dahl made a small choking sound at this.

"Is there a problem, Ensign?" Abernathy said, seeing Dahl for what seemed like the first time in all of this.

"No, sir," Dahl said. "Sorry, sir. A little post-combat nervousness."

"You're Dill," Abernathy said. "From Xenobiology."

"Dahl, sir," Dahl said. "That was my former posting, yes."

"First day on the bridge, then," Abernathy said.

"It is," Dahl said.

"Well, don't worry, it's not always like this," Abernathy said. "Sometimes it's worse."

"Yes, sir," Dahl said.

"Okay," Abernathy said, and then nodded at the prone figure of Jacobs, who was now moaning softly. "Why don't you make yourself useful and take Jackson here to sick bay. He looks like he could use it."

"Right away, sir," Dahl said, and moved to help Jacobs.

"How is he?" Abernathy asked, as Dahl lifted him.

"Banged up," Dahl said. "But I think he'll live."

"Well, good," Abernathy said. "That's more than I can say for the last weapons specialist. Or the one before that. Sometimes, Dill, I wonder what the hell is going on with this ship. It's like it has a goddamned curse."

· · · · ·

"It doesn't prove anything," Finn said, after Dahl recounted the events of the attack. The five of them were huddled around a table in the crew lounge, with their drinks.

"How much more proof do you want?" Dahl asked. "It was like going down a checklist. Wonky inertial dampeners? Check. Exploding bridge stations? Check. Damage to decks six through twelve? Check. Meaningful pause before dropping to commercial? Check."

"No one died," Hanson pointed out.

"Nobody *had* to die," Dahl said. "I think this battle is just an opener. It's what you have before the first commercial break. It's the setup for whatever's supposed to happen next."

"Like what?" Duvall asked.

"I don't know," Dahl said. "*I'm* not writing this thing."

"Jenkins would know," Hester said. "He's got that collection of 'episodes.' "

Dahl nodded. Jenkins had splayed out a timeline of the *Intrepid* that featured glowing hash marks at near regular intervals. *Those are where the Narrative intrudes,* he said, zooming into one of the hash marks, which in detail branched out like a root structure. *It comes and goes, you can see. Each of these smaller events is a scene. They all tie into a narrative arc.* Jenkins zoomed out. *Six years. Twenty-four major events a year, on average. Plus a couple minor ones. I think those are tie-in novels.*

"Not *you*, now," Finn complained to Hester, breaking Dahl's reverie. "It's bad enough Andy is all wrapped up in this. Now you're going over to the crazy side, too."

"Finn, if the shoe fits, I'm going to call it a shoe, all right?" Hester said. "I don't believe his *conclusions,* but his knowledge of the *details* is pretty damn impressive. This last engagement went down like Jenkins said it would. He called the thing right down to the exploding bridge station. Now, maybe we're not actually being *written,* and maybe Jenkins is off his medication. But I bet he's got a good guess where this adventure with that rebel ship takes us."

"So you're going to go running to him every time something happens to find out what you should do next?" Finn asked. "If you really want to follow a cult leader, there are better ones than a guy who hasn't eaten anything but away rations for four years and shits in a portable potty."

"How do *you* explain it, then?" Hester asked Finn.

"I *don't,*" Finn said. "Look. This is a weird damn ship. We all agree on that. But what you're trying to do is impose causality on random events, just like everyone else here has been doing."

"The suspension of the laws of physics isn't a random event, Finn," Hester said.

"And you're a physicist now?" Finn countered, and looked around. "People, we're on a goddamned *spaceship.* Can any of us really explain how the thing works? We encounter all types of alien life on planets we've just discovered. Should we be surprised we don't understand it? We're part of a civilization that spans light-years. That's inherently weird if you give it any thought. It's all inherently unlikely."

"You didn't say any of this when we met with Jenkins," Dahl said.

"I was *going* to," Finn said. "But then you were all 'let's hear what he has to say,' and there was no *point.*"

Dahl frowned, irritated.

"Look, I'm not disagreeing there's something off here," Finn said. "There is. We all know it. But maybe that's because this whole ship is on some sort of insanity feedback loop. It's been feeding on itself for years now. In a situation like that, if you're looking for patterns to connect unlikely events, you're going to find them. It doesn't help there's someone like Jenkins, who is crazy but just coherent enough to whip up an explanation that makes some sort of messed-up sense in hindsight. Then he goes rogue and starts tracking the officers for the rest of the crew, which just feeds the insanity. And into this comes Andy, who is trained to believe this sort of mumbo jumbo."

"What does that mean?" Dahl said, stiffening.

"It means you spent years in a seminary, neck-deep in mysticism," Finn said. "And not just run-of-the-mill human mysticism but genuinely *alien* mysticism. You stretched your mind out there, my friend, just wide enough to fit Jenkins' nutbrained theory." He put up his hands, sensing Dahl's irritation. "I like you, Andy, don't get me wrong. I think you're a good guy. But I think your history here is working against you. And I think whether you know it or not, you're leading our pals here into genuinely bugshit territory."

"Speaking of personal history, that's the thing that creeped me out most about Jenkins," Duvall said.

"That he knows about us?" asked Hanson.

"I mean how *much* he knew about each of us," Duvall said. "And what he thought it meant."

You're all extras, but you're glorified *extras,* Jenkins had told them. *Your average extra exists just to get killed off, so he or she doesn't have a backstory. But each of you do.* He pointed to each in turn. *You were a novitiate to an alien religion. You're a scoundrel who's made enemies across the fleet. You're the son of one of the richest men in the universe. You left your last ship after having an altercation with your superior officer, and you're sleeping with Kerensky now.*

"You're just pissed he told the rest of us that you were boinking Kerensky," Hester said. "Especially after you had already blown him off in front of us."

Duvall rolled her eyes. "I have needs," she said.

"He's had three STDs in his recent history," Finn said.

"I had him get a new round of shots, trust me," Duvall said, and then looked over at Dahl. "And anyway, don't get on me for scratching an itch. None of *you* were exactly stepping up."

"Hey, I was in sick bay when you started with Kerensky," Dahl said. "Don't blame me."

Duvall smirked at that. "And it wasn't that part that bothered me, anyway," she said. "It was the other part."

You're not just going to get killed off, Kerensky told them. It's not enough for a television audience just to kill off some poor random bastard every episode. Every once in a while they have to make it seem like a real person is dying. So they take a smaller character, build them up long enough for the audience to care about them, and then snap them off. That's you guys. Because you come with backstories. You're probably going to have an entire episode devoted to your death.

"More complete bullshit," Finn said.

"Easy for you to say," Hester said. "I'm the only one of us without an interesting backstory. I've got nothing. The next away team I'm on, I'm fucking *doomed*."

Finn pointed at Hester and looked at Dahl. "See, this is what I'm talking about right here. You've overwhelmed a weak and febrile mind."

Dahl smiled at this. "And you're the lone voice of sanity."

"Yes!" Finn said. "I want you to think about what it means

when *I* am the person in a group who is making the case for reality. I'm the least responsible person I know. I resent having to be the voice of reason. I resent it a lot."

" 'Weak and febrile,' " Hester muttered.

"You were the one calling a shoe a shoe," Finn said.

Duvall's phone pinged and she stepped away for a moment. When she returned, she was pale. "All right," she said. "That was altogether too *damned* coincidental for my tastes."

Dahl frowned. "What is it?"

"That was Kerensky," she said. "I'm wanted for a senior officer briefing."

"What for?" Hanson asked.

"When the *Intrepid* was attacked by that rebel ship, our engines got knocked out, so they sent another ship to escort the Calendrian pontifex's ship to the peace talks," Duvall said. "That ship just attacked the pontifex's ship and crippled it."

"What ship is it?" Dahl asked.

"The *Nantes*," Duvall said. "The last ship I was stationed on."

CHAPTER ELEVEN

"Trust me, Andy," Finn said, walking with Dahl toward Duvall's barracks. "She doesn't want to talk to you."

"You don't know that," Dahl said.

"I do know that," Finn said.

"Yeah?" Dahl asked. "How?"

"When I saw her just after she came out of her briefing, she said to me, 'If I see Andy, I swear to God I'm going to break his nose,'" Finn said. Dahl smiled.

The two of them reached Duvall's barracks and entered the room, which was empty except for Duvall, sitting on her bunk.

"Maia," Dahl began.

"Andy," Duvall said, stood, and punched Dahl in the face. Dahl collapsed to the deck, holding his nose.

"I told you," Finn said to Dahl, on the deck. He looked over to Duvall. "I *did* tell him."

"I thought you were kidding!" Dahl said from the deck.

"Surprise," Finn said.

Dahl pulled his hand back from his face to see if there was any blood on it; there wasn't. "What was that for?" he asked Duvall.

"It's for your conspiracy theories," Duvall said.

"They're not my theories," Dahl said. "They're Jenkins' theories."

"For Christ's sake, it doesn't matter who thought up the fucking things!" Duvall snapped. "I'm in that goddamned meeting today, telling them what I know about the *Nantes,* and all the time I'm doing that I'm thinking, 'This is it, this is the episode where I die.' And then I look over at Kerensky, and he's making cow eyes at me, like we're married instead of just screwing. And then I know I'm doomed, because if that son of a bitch has a crush on me, it makes it perfect if I get killed off. Because then he can be *sad* at the end of the episode."

"It doesn't have to work that way, Maia," Dahl said, and started to get up. She pushed him back down.

"Shut *up*, Andy," she said. "Just shut up. You're not getting it. It doesn't *matter* if it's going to work that way. What matters is now I'm buying into your paranoia. Now some part of my brain is thinking about buying it on an away mission. It's thinking about it all the time. It's like waiting for the other shoe to drop. And you fucking did it to me. Thank you so *very* much." Duvall sat down on her bunk, pissed.

"I'm sorry," Dahl said, after a minute.

"*Sorry*," Duvall said, and laughed a small laugh. "Jesus, Andy."

"What went on in the officer briefing?" Finn asked.

"I briefed them about the *Nantes* and its crew," Duvall said. "The Calendrian rebels have a spy or turncoat in the crew, someone who could hack into the weapons systems and fire on the pontifex's ship, and then shut down communications. We've heard nothing from the *Nantes* since the attack."

"Why would they put a spy on the *Nantes*?" Finn asked. "It was the *Intrepid* that was supposed to escort the pontifex's ship."

"They must have known the *Nantes* was the backup ship for this mission," Duvall said. "And it's easier to sneak a spy on the *Nantes* than on the flagship of the Universal Union. So they send a ship to attack us, knock us out of the mission, and then the *Nantes* is in a perfect position to take a shot at the pontifex's ship. And that's the *other* thing—" Duvall pointed at Dahl. "Because when we're being told this in the briefing, I'm thinking 'How far ahead would you have to plant a spy? How could they have known the *Nantes* would be the backup ship for a mission that was just assigned a couple of days ago? How *likely* is that?' And then I think 'This episode needs to be better edited.'" She looked down at Dahl. "And that's when I decided I was going to punch you in the head the next time I saw you."

"Jenkins did say he didn't think the show was very good," Dahl said.

Duvall cocked back her arm. "Don't make me do it again, Andy," she said.

"Is there an away team?" Finn asked.

"Yes," Duvall said. "And I'm on it. The *Nantes* is silent and it isn't moving, so the *Intrepid* has been ordered to investigate the situation on the *Nantes* and to defend the pontifex's ship from any further attack. I was stationed on the *Nantes* and I was a ground trooper, so that makes me the guide for the away team. And I'm likely to get everyone on the team killed now, since thanks to Andy I'm convinced this is when it makes *dramatic sense* for me to get shot between the eyes."

"When do we arrive?" Finn asked.

"About two hours," Duvall said. "Why?"

Finn fished in his pocket and pulled out a small blue oblong pill. "Here, take this."

Duvall peered at it. "What is it?"

"It's a mood leveler made from the orynx plant," Finn said. "It's very mild."

"I don't need a mood leveler," Duvall said. "I just need to smack Andy again."

"You can do both," Finn said. "Trust me, Maia. You're a wreck right now, and you know it. And like you said, that's going to put your away team at risk."

"And taking a drug won't?" Duvall said.

"Not this one," Finn said. "Like I said, it's very mild. You'll hardly notice the effect. All you'll notice is that you'll *unclench* a little. Just enough to focus on your job and not on your state of mind. It won't affect anything else. You'll still be sharp and aware." He held the pill closer to Duvall.

She peered at it again. "There's lint on it," she said.

Finn dusted the lint off. "There," he said.

"All right," Duvall said, taking the pill. "But if I start seeing talking lizards, I'm going to punch you."

"Fair enough," Finn said. "Should I get you some water?"

"I'm fine," Duvall said, and dry swallowed. Then she leaned over and smacked Dahl across the face with an open palm slap.

"What was that one for?" Dahl asked.

"Finn said I could take the pill *and* slap you," Duvall said, and then frowned. She looked up at Finn. "What was this pill made of?"

"The orynx plant," Finn said.

"And its effects are mild," Duvall said.

"Usually," Finn said.

"Because I'll tell you what, I'm getting some pretty strong effects all of a sudden," Duvall said, and then slumped off her bunk. Dahl caught her before she collapsed onto the deck.

"What did you do?" Dahl asked Finn, struggling with Duvall's unconscious body.

"Quite obviously, I knocked her out," Finn said, walking over to assist Dahl.

"I thought you said that pill was *very mild*," Dahl said.

"I lied," Finn said, and took Duvall's legs. The two of them maneuvered her back onto her bunk.

"How long is she going to be out?" Dahl asked

"A dose like that will knock out a good-sized man for about eight hours," Finn said, "so she'll probably be down for at least ten."

"She'll miss her away team," Dahl said.

"Yes, she will. That's the *point*," Finn said, and then nodded down at Duvall. "Andy, you've got Duvall and our other friends so fucked up about this television thing that it's messing with their heads. If you want to go down that road, that's fine. I'm not going to stop you. But I want to make sure the rest of them see a counterargument in action."

"By drugging Maia?" Dahl said.

"That's the means to an end," Finn said. "The end is making the point that even without Maia, the away team is going to go over to the *Nantes* and do their job. Life goes on even when Jenkins' 'Narrative' is supposed to apply. Once Maia, Jimmy and Hester see that, maybe they'll stop freaking out. And who knows? Maybe you'll come to your senses, too."

Dahl nodded to Duvall. "She's still going to get in trouble for missing her mission," he said. "That's a court-martial offense. I'm not sure she'll appreciate that."

Finn smiled. "I like how you think I didn't plan for that," he said.

"And just how did you plan for that?" Dahl said.

"You're about to find out," Finn said. "Because you're part of it."

· · · · ·

"Where's Maia?" Kerensky asked.

"Who?" Finn said, innocently.

"Duvall," Kerensky said somewhat impatiently. "She's supposed to be on this away team."

"Oh, her," Finn said. "She's been waylaid with Orynxian Dropsy. She's out for a couple of days. Dahl here and I are replacing her on the team. Check your orders, sir."

Kerensky looked at Finn appraisingly, then pulled out his phone and checked the away team order. After a moment he grunted and motioned them toward the shuttle. Finn and

Dahl got on. Dahl didn't know how Finn had forged the away team order and didn't feel the need to ask too deeply about it.

Inside the shuttle were Captain Abernathy, Commander Q'eeng and an extraordinarily nervous-looking ensign whom Dahl had never seen before. The ensign had undoubtedly noted the presence of the three senior officers on the away team, had calculated his own odds of survival and didn't like the result. Dahl smiled at the ensign as he sat down; the ensign looked away.

Several minutes later, with Kerensky at the controls, the shuttle was out of its bay and headed toward the *Nantes.*

"Some of you are late additions to this party," Captain Abernathy said, nodding to Finn and Dahl, "so let me review the situation and our plan of attack. The *Nantes* has been out of communication since just before it attacked the pontifex's ship. We think the Calendrian rebel spy was somehow able to take over some systems, cut off communications and fire on the pontifex, but afterward the crew must have been able to get back some control of the ship, otherwise the *Nantes* would have blown the pontifex out of the sky by now. Our job is to get onto the *Nantes,* ascertain the situation and if necessary assist in the capture of the rebel."

"Do we have any information on who this rebel might be, sir?" Dahl heard himself ask, surprised to hear the sound of his own voice. *Oh, shit,* he thought.

"An excellent question, Ensign Dahl," Q'eeng said. "Just before we left the *Intrepid* I requested a crew manifest for the *Nantes.* The crew of the ship has been stable for months, but there was a recent addition to its crew, a Crewman Jer Weston. He's a primary person of interest."

"Wait," Finn said, interrupting the commander. "Did you say Jer Weston?"

"Yes," Q'eeng said, irritated at being interrupted.

"Previously stationed on the *Springfield*?" Finn asked.

"That was his posting prior to the *Nantes,* yes," Q'eeng said. "Why?"

"I know this guy," Finn said. "I knew him on the *Springfield.*"

"My God, man," Abernathy said, leaning forward to Finn. "Tell us about him."

"There's not much to say," Finn said, looking at the captain and then Q'eeng. "He and I worked in the cargo hold together."

"He was your friend?" Q'eeng asked.

"Friend might be a little much, sir," Finn said. "Jer is a dick. 'Friend' isn't part of his vocabulary. But I worked with him for more than a year. I spent time with him. He never seemed like a traitor."

"If spies seemed like traitors they wouldn't be good spies," Q'eeng said.

"Finn, we need to know everything you know about Weston," Abernathy said, intensely. "Anything we can use. Anything that can help us take back control of the *Nantes* before more Calendrian rebel ships converge on this sector. Because if they arrive before the *Nantes* is back in action, the *Intrepid* won't be enough to keep the pontifex safe. And then it won't just be the Calendrians fighting themselves. The whole galaxy will be at war."

There was a long, tense second of silence.

"Uh, okay, sir," Finn said, eventually.

"Great, thanks," Abernathy said. His demeanor was suddenly more relaxed. "Wow. A last-minute replacement for this away team, and you just happen to know the crewman we think is the spy. That's amazing. What are the odds of that?"

"Pretty big odds," Finn said.

"I'll say," Abernathy said.

"Captain, before Crewman Finn briefs us on Weston, I want to discuss the layout of the *Nantes* with you," Q'eeng said. He and Abernathy fell into a discussion.

Dahl turned to Finn. "You okay?" he asked.

"I'm fine," Finn said.

"You're sure," Dahl said.

"Andy, quit it," Finn said. "It's a coincidence, is all it is. I'm going to get through this. You are going to get through this. We're going to get back to the *Intrepid,* we're going to get a drink, and then I'm going to go to Medical when Maia wakes up and kicks my ass. That's my prediction. I'll put money on it if you want."

Dahl smiled. "Okay," he said, and sat back. He looked over at Abernathy and Q'eeng, still in their conversation. Then he looked over to the other ensign. He was looking at Finn with an expression that Dahl couldn't quite read.

After a moment, it came to him. The other ensign looked relieved.

And he looked guilty about it.

CHAPTER TWELVE

The *Nantes* bay was empty except for several automated cargo carts rolling about. "Finn and Dahl, you're with me," Captain Abernathy said, and then pointed at the remaining ensign. "Grover, you're with Kerensky and Q'eeng."

"Yes, sir," Ensign Grover said, and then was flung backward against the shuttle as a pulse beam hit him, fired from one of the automated carts. As he fell, Dahl caught a glimpse of confusion in his eyes.

And then Dahl was running, with Finn and Kerensky, looking for cover under fire. They found it several meters away, behind storage bins. Several armed cargo carts were now rolling toward them, with the others heading toward where Kerensky and Q'eeng had taken cover.

"Anyone have any ideas?" Abernathy asked.

"Those carts are being controlled from a distance," Finn said. "If we can get to the quartermaster's office here in the bay, we can override their signal for the ones in here."

"Yes," Abernathy said, and pointed to a far wall. "If this bay is laid out anything like the *Intrepid*'s, it's over there."

"I can do it," Finn said.

Abernathy held up his hand. "No," he said. "We've already lost one crew member today. I don't want to risk another."

As opposed to risking our captain? Dahl thought, but kept silent.

Abernathy raised his pulse gun. "You two cover me as I run for it. I'm going on three." He started counting. Dahl glanced over to Finn, who shrugged and then readied his pulse gun.

At the three count, Abernathy burst from behind the storage bins like a startled quail and ran in a broken, diving pattern
across the bay. The cargo carts abandoned their previous targets and fired at the captain, narrowly missing him each time.
Dahl and Finn aimed and knocked out one cart each.

Abernathy made it to the quartermaster's office, blasting
the window and jumping through rather than wasting time
opening the door. Several seconds later, the cargo carts nois-
ily deactivated.

"All clear," Abernathy said, coming into view and hoisting
himself over the remains of the window. The members of
the *Intrepid* crew reassembled by the fallen corpse of Grover,
whose face still had a look of disbelief on it.

"Finn, it looks like your friend Jer Weston is now a mur-
derer," Abernathy said, grimly.

"He's not my friend, sir," Finn said.

"But you do *know* him," Abernathy said. "If you find him,
will you be ready to take him down? Alive?"

"Yes, sir," Finn said.

"Good," Abernathy said.

"Captain, we need to move," Q'eeng said. "There may be
others of these carts. In fact, I'm willing to bet that Weston is
using the carts as his own robot army to keep the crew members bottled up."

"Yes, precisely," Abernathy said, and nodded at Q'eeng.
"You and I will make our way to the bridge to see if we can
find Captain Bullington, and then assist her in taking back
the ship. Kerensky, you take Finn and Dahl here and find
Weston. Capture him alive."

"Yes, sir," Kerensky said.

"Good," Abernathy said. "Then let's move." He and Q'eeng
jogged off toward the bay entrance, to wander the crew cor-

ridors, where they would no doubt encounter and fight more armed cargo carts.

Finn turned to Kerensky. "So, what's the plan?" he asked.

"Plan?" Kerensky said, and blinked.

"If there really is a Narrative, it's not on him right now," Dahl said, about Kerensky.

"Right," Finn said, and turned to Dahl. "How about you?"

"You know what I think," Dahl said, and motioned to the cargo carts.

"You think Jer's pulling a Jenkins," Finn said. "Hiding in the walls."

"Bingo," Dahl said.

"A what?" Kerensky said. "What are you two talking about?"

Dahl and Finn didn't answer but instead went about separate tasks—Dahl accessing the ship records while Finn salvaged from the dead cargo carts.

"There," Finn said, holding out his hand after he was done. "Three cart IDs. We're going to have to leave our phones behind so we're not ID'd when we go into the cargo tunnels, and so the armed carts think we're one of them and don't try to kill us."

"Jenkins knew about this trick," Dahl said.

"Yeah, but I took the IDs from deactivated carts," Finn said. "These carts are just recently killed. Their IDs are still in the system. I don't think Jer had time to figure this one out."

"Figure what out?" Kerensky asked.

"I think you're right," Dahl said, and pulled up on his phone a map of the cargo tunnels. "It doesn't look like he's had time to make his hidey-hole disappear from the ship records either, since all of the cart distribution nodes are still on the map."

"So that's seven nodes," Finn said. "Which one do you want to try first?"

Dahl pulled up Weston's information. "His station was here in the bay complex, so I'd say we try the node closest to it," he said, and then returned to the map and highlighted a node. "Let's start here."

"Looks good," Finn said.

"I order you to tell me what you're planning," Kerensky said, plaintively.

"We're about to help you capture Jer Weston," Finn said. "That'll probably get you promoted."

"Oh," Kerensky said, and stood up a bit straighter. "We should definitely do that, then."

"And avenge the death of Grover here," Dahl added, nodding to Grover's still surprised body.

"Yes, that too," Kerensky said, and looked down at the body. "Poor man. This was his last away mission."

"Well, yes," Finn said.

"No, I mean that his term of duty was over in just a couple of days," Kerensky said. "I assigned him to this mission specifically so he could have one more away experience. A last hurrah. He tried to beg off of it, but I insisted."

"That was deeply malicious of you," Dahl said.

Kerensky nodded, either not knowing what *malicious* meant or simply not hearing it, apparently lost in reverie. "A shame, really. He was going to be married, too."

"Oh, please, *stop*," Finn said. "Otherwise I'm going to have to frag you."

"What?" Kerensky said, looking up at Finn.

"I think he means we should probably get going, sir," Dahl said, smoothly.

"Right," Kerensky said. "So, where are we going?"

· · · · ·

"You two wait here," Kerensky whispered at a bend in the corridor, after which came the distribution node they were sneaking up on. "I'll surprise him and stun him, and then we'll contact the captain."

"We can't contact him, we left our phones in the shuttle bay," Finn said.

"And we should probably deactivate all the armed carts first," Dahl said.

"Yes, yes," Kerensky said, mildly irritated. "But *first,* I'll take him down."

"A fine plan," Dahl said.

"We're right behind you," Finn said.

Kerensky nodded and readied his weapon, and then leapt out into the corridor, calling Jer Weston's name. There was an exchange of pulse gun fire, each blast going wide. From the top of the corridor there was a shower of sparks as a pulse gun blast ricocheted through the duct work, which collapsed on Kerensky, pinning him. He groaned and passed out.

"He really *is* completely useless," Finn said.

"What do you want to do now?" Dahl asked.

"I have a plan," Finn said. "Come on." He stood and walked forward, pulse gun behind his back. Dahl followed.

After a few steps the curve of the corridor revealed a disheveled Jer Weston, standing on the distribution node, pulse gun in hand, clearly considering whether or not to kill Kerensky.

"Hey, Jer," Finn said, walking up to him. "It's me, Finn."

Weston squinted. "Finn? Seriously? Here?" He smiled. "Jesus, man. What are the odds?"

"I know!" Finn said, and then shot Weston with a stun pulse. Weston collapsed.

"That was your plan?" Dahl said a second later. "Hoping he'd pause in recognition before he shot you?"

"In retrospect, the plan has significant logistical issues," Finn admitted. "On the other hand, it worked. You can't argue with success."

"Sure you can," Dahl said, "when it's based on stupidity."

"Anyway, this makes my point to you," Finn said. "If I was going to die on this mission, this probably would have been the moment, right? Me squaring off against my former fellow crew member? But I'm alive and he's stunned and captured. So much for 'the Narrative' and dying at dramatically appropriate moments. I hope you take the lesson to heart."

"Fine," Dahl said. "Maybe I've been weirding myself out. I'm still not following you into battle anymore."

"That's probably wise," Finn said, and then glanced over to the small computer at the distribution node, which Weston was probably using to control the cargo carts. "Why don't you disable the killer carts and I'll figure out how we're going to get Jer out of here."

"You could use a cart," Dahl said, going to the computer.

"There's an idea," Finn said.

Dahl disabled the carts across the ship and then heard a groan from Kerensky's direction. "Sounds like someone is up," he said to Finn.

"I'm busy trussing Jer like a turkey," Finn said. "Handle it, if you would."

Dahl walked over to Kerensky, who was still pinned under duct work. "Morning, sir," he said, to Kerensky.

"Did I get him?" Kerensky asked.

"Congratulations, sir," Dahl said. "Your plan worked perfectly."

"Excellent," Kerensky said, and wheezed a bit as the debris on top of him compressed his lungs.

"Would you like some help with your duct work, sir?" Dahl asked.

"Please," Kerensky said.

· · · · ·

"There's nothing in Crewman Weston's file that indicates any sympathy for the Calendrian rebel cause," said Sandra Bullington, captain of the *Nantes*. "I requested a hyperwaved report from the Dub U Investigative Service. Weston isn't religious or political. He doesn't even vote."

Bullington, Abernathy, Q'eeng, Finn and Dahl stood in front of a windowed room in the brig, in which Jer Weston sat. He was confined to a stasis chair, which was itself the only piece of furniture in the room. He looked groggy but was smiling. Kerensky was in sick bay with bruised ribs.

"What about family and friends?" Q'eeng asked.

"Nothing there, either," Bullington said. "He comes from a long line of Methodists from on the other side of the Dub U. None of his known associates have any link to Calendria or its religious or political struggles."

Abernathy looked through the glass at Weston. "Has he explained himself at all?" he asked.

"No," Bullington said. "That son of a bitch killed eighteen crew members and he won't say why. So far he's invoked his right to non-incrimination. But he says he's willing to confess everything under one condition."

"What's that?" Abernathy said.

"That you're the one he gets to confess to," Bullington said.

"Why me?" Abernathy asked.

Bullington shrugged. "He wouldn't say," she said. "If I had to guess, I would say it's because you're the captain of the flagship of the fleet and your exploits are known through the Union. Maybe he just wants to be brought in by a celebrity."

"Sir, I recommend against it," Q'eeng said.

"We've had him physically searched," Bullington said. "There's nothing in his cavities, and even if there were, he's in a stasis chair. He can't move anything below his neck at the moment. If you stay out of biting range, you'll be fine."

"I still recommend against it," Q'eeng said.

"It's worth the risk to get to the bottom of this," Abernathy said, and then looked over to Dahl and Finn. "I'll have these two come in with me, armed. If something happens, I trust one of them will take him down."

Q'eeng looked unhappy but didn't say anything more.

Two minutes later Abernathy, Dahl and Finn came through the door. Weston smiled and addressed Finn.

"Finn, you shot me," he said.

"Sorry," Finn said.

"It's all right," Weston said. "I figured I would get shot. I just didn't know it would be you who did it."

"Captain Bullington said you were ready to confess, but that you wanted to confess to me," Abernathy said. "I'm here."

"Yes you are," Weston said.

"Tell us what your relationship is with the Calendrian rebels," Abernathy said.

"The who what now?" Weston said.

"The Calendrian rebels," Abernathy repeated.

"I have no idea what you're talking about," Weston said.

"You fired on the pontifex's ship after the *Intrepid* was disabled by the rebels," Abernathy said. "You can't honestly expect us to believe that the two were unrelated."

"They are related," Weston said. "Just not that way."

"You're wasting my time," Abernathy said, and turned to go.

"Don't you want to know what the connection is?" Weston asked.

"We know what the connection is," Abernathy said. "It's the Calendrian rebels."

"No," Weston said. "The connection is you."

"What?" Abernathy said, squinting.

Weston turned to Finn. "Sorry you had to be here," he said, and then started blinking one eye at a time, first two left, then three right, then one left, then three right.

"Bomb!" Finn yelled, and Dahl flung himself at the captain as Weston's head exploded. Dahl felt the uniform and skin on his back fry in the heat as the blast wave pushed him into Abernathy, crushing the two of them against the wall.

Some indeterminate time later Dahl heard someone shout his name, looked up and saw Abernathy grabbing and shaking him. Abernathy had burns on his hands and arms but appeared largely fine. Dahl had shielded him from the worst of the blast. Upon realizing that, the whole of Dahl's back seared into painful life.

Dahl pushed Abernathy away from him and crawled over to Finn, on the floor, his face and front burned. He had been closest to the blast. As Dahl made it to his friend, he saw that the one eye Finn had remaining had looked over to him. Finn's hand twitched and Dahl grabbed it, causing Finn to spasm in pain. Dahl tried to break contact but Finn grabbed on. His lips moved.

Dahl moved to his friend's face to hear what he had to say.

"This is just ridiculous," is what Finn whispered.

"I'm sorry," Dahl said.

"Not your fault," Finn eventually said.

"I'm still sorry," Dahl said.

Finn gripped Dahl's hand tighter. "Find a way to stop this," he said.

"I will," Dahl said.

"Okay," Finn breathed, and died.

Abernathy came over to pull Dahl away from Finn. Despite the pain, Dahl took a swing at Abernathy. He missed and lost consciousness before his fist had swung all the way around.

CHAPTER THIRTEEN

"Tell me how to stop this," Dahl said to Jenkins.

Jenkins, who of course knew Dahl was coming to his secret lair, looked him over. "You look healed," he said. "Good. Sorry about your friend Finn."

"Did you know what was going to happen to him?" Dahl asked.

"No," Jenkins said. "It not like whoever is writing this crap sends me the scripts in advance. And this one was particularly badly written. Jer Weston walking around for years with a biological bomb in his head, waiting for an encounter with Captain Abernathy, who he blamed for the death of his own father on an away team twenty years ago, and taking advantage of an unrelated diplomatic incident to do so? That's just hackwork."

"So tell me how to stop it," Dahl said.

"You can't *stop* it," Jenkins said. "There's no stopping it. There's only *hiding* from it."

"Hiding isn't an option," Dahl said.

"Sure it is," Jenkins said, and opened his arms as if to say, *See?*

"*This* is not an option for anyone else but you," Dahl said. "We can't all sneak around in the bowels of a spaceship."

"There are other ways to hide," Jenkins said. "Ask your former boss Collins."

"She's only safe as long as you're around," Dahl said. "And not using the toilet."

"Find a way off this ship, then," Jenkins said. "You and your friends."

"That won't help either," Dahl said. "Jer Weston killed

eighteen members of the *Nantes* crew with his armed cargo carts. *They* weren't safe against what happens here on the *Intrepid,* were they? An entire planet suffered a plague so that we could create a last-minute vaccine for Kerensky. They weren't safe, either. Even you're not safe, Jenkins."

"I'm pretty safe," Jenkins said.

"You're *pretty safe* because your wife was the one who died, and all you were was part of her backstory," Dahl said. "But what happens to you when one of the writers on whatever television show this is thinks about you?"

"They're not going to," Jenkins said.

"Are you sure?" Dahl said. "On the *Nantes,* Jer Weston was using your trick of hiding in the cargo tunnels. That's where we found him. That's where we caught him. Whatever hack thought up that last episode now has it in his brain that the cargo tunnels can be used as hiding spaces. How long until he starts thinking about you?"

Jenkins didn't say anything to this, although Dahl couldn't tell if it was because he was considering the idea of being in a writer's crosshairs or because he mentioned Jenkins' wife.

"None of us are safe from this thing," Dahl said. "You lost your wife to it. I just lost a friend. You say I and all my friends are going to end up dying for dramatic purposes. I say whatever happens to us is going to happen to you, too. All your hiding doesn't change that, Jenkins. It's just delaying it. And meanwhile, you live your life like a rat in the walls."

Jenkins looked around. "I wouldn't say a rat," he said.

"Are you happy living this way?" Dahl asked.

"I haven't been happy since my wife died," Jenkins said. "It was her death that got me on to all of this anyway. Looking at the statistics of deaths on this ship, seeing how events on this ship played themselves out. Figuring that the most logical explanation was that we were part of a television show. Realizing my wife died simply to be a *dramatic moment* before a commercial. That in this television show, she was a bit player. An extra. She probably had about ten seconds of airtime. No one watching that episode probably has any memory of her now. Don't know her first name was Margaret. Or that she liked white wines more than red. Or that I proposed to her in her parents' front yard during a family reunion. Or that we were married for seven years before some hack decided to kill her. But I remember her."

"Do you think she'd be happy with how you're living?" Dahl asked.

"I think she'd understand why I do it," Jenkins said. "What I do on this ship keeps people alive."

"Keeps *some* people alive," Dahl said. "It's a zero-sum game. Someone is always going to have to die. Your alert system keeps the old hands here alive, but makes it more likely the new crew get killed."

"It's a risk, yes," Jenkins said.

"Jenkins, how long were you and your wife stationed on the *Intrepid* before she died?" Dahl asked.

Jenkins opened his mouth to respond and then shut it like a trap.

"It wasn't very long, was it?" Dahl asked.

Jenkins shook his head to say no, and then looked away.

"People on this ship figured it out before you came on it," Dahl said. "Maybe they didn't come to the same conclusions you did, but they saw what was happening and guessed their odds of survival. Now you're giving them better tech to do the same thing to new crew that they did to your wife."

"I think you should leave now," Jenkins said, still turned away from Dahl.

"Jenkins, listen to me," Dahl said, leaning in. "There's no way to hide from this. There's no way to run from it. There's no way to avoid fate. If the Narrative exists—and you and I know it does—then in the end we don't have free will. Sooner or later the Narrative will come for each of us. It'll use us however it wants to use us. And then we'll die from it. Like Finn did. Like Margaret did. Unless we stop it."

Jenkins looked back over at Dahl, eyes wet. "You're a man of faith, aren't you, Dahl?" he said.

"You know my history," Dahl said. "You know I am."

"How can you still be?" Jenkins said.

"What do you mean?" Dahl asked.

"I mean that you and I know that in this universe, God is a *hack*," he said. "He's a writer on an awful science fiction television show, and He can't plot His way out of a box. How do you have faith when you know that?"

"Because I don't think that's actually God," Dahl said.

"You think it's the show's producer, then," Jenkins said. "Or maybe the president of the network."

"I think your definition of what a god is and what my definition is probably differ," Dahl said. "But I don't think any of this is the work of God, or of a god of any sort. If this is a television show, then it was made by people. Whatever and however they're doing this to us, they are just like us. And that means we can stop them. We just have to figure out how. *You* have to figure it out, Jenkins."

"Why me?" Jenkins asked.

"Because you know this television show we're trapped in better than anyone else," Dahl said. "If there's a solution or a loophole, you're the only one who can find it. And soon. Because I don't want any more of my friends to die because of a hack writer. And that includes you."

. . . . .

"We could just blow up the *Intrepid,*" said Hester.

"It wouldn't work," said Hanson.

"Of course it would work," Hester said. "Ka-plooey, there goes the *Intrepid,* there goes the show."

"The show's not about the *Intrepid,*" Hanson said. "It's about the characters on it. Captain Abernathy and his crew."

"Some of them, anyway," Duvall said.

"The five main characters," Hanson amended. "If you blow up the ship, they'll just get another ship. A better ship. They'll just call it the *Intrepid-A* or something like that. It's happened on other science fiction shows."

"You've been studying?" Hester said, mockingly.

"Yes, I have," Hanson said, seriously. "After what happened to Finn, I went and learned about every science fiction television show I could find."

"What did you find out?" Dahl asked. He had already briefed his friends on his latest encounter with Jenkins.

"That I think Jenkins is right," Hanson said.

"That we're on a television show?" Duvall asked.

"No, that we're on a *bad* one," Hanson said. "As far as I can tell, the show we're on is pretty much a blatant rip-off of that show Jenkins told us about."

"*Star Wars,*" Hester said.

"*Star Trek,*" Hanson said. "There was a *Star Wars,* though. It was different."

"Whatever," Hester said. "So not only is this show we're on bad, it's plagiarized. And now my life is even more meaningless than it was before."

"Why would you make a show a knockoff of another show?" Duvall asked.

"*Star Trek* was very successful in its time," Hanson said. "So someone else came along and just reused the basic ideas. It worked because it worked before. People would still be entertained by the same stuff, more or less."

"Did you find our show in your research?" Dahl asked.

"No," Hanson said. "But I didn't think I would. When you create a science fiction show, you create a new fictional timeline, which starts just before the production date of that television show. That show's 'past' doesn't include the television show itself."

"Because that would be recursive and meta," Duvall said.

"Yes, but I don't think they thought about it that hard," Hanson said. "They just wanted the shows to be realistic in their own context, and you can't be realistic if there's a television show version of you in your own past."

"I hate that we now have conversations like this," Hester said.

"I don't think any of us like it," Dahl said.

"I don't know. I think it's interesting," Duvall said.

"It would be interesting if we were sitting in a dorm room, getting stoned," Hester said. "Talking about it seriously after our friend has died sort of takes the *fun* out of it."

"You're still angry about Finn," Hanson said.

"Of course I am," Hester spat. "Aren't you?"

"I recall you and him not getting along when you came on the *Intrepid*," Dahl said.

"I didn't say I always *liked* him," Hester said. "But we got better with each other while we were here. And he was one of us. I'm angry about what happened to him."

"I'm still pissed at him for knocking me out with that pill," Duvall said. "And I feel guilty about it, too. If he hadn't done that, he might still be alive."

"And you might be dead," Dahl pointed out.

"Not if I wasn't written to die in the episode," Duvall said.

"But Finn *was* written into the episode," Hanson said. "He was always going to be there. He was always going to be in that room when that bomb went off."

"Remember when I said I hated the conversations we have these days?" Hester said. "Just now? This is *exactly* the sort of conversation I'm talking about."

"Sorry," Duvall said.

"Jimmy, you said that whenever the show started, it created a new timeline," Dahl said, and ignored Hester throwing up his hands helplessly. "Do we know when that happened?"

"You think that might help us?" Hanson asked.

"I'm just curious," Dahl said. "We're an alternate timeline from 'reality,' whatever that is. I'd like to know when that branching off happened."

"I don't think we can know," Hanson said. "There's nothing that would signal where that timeline twist happened because from our perspective there's never been a break. We don't have any alternate timelines to compare ourselves to. We can only see our timeline."

"We could just start looking for when completely ridiculous shit started happening in our universe," Hester said.

"But define 'completely ridiculous shit,'" Duvall said. "Does space travel count? Contact with alien races? Does quantum physics count? Because I don't understand that crap at all. As far as I'm concerned, quantum physics could have been written by a hack."

"The first science fiction television show I found information about was something called *Captain Video,* and that was in 1949," Hanson said. "The first *Star Trek* show was twenty years after that. So, probably this show was made sometime between the late 1960s and the end of television broadcasting in 2105."

"That's a lot of time to cover," Dahl said.

"Assuming that *Star Trek* actually *exists*," Hester said. "There are all sorts of entertainment programs today that exist only in our timeline. The timeline we exist in could go back before this *Star Trek* show was actually made, and it exists in this timeline basically to *taunt* us."

"Okay, now, *that* is recursive and meta," Duvall said.

"I think that's probably what it is," Hester said. "We've already established whoever is writing us is an asshole. This sounds like just the sort of thing an asshole writer would do."

"I have to give you that," Duvall said.

"This timeline sucks," Hester said.

"Andy," Hanson said, and motioned away from the table. A cargo cart was rolling up to the table they were sitting at. Inside of it was a note. Dahl took the note; the cargo cart rolled away.

"A note from Jenkins?" Duvall asked.

"Yeah," Dahl said.

"What does it say?" Duvall asked.

"It says he thinks he's come up with something that might work," Dahl said. "He wants to talk to us about it. All of us."

CHAPTER FOURTEEN

I want to warn you that this sounds like a crazy idea," Jenkins said.

"I'm amazed you feel the need to say that anymore," Hester said.

Jenkins nodded, as if to say, *Point.* Then he said, "Time travel."

"Time travel?" Dahl said.

Jenkins nodded and fired up his holographic display, showing the timeline of the *Intrepid* and the tentacles branching down, signifying the collection of episodes. "Here," he said, pointing to a branching node of tendrils. "In the middle of what I think was this show's fourth season, Abernathy, Q'eeng and Hartnell took a shuttle and aimed it toward a black hole, using its gravity-warping powers to go backward in time."

"That makes no sense at all," Dahl said.

"Of course it doesn't," Jenkins said. "It's yet another violation of physics caused by the Narrative. The point is not that they violated physics in a nonsensical way. The point is they went back in time. And they went back in time to a specific time. A specific year. They went back to 2010."

"So?" Hester said.

"So, I think the reason they went back to that year was because that was the current year of this show's production," Jenkins said.

"Science fiction shows had their people going back in time all the time," Hanson said. "They were always having them meet famous historical people or take part in important events."

Jenkins pointed his finger excitedly at Hanson. "But that's

just *it,*" he said. "If a show goes back to a specific time in its actual past, they'll usually key it to a specific important historical person or event, because they have to give the audience something it knows about history, or else it won't care. But if the show goes back to the *present,* then it doesn't do that. It just shows that time and the characters reacting to it. It's a dramatic irony thing."

"So if the show just has them wandering around a past time, if they meet someone famous, it's the past, but if they don't, it's the present," Duvall said. "Their present."

"More or less," Jenkins said.

"That's some great show trivia," Duvall said, "but what does it have to do with us?"

"If we go back to the present, we can find a way to stop it," Dahl said suddenly.

Jenkins smiled and touched his nose.

Duvall looked at the two of them, not quite getting it. "Explain this to me, Andy," she said, "because right now it just looks like you and Jenkins are sharing a crazy moment."

"No, this makes sense," Dahl said. "We know when the present is for the show. We know how to time travel to get back to the show's present. We go back to the present, we can stop the people who are making the show."

"If we stop the show, then *everything* stops," Hester said.

"No," Dahl said. "When the Narrative doesn't need us, we still exist. And this timeline existed before the Narrative started intruding on it." He paused, and turned to Jenkins. "Right?"

"Maybe," Jenkins said.

"Maybe?" Hester said, suddenly very concerned.

"There's actually an interesting philosophical argument about whether this timeline exists independently, and the Narrative accesses it, or whether the creation of the Narrative also created this timeline, causing its history to appear instantly even if to us on the inside it appears that the passage of time has actually occurred," Jenkins said. "It's very much a corollary to the Strong Anthropic Principle—"

"Jenkins," Dahl said.

"—but we can talk about that some other time," Jenkins said, getting the hint. "The point is, yes, whether it existed before the Narrative or was created by it, this timeline now exists and is persistent even when the Narrative does not impose itself."

"Okay," Hester said.

"Probably," Jenkins said.

"I really want to throw things at him," Hester said to Dahl.

"I'm going to vote for the idea we exist and will continue to exist even when this show stops," Dahl said. "Because otherwise we're all doomed anyway. All right?"

No one offered a disagreement.

"In which case, to get back to what I was saying, if we go back in time and stop the show, then the *Intrepid* stops being a focus of the Narrative," Dahl said. "It goes back to just being a ship. We stop being glorified extras in our own lives."

"So we won't die," Duvall said.

"Everybody dies," Jenkins said.

"Thank you for that news flash," Duvall said, irritated. "I mean we won't die just to give an audience a thrill."

"Probably not," Jenkins said.

"If we really are in a television series, then it's going to be hard to stop," Hanson said, and looked to Dahl. "Andy, a really successful television series could be worth a lot of money, just like a good drama series today can be. It's not just the show, it's everything around it, including things like merchandising."

"Your boyfriend has an action figure," Hester said to Duvall.

"Yeah, and you *don't*," Duvall shot back. "In this universe that's a problem."

"I'm saying that even if we do travel back in time and find the people making this show, we might not be able to stop it," Hanson said. "There might be too much money involved."

"What other option do we have?" Dahl said. "If we stay here, the only thing to do is wait for the Narrative to kill us off. We might have a slim chance of stopping the show, but a slim chance there is better than a certainty of a dramatic death here."

"Why even bother trying to stop the show?" Hester said. "Look, if we really are extras, then we're not actually needed here. I say we go back in time and just stay there."

"Do you really want to live in the early twenty-first century?" Duvall asked. "It wasn't exactly the most cheerful time to be alive. It's not like they had a cure for cancer then."

"Whatever," Hester said.

"Or baldness," Duvall said.

"This is my original hair," Hester said.

"You can't stay in the past," Jenkins said. "If you do, you'll dissolve."

"What?" Hester said.

"It has to do with conservation of mass and energy," Jenkins said. "All the atoms you're using now are being used in the past. If you stay in the past, then the atoms have to be in two places at the same time. This creates an imbalance and the atoms have to decide where to be. And eventually they'll choose their then-present configuration because technically speaking, you're from the future, so you don't actually exist yet."

"What's 'eventually' here?" Dahl asked.

"About six days," Jenkins said.

"That's completely idiotic!" Hester said.

"I don't make up the rules," Jenkins said. "It's just how it worked last time. It makes sense in the Narrative, though—it gave Abernathy, Q'eeng and Hartnell a reason to get their mission done in a certain, dramatic amount of time."

"This timeline sucks," Hester said.

"If you brought atoms forward, they would have the same problem," Jenkins said. "And in that case they'd choose the present, which means the thing from the past would dissolve. It's a pretty problem, actually. Mind you, that's just one of your problems."

"What else is there?" Dahl asked.

"Well, you'll need to acquire a shuttle, which will be no small matter," Jenkins said. "It's not like they'll let you borrow one for a lazy excursion. But that's not actually the hard part."

"What's the hard part?" Duvall asked.

"You're going to have to get one of the five stars of the show to come with you," Jenkins said. "Take your pick: Abernathy, Q'eeng, West, Hartnell or Kerensky."

"What do we need one of them for?" Hester asked.

"You said it yourself," Jenkins said. "You're extras. If *you* try to aim a shuttle at a black hole, you know what will happen? The gravitational forces will rip apart the shuttle, you'll spaghettify into a long stream of atoms sucking down to the singularity, and you'll die. You'll be dead long before the spaghettification, of course. That's the end event for you. But you get my point."

"And that won't happen if we have one of the main characters in the show," Dahl said.

"No, because the Narrative needs them for later," Jenkins said. "So in that case when you zoom toward a black hole you'll switch over to Narrative physics."

"And we're *sure* main characters never die," Hester said.

"Oh, they can die," Jenkins said, and Hester gave him another look like he wanted to punch him. "But not like *this*. When a main character dies they'd make a big deal out of it. The idea that the Narrative would let one of them die on a mission to go back in time to stop their own show from being made just doesn't seem very likely in the grand scheme of things."

"It's nice at least *something* is unlikely at this point," Hester said.

"So, to recap," Dahl said. "Kidnap a senior officer, steal a shuttle, fly dangerously close to a black hole, go back in time, find the people making the show, stop them from making it anymore, and then come back to our own time before our atoms divorce us and we disintegrate."

"That's what I've got for you, yes," Jenkins said.

"It's a little crazy," Dahl said.

"I told you that going in," Jenkins reminded him.

"And you didn't disappoint," Dahl said.

"So what do we do now?" Duvall asked.

"I think we have to work the problem a step at a time," Dahl said. "And the first step is: How do we get that shuttle?"

Dahl's phone rang. It was Science Officer Q'eeng, ordering him to the senior officer briefing room.

· · · · ·

"The religious war on Forshan is heating up," Q'eeng said, with Captain Abernathy nodding beside him. "The Universal Union is trying to negotiate a cease-fire, but we're limited by a lack of live translators. Our diplomatic team has computer translators, of course, but they only translate the first dialect with any accuracy and even then it lacks the ability to handle idiom. We run the risk of unintentionally offending the Forshan at the worst possible time."

"Q'eeng here tells me you speak all four dialects," Abernathy said.

"That's correct, sir," Dahl said.

"Then there's no time to lose," Abernathy said. "We need you to go to Forshan immediately and start acting as a translator for our diplomats."

"Yes, sir," Dahl said, and felt a chill. *It's come for me*, he thought. *The Narrative has finally come for me. Just as we figured out how to stop it.* "How long until the *Intrepid* reaches Forshan?" he asked.

"The *Intrepid* isn't," Q'eeng said. "We have a mission to the Ames system which can't be put off. You'll have to go yourself."

"How?" Dahl asked.

"You'll be taking a shuttle," Q'eeng said.

Dahl burst out laughing.

"Ensign Dahl, are you all right?" Q'eeng asked, after a moment.

"Sorry, sir," Dahl said. "I was embarrassed that I asked such an obvious question. When do I leave?"

"As soon as we assign a shuttle pilot for you," Abernathy said.

"If I may beg the captain's indulgence, I would like to select my own pilot," Dahl said. "In fact, it might be best if I selected my own team for this mission."

Abernathy and Q'eeng both frowned. "I'm not sure you need an entire away team for this mission," Q'eeng said.

"Respectfully, sir, I do," Dahl said. "As you note, this is a critical mission. I am one of the few humans who can speak all four Forshan dialects, so I expect I will be used exhaustively by our diplomats. I will need my own team for errands and to send communiqués between diplomatic teams. I'll also need to retain the pilot and shuttle in case I am called to travel on Forshan itself, between those diplomatic teams."

"How large of a team do you need?" Q'eeng asked.

Dahl paused and looked up, as if thinking. "A pilot and two aides should probably do it," he said.

Q'eeng looked at Abernathy, who nodded. "Fine," Q'eeng said. "But ensign rank and below only."

"I have just the people in mind," Dahl said. "Although I wonder if it might be useful to have a senior officer on the team as well."

"Such as?" Abernathy asked.

"Lieutenant Kerensky," Dahl said.

"I'm not sure how an astrogator would be of much use on this mission, Ensign," Q'eeng said. "We do try to have away team members have relevant skills."

Dahl paused ever so slightly at this but then moved on. "Then perhaps you, sir," he said to Q'eeng. "You have some familiarity with the Forshan language, after all."

"I know what this is about," Abernathy said.

Dahl blinked. "Sir?" he said.

"I know what this is about," Abernathy repeated. "You were with me on the *Nantes*, Dill."

"Dahl," said Dahl.

"Dahl," Abernathy said. "You were there when your friend was killed when that madman tried to assassinate me. You saw firsthand the risks of an away team. Now you're being asked to lead an away team and you're worried about the responsibility, you're worried about someone dying on your watch."

"I'm pretty sure it's not that," Dahl said.

"I'm telling you not to worry about that," Abernathy said, not hearing Dahl. "You're an officer, Dill. Dahl. Sorry. You're an officer and you've been trained to lead. You don't need me or Q'eeng or Kerensky to tell you what you already know. Just do it. I believe in you, damn it."

"You're very inspiring, sir," Dahl said, after a moment.

"I see good things for you, Ensign," Abernathy said. "It wouldn't surprise me one day to have you as one of my senior staff."

"I should live so long," Dahl said.

"So," Abernathy said. "Assemble your team, brief them and have them ready to go in four hours. Think you can handle that?"

"I do, sir," Dahl said. "Thank you, sir." He stood and saluted. Abernathy returned the salute. Dahl nodded to Q'eeng and then left as quickly as he could, and then called Hester as soon as he was ten steps away from the briefing room.

"So what happened?" Hester asked.

"Our schedule just got drastically tightened," Dahl said. "Listen, do you still have Finn's effects?"

"Are you talking about the same effects I think you're talking about?" Hester asked, carefully.

"Yeah," Dahl said.

"Then yes," Hester said. "It would have been awkward to hand them over."

"Find a small blue oblong effect," Dahl said. "And then meet me at Maia's barracks. As quickly as you can."

CHAPTER FIFTEEN

Three hours and thirty minutes later, Dahl knocked on the door of Lieutenant Kerensky's private berth. Hester and Hanson were behind him, storage crate and cargo cart in tow.

The berth door slid open and Duvall was inside. "For God's sake, get in here," she said.

Dahl looked into the berth. "We're not all going to fit in there," he said.

"Then *you* get in here," she said. "And bring the crate." She looked at Hester and Hanson. "You two try to look like you're not doing something that will get us shot."

"Swell," Hester said. Dahl pushed the storage crate into the berth, followed it and then closed the door behind him.

Inside was Lieutenant Kerensky, pantless and passed out.

"You couldn't put his pants back on him?" Dahl asked.

"Andy, the next time *you* want to drug into unconsciousness the person you're screwing, you can do it the way you want to," Duvall said. "Which reminds me to reiterate that this is definitely a 'you owe me a fuck' level of favor."

"That's ironic, considering," Dahl said, nodding in the direction of Kerensky.

"Very funny," Duvall said.

"How long has he been out?" Dahl asked.

"Not even five minutes," Duvall said. "It was completely unbelievable. I tried to get him to have a drink with me first—I put that little pill in his tumbler—but he just wanted to get at it. I could tell you what I had to do to get him to take a drink, but that's more about me than I think you want to know."

"I'm trying to imagine what that could even mean and I have to tell you I'm drawing a blank," Dahl said.

"It's better that way," Duvall said. "Anyway. He's out now and if I'm any indication of how effective these little pills are, he'll be down for several hours at least."

"Good," Dahl said. "Let's get to work." Duvall nodded and stripped Kerensky's bunk, lining the bottom of the crate with the sheets and blanket.

"Will he have enough air?" she asked.

"It's not airtight," Dahl said. "But maybe you should put his pants back on him now."

"Not yet," Duvall said.

"I'm not sure where this is leading," Dahl said.

"Shut up and let's get him into this thing," Duvall said.

Five minutes later, Dahl and Duvall had contorted Kerensky into the storage crate. Duvall took Kerensky's pants and jacket and stuffed them into a duffel bag.

"Where's his phone?" Dahl asked. Duvall grabbed it off Kerensky's desk and tossed it to Dahl, who opened up the text messaging function, typed a note and sent it. "There," he said. "Kerensky just sent a note that he is on sick leave for his next shift. It'll be twelve hours at least before anyone comes looking for him."

"Poor bastard," Duvall said, looking at the crate. "I do feel bad about this. He's dim and self-centered, but he's not really a bad guy. And he's decent enough in the cot."

"Don't need to know," Dahl said.

"Prude," Duvall said.

"You can make it up to him later," Dahl said, and opened the door, on the other side of which stood Hester.

"Thought you guys had started up a game of Parcheesi in there," he said.

"Don't you start," Duvall said. "Let's get him up on that cart."

A few minutes later, the four of them and their unconscious cargo were at the door of the shuttle bay.

"Get the shuttle ready," Dahl said to Hester, then turned to Hanson and Duvall. "And get the cargo into the shuttle as quietly as possible, please."

"Look who's all authoritative now," Duvall said.

"For now let's just pretend you actually respect my authority," Dahl said.

"Where are you going?" Hanson asked.

"I have one more quick stop to make," Dahl said. "Have to pick up some extra supplies." Hanson nodded and backed the cargo cart into the shuttle bay, Duvall and Hester following. Dahl walked until he found a quiet cargo tunnel and quietly opened the access door to it.

Jenkins was on the other side.

"You know that's creepy," Dahl said.

"I'm trying not to waste your time," Jenkins said. He held up a briefcase. "The leftovers from that mission Abernathy, Q'eeng and Hartnell went on," he said. "Phones and money. The phones will work with that era's communication and information networks. Those networks will be slow and rudimentary. Be patient with them. The money is physical money, which they still use where you're going."

"Will they be able to tell it's not real?" Dahl asked.

"They couldn't last time," Jenkins said.

"How much is in there?" Dahl asked.

"About ninety-three thousand dollars," Jenkins said.

"Is that a lot?" Dahl asked.

"It'll be enough to get you through six days," Jenkins said. Dahl took the suitcase and turned to go.

"One other thing," Jenkins said, and then handed him a small box.

Dahl took it. "You really want me to do this," he said.

"I'm not going with you," Jenkins said. "So you have to do it for me."

"I may not have time," Dahl said.

"I know," Jenkins said. "If you have time."

"And it won't last," Dahl said. "You know it won't."

"It doesn't have to last," Jenkins said. "It just has to last long enough."

"All right," Dahl said.

"Thanks," Jenkins said. "And now I think you better get off the ship as soon as you can. Leaving that note from Kerensky was smart, but don't tempt fate any more than you have to. You're already tempting it enough."

· · · · ·

"You can't do this to me," Kerensky said, in a muffled fashion, from inside the crate. He had woken up five minutes earlier, after sleeping more than ten hours. Hester had been taunting him since.

"That's a funny thing to say," Hester said, "considering where you are."

"Let me out," Kerensky said. "That's an order."

"You keep saying funny things," Hester said. "From *inside a crate*. Which you can't escape from."

There was a moment of silence at that.

"Where are my pants?" Kerensky asked, plaintively.

Hester glanced over at Duvall. "I'm going to let you field that one," he said. Duvall rolled her eyes.

"I really have to pee," Kerensky said. "Really bad."

Duvall sighed. "Anatoly," she said. "It's me."

"Maia?" Kerensky said. "They got you too. Don't worry. I won't let these bastards do anything to you. Do you hear me, you sons of bitches?"

Hester looked over to Dahl disbelievingly. Dahl shrugged.

"Anatoly," Maia said, more forcefully. "They didn't get me too."

"What?" Kerensky said. Then, after a minute, *"Oh."*

"'Oh,'" Duvall agreed. "Now, listen, Anatoly. I'm going to open up the crate and you can come out, but I really need you not to be stupid or to panic. Do you think you can do that?"

There was a pause. "Yes," Kerensky said.

"Anatoly, that little pause you just did suggests to me that what you're really planning to do is something stupid as soon as we uncrate you," Duvall said. "So just to be sure, two of my friends here have pulse guns trained on you. If you do anything particularly idiotic, they'll just blast you. Do you understand?"

"Yes," Kerensky said, sounding somewhat more resigned.

"Okay," Duvall said. She walked over to the crate.

"'Pulse guns'?" Dahl asked. No one had pulse guns with them. It was Duvall's turn to shrug.

"You know he's lying," Hester said.

"That's why I have his pants," Duvall said, and started unlatching the hinges.

Kerensky burst out of the crate, rolled, spied the door and sprinted toward it, flinging it open and throwing himself through it. Everyone else in the room watched him go.

"What do we do now?" Hanson asked.

"Window," Dahl said. They stood up and walked toward the window, cranking the louvers so they were open to the outside.

"This should be good," Hester said.

Thirty seconds later Kerensky burst into view, running into the street, whereupon he stopped, utterly confused. A car honked at him to get out of the way. He backed up onto the sidewalk.

"Anatoly, come back in," Duvall said through the window. "For God's sake, you're not wearing pants."

Kerensky turned around, following her voice. "This isn't a ship," he yelled up to the window.

"No, it's the Best Western Media Center Inn and Suites," Duvall said. "In Burbank."

"Is that a planet?" Kerensky yelled. "What system is it in?"

"Oh, for Christ's sake," Hester muttered. "You're on *Earth,* you moron," he yelled at Kerensky.

Kerensky looked around disbelievingly. "Was there an apocalypse?" he yelled.

Hester looked at Duvall. "You actually have sex with this imbecile?"

"Look, he's had a rough day," Duvall said, and then turned her attention to Kerensky. "We went back in time, Anatoly," she said. "It's the year 2012. This is what it looks like. Now come back inside."

"You drugged me and kidnapped me," Kerensky said, accusingly.

"I know, and I'm really sorry about that," Duvall said. "I was kind of in a rush. But listen, you have to come back inside. You're half-naked. Even in 2012, you can get arrested for that. You don't want to get arrested in 2012, Anatoly. It's not a nice time to be in jail. Come back inside, okay? We're in room 215. Just take the stairs."

Kerensky looked around, looked down at his pantless lower half, and then sprinted back into the Best Western.

"I'm not rooming with him," Hester said. "I just want to be clear on that."

A minute later there was a knock on the door. Hanson went to open it. Kerensky strode into the room.

"First, I want my pants," Kerensky said.

Everyone turned to Duvall, who gave everyone a *what?* expression and then pulled Kerensky's pants out of her duffel and threw them at him.

"Second," Kerensky said, fumbling into his pants, "I want to know why we're here."

"We're here because we landed and hid the shuttle in Griffith Park, and this was the closest hotel," Hester said. "And it was a good thing it was so close, because your crated ass was *not* light."

"I don't mean the *hotel*," Kerensky spat. "I mean here. On Earth. In 2012. In *Burbank*. Someone needs to explain this to me *now*."

This time everyone turned to Dahl.

"Oh," he said. "Well, it's complicated."

· · · · ·

"Eat something, Kerensky," Duvall said, pushing the remains of the pizza at him. They were in a booth at the Numero Uno Pizza down the street from the Best Western. Kerensky was now wearing pants.

Kerensky barely glanced at the pizza. "I'm not sure it's safe," he said.

"They did have food laws in the twenty-first century," Hanson said. "Here in the United States, anyway."

"I'll pass," Kerensky said.

"Let him starve," Hester said, and reached for the last piece. Kerensky's hand shot out and he grabbed it.

"Got it," Dahl said, and turned his phone—his twenty-first-century phone—around, showing the article to the rest of them. " 'Chronicles of the Intrepid.' " He turned the phone back around to him. "Shows every Friday at nine on something called the Corwin Action Network, which is apparently something called a 'basic cable channel.' It started in 2007, which means it's now in its sixth season."

"This is completely ridiculous," Kerensky said, around his pizza.

Dahl looked over to him, and then pressed the screen to open up another article. "And playing Lieutenant Anatoly Kerensky on Chronicles of the Intrepid is an actor named Marc Corey," he said, flipping the screen around to show Kerensky the picture of a smiling doppelgänger in a stylish blazer and open-collared dress shirt. "Born in 1985 in Chatsworth, California. I wonder if that's anywhere near here."

Kerensky grabbed the phone and read the article sullenly. "This doesn't prove anything," he said. "We don't know how accurate any of this information is. For all we know, this"—he scrolled up on the phone screen to find a label—"this Wikipedia information database here is compiled by complete idiots." He handed back the phone.

"We could try to track down this Corey fellow," Hanson said.

"I want to try someone else first," Dahl said, and started poking at his phone again. "If Marc Corey is a regular on a show, he's probably going to be hard to get to. I think we should probably aim lower."

"What do you mean?" Duvall said.

"I mean, I think we should start with me," Dahl said, and then turned the phone around again, to a picture of what appeared to be his own face. "Meet Brian Abnett."

Dahl's friends looked at the picture. "It's a little unsettling, isn't it?" Hanson said, after a minute. "Looking at a picture of someone who is exactly like you but isn't."

"No kidding," Dahl said. "Of course, you all have your own people, too."

At that, the rest of them started to power up their own phones.

"What does Wikipedia say about *him*?" Kerensky sneered. He did not have his own phone.

"Nothing," Dahl said. "He apparently doesn't meet the standard. I followed the link on the *Chronicles of the Intrepid* page to a database called IMDB, which had information about the actors on the series. He has a page there."

"So how do we contact him?" Duvall said.

"It doesn't have contact information on that page," Dahl said. "But let me put his name in the search field."

"I just found myself," Hanson said. "I'm some guy named Chad."

"I knew a Chad once," Hester said. "He used to beat me up."

"I'm sorry," Hanson said.

"It wasn't *you*," Hester said. "Either of you."

"He has his own page," Dahl said.

"Chad?" Hanson asked.

"No, Brian Abnett," Dahl said. He scrolled through the page until he found a tab that said 'Contact.'" Dahl pressed it and an address popped up.

"It's for his agency," Dahl said.

"Wow, actors had agents even then," Duvall said.

"Even *now*, you mean," Dahl said, and pressed his screen again. "His agency is only a couple of miles from here. We can walk it."

"What are we going to do when we get there?" Duvall asked.

"I'm going to get his address from them," Dahl said.

"You think they'll give it you?" Hester asked.

"Of course they will," Dahl said. "I'm him."

CHAPTER SIXTEEN

O kay, I see him," Duvall said, pointing up Camarillo Street. "He's the one on the bicycle."

"Are you sure?" Dahl asked.

"I know what you look like, even wearing a bicycle helmet," Duvall said. "Trust me."

"Now, remember not to freak him out," Dahl said. He had on a baseball cap he had bought and was holding a copy of the day's *Los Angeles Times* in his hand. The two of them were standing in front of the condominium complex Brian Abnett lived in.

"You're telling *me* not to freak him out," she said. "You're the one who's his clone."

"I don't want him freaking out *until* he sees me," Dahl said.

"Don't worry, I'm good with men," Duvall said. "Now go stand over there and try not to look . . ." She paused.

"Try not to look what?" asked Dahl.

"Try not to look so clone-y," Duvall said. "At least not for a couple more minutes." Dahl grinned, stepped back and raised his newspaper.

"Hey," Dahl heard Duvall say a minute later. He peeked over the top of the newspaper just enough to see her walk up to Brian Abnett, who was getting off his bike and unlatching his helmet.

"Hey," Abnett said, and then took another look at her. "Wait, don't tell me," he said, smiling. "We've worked together."

"Maybe," Duvall said, coyly.

"Recently," Abnett said.

"Maybe," Duvall said again.

"That hemorrhoid cream commercial," Abnett said.

"No," Duvall said, flatly.

"Wait!" Abnett said, pointing. "*Chronicles of the Intrepid.* A few months ago. You and I did that scene together where we were being chased by killer robots. Tell me I'm right."

"It's very close to what I remember," Duvall said.

"Thank you," Abnett said. "I hate it when I forget people I've worked with. You're still doing work with them, right? I think I've seen you around the set since then."

"You could say so," Duvall said. "What about you?"

"I've got a small character arc on the show," Abnett said. "It's only been a few shots through the season, and of course they're killing off my character a couple of episodes from now, but until then it's nice work." He motioned at the condominium building. "Means I get to stay here through the year, anyway."

"So they're going to kill you off?" Duvall asked. "You're sure about that?"

"That's what the agent tells me," Abnett said. "She says they're still writing the episode, but it's pretty much a done deal. Which is fine, since she wants to put me up for a couple of film roles and staying on *Intrepid* will just get in the way of that."

"Sad about the character, though," Duvall said.

"Well, that's science fiction television for you, though," Abnett said. "Someone's got to be the red shirt."

"The what?" Duvall said.

"The red shirt," Abnett said. "You know, in the original *Star Trek,* they always had Kirk and Bones and Spock and then some poor dude in a red shirt who got vaporized before the first commercial. The moral of the story was not to wear a red shirt. Or go on away missions when you're the only one whose name isn't on the opening credits."

"Ah," Duvall said.

"You never watched *Star Trek*?" Abnett asked, smiling.

"It was a little before my time," Duvall said.

"So what brings you to my neighborhood, uh . . . ," Abnett said.

"Maia," Duvall said.

"Maia," Abnett repeated. "You aren't looking at the condo that's for sale in the building, are you? I probably shouldn't say this, but I think you might want to look at other places. The last guy in that condo I'm pretty sure was making meth in the bathtub. It's a miracle the entire building didn't go up."

"Oh, I won't be staying for very long," Duvall said. "Actually, I came looking for you."

"Really," Abnett said, with an expression that flickered between being flattered that an attractive woman came looking for him, and worry that the woman, who might be crazy, knew where he lived.

Duvall read the flicker of expression perfectly. "I'm not stalking you," she assured Abnett.

"Okay, that's a relief," Abnett said.

Duvall motioned with her head toward Dahl, still semi-obscured by the hat and newspaper. "In fact, my friend over there is a big fan of yours and he just wanted to meet you for a second. If that's okay. It would really make his day."

"Yeah, okay, sure," Abnett said, still looking at Duvall. "What's your friend's name?"

"Andy Dahl," Duvall said.

"Really?" Abnett said. "That's so weird. That's actually the name of my character on *Chronicles of the Intrepid*."

"That's why he wants to meet you," Duvall said.

"And it's not the only thing we share in common," Dahl said. He walked up to Abnett, took off the cap and dropped the *Times*. "Hello, Brian. I'm you. In red shirt form."

· · · · ·

"I'm still having trouble with this," Abnett said. He was sitting in the Best Western suite with the crew members of the *Intrepid*. "I mean, really really *really* having trouble with this."

"You think *you're* having trouble," Hester said. "Think about us. At least you're not *fictional*."

"Do you know how unreal this is?" Abnett said.

"We've been living with this for a while now, yes," Dahl said.

"So you understand why I'm freaking out about it," Abnett said.

"We could do another freckle check if you like," Dahl said, referring to the moment, shortly after he introduced himself, where Abnett checked every visible freckle, mole and blemish on both of them to confirm that they matched exactly.

"No, I've just got to sit with this," Abnett said. Hester looked over to Dahl, quickly to Abnett and then back to Dahl, conveying the message *The other you is a flake* with his expression. Dahl shrugged. Actors were actors.

"You know what convinces me that you might be telling the truth," Abnett said.

"The fact you're sitting in a room with an exact copy of yourself?" Hester said.

"No," Abnett said. "Well, yes. *That*. But what's really helping me wrap my head around the idea you're telling the truth is *him*." Abnett pointed at Kerensky.

"Me?" Kerensky said, surprised. "Why me?"

"Because the real Marc Corey wouldn't be caught dead in a Best Western attempting to prank an extra whose name he can't be bothered to remember," Abnett said. "No offense, but the other you is a complete asshole."

"So's this one," Hester said.

"Hey," Kerensky said.

"Having another me around is hard to swallow," Abnett said, and pointed to Kerensky again. "But another one of him? That's actually easier to accept."

"You believe us, then," Duvall said.

"I don't know if I *believe* you," Abnett said. "What I do know is that this is very definitely the strangest damn thing that's ever happened to me, and I want to find out what happens next."

"So you'll help us," Dahl said.

"I *want* to help you, but I don't know if I *can* help you," Abnett said. "Look, I'm just an extra. They allow me onto the set for work, but it's not like I can bring anyone else in with me. I get a few lines with the regular cast, but otherwise we're told not to bother them. And I don't talk to the show runners or other producers at all. I couldn't get you in to see any of them if I wanted to. And even if I did, I don't think any of them would believe you. This is Hollywood. We make things up for a living. And the story you're telling is completely nuts. I tell it to anyone, they'll just throw me off the set."

"That might keep you from getting killed a couple of episodes from now," Hanson said, to Dahl.

Abnett shook his head. "No, they'll just recast the part with someone who looks enough like me to work," he said. "You'll still be killed off. Unless you stay here."

Dahl shook his head. "We expire in five days."

"Expire?" Abnett asked.

"It's complicated," Dahl said. "It involves atoms."

"Five days is not a lot of time," Abnett said. "Especially if you want to kill a show."

"Tell us something we don't know," Hester said.

"Maybe you can't help us directly," Duvall said. "But do

you know someone who could? Even as an extra, you know the people who work high up the food chain."

"That's what I'm telling you," Abnett said. "I don't. I don't know anyone on the show who could move you up the ladder." His gaze rested on Kerensky, and he suddenly cocked his head. "But you know what, maybe I know someone *outside* the show who could help you."

"Why are you looking at me like that?" Kerensky asked, unsettled by Abnett's gaze.

"Are those the only clothes you have?" Abnett asked.

"I wasn't given the option of packing," Kerensky said. "Why? What's wrong with the uniform?"

"There's nothing wrong with the uniform if you're at Comic-Con, but it's not going to work for the club I'm thinking of," Abnett said.

"Which club?" Dahl asked.

"What's Comic-Con?" Kerensky asked.

"The Vine Club," Abnett said. "One of those very secret clubs mere mortals can't get into. I can't get into it. But Marc Corey rates, barely."

"Barely," Dahl said.

"That means he has first-floor access but not second-floor, and definitely not basement," Abnett said. "For second-floor you have to be the star of your own show, not part of the supporting cast. For the basement, you have to make twenty million a film and get a slice of the gross."

"I still want to know what Comic-Con is," Kerensky said.

"Later, Kerensky," Hester said. "Jesus." He turned to Abnett. "So, what? We get Kerensky to pose as Marc Corey and get into the club? What does that do?"

Abnett shook his head. "He doesn't pose as Corey. You have him go to the club and do to him what Andy here did to me. Draw him out and get him interested and maybe he will help you. I wouldn't tell him you want to kill the show, since that means he'd be out of a regular job. But otherwise maybe you can get him to introduce you to Charles Paulson. He's the show's creator and executive producer. He's the one you have to talk to. He's the one you have to convince."

"So you can get us into this club," Dahl said.

"I can't," Abnett said. "Like I said, I don't rate. But I have a friend who's a bartender there, and I got him a commercial gig last summer. Kept him from going into foreclosure. So he owes me big. He can get you in." He looked at them all, and then pointed at Kerensky. "Well, get *him* in." He pointed at Duvall next. "And maybe her, too."

"You keep your friend from losing his house, and he lets two people into a club, and these are equal favors?" Hester said.

"Welcome to Hollywood," Abnett said.

"We'll take it," Dahl said. "And thank you, Brian."

"Happy to help," Brian said. "I mean, I've sort of become attached to you. Seeing that you're actually real and all."

"I'm glad to hear that," Dahl said.

"Can I ask you a question?" Abnett said.

"Sure," Dahl said.

"The future," Abnett said. "It really is like it is on the show?"

"The future really is like it is on the show," Dahl said. "But I don't know if it's really the future."

"But this is your past," Abnett said. "We're part of your past. The year 2012, I mean."

"2012 is in our past, but not *this* 2012," Dahl said. "There's no *Chronicles of the Intrepid* television show in our past. It doesn't exist in our timeline."

"So that means that *I* might not exist in your timeline," Abnett said.

"Maybe not," Dahl said.

"So you're the only part of me there," Abnett said. "The only part of me that's *ever* existed there."

"I guess that's possible," Dahl said. "Just like you're the only part of me that's ever existed here."

"Doesn't that mess with you?" Abnett asked. "Knowing that you exist, and don't exist, and are real and aren't, all at the same time?"

"Yes, and I have training dealing with deep, existential questions," Dahl said. "The way I'm dealing with it right now is this: I don't care whether I really exist or don't, whether I'm real or fictional. What I want right now is to be the person who decides my own fate. That's something I can work on. It's what I'm working on now."

"I think you might be smarter than me," Abnett said.

"That's okay," Dahl said. "I think you're better looking than me."

Abnett smiled. "I'll take that," he said. "And speaking of which, it's time to take you folks clothes shopping. Those uniforms work in the future, but here and now, they'll get you branded as geeks who don't get out of the basement enough. Do you have money?"

"We have ninety-three thousand dollars," Hanson said. "Minus seventy-eight dollars for lunch."

"I think we can work with that," Abnett said.

CHAPTER SEVENTEEN

I hate these clothes," Kerensky said.

"You look good," Dahl said, assuring him.

"No, I don't," Kerensky said. "I look like I dressed in the dark. How did people wear this?"

"Stop whining," Duvall said. "It's not like you don't wear civvies back where we come from."

"This underwear is *itchy*," Kerensky said, tugging.

"If I knew you were this whiny, I never would have slept with you," Duvall said.

"If I knew you were going to drug me, kidnap me and take me back to the dark ages *without my pants,* I never would have slept with *you*," Kerensky shot back.

"Guys," Dahl said, and motioned with his eyes to the cabbie, who was studiously ignoring the weirdos in his backseat. "Not so much with the dark ages talk."

The cab, on Sunset, took a left onto Vine.

"So we're sure Marc Corey's still there, right?" Kerensky asked.

"Brian said his friend called as soon as he got there, and would call if he left," Dahl said. "Brian hasn't called me since then, so we can assume he's still in there."

"I don't think this is going to work," Kerensky said.

"It'll work," Dahl said. "I know."

"That was with your guy," Kerensky said. "This guy could be different."

"Please," Duvall said. "If he's anything like you, he'll be totally infatuated with you. It'll be like looking into a mirror he can poke."

"What is that supposed to mean?" Kerensky said.

"It means that you being fascinated with yourself isn't going to be a problem," Duvall said.

"You don't actually like me, do you?" Kerensky said, after a second.

Duvall smiled and patted his cheek. "I like you just fine, Anatoly," she said. "I really do. But right now, I need you to focus. Think of this as another away mission."

"I always get hurt on away missions," Kerensky said.

"Maybe," Duvall said. "But you always survive."

"The Vine Club," the cabbie said, pulling up to the sidewalk.

The three of them got out of the cab, Dahl pausing to pay the cabbie. From inside the club, music thumped. A line of young, pretty, studiously posed people waited outside.

"Come on," Dahl said, and walked up to the bouncer. Duvall and Kerensky followed.

"Line starts over there," the bouncer said, motioning to the pretty, posed people.

"Yes, but I was told to talk to you," Dahl said, and held out his hand with the hundred-dollar bill folded in it, like Abnett told him to do. "Mitch, right?"

Mitch the bouncer glanced down almost imperceptibly at Dahl's hand, then shook it, deftly scraping the bill out of it as he did so. "Right," Mitch said. "Talk to me, then."

"I'm supposed to tell you that these two are Roberto's friends," Dahl said, mentioning the name of Abnett's bartender friend, and nodding back to Kerensky and Duvall. "He's expecting them."

Mitch looked over at Kerensky and Duvall. If he noted Kerensky's resemblance to Marc Corey, he kept it to himself. He turned his gaze back to Dahl. "First floor only," he said. "If they try for the second floor, they're out on their ass. If they go for the basement, they're out on their ass minus teeth."

"First floor," Dahl repeated, nodding.

"And not you," Mitch said. "No offense."

"None taken," Dahl said.

Mitch motioned to Kerensky and Duvall and unlatched the rope; audible protests came from the line of pretty, posed people.

"You got this?" Dahl asked Duvall, as she walked by.

"Trust me, I got this," she said. "Stick by your phone."

"I will," Dahl said. The two of them disappeared into the dark of the Vine Club. Mitch latched the rope behind them.

"Hey," Dahl said to him. "Where can a normal human go get a drink?"

Mitch smiled at this and pointed. "Irish pub right up there," he said. "The bartender's name is Nick. Tell him I sent you."

"Thanks," Dahl said, and headed up the street.

The pub was noisy and crowded. Dahl worked his way to the bar and then fished in his pocket for money.

"Hey, Brian, right?" someone said to him.

Dahl looked up to see the bartender staring back at him, smiling.

"Finn," Dahl said.

"Nick," the bartender said.

"Sorry," Dahl said, after a second. "Brain freeze."

"Occupational hazard," Nick said. "You get known by your part."

"Yeah," Dahl said.

"Hey, are you all right?" Nick asked. "You seem a little"—he wiggled his hands—"dazed."

"I'm fine," Dahl said, and made the effort to smile. "Sorry. Just a little strange to see you here."

"It's the life of an actor," Nick said. "Out of work and bartending. What are you having?"

"Pick a beer for me," Dahl said.

"Brave man," Nick said.

"I trust you," Dahl said.

"Famous last words," Nick said, and then headed off to the taps. Dahl watched him working the taps and tried very hard not to freak out.

"Here you go," Nick said a minute later, handing over a pint glass. "Local microbrew. It's called a Starlet Stout."

Dahl tried it. "It's not bad," he said.

"I'll tell the brew master you said so," Nick said. "You might remember him. The three of us were in a scene together. He got killed by a swarm of robots."

"Lieutenant Fischer," Dahl said

"That's the one," Nick said, and nodded at Dahl's glass. "Real name is Jake Klein. His microbrewery's taking off, though. He's mostly doing that now. I'm thinking of joining him."

"And stop being an actor?" Dahl said.

Nick shrugged. "It's not like they're tearing down the doors to get at me," he said. "I've been out here nine years now and that gig on *Intrepid* was the best thing I've gotten so far, and it wasn't all that great. I got killed by an exploding head."

"I remember," Dahl said.

"That was what did it for me, actually," Nick said. He started washing glasses in the bar sink to give the appearance of being busy as he talked. "We did ten takes of that scene. Every time we did it I had to toss myself backward like there was an actual explosion. And around take seven I thought to myself, 'I'm thirty years old and what I'm doing with my life is pretending to die on a TV show that I wouldn't watch if I wasn't on it.' At a certain point you have to ask yourself why you do it. I mean, why do *you* do it?"

"Me?" Dahl asked.

"Yeah," Nick said.

"I do it because for a long time I didn't know I had a choice," Dahl said.

"That's just it, though," Nick said. "You do. You still on the show?"

"For now," Dahl said.

"But they're going to kill you off too," Nick said.

"In a couple of episodes," Dahl said. "Unless I can avoid it."

"Don't avoid it," Nick said. "Die and then figure out the rest of your life."

Dahl smiled. "It's not as simple as that for some of us," he said, and took a drink.

"Mortgage, huh," Nick said.

"Something like that," Dahl said.

"C'est la vie," Nick said. "So what brings you down to Hollywood and Vine? I think you told me you were in Toluca Lake."

"I had some friends who wanted to go to the Vine Club," Dahl said.

"They didn't let you in?" Nick asked. Dahl shrugged. "You should have let me know. My friend's the bouncer there."

"Mitch," Dahl said.

"That's him," Nick said.

"He's the one who told me to come down here," Dahl said.

"Ouch," Nick said. "Sorry."

"I'm not," Dahl said. "It's really good to see you again."

Nick grinned and then went to tend to other customers.

Dahl's phone vibrated. He fished it out of his pocket and answered it.

"Where are you?" Duvall asked.

"I'm at a pub down the street," Dahl said. "Having a very weird time. Why?"

"You need to come back down here. We just got kicked out of the club," Duvall said.

"You and Kerensky?" Dahl asked. "How did that happen?"

"Not just me and Kerensky," Duvall said. "Marc Corey too. He attacked Kerensky."

"What?" Dahl said.

"We walked up to Corey in his booth, he saw Kerensky and said, 'So you're the fucker whose picture is on Gawker,' and lunged at him," Duvall said.

"What the hell is a Gawker?" Dahl asked.

"Don't ask me, it's not my century," Duvall said. "We all got thrown out and now Corey's passed out on the sidewalk. He was already drunk off his ass when we got there."

"Scrape him off the sidewalk and fish through his pockets for his valet ticket," Dahl said. "Get all of you in his car and then wait for me. I'll be there in just a couple of minutes. Try not to get yourselves arrested."

"I promise nothing," Duvall said, and hung up.

"Problem?" Nick asked. He had come back up while Dahl was on the phone.

"My friends got into a fight at the Vine Club and got kicked out," Dahl said. "I need to go get them before the police arrive."

"You're having an interesting night," Nick said.

"You have no idea," Dahl said. "What do I owe you for the beer?"

Nick waved him off. "On the house," he said. "Your one good thing for the evening."

"Thank you," Dahl said, and then paused, looking at his phone and then looking up at Nick. "Would you mind if I took a picture of the two of us?"

"Now you're getting weird," Nick said, but smiled and leaned in. Dahl held the phone out and took the picture.

"Thanks," Dahl said again.

"No problem," Nick said. "Now you better go before your friends are hauled away."

Dahl hurried out.

Two minutes later he was outside the Vine Club, watching Duvall and Kerensky wrestling with Marc Corey by a black, sleek automobile, while Mitch and a valet looked on. The pretty, posed people had their phones out, taking video of it all.

"Man, what the hell is this?" Mitch asked as Dahl walked up. "Your pals are in there not ten minutes and this chump tries to wreck the place getting at them."

"Sorry about that," Dahl said.

"And this clone action is just freaky," Mitch said.

"My friends were in there to get Marc," Dahl lied, and pointed at Kerensky. "That's his public double. They use him for publicity sometimes. We heard he was getting a little rowdy and came to get him because he's got to be on set tomorrow."

"He wasn't rowdy until your friends showed up," Mitch said. "And what does that dude need a double for? He's a supporting actor on a basic cable science fiction show. It's not like he's actually *famous*."

"You should see him at Comic-Con," Dahl said.

Mitch snorted. "He better enjoy that, then, because he's banned here," he said. "When your friend is coherent tell him that if he shows up again, he'll achieve warp speed thanks to my foot in his ass."

"I'll use those words exactly," Dahl said.

"Do that," Mitch said, and turned back to his duties.

Dahl walked over to Duvall. "What's the problem?" he asked.

"He's drunk and has no bones," Duvall said, struggling with Corey. "And he's woken up enough to argue with us."

"You can't handle a boneless drunk?" Dahl asked.

"Of course I can," Duvall said. "But you said you didn't want us to get arrested."

"A little help here would be nice," Kerensky said, as Corey's drunken hand stabbed a finger up his nose.

Dahl nodded, opened the door to the black car and pulled the front seat forward. Duvall and Kerensky got a better grip on Corey, steadied him and then hurled him into the backseat. Corey jammed in, head into the far corner of the backseat, ass in the air. He whimpered for a second and then made a flabby exhaling sound. He was out again.

"I'm not sitting with him," Kerensky said.

"No you're not," Dahl agreed, reached into the car and pulled Corey's wallet out of his pants. He held it out to Kerensky. "You're driving."

"Why am I driving?" Kerensky asked.

"Because then if we get pulled over, you're him," Dahl said.

"Right," Kerensky said, taking the wallet.

"I'll pay the valet," Duvall said.

"Tip well," Dahl said.

A minute later Kerensky figured out what "D" meant on the shift column and the four of them were driving up Vine.

"Keep to the speed limit," Dahl said.

"I have no idea where I'm going," Kerensky said.

"You're an astrogator," Duvall said.

"This is a *road*," Kerensky said.

"Hold on," Duvall said, and pulled out her phone. "This thing's got a map function. Let me get it working." Kerensky grunted and kept driving.

"Well, we had a fun evening," Duvall said to Dahl, as she entered the address of the Best Western into her phone. "What did you do?"

"I saw an old friend," Dahl said, and showed Duvall the picture of him and Nick.

"Oh," Duvall said, taking the phone. She reached into the backseat and grabbed his hand. "Oh, Andy. You okay?"

"I'm okay," he said.

"He looks just like him," Duvall said, looking at the picture again.

"He would," Dahl said, and looked out the window.

CHAPTER EIGHTEEN

He's slept long enough," Dahl said, nodding to Marc Corey's unconscious form on the bed. "Wake him up."

"That would mean touching him," Duvall said.

"Not necessarily," Hester said. He reached over and took one of the pillows Corey wasn't using, and then hit him on the head with it. Corey woke up with a start.

"Nicely done," Hanson said, to Hester. He nodded in acknowledgment.

Corey sat up and looked around, disoriented. "Where am I?" he asked, to no one in particular.

"In a hotel," Dahl said. "The Best Western in Burbank."

"Why am I here?" Corey said.

"You passed out at the Vine Club after you attacked a friend of mine," Dahl said. "We got you in your car and drove you here."

Corey looked down and furrowed his brow. "Where are my *pants*?" he said.

"We took them from you," Dahl said.

"Why?" Corey said.

"Because we need to talk to you," Dahl said.

"You could do that without taking my pants," Corey said.

"In a perfect world, yes," Dahl said.

Corey peered at Dahl, groggily. "I know you," he said after a minute. "You're an extra on my show." He looked at Duvall and Hanson. "So are you two." His gaze turned to Hester. "You I've never seen before."

Hester looked slightly exasperated at this. "We had a scene together," he said to Corey. "You were attacked by swarm bots."

"Dude, I have a lot of scenes with extras," Corey said. "That's why they're called 'extras.'" He turned his attention back to Dahl. "And if any of you ever want to work on the show again, you will give me my pants and my car keys, right now."

"Your pants are in the restroom," Hanson said. "Drying."

"You were so drunk you pissed yourself," Hester said.

"Besides taking your pants for discussion purposes, we figured you might not want to go into work with clothes that smelled like urine," Dahl said.

Corey looked puzzled at this, glanced down at the under-wear on his body, and then bent over at the waist, sniffing. Both Duvall and Hester gave up looks of mild disgust; Dahl watched impassively.

"I smell fine," Corey said.

"New underwear," Dahl said.

"Whose?" Corey said. "Yours?"

"No, mine," Kerensky said. All this time he had been sitting silently in a suite chair with its back to the bed. Now he stood and turned to face Corey. "After all, you and I are the same size."

Corey gazed up at Kerensky, dumbly. "You," he said, finally.

"Me," Kerensky agreed. "Who is also 'you.'"

"It's you I saw on Gawker yesterday," Corey said.

"I don't know what that means," Kerensky said.

"There was a video of someone who looked like me stand-ing in the street without pants," Corey said. "Someone took the video on their phone and sent it to the Gawker Web site. Our show had to confirm I was on the set before anyone would believe it wasn't me. It was you."

"Yes, it was probably me," Kerensky said.

"Who are you?" Corey asked.

"I'm you," Kerensky said. "Or who you pretend to be, any-way."

"That doesn't make any sense," Corey said.

"Well, you talking about this Gawker thing doesn't make any sense to me, either, so we're even," Kerensky said.

"Why were you running around in the street without pants?" Corey asked.

Kerensky motioned to the others in the room. "They took my pants," he said.

"Why?" Corey asked.

"Because we needed to talk to him," Dahl said.

Corey tore his eyes away from Kerensky. "What is wrong with you people?" he asked.

"You're still here," Dahl pointed out.

But Corey was ignoring him again. He got out of the bed and walked over to Kerensky, who stood there, watching him. Corey looked him all over. "It's amazing," Corey said. "You look exactly like me."

"I *am* exactly like you," Kerensky said. "Down to the last detail."

"That's not possible," Corey said, staring into Kerensky's face.

"It's possible," Kerensky said, and stepped closer to Corey. "Take a closer look." The two of them stood an inch apart while Corey examined Kerensky's body.

"Okay, *this* is getting creepy," Hester said, quietly, to Dahl.

"Marc, we need your help," Dahl said to Corey. "We need you to get us in to talk to Charles Paulson."

"Why?" Corey said, not taking his eyes off Kerensky.

"There's something about the show we need to discuss with him," Dahl said.

"He's not seeing people right now," Corey said, turning. "A month ago his son was in a motorcycle accident. Son's in a coma right now and they don't think he's going to pull through. Paulson gave his son the bike for a birthday gift. The rumor is Paulson goes to his office in the morning, sits down and stares at the walls until six o'clock and then goes home again. He's not going to see you." He turned back to Kerensky.

"We need to try," Dahl said. "And that's why we need you. He can avoid dealing with nearly everyone else, but you're a star on his show. He has to see you."

"He doesn't have to see anybody," Corey said.

"You could make him see you," Duvall said.

Corey glanced over, and then broke away from Kerensky to step over to her. "And why would I do that?" he asked. "You're right, if I threw a fit and demanded to see Paulson, he'd make time to see me. But if I saw him and wasted his time, he might kick me off the show. He might have my character killed off in some horrible way just to get a quick ratings boost out of it. And then I'd be out of a job. Do you know how hard it is to get a regular series gig in this town? I was a waiter before I got this. I'm not going to do anything for you people."

"It's important," Dahl said.

"*I'm* important," Corey said. "My career is important. It's more important than whatever *you* want."

"If you help us, we can give you money," Hanson said. "We've got ninety thousand dollars."

"That's less than what I make an episode," Corey said, and looked back toward Kerensky. "You'll have to do better than that."

Dahl opened his mouth to speak.

"I'll handle this," Kerensky said, and looked at the others. "Let me talk to Marc."

"So talk," Hester said.

"Alone," Kerensky said.

"Are you sure?" Dahl said.

"Yes," Kerensky said. "I'm sure."

"All right," Dahl said, and motioned to Duvall, Hanson and an incredulous Hester to clear the room.

"Tell me I'm not the only one who thinks something *unseemly* is about to happen in there," Hester said, in the hall.

"It's only you," Dahl said.

"No it's not," Duvall said. Hanson also shook his head. "You can't tell me you weren't seeing how Corey was responding to Anatoly, Andy," Duvall said.

"I must have missed it," Dahl said.

"Right," Hester said.

"You really *are* a prude, aren't you," Duvall said to Dahl.

"I just prefer to think there is a sober, reasoned discussion going on in there and that Kerensky is making some very good points."

From the other side of the door there was a muffled *thump*.

"Yes, *that's* it," Hester said.

"I think I'm going to wait in the lobby," Dahl said.

· · · · ·

Two hours later, as dawn broke, a tired-looking Kerensky came down to the lobby.

"Marc needs his keys," he said. "He's got a six-thirty makeup call."

Dahl dug in his pocket for the keys. "So he'll help us?" he asked.

Kerensky nodded. "He's going to put in a call as soon as he gets to the set," he said. "He'll tell Paulson that unless he schedules a meeting today, he's going to quit."

"And just how did you manage to get him to agree to that?" Hester said.

Kerensky fixed Hester with a direct stare. "Are you actually interested?"

"Uh," Hester said. "Actually, no. No, I'm not."

"Didn't think so," Kerensky said. He took the keys from Dahl.

"I am," Duvall said.

Kerensky sighed, and turned to Duvall. "Tell me, Maia: Have you ever met someone who you know so completely, so exactly and so perfectly that it's like the two of you share the same body, thoughts and desires? And had that feeling compounded by the knowledge that how you feel about them is exactly how they feel about you, right down to the very last atom of your being? Have you?"

"Not really," Duvall said.

"I pity you," he said, and then headed back to the hotel room.

"You *had* to ask," Hester said to Duvall.

"I was curious," Duvall said. "Sue me."

"Now I have *images*," Hester said. "They are in my *mind*. They will never leave me. I blame you."

"It's certainly a side of Kerensky we haven't seen before," Dahl said. "I never saw him being interested in men."

"It's not that," Hanson said.

"Did you *miss* the last couple of hours?" Hester said. "And the thumping?"

"No, Jimmy's right," Duvall said. "He's not interested in men. He's interested in himself. Always has been. Now he's gotten the chance to follow through on that."

"Ack," Hester said.

Duvall looked over at him. "Wouldn't you, if you had the chance?" she asked.

"I didn't," Dahl pointed out.

"Yes, but we already established you're a prude," Duvall said.

Dahl grinned. "Point," he said.

The elevator opened and Corey came out, followed by Kerensky. Corey walked up to Dahl. "I need your phone number," he said. "So I can call you when I set up the meeting today."

"All right," Dahl said, and gave it to him. Corey added it to his contacts and then looked at them all.

"I want you to appreciate what I'm doing for you," he said. "By getting you this meeting, I'm putting my ass on the line. So if you do anything that puts me or my career at risk, I swear I will find you and make you miserable for the rest of your lives. Are you all clear on this?"

"We're clear," Dahl said. "Thank you."

"I'm not doing it for you," Corey said, and then nodded over to Kerensky. "I'm doing it for him."

"Thank you anyway," Dahl said

"Also, if anyone asks, the reason you guys were helping me into my car last night is because I had an allergic reaction to the tannins in the wine I was drinking at the Vine Club," Corey said.

"Of course," Dahl said.

"That's the truth, you know," Corey said. "People are allergic to all sorts of things."

"Yes," Dahl said.

"You didn't see if anyone was taking video while you were putting me into the car, did you?" Corey asked.

"There might have been a couple," Dahl allowed.

Corey sighed. "Tannins. Remember it."

"Will do," Dahl said.

Corey nodded at Dahl, and then walked over to Kerensky and enveloped him in a passionate hug. Kerensky reciprocated.

"I wish we had more time," Corey said.

"So do I," Kerensky said. They hugged again and separated. Corey walked out of the lobby. Kerensky watched him go.

"Wow," Hester said. "You've got it bad, Kerensky."

Kerensky wheeled around. "What is *that* supposed to mean?"

Hester held up his hands. "Look, I'm not judging," he said.

"Judging what?" Kerensky said, and looked at the others. "What? You all think I had *sex* with Marc?"

"Didn't you?" Duvall asked.

"We *talked*," Kerensky said. "The most amazing conversation I have ever had with anyone in my entire life. It was like meeting the brother I never had."

"Come on, Anatoly," Hester said. "We heard *thumps*."

"Marc was putting on his pants," Kerensky said. "I gave him back his pants, and he was still unsteady, and he fell over. That was *it*."

"All right," Hester said. "Sorry."

"Jesus," Kerensky said, looking around. "You people. I have one of the most incredible experiences I'll *ever* have, talking with the one person who really gets me—who really *understands* me—and you're all down here thinking I'm performing some sort of time-traveling incestuous masturbation thing. Thanks so very much for crapping on my amazing, life-altering experience. You all make me sick." He stormed off.

"Well, that was interesting," Duvall said.

Kerensky stormed back in and pointed at Maia. "And we're through," he said.

"Fair enough," Duvall said. Kerensky stormed off a second time.

"I'd just like to point out that I was right," Dahl said, after a minute. Duvall walked over and smacked him on the head.

CHAPTER NINETEEN

Charles Paulson's private offices were in Burbank, off the studio lot, in a building that housed three other production companies, two agencies, a tech start-up and a nonprofit dedicated to fighting thrush. Paulson's offices filled the third floor; the group took the elevator.

"I shouldn't have eaten that last burrito," Hester said as they entered the elevator, a pained look on his face.

"I told you not to," Hanson said.

"You also said that the twenty-first century had food safety laws," Hester said.

"I don't think food safety laws are going to protect you from a third carnitas burrito," Hanson said. "That's not about food safety. It's about pork fat overload."

"I need a bathroom," Hester said.

"Can this wait?" Dahl said, to Hester. The elevator reached the third floor. "This is kind of an important meeting."

"If I don't find a bathroom, you're not going to want me at the meeting," Hester said. "Because what would happen would be grim."

The elevator doors opened and the five of them stepped off. Down the hallway to the right was a sign for the men's bathroom. Hester made his way toward it, quickly but stiffly, and disappeared through its door.

"How long do you think this is going to take?" Duvall asked Dahl. "Our meeting is in about a minute."

"Have you ever had a carnitas incident?" Dahl asked Duvall.

"No," Duvall said. "And from the looks of it I should be glad."

"He'll probably be in there a while," Dahl said.

"We can't wait," Kerensky said.

"No," Dahl said.

"You guys go ahead," Hanson said. "I'll stay and make sure Hester's all right. We'll wait for you in the office lobby when he's done."

"You're sure?" Dahl asked.

"I'm sure," Hanson said. "Hester and I were just going to be spectators in the meeting anyway. We can wait in the lobby just as easily, and read magazines. It's always fun to catch up on three-hundred-and-fifty-year-old gossip."

Dahl smiled at this. "All right," he said. "Thanks, Jimmy."

"If Hester's intestines explode, you let us know," Duvall said.

"You'll be the first," Hanson said, and headed toward the bathroom.

The receptionist at Paulson Productions smiled warmly at Kerensky as he, Dahl and Duvall entered the office lobby. "Hello, Marc," she said. "Good to see you again."

"Uh," Kerensky said.

"We're here to see Mr. Paulson," Dahl said, stepping into Kerensky's moment of awkwardness. "We have an appointment. Marc set it up."

"Yes, of course," the receptionist said, glancing at her computer screen. "Mr. Dahl, is it?"

"That's me," Dahl said.

"Have a seat over there and I'll let him know you're here," she said, smiling at Kerensky again before picking up her handset to call Paulson.

"I think she was flirting with you," Duvall said to Kerensky.

"She thought she was flirting with Marc," Kerensky pointed out.

"Maybe there's a history there," Duvall said.

"Stop it," Kerensky said.

"Just trying to help you rebound after the breakup," Duvall said.

"Mr. Dahl, Marc, ma'am," the receptionist said. "Mr. Paulson will see you now. Follow me, please." She led them down the corridor to a large office, in which sat Paulson, behind a large desk.

Paulson looked at Kerensky, severely. "I'm supposed to be talking to these people of yours, not you," he said. "You're supposed to be at work."

"I am at work," Kerensky said.

"This is not work," Paulson said. "Your work is at the studio. On the set. If you're not there, we're not shooting. If we're not shooting, you're wasting production time and money. The studio and the Corwin are already riding me because we're behind on production this year. You're not helping."

"Mr. Paulson," Dahl said, "perhaps you should call your show and see if Marc Corey is there."

Paulson fixed on Dahl, seeing him for the first time. "You look vaguely familiar. Who are you?"

"I'm Andrew Dahl," he said, sitting on one of the chairs in front of the desk, and then motioned to Duvall, who sat on the other. "This is Maia Duvall. We work on *Intrepid*."

"Then you should be on set as well," Paulson said.

"Mr. Paulson," Dahl repeated. "You should really call your show and see if Marc Corey is there."

Paulson pointed at Kerensky. "He's right *there*," he said.

"No, he's not," Dahl said. "That's why we're here to talk to you."

Paulson's eyes narrowed. "You people are wasting my time," he said.

"Jesus," Kerensky said, exasperated. "Will you just call the damn set? Marc's *there*."

Paulson paused to stare at Kerensky for a moment, and then picked up his desk phone and punched a button. "Yeah, hi, Judy," he said. "You on the set? . . . Yeah, okay. Tell me if you see Marc Corey there." He paused, and then looked at Kerensky again. "Okay. How long has he been there? . . . Okay. He been acting weird today? Out of character? . . . Yeah, okay. . . . No. No, I don't need to speak to him. Thanks, Judy." He hung up.

"That was my show runner, Judy Melendez," Paulson said. "She says Marc's been on set since the six-thirty makeup call."

"Thank you," Kerensky said.

"All right, I'll bite," Paulson said, to Kerensky. "Who the hell are you? Marc obviously *knows* you, or he wouldn't have set up this meeting. You could be his identical twin, but I know he doesn't have any brothers. So, what? Are you his cousin? Do you want to be on the show? Is this what this is about?"

"Do you put family members on the show?" Dahl asked.

"We don't go out of our way to advertise it, but sure," Paulson said. "A season ago I gave my uncle a part. He was about to lose his SAG insurance, so I put him in for the part of an admiral who tried to have Abernathy court-martialed. I also put in a small role for my son—" He stopped speaking, abruptly.

"We heard about your son," Dahl said. "We're very sorry."

"Thank you," Paulson said, and paused again. His demeanor had transformed from aggressive producer to something more tired and small. "Sorry," he said, after a moment. "It's been difficult."

"I can't imagine," Dahl said.

"Be glad that you can't," Paulson said, and reached over on his desk for a picture frame, looked at it, and held it in his hand. "Stupid kid. I told him to be careful handling the bike in the rain." He turned the frame briefly, showing a picture of him and a younger man, dressed in motorcycle leathers, smiling at the camera. "He never did listen to me," he said.

"Is that your son?" Duvall asked, reaching out for the frame.

"Yes," Paulson said, handing over the picture. "Matthew. He had just gotten his master's in anthropology when he tells me he wants to try being an actor. I said to him, if you wanted to be an actor, why did I just pay for you to get a master's in anthropology? But I put him on the show. He was an extra on a couple of episodes before . . . well."

"Andy," Duvall said, handing the picture to Dahl. He started at it.

Kerensky came over and looked at the picture Dahl was holding. "You have *got* to be kidding me," he said.

"What?" Paulson said, looking at the three of them. "Do you know him? Do you know Matthew?"

All three of them looked at Paulson.

"Matthew!" screamed a woman's voice, from out of the room and down the hall.

"Oh, shit," Duvall said, and launched herself out of her chair and out of the room. Dahl and Kerensky followed.

In the lobby, the receptionist had attached herself to Hester, sobbing in joy. Hester stood there, wearing a receptionist, deeply confused.

Hanson saw his three crewmates and came over to them. "We walked into the lobby," he said. "That's all we did. We walked into the lobby, and she screams a name and then almost leaps over her desk to get at Hester. What's going on?"

"I think we found the actor who plays Hester," Dahl said.

"Okay," Hanson said. "Who is he?"

"Matthew?" Paulson said, from the hall. He had followed his three guests out of the room to find out what was going on. "Matthew! *Matthew!*" He rushed to Hester, hugged him furiously and started kissing him on the cheek.

"He's Charles Paulson's kid," Duvall said to Hanson.

"The one who's in a coma?" Hanson said.

"That's the one," Dahl said.

"Oh, wow," Hanson said. "Wow."

All three of them looked at Hester, who whispered, "Help me."

"Someone's going to have to tell them who Hester really is," Kerensky said. He, Hanson and Duvall all looked at Dahl.

Dahl sighed, and moved toward Hester.

. . . . .

"Are you all right?" Dahl asked Hester. They were in a private hospital room, in which Matthew Paulson lay on a bed, tubes keeping him alive. Hester was staring at his comatose double.

"I'm better off than he is," Hester said.

"Hester," Dahl said, and looked out the doorway, where he was standing, to see if Charles Paulson was close enough in the hall to have heard Hester's comment. He wasn't. He was in the waiting area with Duvall, Hanson and Kerensky. Matthew Paulson could have only two visitors at a time.

"Sorry," Hester said. "I didn't mean it to be an asshole. It's just . . . well, now it all makes sense, doesn't it?"

"What do you mean?" Dahl asked.

"About me," Hester said. "You and Duvall and Hanson and Finn all are *interesting*, because you had to have interesting backstories, so you could all get killed off in a contextual way. Finn getting killed by someone he knew, right? You, about to be killed when you go back to Forshan. But I didn't have anything unusual about me. I'm just some guy from Des Moines who had a B minus average in high school, who joined the Dub U Fleet to see some of the universe before he came back home and stayed. Before I came on the *Intrepid* I was just another sarcastic loner.

"And now that makes sense, because I was never *meant* to do anything special, was I? I really was an extra. A placeholder character who Paulson could pour his kid into until his kid got bored with playing actor and went back to school to get a doctorate. Even the one thing I can do—pilot a shuttle—is just something that got stuck in because the show needed someone in that seat, and why not give it to the producer's kid? Make him feel *special*."

"I don't think it's like that," Dahl said.

"It's *exactly* like that," Hester said. "I'm meant to fill a spot and that's it."

"That's not true at all," Dahl said.

"No?" Hester looked up at Dahl. "What's my first name?"

"What?" Dahl asked.

"What's my first name?" Hester repeated. "You're Andy Dahl. Maia Duvall. Jimmy Hanson. Anatoly Kerensky, for Christ's sake. What's *my* first name, Andy? You don't know, do you?"

"You *have* a first name," Dahl said. "I could look on my phone and find it."

"But you don't *know* it," Hester said. "You never used it. You never call me by it. We're *friends,* and you don't even know my full name."

"I'm sorry," Dahl said. "I just never thought about calling you anything other than 'Hester.' "

"My point exactly," Hester said. "If even my *friends* never think about what my first name might be, that points out my role in the universe pretty precisely, doesn't it?" He went back to looking at Matthew Paulson, in his coma.

"So, what *is* your first name?" Dahl finally asked.

"It's Jasper," Hester said.

"Jasper," Dahl said.

"Family name," Hester said. "Jasper Allen Hester."

"Do you want me to call you Jasper from now on?" Dahl asked.

"Fuck, no," Hester said. "Who wants to be called Jasper? It's a ridiculous fucking name."

Dahl tried to stifle a laugh and failed. Hester smiled at this.

"I'll keep calling you Hester," Dahl said. "But I want you to know that inside, I'll be saying Jasper."

"If it makes you happy," Hester said.

"Jasper Jasper Jasper," Dahl said.

"All right," Hester said. "Enough. I'd hate to kill you in a hospital."

They returned their attention to Matthew Paulson.

"Poor kid," Hester said.

"He's your age," Duvall said.

"Yeah, but I'm likely to outlive him," Hester said. "There's a change for one of us."

"I suppose it is," Dahl said.

"That's the problem with living in the twenty-first century," Hester said. "In our world, if he got in the same accident, we could fix him. I mean, hell, Andy, think of all the horrible things that happened to you, and you survived."

"I survived because it wasn't time for me to die yet," Dahl said. "It's like Kerensky and his amazing powers of recovery. It's all thanks to the Narrative."

"Does it matter why?" Hester said. "I mean, really, Andy. If you're just about dead and you survive and are healed by entirely fictional means, do you really give a shit? No, because you're not dead. The Narrative knocks us off when it's convenient. But it's not all bad."

"You were just talking about how it all made sense you were a nobody," Dahl said. "That didn't sound like you were in love with the Narrative."

"I didn't say I was," Hester said. "But I think you're forgetting that this meant I was the only one of us not absolutely fated to die horribly for the amusement of others."

"This is a good point," Dahl said.

"This show we're on, it's crap," Hester said. "But it's crap that sometimes works to our advantage."

"Until it finally kills us," Dahl said.

"Kills *you*," Hester reminded him. "*I* might survive, remember." He motioned to Matthew Paulson. "And if he lived in our world, he might have been saved, too."

Dahl was silent at this. Hester looked up at him eventually to see Dahl looking at him curiously. "What?"

"I'm thinking," Dahl said.

"About what?" Hester said.

"About using the Narrative to our advantage," Dahl said.

Hester squinted. "This involves me in some way, doesn't it," he said.

"Yes, Jasper," Dahl said. "Yes it does."

CHAPTER TWENTY

Charles Paulson opened the door to the conference room where the five of them sat, waiting, followed by another man. "Sorry about the wait," he told them, and then motioned to the other man. "You wanted to see the show's head writer, here he is. This is Nick Weinstein. I've explained to him what's going on."

"Hello," Weinstein said, looking at the five of them. "Wow. Charles really wasn't kidding."

"Now, *that's* funny," Hester said, breaking up the slack-jawed staring four of the five of them were doing.

"What's funny?" Weinstein asked.

"Mister Weinstein, were you ever an extra on your show?" Dahl asked.

"Once, a few seasons ago," Weinstein said. "We needed a warm body for a funeral scene. I happened to be on the set. They threw a costume on me and told me to act sad. Why?"

"We know the man you played," Dahl said. "His name is Jenkins."

"Really?" Weinstein said, and smiled. "What's he like?"

"He's a sad, crazed shut-in who never got over the loss of his wife," Duvall said.

"Oh," Weinstein said, and stopped smiling. "Sorry."

"You're better groomed, though," Hanson said, encouragingly.

"That's probably the first time anyone's ever said that about me," Weinstein said, motioning at his beard.

"You said you had something you wanted to talk to me and Nick about," Paulson said, to Dahl.

"I do," Dahl said. "We do. Please sit."

"Who is Jenkins?" Kerensky whispered to Dahl, as Paulson and Weinstein took their chairs.

"Later," Dahl said.

"So," Paulson said. His eyes flickered involuntarily over to Hester every few seconds.

"Mister Paulson, Mister Weinstein, there's a reason we came back to your time," Dahl said. "We came to convince you to stop your show."

"What?" Weinstein said. "Why?"

"Because otherwise we're dead," Dahl said. "Mister Weinstein, when you kill off an extra in one of your scripts, the actor playing the extra eventually walks off the set and goes to get lunch. But where we are, that person stays dead. And people are killed off in just about every episode."

"Well, not every episode," Weinstein said.

"Jimmy," Dahl said.

"*Chronicles of the Intrepid* has aired one hundred twenty-eight episodes over six seasons to date," Hanson said. "One or more *Intrepid* crew members have died in ninety-six of those episodes. One hundred twelve episodes have death portrayed in one way or another. You've killed at least four hundred *Intrepid* crew members overall in the course of the series, and when you add in episodes where you've had other ships destroyed or planets attacked or suffering from diseases, your total death count reaches into the millions."

"Not counting enemy deaths," Dahl said.

"No, those would bump up the figure incrementally," Hanson said.

"He's read up a lot on the show," Dahl said to Weinstein, about Hanson.

"All of those deaths aren't my fault," Weinstein said.

"You *wrote* them," Duvall said.

"I didn't write *all* of them," Weinstein said. "There are other writers on staff."

"You're the head writer," Hester said. "Everything in the scripts goes through you for approval."

"The point is not to pin these deaths on you," Dahl said, cutting in. "You couldn't have known. From your point of view you're writing fiction. From our point of view, though, it's real."

"How does that even work?" Weinstein said. "How does what we write here affect your reality? That doesn't make any sense."

Hester snorted. "Welcome to our lives," he said.

"What do you mean?" Weinstein said, turning his attention to Hester.

"Do you think our lives make any sense at all?" Hester said. "You've got us living in a universe where there are killer robots with harpoons walking around a space station, because, sure, it makes perfect sense to have harpoon-launching killer robots."

"Or ice sharks," Duvall said.

"Or Borgovian Land Worms," Hanson said.

Weinstein held up a finger. "I was not responsible for those land worms," he said. "I was out for two weeks with bird flu. The writer who did that script loved *Dune*. By the time I got back, it was too late. The Herbert estate flayed us for those."

"We dove *into a black hole* to get here," Hester said, and jerked a thumb at Kerensky. "And we made sure to kidnap this sad bastard to make sure it would work, because he's a main character on your show and won't die offscreen. Think about that—physics *alters around him*."

"Not that it keeps me from having the crap beaten out of me on a regular basis," Kerensky said. "I used to wonder why bad things kept happening to me. Now I know it's because at least one of your main characters has to be made to suffer. That just sucks."

"You even make him heal super quickly so you can beat him up again," Duvall said. "Which now that I think about it seems cruel."

"And there's the Box," Hanson said, motioning to Dahl.

"The Box?" Weinstein said, looking at Dahl.

"Whenever you write bad science into the show, the way it gets resolved is that we feed the problem into the Box, and then when it's dramatically appropriate it spits out an answer," Dahl said.

"We never wrote a Box into the series," Weinstein said, confused.

"But you do write bad science into the series," Dahl said. "All the time. So there's a Box."

"Did they teach you science in school?" Hester asked. "I'm just wondering."

"I went to Occidental College," Weinstein said. "It has really good science classes."

"Yeah, but did you *go* to any?" Duvall said. "Because I have to tell you, our universe is a mess."

"Other science fiction shows had science advisers and consultants," Hanson pointed out.

"It's science *fiction,*" Weinstein said. "The second part of that phrase matters too."

"But you're making it *bad* science fiction," Hester said. "And *we* have to live in it."

"Guys," Dahl said, interrupting everyone again. "Let's try to stay on target here."

"What *is* the target?" Paulson asked. "You said you had an idea you wanted to talk about, and all I'm hearing so far is a bitch session at my head writer."

"I'm feeling a little defensive," Weinstein said.

"Don't," Dahl said. "Again: You couldn't have known. But now you know where we are coming from, and why we came back to stop your show."

Paulson opened his mouth at this, probably to object and offer any number of reasons why that would be impossible. Dahl held up his hand to forestall the objection. "Now that we're here, I know that just stopping the show can't happen. It was a long shot anyway. But now I don't want the show to end, because I can see a way for it to work to our advantage. Both ours and yours."

"Get to it, then," Paulson said.

"Charles, your son's in a coma," Dahl said.

"Yes," Paulson said.

"There's no chance for him ever coming out of it," Dahl said.

"No," Paulson said after a minute, and looked around, eyes wet. "No."

"You didn't say anything about this," Weinstein said. "I thought there was still a chance."

"No," Paulson said. "Doctor Lo told me yesterday that the scans show his brain function continuing to deteriorate, and that it's the machines keeping his body alive at this point. We're waiting until we have the family together so we can say good-bye. We'll have him taken off the machines then." He looked over at Hester, who sat there silently, and then back at Dahl. "Unless you have another idea."

"I do," Dahl said. "Charles, I think we can save your son."

· · · · ·

"Tell me how," Paulson said.

"We take him with us," Dahl said. "Back to the *Intrepid*. We can cure him there. We have the technology there to do it. And even if we didn't"—he pointed at Weinstein—"we have the Narrative. Mister Weinstein here writes an episode in which Hester is injured but survives and is taken to sick bay to be healed. It gets done. Hester survives. Your son survives."

"Take him into the show," Paulson said. "That's your plan."

"That's the idea," Dahl said. "Sort of."

"Sort of," Paulson said, frowning.

"There are some logistical issues," Dahl said. "As well as some that are, for lack of a better word, teleological."

"Like what?" Paulson said.

Dahl turned to Weinstein, who was also frowning. "I'm guessing you're thinking of a few right now," he said.

"Yeah," Weinstein said, and motioned to Hester. "The first is that you'll have two of him in your universe."

"You can make up an excuse for that," Paulson said.

"I could, yes," Weinstein said. "It would be messy and nonsensical."

"This is a problem for you?" Hester asked.

"But the thing is that two of him in their universe means none of him in this one," Weinstein said, ignoring Hester's comment. "You had—have, sorry—your son playing this character here. If they both go, there's no one to play the character."

"We'll recast the role," Paulson said. "Someone who looks like Matthew."

"But then the problem is which of the—" Weinstein looked at Hester.

"Hester," he said.

"Which of the Hesters the new one back here affects," Weinstein said. "Besides that, and I'm the first to admit that I have no idea how this screwy voodoo works, but if I were trying to do this, I wouldn't be using a substitute Hester, because who knows how that would affect your son's healing process. He might not end up himself."

"Right," Dahl said. "Which is why we offer the following solution."

"I stay behind," Hester said.

"So, you stay behind, pretend to be my son," Paulson said. "You make a miraculous recovery, then we make the episode where you play my son, and we make you well."

"Sort of," Hester said.

"What is it with these 'sort ofs'?" Paulson snapped. "What's the problem?"

Dahl looked over at Weinstein again. "Tell him," he said.

"Oh, shit," Weinstein said, straightening up in his chair. "This is about that atom thing, isn't it?"

"Atom thing?" Paulson said. "What 'atom thing'?"

Weinstein grabbed his head. "So *stupid*," he said to himself. "Charles, when we wrote the episode where Abernathy and the others came back in time, we did this thing where they could only be here six days before their atoms reverted to their current positions in the timeline."

"I have no idea what that means, Nick," Paulson said. "Talk normal human to me."

"It means that if we stay in this timeline for six days, we die," Dahl said. "And we're already on day three."

"It also means that if Matthew goes to their timeline, he only has six days before the same thing happens to him," Weinstein said.

"What a stupid fucking idea!" Paulson exploded at Weinstein. "Why the fuck did you do that?"

Weinstein held his hands out defensively. "How was I supposed to know one day I'd be here talking about this?" he said, plaintively. "Jesus, Charles, we were just trying to get through the damn episode. We needed them to have a reason to get everything done on a schedule. It made sense at the time."

"Well, change it," Paulson said. "New rule: People traveling through time can take as much fucking time as they want."

Weinstein looked over at Dahl, pleadingly. "It's too late for that," Dahl said, interpreting Weinstein's look. "The rule was in effect when we came through time, and besides, this isn't an episode. We're acting outside the Narrative, which means that even if you could change it, it wouldn't have an effect because it's not being recorded. We're stuck with it."

"They're right," Paulson said to Weinstein, motioning at the *Intrepid* crew. "The universe you've written sucks." Weinstein looked cowed.

"He didn't know," Dahl said to Paulson. "You can't blame him. And we need him, so please don't fire him."

"I'm not going to fire him," Paulson said, still staring at Weinstein. "I want to know how we *fix* this."

Weinstein opened his mouth, then closed it, then turned to Dahl. "Help would be appreciated," he said.

"This is where it gets a little crazy," Dahl said.

"Gets?" Weinstein said.

Dahl turned to Paulson. "Hester stays behind," he said. "We take your son with us. We go back to our time and our universe, but he"—Dahl pointed at Weinstein—"writes that the person in the shuttle is Hester. We don't try to sneak him in or have him be another extra. He has to be central to the plot. We call him out by name. His full name. Jasper Allen Hester."

"Jasper?" Duvall said, to Hester.

"Not now," Hester said.

"So we call him Jasper Allen Hester," Paulson said. "So what? He'll still be my son, not your friend."

"No," Dahl said. "Not if we say he isn't. If the Narrative says it's Hester, then it's Hester."

"But—" Paulson cut himself short and looked at Weinstein. "This makes no fucking sense to me at all, Nick."

"No, it doesn't," Weinstein said. "But that's the thing. It doesn't *have* to make sense. It just has to *happen*." He turned to Dahl. "You're using the shoddy world building of the series to your advantage."

"I wouldn't have put it that way, but yes," Dahl said.

"What about this atom thing?" Paulson said. "I thought this was a problem."

"If it was Hester here and your son there, then it would be," Weinstein said. "But if it's definitely Hester there, then it will definitely be your son here, and all their atoms will be where they should be." He turned to Dahl. "Right?"

"That's the idea," Dahl said.

"I *like* this plan," Weinstein said.

"And we're sure this will work," Paulson said.

"No, we're not," Hester said. Everyone looked at him. "What?" he said. "We don't know if it will work. We could be wrong about this. In which case, Mister Paulson, your son will still die."

"But then you will die, too," Paulson said. "You don't have to die."

"Mister Paulson, the fact of the matter is that if your son hadn't gone into his coma, you would have eventually killed me off as soon as he got bored being an actor," Hester said, and then pointed at Weinstein. "Well, *he* would kill me off. Probably by being eaten by a space badger or something else completely asinine. Your son is in a coma now, so it's possible I'll live, but then again one day I might be on deck six when the *Intrepid* gets into a space battle, in which case I'll be just some anonymous bastard sucked into space. Either way, I would have died pointlessly."

He looked around the table. "I figure this way, *if* I die, I die trying to do something useful—saving your son," he said, looking back at Paulson. "My life will actually be good for something, which it's avoiding being so far. And if this works, then both your son and I get to live, which wasn't going to happen before. Either way I figure I'm better off than I was before."

Paulson got up, crossed the room to where Hester was sitting and collapsed into him, sobbing. Hester, not quite knowing what to do with him, patted him on the back gingerly.

"I don't know how I can make this up to you," Paulson said to Hester, when he finally disengaged. He looked over to the rest of the crew. "How I'm going to make it up to all of you."

"As it happens," Dahl said, "I have some suggestions on that."

CHAPTER TWENTY-ONE

The taxi turned off North Occidental Boulevard onto East-erly Terrace and slowed to a stop in front of a yellow bun-galow.

"Your stop," the taxi driver said.

"Would you mind waiting?" Dahl asked. "I'm only going to be a few minutes."

"I have to run the meter," the driver said.

"That's fine," Dahl said. He got out of the car and walked up the brick walkway to the house door and knocked.

After a moment a woman came to the door. "I don't need any more copies of *The Watchtower*," she said.

"Pardon?" Dahl said.

"Or the Book of Mormon," she said. "I mean, thank you. I appreciate the thought. But I'm good."

"I do have something to deliver, but it's neither of those things," Dahl said. "But first, tell me if you're Samantha Mar-tinez."

"Yes," she said.

"My name is Andy Dahl," Dahl said. "You could say that you and I almost have a friend in common." He held out a small box to her.

She didn't take it. "What is it?" she said.

"Open it," Dahl suggested.

"I'm sorry, Mister Dahl, but I am a little suspicious of strange men coming to my door on a Saturday morning, asking my name and bearing mysterious packages," Martinez said.

Dahl smiled at this. "Fair enough," he said. He opened the package, revealing a small black hemisphere that Dahl recognized as a holographic image projector. He activated it; the image of someone who looked like Samantha Martinez appeared and hovered in the air over the projector. She was in a wedding dress, smiling, standing next to a man who looked like a clean-shaven version of Jenkins. Dahl held it out for her to see.

Martinez looked at the image quietly for a minute. "I don't understand," she said.

"It's complicated," Dahl admitted.

"Did you Photoshop my face into this picture?" she asked. "And how are you doing this?" She motioned to the floating projection. "Is this some new Apple thing?"

"If you're asking if I've altered the image, the answer is no," Dahl said. "And as for the projector, it's probably best to say it's something like a prototype." He touched the surface of the projector and the image shifted, to another picture of Jenkins and Martinez's double, looking happily at each other. After a few seconds the picture changed to another.

"I don't understand," Martinez said again.

"You're an actress," Dahl said.

"Was an actress," Martinez said. "I did it for a couple of years and didn't get anywhere. I'm a teacher now."

"When you were an actress, you had a small role on *Chronicles of the Intrepid*," Dahl said. "Do you remember?"

"Yes," Martinez said. "My character got shot. I was in the episode for about a minute."

"This is that character," Dahl said. "Her name was Margaret. The man in the picture is her husband." He held the projector out to Martinez. She took it, looked at it again and then set it down on a small table on the other side of the door. She turned back to Dahl.

"Is this some kind of a joke?" she said.

"No joke," Dahl said. "I'm not trying to trick you or sell you anything. After today, you won't see me again. All I'm doing is delivering this to you."

"I don't understand," Martinez said again. "I don't understand how you have all these pictures of me, with someone I don't even know."

"They're not my pictures, they're his," Dahl said, and held out the box the projector came in to Martinez. "Here. There's a note in the box from him. It'll explain things better than I can, I think."

Martinez took the box and took out a folded sheet, dense with writing. "This is from him," she said.

"Yes," Dahl said.

"Why isn't he here?" Martinez asked. "Why didn't he deliver it himself?"

"It's complicated," Dahl repeated. "But even if he could have been, I think he would have been afraid to. And I think seeing you might have broken his heart."

"Because of her," Martinez said.

"Yes," Dahl said.

"Does he want to meet me?" Martinez asked. "Is this his way of introducing himself?"

"I think it's his way of introducing himself, yes," Dahl said. "But I'm afraid he can't meet you."

"Why?" Martinez asked.

"He has to be somewhere else," Dahl said. "That's the easiest way to put it. Maybe his letter will explain it better."

"I'm sorry I keep saying this, but I still don't understand," Martinez said. "You show up at my door with pictures of someone who looks just like me, who you say is the person I played for a minute in a television show, who is dead and who has a husband who sends me gifts. You know how crazy that sounds?"

"I do," Dahl said.

"Why would he do this?" Martinez said. "What's the point of it?"

"Are you asking my opinion?" Dahl asked.

"I am," Martinez said.

"Because he misses his wife," Dahl said. "He misses his wife so much that it's turned his life inside out. In a way that's hard to explain, you being here and being alive means that in some way his wife's life continues. So he's sending her to you. He wants to give you the part of her life he had with her."

"But why?" Martinez said.

"Because it's his way of letting her go," Dahl said. "He's giving her to you so he can get on with the rest of his life."

"He said this to you," Martinez said.

"No," Dahl said. "But I think that's why he did it."

Martinez stepped away from the door, quickly. When she came back a minute later, she had a tissue in her hand, with which she had dried her eyes. She looked up at Dahl and smiled weakly.

"This is definitely the strangest Saturday morning I've had in a while," she said.

"Sorry about that," Dahl said.

"No, it's fine," Martinez said. "I still don't understand. But I guess I'm helping your friend, aren't I?"

"I think you are," Dahl said. "Thank you for that."

"I'm sorry," Martinez said, and stepped aside slightly. "Would you like to come in for a minute?"

"I would love to, but I can't," Dahl said. "I have a taxi running its meter, and I have people waiting for me."

"Going back to your mysterious, complicated place," Martinez said.

"Yes," Dahl said. "Which reminds me. That projector and that letter will probably disappear in a couple of days."

"Like, vaporize?" Martinez said. "As in 'this letter will self-destruct in five seconds'?"

"Pretty much," Dahl said.

"Are you a spy or something?" Martinez said, smiling.

"It's complicated," Dahl said once more. "In any event, I suggest making copies of everything. You can probably just project the pictures against a white wall and take pictures of them, and scan the letter."

"I'll do that," Martinez said. "Thanks for telling me."

"You're welcome," Dahl said, and turned to go.

"Wait a second," Martinez said. "Your friend. Are you going to see him when you get back?"

"Yes," Dahl said.

Martinez stepped out of the doorway to Dahl and gave him a small kiss on the cheek. "Give him that for me," she said. "And tell him that I said thank you. And that I'll take good care of Margaret for him."

"I will," Dahl said. "I promise."

"Thank you." She leaned up and gave him a peck on the other cheek. "That's for you."

Dahl smiled. "Thanks."

Martinez grinned and went back into the bungalow.

· · · · ·

"So, you're ready for this," Dahl asked Hester, in the shuttle.

"Of course not," Hester said. "If everything goes according to plan, then the moment you guys go back to our universe, I'll be transported from this perfectly functioning body to one that has severe physical and brain damage, at which point all I can hope for is that we're not wrong about twenty-fifth-century medicine being able to cure me. If everything *doesn't* go according to plan, then in forty-eight hours all my atoms go pop. I want to ask you how you think one gets *ready* for either scenario."

"Good point," Dahl said.

"I want to know how you talked me into this," Hester said.

"I'm apparently very persuasive," Dahl said.

"Then again, I'm the guy who got talked into holding Finn's drugs for him because he convinced me they were candy," Hester said.

"If I recall correctly, there *were* candied," Dahl said.

"I'm gullible and weak-willed, is what I'm saying," Hester said.

"I disagree with that assessment," Dahl said.

"Well, you *would* say that," Hester said, "now that you've talked me into your ridiculous plan."

The two of them stood over the body of Matthew Paulson, whose stretcher was surrounded by mobile life support apparatus. Duvall was checking the equipment and the comatose body it was attached to.

"How is he?" Dahl asked.

"He's stable," Duvall said. "The machines are doing the hard work for the moment, and the shuttle has adapters I could use, so we don't have to worry about depleting any batteries. As long as he doesn't have any major medical emergencies between now and when we make the transition back, we should be fine."

"And if he does?" Hester asked.

Duvall looked at him. "Then I'll do my best with the training I have," she said. She reached over and slapped his shoulder. "Don't worry. I'm not going to let you down."

"Guys, it's time to go," Kerensky said, from the pilot seat of the shuttle. "Our trip over from Griffith Park did not go unnoticed, and I've got at least three aircraft coming our way. We've got another couple of minutes before things get messy."

"Got it," Dahl said, and looked back to Hester. "So, you're ready for this," he said.

"Yes," Hester said. The two of them walked outside, into the lawn of Charles Paulson's Malibu estate. Charles and his family were there, waiting for Hester. Hanson, who had been keeping them company, broke off and joined Dahl. Hester walked over to join Paulson's family.

"When will we know?" Paulson asked Dahl.

"We're taking the engines to maximum capacity to the black hole we're using," Dahl said. "It will be within the day. I suppose you'll know when your son starts acting like your son again."

"If it works," Paulson said.

"If it works," Dahl agreed. "Let's work on the assumption it will."

"Yes, let's," Hester said.

"Now," Dahl said, to Paulson. "We're agreed on everything."

"Yes," Paulson said. "None of your characters will be killed off going forward. The show will stop randomly killing off extras. And the show itself will wrap up next season and we won't make any new shows in the universe within a hundred years of your timeline."

"And this episode?" Dahl said. "The one where everything we planned happens."

"Nick messaged me about it just a few minutes ago," Paulson said. "He says he's almost got a rough version done. As soon as it's done he and I will work on a polish, and then we'll get it into production as soon as . . . well, as soon as we know whether or not your plan worked."

"It'll work," Dahl said.

"It's going to make hell with our production schedule," Paulson said. "I'm going to end up having to pay for this episode out of my own pocket."

"It'll be worth it," Dahl said.

"I know," Paulson said. "If everything works, it'll be a hell of a show for you."

"Of course," Dahl said. Hester rolled his eyes a little.

"I hear helicopters," Hanson said. From the shuttle came the sound of engines primed to move. Dahl looked at Hester.

"Good luck," Hester said.

"See you soon," Dahl said, and made his way to the shuttle. They were gone before the helicopters could get to them.

· · · · ·

"It's time," Kerensky said, as they approached the black hole. "Everyone get ready for the transition. Dahl, come take the co-pilot seat."

"I can't fly a shuttle," Dahl said.

"I don't need you to fly it," Kerensky said. "I need you to hit the automatic homing and landing sequence in case that asshole writer has something explode and knock me out."

Dahl got up and looked over to Duvall. "Hester doing okay?" he asked.

"He's fine, everything's fine," Duvall said. "He's not Hester yet, though."

"Call him Hester anyway," Dahl said. "Maybe it'll matter."

"You're the boss," Duvall said.

Dahl sat down in the co-pilot seat. "You remember how to do this," he said to Kerensky.

"Aim for the gap between the accretion disk and the Schwartzchild radius and boost engines to one hundred ten percent," Kerensky said, testily. "I've got it. Although it might have been helpful for me to observe the last time we did it. But no, you had me in a crate. Without my pants."

"Sorry about that," Dahl said.

"Not that it matters anyway," Kerensky said. "I'm your

good-luck charm, remember? We'll make it through this part just fine."

"Hopefully the rest of it, too," Dahl said.

"If this plan of yours works," Kerensky said. "How will we know that it's worked?"

"When we revive Hester, and he's Hester," Dahl said.

A sensor beeped. "Transition in ten seconds," Kerensky said. "So we won't know until we're back on the *Intrepid*."

"Probably," Dahl said.

"Probably?" Kerensky said.

"I thought of one way we might know if the transfer didn't take," Dahl said.

"How?" Kerensky asked.

The shuttle jammed itself into the ragged edge between the accretion disk and the Schwartzchild radius and transitioned instantly.

In the view screen the planet Forshan loomed large, and above it a dozen ships, including the *Intrepid*, were locked in battle.

Every single sensor on the shuttle flashed to red and began to blare.

One of the nearby starships sparkled, sending a clutch of missiles toward the shuttle.

"When we come through, it might look like *this*," Dahl said.

Kerensky screamed, and Dahl then felt ill as Kerensky plunged the shuttle into evasive maneuvers.

CHAPTER TWENTY-TWO

Five missiles coming," Dahl said, fighting the sickness in his stomach from the shuttle's dive to read the co-pilot's panel.

"I know," Kerensky said.

"Engines minimal," Dahl said. "We burned them coming through."

"I *know*," Kerensky said.

"Defense options?" Dahl asked.

"It's a *shuttle*," Kerensky said. "I'm doing them." He corkscrewed the shuttle violently. The missiles changed course to follow, spreading out from their original configuration.

A message popped up on Dahl's screen. "Three missiles locked," he said. "Impact in six seconds."

Kerensky looked up, as if toward the heavens. "Goddamn it, I'm a *featured character*! Do something!"

A beam of light lanced from the *Intrepid*, vaporizing the nearest missile. Kerensky yanked the shuttle over to avoid the explosion and debris. The *Intrepid*'s pulse beam touched the four other missiles, turning them into atoms.

"Holy shit, that *worked*," Kerensky said.

"If only you knew before, right?" Dahl said, amazed himself.

The shuttle's phone activated. "Kerensky, come in," it said. It was Abernathy on the other end.

"Kerensky here," he said.

"Not a lot of time here," Abernathy said. "Do you have the carrier?"

The carrier? Dahl thought—and then remembered that Hester carried in his body invasive cells whose DNA was a coded message detailing the final will and testament of the leader of the Forshan's rightward schism—which if unlocked could end the religious wars on Forshan—which would not be convenient to any number of leaders on either side of the conflict—which was why all those ships were out there: to bring the shuttle down.

Then Dahl remembered that until that very second, absolutely none of that was true.

But it was now.

"We have the carrier," Kerensky said. "Crewman Hester. Yes. But he's awfully sick, Captain. We're barely keeping him alive."

A panel on Dahl's co-pilot screen flashed. "Three new missiles away!" he said to Kerensky, who spun the shuttle into new evasive maneuvers.

"Kerensky, this is Chief Medical Officer Hartnell," a new voice said. "Crewman Hester's immune system is fighting those cells and losing. If you don't get him to the ship now, they're going to kill him, and then the cells will die too."

"We're being fired on," Kerensky said. "It makes travel difficult."

A new pulse beam flickered out of the *Intrepid,* vaporizing the three new missiles.

"You worry about getting to the *Intrepid,* Kerensky," Abernathy said. "We'll worry about the missiles. Abernathy out."

" 'The carrier'?" Duvall said, from the back of the shuttle. "He's got cells in his body with an encoded message in his DNA? That doesn't even make sense!"

"Nick Weinstein had to write the episode really quickly," Dahl said. "Cut him a break."

"He also wrote *this?*" Kerensky said, motioning out the view screens to the space battle in front of them. "If I ever see him again I'm going to kick his ass."

"Focus," Dahl said. "We need to get to the *Intrepid* without dying."

"Do you think Paulson's son is in Hester's old body?" Kerensky said.

"What?" Dahl said.

"Do you think the switch worked?" Kerensky asked, glancing at Dahl.

Dahl looked back at the body on the stretcher. "I don't know," he said. "Maybe?"

" 'Maybe' works for me," Kerensky said, stopped the shuttle's evasive maneuvers and jammed it as fast as it would go, straight toward the *Intrepid*. All around them Forshan spacecraft fired missiles, beams and projectiles. The *Intrepid* lit up like a Christmas tree, firing all available weapons to shoot down missiles and disable beams and projectile weapons on the Forshan spacecraft.

"This is a bad idea," Dahl said to Kerensky, who was grimly staring forward, keeping the *Intrepid* squarely in his sights.

"We're going to live or die," Kerensky said. "Why fuck around?"

"I liked you better before you were a fatalist," Dahl said.

A missile erupted starboard, knocking the shuttle off its course. The shuttle's inertial dampeners flickered, hurling Hester, Duvall and Hanson around the rear of the shuttle.

"Don't fly into missiles!" Duvall shouted.

"Blame the writer!" Kerensky shot back.

"That's a shitty excuse!" Duvall said. The shuttle rocked again as another missile scored a near miss.

The shuttle ran through the gauntlet of ships, breaking through toward the *Intrepid*.

"The shuttle bay is aft," Dahl said. "We're not aimed at aft."

"Here's where we find out just how hot a shuttle pilot that

writer thinks I am," Kerensky said, and threw the shuttle into a reverse Fibonacci spiral, over the top of the *Intrepid*. Dahl groaned as the *Intrepid* wheeled and grew in the view screen. Missiles vibrated the shuttle as they zoomed by, narrowly missing the arcing shuttle. Dahl was certain they were going to smash against the *Intrepid*'s hull, and then they were in the shuttle bay, slamming into the deck. The shuttle screeched violently and something fell off of it outside.

Kerensky whooped and shut down the engines. *"That's good television,"* he said.

"I'm never flying with you again," Duvall said, from the back of the shuttle.

"There's no time to waste," Kerensky said, changing his demeanor so suddenly that Dahl had no doubt he'd just been gripped by the Narrative. "We've got to get Hester to sick bay. Dahl, you're with me on the left side of the stretcher. Duvall, Hanson, take the right. Let's run, people."

Dahl unbuckled and scrambled over to the stretcher, unexpectedly giddy. Kerensky had used Hester's name while under the influence of the Narrative.

As they raced through the corridors with the stretcher, they heard the booms and thumps of the *Intrepid* under attack.

"Now that we're on board, all those ships are attacking the *Intrepid*," Kerensky said. "We need to hurry." The ship shook again, more severely.

"Took you long enough," Medical Officer Hartnell said, as the four of them wheeled the stretcher into sick bay. "Any longer and there wouldn't be a sick bay left. Or any other part of the ship."

"Can't we bug out?" Dahl heard himself say, as they maneuvered the stretcher.

"Engines have been disabled in the attack," Hartnell said. "Nowhere to run. If we don't get this message out of him fast, we're all dead. Lift!" They lifted Hester's body and put it onto a medical table. Hartnell flicked at his tablet and Hester's body stiffened.

"There, he's in stasis," Hartnell said. "He'll be stable until all of this is done." He looked at his medical tablet and frowned. "What the hell are all these fractures and brain trauma?" he said.

"It was a rough shuttle ride," Kerensky said.

Hartnell looked at Kerensky as if he were going to say something, but then the entire ship lurched, throwing everyone but Hester to the deck.

"Oh, that's not good," Duvall said.

Hartnell's phone activated. "This is the captain," Abernathy said through the phone. "What's the status of the carrier?"

"Crewman Hester's alive and in stasis," Hartnell said. "I'm about to take a sample of the invasive cells to start the decoding process."

There was another violent shudder to the ship. "You're going to need to work faster than that," Abernathy said. "We're taking hits we can't keep taking. We need that decoded now."

"Now isn't going to work," Hartnell said. "How much time can you give me?"

Another shudder, and the lights flickered. "I can give you ten minutes," Abernathy said. "Try not to use them all." The captain disconnected.

Hartnell looked at them all. "We're fucked," he said.

Dahl couldn't help smiling crazily at that. *Pretty sure he wasn't in the Narrative when he said that,* he thought.

"Andy," Hanson said. "The Box."

"Shit," Dahl said. "The Box."

"What's a Box?" Hartnell said.

"Take a sample and give it to me," Dahl said to Hartnell.

"Why?" Hartnell asked.

"I'll take it to Xenobiology and run it there," Dahl said.

"We've got the same equipment here—" Hartnell said.

Dahl looked over to Kerensky for help. "Just do it, Hartnell," Kerensky said. "Before you get us all killed."

Hartnell frowned but took his sampler and jammed it into Hester's arm, then took out the sample container and gave it to Dahl. "Here. Now someone please tell me what this is about."

"Andy," Hanson said. "To get to Xenobiology from here you'll need to go through deck six."

"Right," Dahl said, and turned to Kerensky. "Come with me, please."

"Who's going to tell me what's going on?" Hartnell said, and then Dahl and Kerensky were out the door, into the corridor.

"What's with deck six?" Kerensky asked as they ran.

"It has a tendency to blow up when we're attacked," Dahl said. "Like right now."

"You're using me as a good-luck charm again, aren't you?" Kerensky said.

"Not exactly," Dahl said.

Deck six was exploding and on fire.

"The corridors are blocked!" Kerensky said, over the noise.

"Come on," Dahl said, and slapped open an access door to the cargo tunnels. There was a gust as the heated air of deck six blew into the opened door. Kerensky went through and Dahl shut the access door as something erupted in the hall.

"This way," Dahl said, and the two fished their way around

the cargo carts to an access door on the other side of the deck and then back into the main corridors.

Lieutenant Collins did not look happy to see Dahl.

"What are you doing here?" she said. Dahl ignored her and went to the storage room, pulling out the Box.

"Hey, you can't be using that around *Kerensky*," Collins said, moving toward Dahl.

"If she tries to come near me, take her out," Dahl said to Kerensky.

"Got it," Kerensky said. Collins abruptly stopped.

"Take her tablet," Dahl said. Kerensky did.

"How much time?" Dahl asked. He set the Box on an induction pad.

"Seven minutes," Kerensky said.

"That'll work," Dahl said, slipped the sample into the Box and pressed the green button. He walked over to Kerensky, took Collins' tablet, signed her off and signed into his own account.

"Now what?" Kerensky said.

"We wait," Dahl said.

"For how long?" Kerensky said.

"As long as dramatically appropriate," Dahl said.

Kerensky peered at the Box. "So this was the thing that kept me from turning into mush when I got the Merovian Plague?"

"That's it," Dahl said.

"Ridiculous," Kerensky said.

Collins looked at Kerensky, gaping. "You *know*?" she said. "You're not supposed to know."

"At this point, I know a lot more than you," Kerensky said.

The Box pinged and the tablet was flooded with data. Dahl barely glanced at it. "We're good," he said. "Back to sick bay." They ran out of Xenobiology, back to the access corridors to return to deck six.

"Almost there," Kerensky said, as they emerged out of the access corridors into the fires of deck six.

The ship rocked violently and the main corridor of deck six collapsed onto Dahl, crushing him and slicing a jagged shard of metal through his liver. Dahl stared at it for a moment and then looked at Kerensky.

"You *had* to say 'almost there,'" he whispered, the words dribbling out between drips of blood.

"Oh, God, Dahl," Kerensky said, and started trying to move debris off of him.

"Stop," Dahl said. Kerensky ignored him. *"Stop,"* he said again, more forcefully. Kerensky stopped. Dahl pushed the tablet, still in his hands, to Kerensky. "No time. Take the results. Feed them into the sick bay computer. Don't let Hartnell argue. When the sick bay computer has the data, the Narrative will take over. It will be done. But get there. Hurry."

"Dahl—" Kerensky said.

"This is why I brought you with me," Dahl said. "Because I knew whatever happened to me, *you'd* make it back. Now go. Save the day, Kerensky. Save the day."

Kerensky nodded, took the tablet, and ran.

Dahl lay there, pinned through the liver, and in his final moments of consciousness tried to focus on the fact that Hester would live, the ship would be saved and his friends would make it through the rest of their lives without being savaged by the Narrative. And all it needed was one more dramatic death of an extra. His dramatic death.

It's a fair trade, he thought, trying to reconcile himself to how it all played out. A fair trade. Saved his friends. Saved Matthew Paulson. Saved the *Intrepid.* A fair trade.

But as everything went gray and slid into black, a final thought bubbled up from the bottom of what was left of him.

Screw this, I want to live, it said.

But then everything went to black anyway.

· · · · ·

"Stop being dramatic," the voice said. "We know you're awake."

Dahl opened his eyes.

Hester was standing over him, along with Duvall and Hanson.

Dahl smiled at Hester. "It worked," he said. "It's you. It really worked."

"Of course it worked," Hester said. "Why wouldn't it work?"

Dahl laughed weakly at this. He tried to get up but couldn't.

"Stasis medical chair," Duvall said. "You're regrowing a liver and a lot of burned skin and healing a broken rib cage. You wouldn't like what you'd be feeling if you moved."

"How long have I been in this thing?" Dahl asked.

"Four days," Hanson said. "You were a mess."

"I thought I was dead," Dahl said.

"You would have been dead if someone hadn't rescued you," Duvall said.

"Who rescued me?" Dahl asked.

Another face loomed into view.

"Jenkins," Dahl said.

"You were right outside a cargo tunnel," Jenkins said. "I figured, might as well."

"Thank you," Dahl said.

"No thanks necessary," Jenkins said. "I did it purely out of self-interest. If you died, I would never know if you ever delivered that message for me."

"I did," Dahl said.

"How did it go over?" Jenkins asked.

"It went over well," Dahl said. "I'm supposed to give you a kiss for her."

"Well, maybe some other time," Jenkins said.

"What are you two talking about?" Duvall asked.

"I'll tell you later," Dahl said, and then looked back to Jenkins. "So you're out of your hiding place, then."

"Yes," he said. "It was time."

"Good," Dahl said.

"And the great news is we're all heroes," Hester said. "The 'message' was extracted out of my body and broadcast by the *Intrepid*, ending the religious war on Forshan. How lucky is that."

"Amazing," Dahl said.

"Of course, none of it even begins to make sense if you think about it," Hester said.

"It never has," Dahl said.

Later in the day, after his friends had left, Dahl had another visitor.

"Science Officer Q'eeng," Dahl said.

"Ensign," Q'eeng said. "You are healing?"

"So I've been told," Dahl said.

"Lieutenant Kerensky tells me it was you who cracked the code, so the rightward schism leader's last will and testament could be broadcast," Q'eeng said.

"I suppose it was," Dahl said, "although I can't honestly take all the credit."

"Nevertheless, for your bravery and your sacrifice I have written you up for a commendation," Q'eeng said. "If it's approved, which it will be, then you will also be advanced in rank. So let me be the first to say, Congratulations, Lieutenant."

"Thank you, sir," Dahl said.

"There's one other thing," Q'eeng said. "Just a few minutes ago I received a highly classified message from the Universal Union High Command. I was informed that I was to read it to you, and only to you, out loud."

"All right, sir," Dahl said. "I'm ready."

Q'eeng pulled out his phone, pressed the screen and read the words there. "Andy, I don't know if these words will reach you. Nick wrote this scene and we filmed it, but obviously it won't be shown on TV. I don't know if just filming it will be enough, and I guess there is no way for you to tell us if it worked. But if it does work, I want you to know two things. One, I'm sorry for everything you just got put through—Nick felt we had to really push the action in this one or the audience would start to question what was going on. Maybe that's not a great argument to you now, considering where you are. But it made sense at the time.

"Two, no words I can say will ever thank you, Jasper and all of you for what you have done for my family and for me. You gave me my son back, and by giving him back you have given us everything. We will stick to our end of the agreement. Everything we said we would do we will. I don't know what else to say, except this: Thank you for letting us live happily ever after. We will do the same for you. In love and gratitude, Charles Paulson."

"Thank you," Dahl said to Q'eeng, after a moment.

"You are welcome," Q'eeng said, putting away his phone. "A most curious message."

"I suppose you could say it's in code, sir," Dahl said.

"Are you allowed to tell your superior officer what it's about?" Q'eeng asked.

"It's a message from God," Dahl said. "Or someone close enough to Him for our purposes."

Q'eeng looked at Dahl appraisingly. "I sometimes get the feeling there are things happening on the *Intrepid* that I'm not meant to know about," he said. "I suspect this is one of them."

"Sir, and with all due respect," Dahl said, "you don't know how right you are."

CHAPTER TWENTY-THREE

So what now?" Duvall asked. The four of them were in the mess, picking at their midday meal.

"What do you mean?" Hester asked.

"I mean, what now?" Duvall said. She pointed to Hester. "You're transplanted into a new body"—her point changed to Dahl—"he's back from the dead, we've all come back from an alternate reality to keep ourselves from being killed for dramatic purposes. We've won. What now?"

"I don't think it works like that," Hanson said. "I don't think we've won anything, other than being in control of our own lives."

"Right," Hester said. "After everything, what it all means is that if one day we slip in the bathroom and crack our head on the toilet, our last thoughts can be a satisfied, 'Well, I and only I did this to myself.'"

"When you put it that way, it hardly seems worth it," Duvall said.

"I don't mind cracking my head on the toilet," Hester said. "As long as I do it at age one hundred and twenty."

"On your one hundred and twentieth birthday, I'll come over with floor wax," Duvall promised.

"I can't wait," Hester said.

"Andy? You okay?" Hanson asked.

"I'm fine," Dahl said, and smiled. "Sorry. Was just thinking. About being fictional, and all that."

"We're over that now," Hester said. "That was the point of all of this."

"You're right," Dahl said. "I know."

Duvall looked at her phone. "Crap, I'm going to be late," she said. "I'm breaking in a new crew member."

"Oh, the burdens of a promotion," Hester said.

"It's hard, it really is," Duvall said, and got up.

"I'll walk with you," Hester said. "You can tell me more of your woes."

"Excellent," Duvall said. The two of them left.

Hanson looked back at Dahl. "Still thinking about being fictional?" he said, after a minute.

"Sort of," Dahl said. "What I've been really thinking about is you, Jimmy."

"Me," Hanson said.

"Yeah," Dahl said. "Because while I was recuperating from our last adventure, something struck me about you. You don't really fit."

"That's interesting," Hanson said. "Tell me why."

"Think about it," Dahl said. "Think of the five of us who met that first day, the day we joined the crew of the *Intrepid*. Each of us turned out to be critical in some way. Hester, who didn't seem to have a purpose, turned out to be the key to everything. Duvall had medical training and got close to Kerensky, which helped us when we needed it and made him part of our crew when we needed him. Finn gave us tools and information we needed and his loss galvanized us to take action. Jenkins gave us context for our situation and the means to do something about it."

"What about you?" Hanson asked. "Where do you fit in?"

"Well, that's the one I had a hard time with," Dahl said. "I wondered what I brought to the party. I thought maybe I was just the man with the plan—the guy who came up with the basic ideas everyone else went along with. Logistics. But then I started thinking about Kerensky, and what he is to the show."

"He's the guy who gets beat up to show that the main characters can get beat up," Hanson said.

"Right," Dahl said.

"But you can't be Kerensky," Hanson said. "We have a Kerensky. It's Kerensky."

"It's not about Kerensky getting beat up," Dahl said. "It's about Kerensky not dying."

"I'm not following you," Hanson said.

"Jimmy, how many times should I have died since we've been on the *Intrepid*?" Dahl asked. "I count at least three. The first time, when I was attacked at Eskridge colony, when Cassaway and Mbeke died. Then in the *Nantes* interrogation room with Finn and Captain Abernathy. And then on deck six when we returned to the *Intrepid* with Hester. Three times I should have been dead, no ifs, ands or buts. I should *be* dead, three times over. But I'm not. I get hurt. I get hurt really badly. But I don't die. That's when I figured it out. I'm the protagonist."

"But you're an extra," Hanson said. "We all are. Jenkins said it. Charles Paulson said it. Even the actor playing you said it."

"I'm an extra on the show," Dahl said. "I'm the protagonist somewhere else."

"Where?" Hanson said.

"That's what I want you to tell me, Jimmy," Dahl said.

"What?" Hanson said. "What are you talking about?"

"It's like I said: You don't fit," Dahl said. "Everyone else served a strong purpose for the story. Everyone but you. For this, you were just *around*, Jimmy. You have a backstory, but it never really entered in to what we did. You did a few useful things—you looked into show trivia, and talked about people, and occasionally you reminded people to do things. You added just enough that it seemed like you were taking part. But the more I think about it, the more I realize that you don't quite add up the way the rest of us do."

"Life is like that, Andy," Hanson said. "It's messy. We don't all add up that way."

"No," Dahl said. "We *do*. Everyone else does. Everyone else but you. The only way you fit is if the thing you're supposed to do, you haven't done yet. The only way you fit is if there's something else going on here. We're all supposed to think we were real people who found out they were extras on a television show. But I know that doesn't begin to explain me. I should be dead several times over, like Kerensky or any of the show's major characters are supposed to be dead, but aren't, because the universe plays favorites with them. The universe plays favorites with me, too."

"Maybe you're lucky," Hanson said.

"No one is that lucky, Jimmy," Dahl said. "So here's what I think. I think there's no television show. No *real* television show. I think that Charles Paulson and Marc Corey and Brian Abnett and everyone else over there are just as fictional as we were supposed to be. I think Captain Abernathy and Commander Q'eeng, Medical Officer Hartnell and Chief Engineer West are the bit players here, and that me and Maia and Finn and Jasper are the people who really count. And I think in the end, you really exist for just one reason."

"What reason is that, Andy?" Hanson said.

"To tell me that I'm right about this," Dahl said.

"My parents would be surprised by your conclusion," Hanson said.

"My parents would be surprised by all of this," Dahl said. "Our parents are not the point here."

"Andy, we've known each other for years," Hanson said. "I think you know who I am."

"Jimmy," Dahl said. "Please. Tell me if I'm right."

Hanson sat there for a minute, looking at Dahl. "I don't think it would actually make you happier to be told you were right about this," he said, finally.

"I don't want to be happy," Dahl said. "I just want to know."

"And even if you were right," Hanson said, "what do you get out of it? Aren't you better off believing that you've accomplished something? That you've gotten the happy ending you were promised? Why would you want to push that?"

"Because I need to know," Dahl said. "I've always needed to know."

"Because that's the way you are," Hanson said. "A seeker of truth. A spiritual man."

"Yes," Dahl said.

"A man who needs to know if he's really that way, or just written to *be* that way," Hanson said.

"Yes," Dahl said.

"Someone who needs to know if he's really his own man, or—"

"Tell me you're not about to make the pun I think you are," Dahl said.

Hanson smiled. "Sorry," he said. "It was there." He pushed out from his chair and stood up. "Andy, you're my friend. Do you believe that?"

"Yes," Dahl said. "I do."

"Then maybe you can believe this," Hanson said. "Whether you're an extra or the hero, this story is about to end. When it's done, whatever you want to be will be up to you and only you. It will happen away from the eyes of any audience and from the hand of any writer. You will be your own man."

"If I exist when I stop being written," Dahl said.

"There is that," Hanson said. "It's an interesting philosophical question. But if I had to guess, I'd guess that your creator would say to you that he would want you to live happily ever after."

"That's just a guess," Dahl said.

"Maybe a little more than a guess," Hanson said. "But I will say this, though: You were right."

"About what?" Dahl said.

"That now I've done what I was supposed to do," Hanson said. "But now I have to go do the other thing I'm supposed to do, which is assume my post. See you at dinner, Andy?"

Dahl grinned. "Yes," he said. "If any of us are around for it."

"Great," Hanson said. "See you then." And he wandered off.

Dahl sat there for a few more minutes, thinking about everything that had happened and everything that Hanson said. And then he got up and went to his station on the bridge. Because whether fictional or not, on a spaceship, a television show or in something else entirely, he still had work to do, surrounded by his friends and the crew of the *Intrepid*.

And that's just what he did, until the day six months later when a systems failure caused the *Intrepid* to plow into a small asteroid, vaporizing the ship and killing everyone on board instantly.

CHAPTER TWENTY-FOUR

No, no, I'm just fucking with you.
    They all lived happily ever after.
Seriously.

CODA I:

First Person

Hello, Internet.
There isn't any good way to start this, so let me just jump right in.

So, I am a scriptwriter for a television show on a major network who just found out that the people he's been making up in his head (and killing off at the rate of about one an episode) are actually real. Now I have writer's block, I don't know how to solve it, and if I don't figure it out soon, I'm going to get fired. Help me.

And now I just spent 20 minutes looking at that last paragraph and feeling like an asshole. Let me break it down further to explain it to you a little better.

"Hello, Internet": You know that *New Yorker* cartoon that has a dog talking to another dog by a computer and saying, "On the Internet, no one knows you're a dog"? Yeah, well, this is that.

No, I'm not a dog. But yes, I need some anonymity here. Because *holy shit,* look what I just wrote up there. That's not something you can just say out loud to people. But on the Internet? Anonymously? Might fly.

"I am a scriptwriter . . .": I really am. I've been working for several years on the show, which (duh) has been successful enough to have been around for several years. I don't want to go into too much more detail about that right now, because remember, I'm trying to have some anonymity here to work through this thing I've been dealing with. Suffice to say that it's not going to win any major Emmys, but it's still the sort of show that you, my dear Internet,

would probably watch. And that in the real world, I have an
IMDB page. And it's pretty long. So there.

**"Who just found out the people he's been making
up in his head are real":** Yes, I know. I *know*. Didn't I just
say "holy shit" two paragraphs ago about it? Don't you
think I know how wobbly-toothed, speed freak crazy it
sounds? I do. I very very very *very* much do. If I didn't think
it was completely bugfuck crazy, I'd be writing about it on
my own actual blog (if I had my own actual blog, which
I don't, because I work on a weekly television series, and
who has the time) and finding some way to go full Whitley
Strieber on it. I don't want that. That's a lifestyle. A
whacked-out, late night talking to the tinfoil-hatted on your
podcast lifestyle. I don't want that. I just want to be able to
get back to my own writing.

But still: The people I wrote in my scripts exist. I know
because I met them, swear to God, right there in the flesh,
I could reach out and touch them. And whenever I kill one
of them off in my scripts, they actually die. To me, it's just
putting down words on a page. To them, it's falling off a
building, or being hit by a car, or being eaten by a bear or
whatever (these are just examples, they're not necessarily
how I've killed people off).

Think about that. Think about what it means. That just
writing down "BOB is consumed by badgers" in a script
means that somewhere in the universe, some poor bastard
named Bob has just been chased down by ravenous
mustelids. Sure, it sounds funny when I write it like that.
But if you were Bob? It would suck. And then you would be
dead, thanks to me. Which explains the next part:

"Now I have writer's block": You know, I never
understood writer's block before this. You're a writer and you
suddenly can't write because your girlfriend broke up with

you? Shit, dude, that's the *perfect* time to write. It's not like you're doing anything else with your nights. Having a hard time coming up with the next scene? Have something explode. You're done. Filled with existential ennui about your place in the universe? Get over yourself. Yes, you're an inconsequential worm in the grand scope of history. But you're an inconsequential worm who makes shit up for a living, which means that you don't have to lift heavy boxes or ask people if they want fries with that. Grow up and get back to work.

On a good day, I can bang out a first draft of an episode in six hours. Is it good? It ain't Shakespeare, but then, Shakespeare wrote *Titus Andronicus,* so you tell me. Six hours, one script, a good day. And I have to tell you, as a writer, I've had my share of good days.

But now I have writer's block and I can't write a script because *fuck me I kill people when I write.* It's a pretty good excuse for having writer's block, if you ask me. Girlfriend leaving you? Get on with it. You send people to their deaths by typing? Might give you pause. It's given me pause. Now I sit in front of my laptop, Final Draft all loaded up, and just stare at the screen for hours.

"I'm going to get fired": My job is writing scripts. I'm not writing scripts. If I don't start writing scripts again, soon, there's no reason for me to be kept on staff. I've been able to stall a bit because I had one script in the outbox before the block slammed down, but that gives me about a week's insurance. That's not a lot of time. You see why I'm nervous.

"Help me": Look, I need help. This isn't something I can talk to with people I actually know. Because, again: *Bugshit crazy.* I can't afford to have people I work with—or other writers I know, most of whom are unemployed and would be happy to crawl over my carcass to get my television show writing staff position—think that I've lost my marbles. Gigs like this don't grow on trees. But I have to talk to someone about it, because for the life of me I haven't the first damn clue about what I should be doing about this. I need some perspective from outside my own head.

And this is where you come in, Internet. You have perspective. And I'm guessing that some of you might just be bored enough to help out some anonymous dude on the Internet, asking for advice on a completely ridiculous situation. It's either this or Angry Birds, right?

So, what do you say, Internet?

Yours,
Anon-a-Writer

———

So, the good news is that apparently people are reading this. The bad news is people are asking me questions instead of, you know, *helping me*. But then again when you anonymously post on the Internet that the characters you write have suddenly come alive, I suppose you have to answer a few questions first. Fine. So for those of you who need it, a quick run-through of the most common questions I've gotten so far. I'm going to paraphrase some to keep from repeating questions and comments.

Dude, are you serious?

Dude, I am serious. I am not high (being high is more fun), I am not making this up (if I was making things up, I would be getting paid for it), and I am not crazy (crazy would be more fun, too). This is for real.

Really?

Yes.

Really?

Yes.

No, really?

Shut up. Next question.

Why haven't you discussed this with your therapist?

Because contrary to popular belief, not every writer in Los Angeles has been in therapy since before they could walk. All my neuroses are manageable (or were, anyway). I suppose I could get one, but that would be a hell of a first session, wouldn't it, and I'm not entirely convinced I'd get out of there without being sedated and sent off to the funny farm. Call me paranoid.

Isn't this kind of the plot to that movie *Stranger than Fiction*?

Maybe? That's the Will Ferrell movie where he's a character in someone's book, right? (I know I could check this on IMDB, but I'm lazy.) Except for that I'm the writer, not the character. So same concept, different spin. Maybe?

But, look, even if it is, I didn't say what was happening to me was creatively 100% *original*. I mean, there's *The Purple Rose of Cairo,* which had characters coming down off the screen. There's those Jasper Fforde books where everyone's a fairy tale or literary character. There's Denise Hogan's books where she's always arguing with her characters and sometimes they don't listen to her and mess with her plots. My mom loves those. Hell, there's *The Last Action Hero,* for God's sake. Have you seen that? You have? I'm sorry.

There's also the small but telling detail that those are all fictional, and this is *really happening to me*. Like I said, a subtle difference. But an important one. I'm not going for originality here. I'm trying to get this solved.

Hey, is your show [insert name of show here]?

Friend, what part of "I want to be anonymous" don't you understand? Even if you guessed right I'm still not going to

tell you. Want a hint? Fine: It's not *30 Rock*. Also I am not
Tina Fey. Mmmm . . . Tina Fey.

Likewise:

**You know that these days the Internet *does* know
if you're a dog, right?**

Yes, but *this* dog opened this blog account using a
throwaway e-mail address and cruises the Web using Tor.

**Why don't you just write scripts where people don't
get killed?**

Well, I *could* do that, but two things will happen then:

1. The script gets turned in and the producers say, "The
stakes need to be raised in this scene. Kill someone." And
then I have to kill someone in the script, or a co-writer
does, or one of the producers does a quick uncredited wash
of the script, or the director zaps a character during shooting,
and someone dies *anyway*.

2. Even if I don't kill anyone, there still needs to be
drama, and on a show like mine, drama usually means if
someone isn't killed, then they are maimed or mutilated or
given a disease that turns them into a pustule with legs.
Admittedly, turning a character into a pustule is better
than killing them dead, but it's still not *comfortable* for
them, and it's still me doing it to them. So I still have
guilt.

Believe me, there's nothing I'd like to do better than turn
in scripts whether the characters do nothing but lounge on
pillows, eating chocolates and having hot, cathartic sex for
an hour (minus commercial time, your capitalistically
inspired refractory period). I think our audience wouldn't
mind either—it would be inspirational and educational! But
it's not that kind of show, and there's only so edgy basic
cable is going to let us be.

I have to write stuff that's actually like what gets written for our show, basically. If I don't, I'll get canned. I don't want to get canned.

You understand that if what you're saying is actually true, then the existential ramifications are astounding!

Yeah, it's pretty weird shit. I could go on for hours about it—that is, if it wasn't *also* messing with my day-to-day life in a pretty substantial way. You know what it's like? It's like waking up one morning, going outside and finding a *Tyrannosaurus rex* in your front yard, staring at you. For the first five seconds, you're completely amazed that a real live dinosaur is standing in front of you. And then you run like hell, because to a *T. rex,* you're a chewy, crunchy bite-sized snack.

Is there a *T. rex* in your front yard?

No.

Damn.

You're not helping.

For someone who says they're having writing block, aren't you writing a lot?

Yeah, but this isn't real writing, is it? I'm not doing anything creative here, I'm just answering comments and asking for help. Blogs are nice and all, but what I really need to be doing is writing scripts. And I can't do that right now. The creative lobe of my brain is completely blown out. That's where the blockage is.

You mentioned that you were using Final Draft. Have you considered that maybe your software is the problem? I use Scrivener myself. You should try it!

Wow, really? Dude, if someone's having a heart attack in front of you, do you take that opportunity to talk about your amazing low-cholesterol diet, too? Because that would be *awesome.*

The software is not the problem. The problem is that every time I write *I kill someone.* If you're going to try to help, don't suggest a particular brand of sprinkler after the house is already on fire. Grab a hose.

Related to this:

I believe everything you say and I think we should meet so we can discuss this in detail possibly in my SECRET BASEMENT LAIR AT MY MOM'S HOUSE WHERE I LIVE.

Oooooh, man. *That's* another reason to remain safely anonymous, isn't it.

So now that the Q&A session is done, does anyone actually have help for me? Please?

AW

———

Finally! An actual good idea from a comment, which I will now replicate in full:

In your last post you mentioned some movies and books in which the line between the creator and the created had been broken (or at least smudged) in some way. Have you considered that perhaps the people who wrote those movies and books might have had experiences similar to yours? It's possible that they have, and just haven't ever talked about it for the same reason you're trying to stay anonymous, which is, it sounds completely crazy. But if you approached them and your experience is similar to theirs, maybe they would talk to you in confidence. The fact you actually are a screenwriter of some note might keep them from fleeing in terror, at least at first.

The "at least at first" bit is a nice touch, thank you. And I'm glad you have the delusion that a scriptwriter on a weekly basic cable series has any sort of credibility. It warms my heart.

But to answer your question, no, it didn't occur to me at all, because, well, it's nuts, isn't it. And we live in the really real world, where stuff like this doesn't happen. But on the other hand, it happened to *me*, and—no offense to me—I'm not all *that* special, either as a writer or a human being.

So: I have to admit that it's entirely possible that what's happened to me has happened to others. And if it has happened to others, then it's entirely possible they've found some way to deal with it that doesn't involve not writing anymore. And that's the goal here. And now I have a plan: Contact those writers and find out if they've got a secret experience like mine.

Which sounds perfectly reasonable until you think about what that actually means. To give you an idea, let me present to you a quick, one-act play entitled *Anon-a-Writer Presents His Conundrum to Someone Who Is Not the Internet*:

ANON-A-WRITER
Hello! I have been visited by characters from my scripts who inform me that I kill them whenever I write an action scene.
Does this happen to you too?

OTHER WRITER
Hello, Anon-a-Writer! In one hand I have a restraining order, and in the other I have a Taser. Which would you like to meet first?

Yes, I see no way that this perfect plan could ever go wrong.

But on the other hand I don't have a *better* plan, do I. So here's what I'm going to do:

Make a list of writers whose characters break the reality wall one way or another.

Contact them and find out if it's based on their actual

real-world experience, without coming across like a psychotic freakbag.

Profit! Okay, not profit, but if their work *is* based on their real-life experiences, find out from them a way to keep writing.

Off to craft introductions that don't sound too creepy. Wish me luck.

AW

––––––

Guys, seriously now: Stop trying to guess which show I work for. I'm just not going to tell you. Because I don't want to get *fired*. Which is what happens when people like me talk about their jobs to people like you, i.e., the Internet. And especially when people like me are claiming their characters are coming to life and talking to them. I know it's good fun for you to be guessing, but, come on. A little charity, please. I promise you that after this is all done, if everything works out, I'll tell you. Say, in five years. Or after I win an Emmy. Whichever comes first (bet on five years).

Okay? Okay. Thank you.

––––––

Hello, Internet. You're wanting updates. Well, here we go. I've identified some creative types who have written stories similar to my situation, including those we mentioned here earlier: Woody Allen, for *Purple Rose of Cairo,* Jasper Fforde, Zak Penn and Adam Leff (*Last Action Hero*), Zach Helm (*Stranger than Fiction*) and Denise Hogan. The plan here is to approach them credits first—to at least suggest I'm not completely insane—and then to ask them in a *very subtle way* about whether what they've written has any connection to their real-life experiences. Then off they go to the writers. And we'll see if anyone nibbles.

And, to anticipate some of you raising your hands out there in the audience, yes, I'll share with you the responses—after I snip out major identifying details. Oh, don't look at me like that. Remember that anonymity thing I'm striving for? Yeah. Too many details and I'm out of my very peculiar little closet (it's a lovely closet; it smells of pine and desperation). But on the other hand, as you've been helpful, I figure I owe you continuing updates on this thing.

Also, to make no mistake about it, I fully expect that the responses will be, "Wow, you're even crazier than most random people who write me, would you like my suggestion for antipsychotic pharmaceuticals." Because that's how I would respond to this showing up randomly in my inbox. It's how I *have* responded, in fact. You wouldn't *believe* the sort of random crazy gets sent to you when you're a writer on a successful television series. Or maybe you would. Crazy is highly distributed these days.

(insert pause to send off e-mails)

And they're off. Now we get to see how long it takes before anyone responds. Want to start a betting pool?

AW

———

Wow, so that didn't take long at all. The first response. E-mail posted below:

XXX XXXXX <u>via</u> gmail.com   <u>show details</u> 4:33 PM (0 minutes ago)

Dear ANON-A-WRITER:

Hello, I'm XXX XXXXXX, assistant for XXXXX XXXXX. We received your query and wanted to know whether it was some sort of creative

or interview project you're doing for a major magazine or newspaper.
Please let us know.

My response:

Hello, XXX XXXXXX. No, it's not for any newspaper or magazine
or blog (well, it might be for my own personal blog). It's more of
something I'm asking for my own information. Thank you and let me
know if XXXXX XXXXX has time for a chat. It would be very useful
to me.

The assistant's response:

Unfortunately XXXXX XXXXX doesn't have any availability at this time.
Thanks for your interest and good luck on your project.

Translation: Your crazy would be fine if it was for *People*
magazine, or maybe even *Us,* but if it's freelance crazy, we
don't want anything to do with you.

Sigh. There was a time when freelance crazy was respected in this town! I think it was the early 80s. David Lee
Roth was hanging out at the Whisky then. Or so I have
heard. I was, like, *six* at the time.

One down, five to go. . . .

AW

———

New response. This is kind of awesome, actually.

To: ANON-A-WRITER

From: XXXXX X XXXX, Esq., partner, XXXX, XXXXX, XXX and
XXXXX

Dear Mr. Writer:

Your e-mail query to XXXXX XXXXXX was forwarded to us by his assistant, as is every letter for which they feel there is some concern about. Mr. XXXXXX values his privacy considerably and was greatly unsettled by your e-mail, both for its content and because it arrived in an unsolicited manner at a private e-mail.

At this time our client has decided not to escalate the matter by asking the XXXXXXX Police Department to investigate you and your e-mail. However, we request that you do not ever again attempt to contact our client in any way. If you attempt to do so, we will forward all correspondence both to the XXXXXXX Police Department and to the FBI and file for a restraining order against you. I do not need to tell you that such a request would instantly become news, severely impacting your career as a staff writer on XXXXXXXXXX.

We trust that this is the last we will hear from you.

Yours,

XXXXX X XXXX, Esq., partner, XXXX, XXXXX, XXX and XXXXX

Whoa.

Just for the record, the e-mail I sent did *not* begin: "Dear XXXXX, as I happened to be standing over your bed last night, *watching you sleep* . . ." It really didn't. I *swear.*

Either this person gets more crazy e-mails than usual from people who dress up as their cat and then stand outside their house, or this person got spooked by this e-mail for an entirely other reason. Hmmmm.

Is it worth getting the FBI involved to find out?

No. No, it is not.

Not *yet,* anyway. Still curious.

And now I'm fighting off an urge to dress up as this

person's cat and stand outside their house. But it's early yet, and it's a weeknight. Maybe after a few more gin rickeys.

AW

———

From the comments:

I'm not entirely convinced you've seen your characters come alive, but as someone who suffers from writer's block all the time, it's amazing to me that you can joke about your situation as much as you do on this site, especially when your actual job is on the line. If I were you, I would be wetting my pants right about now.

Oh, trust me. I am. I so very *am*. My local Pavilions is entirely out of Depends right about now. I shop for them at night, so my neighbors won't see me. And when I'm done with them I put them in my next door neighbor's trash can so they can't be traced back to me. I'm not proud. Or dry.

I'm going to let you in on a little secret, Internet: Part of the reason I'm writing this blog right now is in fact to keep from shitting myself in abject fear. The last time I went a week without writing something creative was when I was in college and I spent six days in the hospital for a truly epic case of food poisoning. (Dorm food. Not always the freshest. I wasn't the only one. For the rest of the year my dorm was known as the Puke Palace. I digress.) And even then, when I thought I was going to retch my lower intestine right out past my tongue, I was plotting stories and trying out dialogue in my head. Right now, I try plotting a story or thinking about dialogue for a script and a big wall comes down in my brain. I. Just. Cannot. Write.

This has never happened to me before. I am absolutely terrified that *this is it,* that the creative tank is all out of gas and that from here on out there's nothing for me but residuals and occasional teaching gigs at the Learning Annex. I mean, fuck, kill me now. It terrifies me so much that there's only two things I can think to do at the moment:

1. Make a special cocktail of antifreeze and OxyContin and then take a long, luxurious bath with my toaster.

2. Write on this blog like it's a methadone treatment.

One of these options doesn't have me found as a bloated corpse a week later. Guess which one.

As for the joking, well, look. When I was twelve, my appendix burst, and as they were wheeling my ass into the operating room, I asked the doctor, "How will this affect my piano playing?" and he said, "Don't worry, you'll still be able to play the piano," and I said, "Wow! I wasn't able to before!"

And then they gassed me.

My point is that even when I was about to die of imminent peritonitis I was still going for the joke. Failing, but going for it. (Actually, as my father said in the recovery room, "All the jokes in the world you could have made at that moment, and that's the one you go for. You are no son of mine." Dad took his jokes seriously.)

Shorter version of all of the above: If I actually wrote in a way that indicated how bowel-voidingly scared I am at the moment, you would have all fled by now. And I probably would have gone to play in traffic. It's better to joke, I think.

Don't you?

AW

Hey, now we're getting somewhere. The following e-mail from the next person on my list:

Dear Anon-a-Writer:

Your e-mail intrigues me on several levels. In fact, there is some crossover between what happens in my books and what happens in my real life. Your canny ambiguity in asking the question suggests to me you might have some of that same crossover.

As it happens, I'll be coming to LA tomorrow to meet with my film agent about a project we're pitching at XXXXXXXXX Studios. After I'm done with the industry glad-handing, I'd be happy to meet and chat. I'm staying at XXX XXXX XXXXXXX; let's meet in the bar there about 5, if you have the time.

Yours,

XXXXXX XXXXXX

So *that* sounds wildly promising. Now all I have to do is keep myself from *exploding with anxiety* for the next 24 hours or so. Fortunately I have meetings all day tomorrow. And yes, I said *fortunately*—the more meetings I have to sit in at work, the less anyone asks about the scripts I'm supposed to be working on. This is getting harder to keep up. I did suggest to one of the other staff writers that he and I collaborate on a script, and that he bang out the story outline and maybe the first draft. I can make him do the first draft because I'm senior. I can do it without guilt because he owes me money. I question my moral grounding. But at the moment, not as much as I would otherwise.

Hopefully the writer I'm meeting tomorrow will have something useful for me. Meetings and taking advantage of underlings only goes so far.

AW

Okay. I've met with the other writer. She's Denise Hogan. And in order to describe our "conversation," I'm going to use a format I'm used to.

INT. COFFEE SHOP — CORNER TABLE — DAY

Two people are sitting at the table, coffees in hand, the remains of muffins on the table. They are ANON-A-WRITER and DENISE HOGAN. They have been talking for an hour as ANON-A-WRITER has described his crisis to DENISE in detail.

DENISE
That's really a very interesting situation you've gotten yourself into.

ANON-A-WRITER
"Interesting" isn't the word I would use for it. "Magnificently screwed" is the phrase I would use.

DENISE
Yes, that would work, too.

AW
But this has happened to you too, right?
When you write the characters in your novels, they are always arguing with you and ignoring how you want the plot to go and running off and doing their own thing. It's your trademark.
You write it like it actually happens.

DENISE
(gently)
Well, I think we need to have some definition of terms on this.

AW
(draws back)
Definition of terms? That sounds like code for "No, it doesn't
actually happen to me that way, you crazy crazy person."

DENISE
(beat)
AW, may I be honest with you?

AW
Considering what I just splashed out to you over the last hour?
Yes, would you, please.

DENISE
I'm here because I read your blog.

AW
I don't have a blog.

DENISE
You don't have one under your actual name.
You have one as Anon-a-Writer.

AW
(beat)
Oh. Oh, *shit.*

DENISE
(holds up hands)
Relax, I'm not here to out you.

AW

Fuck!

(gets up, thinks about leaving, shuffles back and

forth for a moment, sits back down)

How did you find it?

DENISE

How anyone with an ego finds anything on the Internet.

I have a Google alert tied to my name.

AW

(runs hands through hair)

Fucking *Google,* man.

DENISE

I clicked through to see if it was some sort of feature piece on

writers who break the fourth wall and then I saw what your blog

was really about, and I put it into my RSS feed. I knew you were

going to contact me before you sent your e-mail.

AW

You're not actually in town to see your film agent.

DENISE

Well, no. I had lunch with him today, and we *did* talk about that

Paramount thing. But I called him after I got your e-mail and told

him I was going to be in town. Don't worry, I didn't tell him why

else I was here.

AW

So your characters aren't actually alive and talking to you.

DENISE

Other than the usual thing writers mean about making their
characters come alive, no.

AW

Swell.

(stands up again)

Thank you for wasting a large portion of my day.

Nice to meet you.

DENISE

But you and I have something in common.

AW

Besides the wasted afternoon?

DENISE

(crossly)

Look, I didn't come here to get a close-up look at a freak show.
I already have my first husband for that. I came here because
I think I understand your situation better than you think.
I had writer's block too. A bad one.

AW

How bad?

DENISE

More than a year. Bad enough for you?

AW

Maybe.

DENISE

I think I can help you with yours. Because whether I believe you or
not about your characters being actually real, I think my own
writer's block situation is close to what yours is now.

AW

If you don't believe what I'm saying, I don't see how your situation
could be like mine.

DENISE

Because we both had characters we're scared to do anything with.

AW

(sits back down, warily)
Go on.

DENISE

For whatever reason, you have characters you're scared of killing
or hurting, and it's blocking you. For me, I had characters who I
couldn't make do anything critical. I would push them to a crisis
point in my stories, but when it came time for them to pull the
trigger—to do something significant—I could never get them to do
it. I'd devise all these ways to get them out of the holes I spent
chapters putting them into. The way I was doing wasn't good.
Finally I froze up completely. I just couldn't write.

AW

But that's about *you*—

DENISE

(holds up hand)
Wait, I'm not done. Finally, one day as I was sitting in front of my
laptop, doing nothing with my characters, I typed one of them

JOHN SCALZI

turning to me as the writer and saying, "Would you just fucking make up your mind already? No? Fine. I'll do it, then." And then he did something I didn't expect—that I wasn't even wanting him to do—and when he did it, it was like a huge flood of possibilities broke through the dam of my writer's block. My character did what I was afraid of him doing.

AW

Which is what?

DENISE

Having agency. Doing things that even if they were disastrous in the long run for the character, was still doing something.

AW

Trust me, agency is not a problem with my characters.

DENISE

I didn't say it was. But my characters were also doing something else. They were rebelling against something.

AW

What?

DENISE

My own bad writing. I wouldn't do for my characters what they needed for me to do—be courageous enough in my writing to make them interesting. So they did it themselves. And by they, I mean me, or some part of my writing brain that I wasn't willing to connect with before. Maybe that's something you need to do too.

AW

Wait. Did you just call me a bad writer?

DENISE

I didn't call you a bad writer.

AW

Good.

DENISE

But I've watched your show. Most of the scripts are pretty terrible.

AW

(throws up hands)
Oh, come *on*.

DENISE

(continuing)
And they're terrible for no good reason!

AW

(leaning forward)
Do you write scripts? Do you know how hard it is to work on a
weekly deadline for a television show?

DENISE

No, but you do. Let me ask you: Do you really think you're
making a good effort? Remember, I'm reading your blog. I've read
you make excuses for the quality of your output, even when you
pat yourself on the back for the speed you crank it out.

AW

This doesn't have anything to do with why I'm blocked.

DENISE

Doesn't it? I was blocked because I knew I was writing badly, and
I didn't have the courage to fix it. You know you're writing badly,

but you give yourself an excuse for it. Maybe that block is telling
you the excuse isn't working anymore.

AW
I'm not blocked because I'm writing badly, goddamn it! I'm
blocked because I don't want anyone else to die!

DENISE
(nods)
I believe that's your new excuse, yes.

AW
(standing up again)
I thought I was wasting my time before. Now I know.
Thanks ever so much. I'll be sure not to use your name when
I write this up on the blog.

DENISE
If you actually do put it on your blog, use my name. And then ask
your readers if what I've said makes sense. You said you wanted
their help. I want to see if you're really interested in that help.

ANON-A-WRITER WALKS OUT.

And that's how I completely wasted my evening tonight,
listening to a woman who I thought might actually be
helpful to me explain how I'm a bad writer—oh, wait, not a
bad *writer,* just doing bad *writing.* Because *there's* a distinction
with a difference.

And no, I've never said my writing for the show was bad.
I said it's not Shakespeare. I said it's not Emmy-winning
good. That's not the same as *bad.* I think I'm honest enough
about myself that I would admit to bad writing. But you

don't stay on a writing staff for years if you can't write, or if all you write is bad shit. Believe it or not, there is a minimum level of competence you have to have. I have an M.F.A. in film from USC, people. They don't just *give* those away. I wish they did. I wouldn't have had student loans for six years until I caught my first break. But they don't.

My point is, fuck you, Denise Hogan. I'm not your cheap entertainment in L.A. I came to you with a real problem and your solution is to crap all over me and my work. Thanks so much for that. One day I look forward to returning the favor.

In the meantime, enjoy the Internet knowing how you "helped" me today. I'm sure they're going to love it.

AW

———

So, that was a reporter from Gawker on my cell phone. She told me that they figured out I was Anon-a-Writer based on what I've been writing here, like how my show was on basic cable, it was an hour-long show, it's been on for several seasons, it's a show where a lot of people get killed, and that I'm a USC alum who got his first regular gig in the business six years after graduating.

And also because once I named Denise Hogan, they went on Facebook and did an image search on her name and found a picture of her dated today, at a coffee shop in Burbank, sitting with a guy who looks like me. The picture was taken by a fan of hers with her iPhone. She didn't come up to talk to Denise because she was too nervous. But not too nervous, apparently, that she couldn't upload the damn picture to a social network with half the population of the entire wired world on it.

So that's the story and Gawker's going to be posting it in,

like, twenty minutes. The chipper little Gawker reporter
wanted to know if I had anything I wanted to say about it.
Sure, here's what I want to say:

Fuck.

That is all.

And now I'm going to spend the remaining few hours as
a writer on *The Chronicles of the Intrepid* doing what I
probably should have been doing the moment all this shit
started: sitting on my couch with a big fat bottle of Jim
Beam and getting really fucking drunk.

Thanks, Internet. This little adventure has certainly been
an eye-opener.

Love,

Apparently Not-So-Anon-a-Writer, After All

———

Dear Internet:

First, I'm hung over and you're too damn bright. Tone it
down.

Oh, wait, that's something I can fix on my end. Hold on.

There. Much better.

Second, something important's happened. I need to share
it with you.

And to share it with you I need to go into script mode
again. Bear with me.

EXT — FEATURELESS EXPANSE WITH ENDLESS
GROUND REACHING TO THE HORIZON — POSSIBLY
DAY

ANON-A-WRITE—aw, fuck it, half the Internet already knows
anyway: NICK WEINSTEIN comes to in the expanse, clutching
his head and wincing. ANOTHER MAN is by him, kneeling

casually. Some distance behind him is a crowd of people. They, like the MAN near NICK, are all wearing red shirts.

MAN
Finally.

NICK
(looks around)
Okay, I give up. Where am I?

MAN
A flat, gray, featureless expanse stretching out to nowhere.
A perfect metaphor for the inside of your own brain, Nick.

NICK
(looks at MAN)
You look vaguely familiar.

MAN
(smiles)
I should. You killed me. Not too many episodes ago, either.

NICK
(gapes for a second, then)
Finn, right?

FINN
Correct. And do you remember how you killed me?

NICK
Exploding head.

FINN
Right again.

NICK
Not *your* head exploding, though.

FINN
No, someone else's. I just happened to be in the way.
(stands, points over to the crowd, at one guy in particular)
He's the guy whose head you blew off. Wave, Jer!

JER waves. NICK waves back, cautiously.

NICK
(stands, also, unsteadily, peering)
His head looks pretty good for having been blown off.

FINN
We figured it would be easier for you if you didn't see us all in the
state you killed us in. Jer would be headless, I would be severely
burned, others would be dismembered, partially eaten, have their
flesh melted off their bones from horrible disfiguring diseases. You
know. Messy. We thought you'd find that distracting.

NICK
Thanks.

FINN
Don't mention it.

NICK
I'm assuming this can't be real and that I'm having a dream.

FINN

This is a dream. It doesn't mean it's not also real.

NICK

(rubbing his head)

That's a little deep for my current state of sobriety, Finn.

FINN

Then try this: It's real and taking place in a dream, because how else can your dead talk to you?

NICK

Why do you want to talk to me?

FINN

Because we have something we want to ask of you.

NICK

I'm already not killing any more of you. I've got writer's block, because of you. And I'm about to lose my job, because of the writer's block.

FINN

You've got writer's block, yes. It's not because of us. Not directly, anyway.

NICK

It's my writer's block. I think I know why I have it.

FINN

I didn't say you didn't know why you had it. But you're not admitting the reason why to yourself.

NICK

Don't take this the wrong way, Finn, but your Yoda act is getting
old quick.

FINN

Fine. Then I'll put it this way: Denise Hogan? She was right.

NICK

(Throws up his hands)
Even in my own brain, I get this.

FINN

You're a decent enough writer, Nick. But you're lazy.
(motions toward the crowd)
And most of us are dead because of it.

NICK

Come on, that's not fair. You're dead because it's an action show.
People die in action shows. It's one of the reasons it's called an
action show.

FINN

(looks at NICK, then points to a face in the crowd)
You! How did you die?

REDSHIRT #1
Ice shark!

FINN

(turning to NICK)
Seriously, an ice shark? What's even the biology on that?
(turns back to the crowd)
Anyone else randomly eaten by space animals?

REDSHIRT #2

Pornathic crabs!

REDSHIRT #3

A Great Badger of Tau Ceti!

REDSHIRT #4

Borgovian Land Worms!

NICK

(to REDSHIRT #4)

I didn't write the land worms!

(to FINN)

Seriously, those aren't mine. I keep getting blamed for those.

FINN

That's because you're the senior writer on the show, Nick. You could have raised a flag or two about the random animal attacks, whether you wrote them or not.

NICK

It's a weekly science fiction show—

FINN

It's a weekly science fiction show, but lots of weekly shows aren't *crap,* Nick. Including science fiction shows. A lot of weekly science fiction shows at least *try* for something other than mere sufficiency. You're using schedule and genre as an excuse.

(back to the crowd)

How many of you were killed on decks six through twelve?

Dozens of hands shoot up. FINN turns back to NICK, looking for an answer.

NICK

The ship needs to take damage. The show has to have drama.

FINN

The ship needs to take damage. Fine. It doesn't mean you have to
have some bastard crewman sucked into space every time it
happens. Maybe after the first dozen times it happened, the
Universal Union should have started engineering for space
defenestration.

NICK

Look, I get it, Finn. You're unhappy with being dead. So am I.
That's why I'm blocked!

FINN

You don't get it. None of us are pissed off at being dead.

REDSHIRT #4

I am!

FINN

(to REDSHIRT #4)

Not now, Davis!

(back to NICK)

None of us except for Davis are pissed off at being dead. Death
happens. It happens to everyone. It's going to happen to you. What
we're pissed off about is that our deaths are so completely *pointless*.
When you killed us off, Nick, it doesn't do anything for the story.
It's just a little jolt you give the viewers before the commercial
break, and they've forgotten it before the first Doritos ad fades off
the screen. Our lives had meaning, Nick, if only to us. And you
gave us really shitty deaths. Pointless, shitty deaths.

NICK

Shitty deaths happen all the time, Finn. People accidentally step in front of buses, or slip and crack their head on the toilet, or go jogging and get attacked by mountain lions. That's life.

FINN

That's *your* life, Nick. But you don't have anyone writing you, as far as you know. *We* do. It's you. And when we die on the show, it's because *you've killed us off.* Everyone dies. But we died how you decided we were going to die. And so far, you've decided we'd die because it's easier than writing a dramatic moment whose response is earned in the writing. And you *know* it, Nick.

NICK

I don't—

FINN

You do. We're dead, Nick. We don't have time for bullshit anymore. So admit it. Admit what's actually going on in your head.

NICK

(sits down, dazed)

All right. Fine. All right. I wrote my last script, the one we used to send everyone back, and I remember thinking to myself, 'Wow, we didn't actually kill anyone off this time.' And then I started thinking about all the ways we've killed off crew on the show. Then I started thinking about the fact that for them, they were real deaths. Real deaths of real people. And then I started thinking of all the stupid ways I've killed people off. Not just them being stupid by themselves, but everything around them too. Stupid reasons to get people in a position where I could kill them off. Ridiculous coincidences. Out-of-nowhere plot

twists. All the little shitty tricks I and the other writers
use because we can and no one calls us on it.
Then I went and got drunk—

FINN
(nodding)
And when you woke up you went to do some writing and nothing
came out.

NICK
I thought it was about not wanting to kill people. About being
responsible for their deaths.

FINN
(kneeling again)
It's the fact you weren't acting responsibly when you killed
them that's eating at you. Even if you hadn't written our deaths,
all of us would have died one day. That's a fact. I think
you know it.

NICK
And I gave you bad deaths when I could have given you better
ones.

FINN
Yes. You're not a grim reaper, Nick. You're a general.
Sometimes generals send soldiers to their deaths.
Hopefully they don't do it stupidly.

NICK
(looking back at the crowd)
You want me to write better deaths.

FINN

Yeah. Fewer deaths wouldn't hurt, either. But better deaths. We're
all already dead. It's too late for us. But each of us have people we
care about who are still alive, who might pass under your pen, if
you want to put it that way. We think they deserve better. And now
you know you do too.

NICK

You're assuming I'll still have a job after all this.

FINN

(standing again)

You'll be fine. Just tell everyone you were exploring the boundaries
between fiction and interactive performance in the online media.
It's a perfectly meta excuse, and anyway, no one's going to believe
your characters actually came to life. At most people will think you
were kind of an asshole with this thing. But then some people think
you're kind of an asshole anyway.

NICK

Thanks.

FINN

Hey, I told you, I'm dead. No time for bullshit. Now pass out again
and wake up for real this time. Then get over to your computer.
Try writing. Try writing better. And stop drinking so much. It does
weird things to your head.

NICK nods, then passes out. FINN and his crew of redshirts
disappear (I assume).

And then I woke up.
And then I went and powered up my laptop.

And then I wrote thirty pages of the *best goddamned script* I've ever written for the show.

And then I collapsed because I was still sort of drunk.

And now I'm awake again, and hung over, and writing this crying because I can write again.

———

And this is where I end the blog. It did what it was supposed to—it got me over my writer's block. Now I have scripts to write and writers to supervise and a show to be part of. It's time for me to get back to that.

Some of you have asked—is it really a hoax? Did I ever really have writer's block, or was this an exercise in alternate creativity schemes, a weird little side project from someone who writes too many pages about lasers and explosions and aliens? And did my characters ever actually come to life?

Well, think about it. I trade in fiction. I trade in science fiction. I make up weird shit all the time. What's the most logical explanation in a case like this: more fiction, or everything in the blog being really real, and really happening?

You know what the most logical answer is.

Now you have to ask yourself if you believe it.

Think about it and let me know.

Until then:

Bye, Internet.

Nick Weinstein, Senior Writer,
The Chronicles of the Intrepid

CODA II:

Second Person

Y ou've heard it said that people who have been in horrific accidents usually don't remember the accident—the accident knocks their short-term memory right out of them—but you remember your accident well enough. You remember the rain making the roads slick, and you reining yourself in because of it. You remember the BMW running the red and seeing the driver on his cell phone, yelling, and you knew he wasn't yelling because of you because he never looked in your direction and didn't see your motorcycle until it crushed itself into his front fender.

You remember taking to the air and for the briefest of seconds enjoying it—the surprising sensation of flight!—until your brain had just enough time to process what had happened and douse you in an ice-cold bath of fear before you hit the pavement helmet first. You felt your body twist in ways human bodies weren't supposed to twist and heard things inside your body pop and snap in ways you did not imagine they were meant to pop and snap. You felt the visor of your helmet fly off and the pavement skip and scrape off the fiberglass or carbon fiber or whatever it was that your helmet was made of, an inch from your face.

Twist pop snap scrape and then stop, and then your whole world was the little you could see out of the ruined helmet, mostly facing down into the pavement. You had two thoughts at that moment: one, the observation that you must be in shock, because you couldn't feel any pain; two, that given the crick of your neck, you had a sneaking suspicion that your body had landed in such a way that your legs were bunched up underneath you and your ass was pointing straight up into the sky. The fact that your brain was more concerned about the position of your ass than the overall ability to feel anything only served to confirm your shock theory.

Then you heard a voice screaming at you; it was the driver of the BMW, outraged at the condition of his fender. You tried to glance over at him, but without being able to move your head, you were only able to get a look at his shoes. They were of the sort of striving, status-conscious black leather that told you that the guy had to work in the entertainment industry. Although truth be told it wasn't just the shoes that told you that; there was also the thing about the asshole blowing through a red light in his BMW because he was bellowing into his phone and being gasket-blowing mad at you because you had the gall to hurt his car.

You wondered briefly if the jerk might know your dad before your injuries finally got the best of you and everything went out of focus, the screaming agent or entertainment lawyer or whoever he was softening out to a buzzy murmur that became more relaxing and gentle as you went along.

So that was your accident, which you remember in what you now consider absolutely terrifying detail. It's as clear in your head as a back episode of one of your father's television shows, preserved in high definition on a Blu-ray Disc. At this point you've even added a commentary track to it, making asides to yourself as you review it in your head, about your motorcycle, the BMW, the driver (who as it turns out was an entertainment lawyer, and who was sentenced to two weeks in county jail and three hundred hours of community service for his third violation of California law banning driving while holding a cell phone) and your brief, arcing flight from bike to pavement. You couldn't remember it more clearly.

What you can't remember is what came after, and how you

woke up, lying on your bed, fully clothed, without a scratch on you, a few weeks later.

It's beginning to bother you.

· · · · ·

"You have amnesia," your father said, when you first spoke to him about it. "It's not that unusual after an accident. When I was seven I was in a car accident. I don't remember anything about it. One minute I was in the car going to see your great-grandmother and the next I was in a hospital bed with a cast and my mother standing over me with a gallon of ice cream."

"You woke up the next day," you said to your father. "I had the accident weeks ago. But I only woke up a few days ago."

"That's not true," your father said. "You were awake before that. Awake and talking and having conversations. You just don't remember that you did it."

"That's my point," you said. "This isn't like blacking out after an accident. This is losing memory several weeks after the fact."

"You *did* land on your head," your father said. "You landed on your head after sailing through the air at forty-five miles an hour. Even in the best-case scenario, like yours was, that's going to leave some lingering trauma, Matthew. It doesn't surprise me that you've lost some memories."

"Not *some,* Dad," you said. "All of them. Everything from the accident until when I woke up with you and Mom and Candace and Rennie standing over me."

"I told you, you fainted," your dad said. "We were concerned."

"So I faint and then wake up without a single memory of the last few weeks," you said. "You understand why I might be concerned about this."

"Do you want me to schedule you for an MRI?" your dad asked. "I can do that. Have the doctors look around for any additional signs of brain trauma."

"I think that might be a smart thing to do, don't you?" you said. "Look, Dad, I don't want to come across as overly paranoid about this, but losing weeks of my life bothers me. I want to be sure I'm not going to lose any more of it. It's not a comfortable feeling to wake up and have a big hole in your memory."

"No, Matt, I get it," your dad said. "I'll get Brenda to schedule it as quickly as she can. Fair enough?"

"Okay," you said.

"But in the meantime I don't want you to worry about it too much," your father said. "The doctors told us you would probably have at least a couple of episodes like this. So this is normal."

" 'Normal' isn't what I would call it," you said.

"Normal in the context of a motorcycle accident," your dad said. "Normal such as it is."

"I don't like this new 'normal,' " you said.

"I can think of worse ones," your father said, and did that thing he's been doing the last couple of days, where he looks like he's about to lose it and start weeping all over you.

· · · · ·

While you're waiting for your MRI, you go over the script you've been given for an episode of *The Chronicles of the Intrepid*. The good news for you is that your character plays a central role in the events. The bad news is that you don't have any lines, and you spend the entire episode lying on a gurney pretending to be unconscious.

"That's not true," Nick Weinstein said, after you pointed out these facts to him. He had stopped by the house with revisions, which was a service you suspected other extras did not get from the head writer of the series. "Look"—he flipped to the final pages of the script—"you're conscious here."

"'Crewman Hester opens his eyes, looks around,'" you said, reading the script direction.

"That's consciousness," Weinstein said.

"If you say so," you said.

"I know it's not a lot," Weinstein said. "But I didn't want to overtax you on your first episode back."

You achieved that, you said to yourself, flipping through the script in the MRI waiting room and rereading the scenes where you don't do much but lie there. The episode is action-packed—Lieutenant Kerensky in particular gets a lot of screen time piloting shuttles and running through exploding corridors while redshirts get impaled by falling scenery all around him—but it's even less coherent than usual for *Intrepid,* which is really saying something. Weinstein isn't bad with dialogue and keeping things moving, but neither him nor anyone on his writing staff seems overly invested in plotting. You strongly suspected that if you knew more about the science fiction television genre, you could probably call out all the scenes Weinstein and pals lifted from other shows.

Hey, it paid for college, some part of your brain said. *Not to mention this MRI.*

Fair enough, you thought. But it's not unreasonable to want the family business to be making something other than brainlessly extruded entertainment product, indistinguishable from any other sort of brainlessly extruded entertainment product. If that's all you're doing, then your family might as well be making plastic coat hangers.

"Matthew Paulson?" the MRI technician said. You looked up. "We're ready for you."

You enter the room the MRI machine is in, and the

technician shows you where you can slip into a hospital gown and store your clothes and personal belongings. Nothing metal's supposed to be in the room with the machine. You get undressed, get into your gown and then step into the room, while the technician looks at your information.

"All right, you've been here before, so you know the drill, right?" the technician asked.

"Actually, I don't remember being here before," you said. "It's kind of why I'm here now."

The technician scanned the information again and got slightly red. "Sorry," he said. "I'm not usually this much of an idiot."

"When was the last time I was here?" you asked.

"A little over a week ago," the technician said, and then frowned, reading the information again. "Well, maybe," he said after a minute. "I think your information may have gotten mixed up with someone else's."

"Why do you think that?" you asked.

The technician looked up at you. "Let me hold off on answering that for a bit," he said. "If it *is* a mix-up, which I'm pretty sure it is, then I don't want to be on the hook for sharing another patient's information."

"Okay," you said. "But if it is my information, you'll let me know."

"Of course," the technician said. "It's your information. Let's concentrate on this session for now, though." And with that he motioned for you to get on the table and slide your head and body into a claustrophobic tube.

· · · · ·

"So what do you think that technician was looking at?" Sandra asked you, as the two of you ate lunch at P.F. Chang's. It wasn't your favorite place, but she always had a weakness for it, for reasons passing understanding, and you still have a weakness for her. You met her outside the restaurant, the first time you had seen her since the accident, and she cried on your shoulder, hugging you, before she pulled back and jokingly slapped you across the face for not calling her before this. Then you went inside for upscale chain fusion food.

"I don't know," you said. "I wanted to get a look at it, but after the scan, he told me to get dressed and they'd call with the results. He was gone before I put my pants on."

"But whatever it was, it wasn't good," Sandra said.

"Whatever it was, I don't think it matched up with me walking and talking," you said. "Especially not a week ago."

"Medical record errors happen," Sandra said. "My firm makes a pretty good living with them." She was a first year at UCLA School of Law and interning at the moment at one of those firms that specialized in medical class-action suits.

"Maybe," you said.

"What is it?" Sandra said, after a minute of watching your face. "You don't think your parents are lying to you, do you?"

"Can you remember anything about it?" you asked. "About me after the accident."

"Your parents wouldn't let any of us see you," Sandra said, and her face got tight, the way it did when she was keeping herself from saying something she would regret later. "They didn't even call us," she said after a second. "I found out about it because Khamal forwarded me the *L.A. Times* story on Facebook."

"There was a story about it?" you said, surprised.

"Yeah," Sandra said. "It wasn't really about you. It was about the asshole who ran that light. He's a partner at Wickcomb Lassen Jenkins and Bing. Outside counsel for half the studios."

"I need to find that article," you said.

"I'll send it to you," Sandra said.

"Thanks," you said.

"I resent having to find out you were in a life-threatening accident through the *Los Angeles Times*," Sandra said. "I think I rate better than that."

"My mom never liked you as much after you broke my heart," you said.

"We were sophomores in high school," Sandra said. "And *you* got over it. Pretty quickly, too, since you were all over Jenna a week later."

"Maybe," you said. The Jenna Situation, as you recalled it now, had been fraught with fraughtiness.

"Anyway," Sandra said. "Even if she or your dad didn't tell me, they could have told Naren. He's one of your best friends. Or Kel. Or Gwen. And once we did find out, they wouldn't let any of us see you. They said they didn't want us to see you like that."

"They actually said that to you?" you asked.

Sandra was quiet for a moment. "They didn't say it out loud, but there was subtext there," she said. "They didn't want us to see you in that condition. They didn't want us to have a memory of you like that. Naren was the one who pushed them the most about it, you know. He was ready to come back from Princeton and camp out on your doorstep until they let him see you. And then you got better."

You smiled, remembering the blubbery conversation the two of you had when you called him to let you know you were okay. And then you stopped smiling. "It doesn't make any sense," you said.

"What specifically?" asked Sandra.

"My dad told me that I'd been recovered and awake for days before I got my memory back," you said. "That I was acting like myself during that time."

"Okay," Sandra said.

"So why didn't I call you?" you said. "We talk or see each other pretty much every week when I'm in town. Why didn't I call Naren? I talk to him every other day. Why didn't I update Facebook or send any texts? Why didn't I tell anyone I was okay? It's just about the first thing I did when I *did* regain my memory."

Sandra opened her mouth to respond, but then closed it, considering. "You're right, it doesn't make sense," she said. "You would have called or texted, if for no other reason than that any one of us would have killed you if you didn't."

"Exactly," you said.

"So you *do* think your parents are lying to you," Sandra said.

"Maybe," you said.

"And you think that somehow this is related to your medical information, which shows something weird," Sandra said.

"Maybe," you said again.

"What do you think the connection is?" Sandra asked.

"I have no idea," you admitted.

"You know that by law you're allowed to look at your own medical records," Sandra said. "If you think this is something medical, that's the obvious place to start."

"How long will that take?" you asked.

"If you go to the hospital and request them? They'll make you file a request form and then send it to a back room where it's pecked at by chickens for several days before giving you a précis of your record," Sandra said. "Which may or may not be helpful in any meaningful sense."

"You're smiling, so I assume there's an Option B," you said to Sandra.

Sandra, who was indeed smiling, picked up her phone and made a call, and talked in a bright and enthusiastic voice to whoever was on the other end of the line, passing along your name and pausing only to get the name of the hospital from you. After another minute she hung up.

"Who was that?" you asked.

"Sometimes the firm I'm interning for needs to get information more quickly than the legal process will allow," Sandra said. "That's the guy we use to get it. He's got moles in every hospital from Escondido to Santa Cruz. You'll have your report by dinnertime."

"How do you know about this guy?" you asked.

"What, you think a *partner* is going to get caught with this guy's number in his contact list?" Sandra said. "It's always the intern's job to take care of this sort of thing. That way, if the firm gets caught, it's plausible deniability. Blame it on the stupid, superambitious law student. It's brilliant."

"Except for you, if your guy gets caught," you noted.

Sandra shrugged. "I'd survive," she said. You're reminded that her father sold his software company to Microsoft in the late 1990s for $3.6 billion and cashed out before the Internet bubble burst. In a sense, law school was an affectation for her.

Sandra noted the strange look on your face. "What?" she asked, smiling.

"Nothing," you said. "Just thinking about the lifestyles of the undeservingly rich and pampered."

"You'd better be including yourself in that thought, Mr. I-changed-my-major-eight-times-in-college-and-still-don't-know-what-I-want-to-do-with-my-life-sad-bastard," Sandra said. "I'm not so happy to see you alive that I won't kill you."

"I do," you promised.

"You've been the worst of us," Sandra pointed out. "I only changed my major four times."

"And then took a couple of years off farting around before starting law school," you said.

"I founded a start-up," Sandra said. "Dad was very proud of me."

You said nothing, smiling.

"All right, fine, I founded a start-up with angel investing from my dad and his friends, and then proclaimed myself 'spokesperson' while others did all the real work," Sandra said. "I hope you're happy now."

"I am," you said.

"But it was still *something*," Sandra said. "And I'm doing something now. Drifting through grad school hasn't done you any favors. Just because you'll never have to do anything with your life doesn't mean you *shouldn't* do anything with your life. We both know people like that. It's not pretty."

"True," you agreed.

"Do you know what you want to do with your life now?" Sandra asked.

"The first thing I want to do is figure out what's happening to me right now," you said. "Until I do, it doesn't feel like I have my life back. It doesn't even feel like it's really my life."

· · · · ·

You stood in front of your mirror, naked, not because you are a narcissist but because you are freaking out. On your iPad are the medical records Sandra's guy acquired for you, including the records from your car crash. The records include pictures of you, in the hospital, as you were being prepped for the surgery, and the pictures they took of your brain after they stabilized you.

The list of things that were broken, punctured or torn in your body reads like a high school anatomy test. The pictures of your body look like the mannequins your father's effects crews would strew across the ground in the cheapo horror films he used to produce when you were a kid. There is no way, given the way in which you almost died and what they had to do to keep you alive, that your body should, *right now*, be anything less than a patchwork of scars and bruises and scabs parked in a bed with tubes and/or catheters in every possible orifice.

You stood in front of your mirror, naked, and there was not a scratch on you.

Oh, there are a few things. There's the scar on the back of your left hand, commemorating the moment when you were thirteen that you went over your handlebars. There's the small, almost unnoticeable burn mark below your lower lip from when you were sixteen and you leaned over to kiss Jenna Fischmann at the exact moment she was raising a cigarette to her mouth. There's the tiny incision mark from the laparoscopic appendectomy you had eighteen months ago; you have to bend over and part your pubic hair to see it. Every small record of the relatively minimal damage you've inflicted on your body prior to the accident is there for you to note and mark.

There's nothing relating to the accident at all.

The abrasions that scraped the skin off much of your right arm: gone. The scar that would mark where your tibia tore through to the surface of your left leg: missing. The bruises up and down your abdomen where your ribs popped and snapped and shredded muscle and blood vessels inside of you: not a hint they ever existed.

You spent most of an hour in front of the mirror, glancing at your medical records for specific incidents of trauma and then looking back into the glass for the evidence of what's written there. There isn't any. You are in the sort of unblemished health that only someone in their early twenties can be. It's like the accident never happened, or at the very least, never happened to you.

You picked up your iPad and turned it off, making a special effort not to pull up the images of your latest MRI, complete with the MRI technician's handwritten notation of, "Seriously, WTF?" because the disconnect between what the previous set of MRIs said about your brain and what the new ones said is like the disconnect between the shores of Spain and the eastern seaboard of the United States. The previous MRI indicated that your future would be best spent as an organ donor. The current MRI showed a perfectly healthy brain in a perfectly healthy body.

There's a word for such a thing.

"Impossible." You said it to yourself, looking at yourself in the mirror, because you doubted that at this point anyone else would say it to you. "Just fucking impossible."

You looked around your room, trying to see it like a stranger. It's larger than most people's first apartments and is strewn with the memorabilia of the last few years of your life and the various course corrections you've made, trying to figure out what it was you were supposed to be doing with yourself. On the desk, your laptop, bought to write screenplays but used primarily to read Facebook updates from your far-flung friends. On the bookshelves, a stack of anthropology texts that stand testament to a degree that you knew you would never use even as you were getting it; a delaying tactic to avoid facing the fact you didn't know what the hell you were doing.

On the bedside table is the Nikon DSLR your mother gave you as a gift when you said you were giving some thought to photography; you used it for about a week and then put it on the shelf and didn't use it again. Next to it, the script from *The Chronicles of the Intrepid*, evidence of your latest thing, dipping your toe into the world of acting to see if it might be for you.

Like the screenwriting and anthropology and photography, it's not; you already know it. As with everything else, though, there'd be the period between when you discovered the fact and when you could exit gracefully from the field. With anthropology, it was when you received the degree. With the screenwriting, it was a desultory meeting with an agent who was giving you twenty minutes as a favor to your father. With acting, it will be doing this episode of the show and then bowing out, and then returning to this room to figure out what the next thing will be.

You turned back to the mirror and looked at yourself one more time, naked, unblemished, and wondered if you would have been more useful to the world as an organ donor than you are right now: perfectly healthy, perfectly comfortable and perfectly useless.

· · · · ·

You lay on your stretcher on the set of *The Chronicles of the Intrepid,* waiting for the crew to move around to get another shot and becoming increasingly uncomfortable. Part of that was your makeup, which was designed to make you look pallid and sweaty and bruised, requiring constant application of a glycerin substance that made you feel as if you were being periodically coated in personal lubricant. Part of it was that two of the other actors were spending all their time staring at you.

One of them was an extra like you, a guy named Brian Abnett, and you mostly ignored him because you knew it was common knowledge on the set that you're the son of the show's producer, and you knew that there was a certain type of low-achieving actor who would love to become chummy with you on the idea that it would advance their own status, a sort of work-through-entourage thing. You knew what he's about and it's not anything you wanted to deal with.

The other, though, was Marc Corey, who was one of the stars of the show. He was already in perfectly well with your father, so he didn't need you to advance his career, and what you knew of him from Gawker, TMZ and the occasional comment from your father suggested that he's not the sort of person who would be wasting any of his precious, precious time with you. So the fact he couldn't really keep his eyes off of you is disconcerting.

You spent several hours acting like a coma patient while Corey and a cast of extras hovered over your stretcher during a simulated shuttle attack, ran with it down various hallway sets, and swung it into the medical bay set, where another set of extras, in medical staff costumes, pretend to jab you with space needles and waved fake gizmos over you like they were trying to diagnose your condition. Every now and again you cracked open an eye to see if Abnett or Corey was still gawking at you. One or the other usually was. Your one scene of actual acting had you opening your eyes as if you were coming out of a bout of unconsciousness. This time they were both staring at you. They were supposed to be doing that in the script. You still wondered if either or both of them were thinking of hitting on you after the show wraps for the day.

Eventually the day was done, and you scraped off the KY and bruise makeup, formally ending your acting career forever. On your way out, you saw Abnett and Corey talking to each other. For a reason you couldn't entirely explain to yourself, you changed your course and walked right up to the both of them.

"Matt," Marc said to you as you walked up.

"What's going on?" you asked, in a tone that made it clear

that the phrase was not a casual greeting but an actual inter-
rogative.

"What do you mean?" Marc said.

"The two of you have been staring at me all day," you said.

"Well, yes," Brian Abnett said. "You've been playing a character in a coma. We've been carting you around on a stretcher
all day. That requires us to look at you."

"Spare me," you said to Abnett. "Tell me what's going on."

Marc opened his mouth to say something, then closed it
and turned to Abnett. "I still have to work here after today,"
he said.

Abnett smiled wryly. "So I get to be the redshirt on this
one," he said to Marc.

"It's not like that," Marc said. "But he needs to know."

"No, I agree," Abnett said. He slapped Marc on the shoulder. "I'll take care of this, Marc."

"Thanks," Marc said, and then turned to you. "It's good to
see you, Matt. It really is." He walked off quickly.

"I have no idea what that was about," you said to Abnett,
after Marc walked off. "Before today I'm pretty sure he never
gave me a thought whatsoever."

"How are you feeling, Matt?" Abnett said, not directly answering you.

"What do you mean?" you asked.

"I think you know what I mean," Abnett said. "You feeling
good? Healthy? Like a new man?"

You felt a little cold at that last comment. "You know," you
said.

"I do," Abnett said. "And now I know that you know, too.
Or at least, that you know something."

"I don't think I know as much as you do," you said.

Abnett looked at you. "No, you probably don't. In which

case, I think you and I need to get out of here and go somewhere we can get a drink. Maybe several."

. . . . .

You returned to your room late in the evening and stood in
the middle of it, searching for something. Searching for the
message that had been left for you.

"Hester left you a message," Abnett had told you, after he
explained everything else that had happened, every other
absolutely impossible thing. "I don't know where it is because
he didn't tell me. He told Kerensky, who told Marc, who told
me. Marc says it's somewhere in your room, somewhere you
might find it but no one else would look—and someplace you
wouldn't look, unless you went looking for it."

"Why would he do it that way?" you had asked Abnett.

"I don't know," Abnett had said. "Maybe he figured there
was a chance you wouldn't actually figure it out. And if you
didn't figure it out, what would be the point in telling you?
You probably wouldn't believe it anyway. I barely believe it,
and I met my guy. *That* was some weirdness, I'll tell you. You
never met yours. You could very easily doubt it."

You didn't doubt it. You had the physical evidence of it.
You had you.

You went first to your computer and looked through the
folders, looking for documents that had titles you didn't remember giving any. When you didn't find any, you rearranged
the folders so you could look for files that were created since
you had your accident. There were none. You checked your
e-mail queue to see if there were any e-mails from yourself.
None. Your Facebook page was jammed with messages from
friends from high school, college and grad school, who heard
you were back from your accident. Nothing from yourself, no

new pictures posted into your albums. No trace of you leaving a message for you.

You stood up from your desk and turned around, scanning the room. You went to your bookshelves. There you took down the blank journals that you had bought around the time you decided to be a screenwriter, so you could write down your thoughts and use them later for your masterworks. You thumbed through them. They were as blank as they had been before. You placed them back on the shelf and then ran your eyes over to your high school yearbooks. You pulled them down, disturbing the dust on the bookshelf, and opened them, looking for a new inscription among the ones that were already there. There were none. You returned them to the shelf, and as you did so you noticed another place on the bookshelf where the dust had been disturbed, but not in the shape of a book.

You looked at the shape of the disturbance for a minute, and then you turned around, walked to your bed table and picked up your camera. You slid open the slot for the memory card, popped it out, took it to your computer and opened up the pictures folder, arranging it so you could see the picture files by date.

There were three new files made since your accident. One photo and two video files.

The picture file was of someone's legs and shoes. You smiled at this. The first video file consisted of someone panning across the room with the camera, swinging it back and forth as if they were trying to figure out how the thing worked.

The third video was of you. In it, your face appeared, followed by some wild thrashing as you set down the camera and propped it up so you would stay in the frame. You were sitting. The autofocus buzzed back and forth for a second and then settled, framing you sharply.

"Hi, Matthew," you said. "I'm Jasper Hester. I'm you. Sort of. I've spent a couple of days with your family now, talking to them about you, and they tell me you haven't touched this camera in a year, which I figure means it's the perfect place to leave you a message. If you wake up and just go on with your life, then you'll never find it and there's no harm done. But if you do find this, I figure it's because you're looking for it.

"If you are looking for it, then I figure either one of two things have happened. Either you've figured out something's weird and no one will tell you anything about it, or you've been told about it and you don't believe it. If it's the first of these, then no, you're not crazy or had some sort of weird psychotic break with your life. You haven't had a stroke. You did have a massive brain injury, but not with the body you're in now. So don't worry about that. Also, you don't have amnesia. You don't have any memory of this because it's not you doing it. I guess that's pretty simple.

"If you've been told what happened and you don't believe it, hopefully this will convince you. And if it doesn't, well, I don't know what to tell you, then. Believe what you want. But in the meantime indulge me for a minute."

In the video Hester who is not you but also is ran his fingers through his hair and looked away, trying to figure what to say next.

"Okay, here's what I want to say. I think I exist because you exist. Somehow, in a way I really couldn't ever try to explain in any way that makes any sense, I believe that the day you asked your dad if you could try acting in his show, on that day something happened. Something happened that meant that in the universe I live in, events twisted and turned and did whatever they do so that I was born and I lived a life that you could be part of, as me, as a fictional character, in your world. I don't know how it works or why, but it does. It just does.

"Our lives are twisted together, because we're sort of the same person, just one universe and a few centuries apart. And because of that, I think I can ask you this next question.

"Honestly, Matthew, what the *fuck* are we doing with our lives?

"I've been talking to your family about you, you know. They love you. They all do. They love you and when you had your accident it was like someone came along and stabbed them in the heart. It's amazing how much love they have for you. But, and again, I can tell you this because you're me, I can tell they think you need to get your ass in gear. They talk about how you have so many interests, and how you're waiting for that one thing that will help you achieve your potential, and what I hear is what they won't say: You need to grow up.

"I know it because I'm the same way. Of course I'm the same way, I'm *you*. I've been drifting along for years, Matthew. I joined the Universal Union navy not because I was driven but because I didn't know what to do with myself. And I figured as long as I didn't know what I wanted to do with myself I might as well see the universe, right? But even then I've always just done the bare minimum of what I had to do. There wasn't much point to doing more.

"It wasn't bad. To be honest I thought I was pretty clever. I was getting away with something in my own way. But then I get here and saw you, brain-dead and with tubes coming out of every part of your body. And I realized I wasn't getting away with anything. Just like you didn't get away with anything. You were just born, fucked around for a while, got hit by a car and died, and that's your whole life story right there. You don't win by getting through all your life not having done anything.

"Matthew, if you're looking at this now it's because one of us finally did something useful with his life. It's me. I decided to save your life. I swapped bodies with you because I think the way it works means that I'll survive in my world in your messed-up body, and you'll survive in mine. If I'm wrong and we both die, or you survive and I die, then I'll have died trying to save you. And yes, that sucks for me, but my life expectancy because of your dad's show wasn't all that great to begin with. And all things considered, it was one of the best ways I could have died.

"But I'm going to let you in on a secret. I think this is going to work. Don't ask me why—hell, don't ask me why about *any* of this situation—I just think it will. If it does, I have only one thing I want from you. That you do something. Stop drifting. Stop trying things until you get bored with them. Stop waiting for that one thing. It's stupid. You're wasting time. You almost wasted all of your time. You were lucky I was around, but I get a feeling this isn't something we'll get to do twice.

"I'm going to do the same thing. I'm done drifting, Matthew. Our lives are arbitrary and weird, but if I pull this off—if me and all my friends from the *Intrepid* pull this off—then we get something that everyone else in our universe doesn't get: a chance to make our own fate. I'm going to take it. I don't know how yet. But I'm not going to blow it.

"Don't you blow it either, Matthew. I don't expect you to know what to do with yourself yet. But I expect you to figure it out. I think that's a fair request from me, all things considered.

"Welcome to your new life, Matthew. Don't fuck this one up."

Hester reached over and turned off the camera.

You clicked out of the video window, closed the laptop

and turned around to see your father, standing in the doorway.

"It's not amnesia," he said. There were tears on his face.

"I know," you said.

CODA III:

Third Person

Samantha Martinez sits at her computer and watches a short video of a woman who could be her reading a book on a beach. It's the woman's honeymoon and the videographer is her newlywed husband, using a camera the two of them received as a wedding gift. The content of the video is utterly unremarkable—a minute of the camera approaching the woman, who looks up from her book, smiles, tries to ignore the camera for several seconds and then puts her book down and stares up at the camera. What could be the Santa Monica Pier, or some iteration of it, hovers not too distantly in the frame.

"Put that stupid thing down and come into the water with me," the woman says, to the cameraman.

"Someone will take the camera," says her husband, off-screen.

"Then they take the camera," she says. "And all they'll have is a video of me reading a book. You get to have me."

"Fair point," says the husband.

The woman stands up, drops her book, adjusts her bikini, looks at her husband again. "Are you coming?"

"In a minute," the husband says. "Run to the water. If someone does steal the camera, I want them to know what they're missing."

"Goof," the woman says, and then for a minute the camera wheels away as she comes toward the husband to get a kiss. Then the picture steadies again and the camera watches her as she jogs to the water. When she gets there, she turns around and makes a beckoning motion. The camera switches off.

Samantha Martinez watches the video three more times before she gets up, grabs her car keys and walks out of the front door of her house.

· · · · ·

"Samantha," Eleanor, her sister, says, waving her hand to get Samantha's attention. "You're doing that thing again."

"Sorry," Samantha says. "What thing again?"

"That thing," Eleanor says. "That thing when no matter what someone else is saying you phase out and stare out the window."

"I wasn't staring out of a window," Samantha says.

"You were phased out," Eleanor says. "The staring out the window part isn't really the important part of that."

The two of them are sitting in the Burbank P.F. Chang's, which is empty in the early afternoon except for a young couple in a booth, across the entire length of the restaurant from them. Eleanor and Samantha are sitting at a table near the large bank of windows pointing out toward a mall parking structure.

Samantha is in fact not looking out the window; she's looking at the couple and their discussion. Even from a distance she can see the two aren't really a couple, although they might have been once, and Samantha can see that the young man, at the very least, wouldn't mind if they were again. He is bending toward her almost imperceptibly while they sit, telling her that he'd be willing. The young woman doesn't notice, yet; Samantha wonders if she will, and whether the young man will ever bring it to her attention.

"Samantha," Eleanor says forcefully.

"Sorry," Samantha says, and snaps her attention to her sister. "Really, E, sorry. I don't know where my head is these last few days."

Eleanor turns to look behind her and sees the couple in the booth. "Someone you know?" she asks.

"No," Samantha says. "I'm just watching their body language. He likes her more than she likes him."

"Huh," Eleanor says, and turns back to Samantha. "Maybe you should go over there and tell him not to waste his time."

"He's not wasting his time," Samantha says. "He just hasn't let her know how important she is to him yet. If I was going to tell him anything, that's what I would tell him. Not to stay quiet about it. Life is too short for that."

Eleanor stares at her sister, strangely. "Are you okay, Sam?" she asks.

"I'm fine, E," Samantha says.

"Because what you just said is the sort of line that comes out of a Lifetime movie character after she discovers she has breast cancer," Eleanor says.

Samantha laughs at this. "I don't have breast cancer, E," she says. "I swear."

Eleanor smiles. "Then what is going on, sis?"

"It's hard to explain," Samantha says.

"Our waiter is taking his time," Eleanor says. "Try me."

"Someone sent me a package," Samantha says. "It's pictures and videos and love letters from a husband and wife. I've been looking through them."

"Is that legal?" Eleanor asks.

"I don't think that's something I need to worry about," Samantha says.

"Why would someone send those to you?" Eleanor asks.

"They thought they might mean something to me," Samantha says.

"Some random couple's love letters?" Eleanor asks.

"They're not random," Samantha says, carefully. "It made sense to send them to me. It's just been a lot to sort through."

"I get the sense you're skipping a whole bunch of details here," Eleanor says.

"I did say it was hard to explain," Samantha says.

"So what's it been like, going through another couple's mail?" Eleanor asks.

"Sad," Samatha says. "They were happy, and then it was taken away."

"It's good they were happy first, then," Eleanor says.

"E, don't you ever wonder about how your life could have been different?" Samantha asks, changing the subject slightly. "Don't you ever wonder, if things just happened a little differently, you might have a different job, or different husband, or different children? Do you think you would have been happier? And if you could see that other life, how would it make you feel?"

"That's a lot of philosophy at one time," Eleanor says, as the waiter finally rolls up and deposits the sisters' salads. "I don't actually wonder how my life could be different, Sam. I like my life. I have a good job, Braden's a good kid and most days I don't feel like strangling Lou. I worry about my little sister from time to time, but that's as bad as it gets."

"You met Lou at Pomona," Samantha says, mentioning her sister's alma mater. "But I remember you flipping a quarter for your college choice. If the coin had landed on heads instead of tails, you would have gone to Wesleyan. You never would have met Lou. You wouldn't have married him and had Braden. One coin toss and everything in your life would have gone another way completely."

"I suppose so," Eleanor says, spearing leaves.

"Maybe there's another you out there," Samantha says. "And for her the coin landed another way. She's out there leading your other life. What if you got to see that other life? How would that make you feel?"

Eleanor swallows her mouthful of greens and points her fork at her sister. "About that coin toss," she says. "I faked it. Mom's the one who wanted me to go to Wesleyan, not me. She was excited about the idea of two generations of our family going there. I always wanted to go to Pomona, but Mom kept begging me to consider Wesleyan. Finally I told her I would flip a coin over it. It didn't matter which way the coin would have landed, I was still going to choose Pomona. It was all show to keep her happy."

"There are other places your life could have changed," Samantha says. "Other lives you could have led."

"But it didn't," Eleanor says. "And I don't. I live the life I live, and it's the only life I have. No one else is out there in the universe living my alternate lives, and even if they were, I wouldn't be worrying about them because I have my life to live here, now. In my life, I have Lou and Braden and I'm happy. I don't worry about what else could have been. Maybe that's lack of imagination on my part. On the other hand, it keeps me from being mopey."

Samantha smiles again. "I'm not mopey," she says.

"Yes you are," Eleanor says. "Or maudlin, which is the slightly more socially respectable version. It sounds like watching these couple's home videos is making you wonder if they're happier than you are."

"They're not," Samantha says. "She's dead."

· · · · ·

A letter from Margaret Jenkins to her husband Adam:

Sweetheart:
I love you. I'm sorry that you're upset. I know the Viking *was supposed to be back to Earth in time for our anniversary but I don't have any control of our missions, including the*

emergency ones, like this one is. This was part of the deal
when you married a crewman on a Dub U ship. You knew
that. We discussed it. I don't like being away from you any
more than you like it, but I also love what I do. You told me
when you proposed to me that you knew this would be
something you would have to live with. I'm asking you to
remember you said that you would live with it.

You also said that you would consider joining the navy
yourself. I asked Captain Feist about the Special Skills
intake process and she tells me that the navy really needs
people who have experience with large-scale computer
systems like you do. She also tells me that if you make it
through the expedited training and get on a ship, the Dub U
will pick up the tab for your college loans. That would be
one less thing hanging over us.

Captain also tells me that she suspects there'll be an
opening on the Viking for a systems specialist in the next
year. No guarantees but it's worth a shot and the Dub U
does make an effort to place married couples on the same
ship. It believes it's good for morale. I know it would be
good for my morale. Monogamy sucks when you can't
exercise the privilege. I know you feel the same way.

I love you. Think about it. I love you. I'm sorry I can't be
there with you. I love you. I wish I was. I love you. I wish
you were here with me. I love you. Maybe you could be. I
love you. Think about it. I love you.

Also: I love you.

(I) love (you),
M

. . . . .

To placate Eleanor, who became more worried about her sister
the more she thought about their conversation at P.F. Chang's,

Samantha sets off on a series of blind dates, selected by Eleanor apparently at random.

The dates do not go well.

The first date is with an investment banker who spends the
date rationalizing the behavior of investment bankers in the
2008 economic meltdown, interrupting himself only to answer "urgent" e-mails sent to him, or so he claims, from associates in Sydney and Tokyo. At one point he goes to the bathroom
without his phone; Samantha pops open the back and flips the
battery in the compartment. Her date, enraged that his phone
has inexplicably stopped working, leaves, barely stopping to
ask Samantha if she minds splitting the bill before stalking off
in search of a Verizon store.

The second date is with a junior high English teacher from
Glendale who is an aspiring screenwriter and who agreed to
the date because Eleanor hinted that Samantha might still
have connections at *The Chronicles of the Intrepid,* one of the
shows she had been an extra on. When Samantha explains
that she had only been an extra, and that was years ago, and
she had gotten the gig through a casting director and not
through personal connections, the teacher is silent for several minutes and then begs Samantha to read the script anyway and give him feedback. She does, silently, as dinner is
served. It is terrible. Out of pity, Samantha lies.

The third date is with a man so boring that Samantha literally cannot remember a thing about him by the time she
gets back to her car.

The fourth date is with a bisexual woman co-worker of
Eleanor's, whose gender Eleanor obfuscated by referring to
her as "Chris." Chris is cheerful enough when Samantha explains the situation, and the two have a perfectly nice dinner. After the dinner Samantha calls her sister and asks her
what she was thinking. "Honey, it's been so long since you

had a relationship, I thought maybe you just weren't telling me something," Eleanor says.

The fifth date is a creep. Samantha leaves before the entrée.

The sixth date is with a man named Bryan who is polite and attentive and charming and decent looking and Samantha can tell he has absolutely no interest in her whatsoever. When Samantha says this to him, he laughs.

"I'm sorry," he says. "I was hoping it wasn't obvious."

"It's all right," Samantha says. "But why did you agree to the date?"

"You've met your sister, right?" Bryan says. "After five minutes it was easier just to say yes than to find excuses to say no. And she said you were really nice. She was right about that, by the way."

"Thank you," Samantha says, and looks at him again silently for a few seconds. "You're a widower," she says, finally.

"Ah," Bryan says. "Eleanor told you." He takes a sip of his wine.

"No," Samantha says. "I just guessed."

"Eleanor should have told you, then," Bryan says. "I apologize that she didn't."

"It's not your fault," Samantha says. "Eleanor didn't mention to me that she had set me up on a date with a woman two weeks ago, so it's easy to see how she might skip over you being widower."

They both laugh at this. "I think maybe you ought to fire your sister from matchmaking," Bryan says.

"How long has it been?" Samantha asks. "That you've been widowed, I mean."

Bryan nods to signal that he knows what she means. "Eighteen months," he says. "It was a stroke. She was running a half-marathon and she stumbled and died at the hospital. The doctors told me the blood vessels in her brain had probably been thin her whole life and just took that moment to go. She was thirty-four."

"I'm sorry," Samantha says.

"So am I," Bryan says, and takes another small drink from his wine. "A year after Jen died, friends started asking me if I was ready to date again. I can't think of a reason to say no. Then I go on them and I realize I don't want anything to do with them. No offense," he says quickly. "It's not you. It's me."

"No offense taken," Samantha says. "It must have been love."

"That's the funny thing," Bryan says, and suddenly he's more animated than he's been the entire evening and, Samantha suspects, more than he's been for a long time. "It wasn't love, not at first. Or it wasn't for me. Jen always said that she knew I was going to be hers from the first time she saw me, but I didn't know that. I didn't even much like her when I met her."

"Why not?" Samantha asks.

"She was *pushy*," Bryan says, smiling. "She didn't mind telling you what she thought, whether you had asked for an opinion or not. I also didn't think she was that attractive, to be entirely honest. She definitely wasn't the sort of woman I thought was my type."

"But you came around," Samantha says.

"I can't explain it," Bryan admits. "Well, that's not true. I can. Jen decided I was a long-term project and invested the time. And then the next thing I knew I was under a chuppah, wondering how the hell I had gotten myself there. But by then, it was love. And that's all I can say. Like I said, I can't explain it."

"It sounds wonderful," Samantha says.

"It was," Bryan says. He finishes his wine.

"Do you think that's how it works?" Samantha asks. "That you have just that one person you love?"

"I don't know," Bryan says. "For everyone in world? I don't think so. People look at love all sorts of ways. I think there are some people who can love someone, and then if they die, can love someone else. I was best man to a college friend whose wife died, and then five years later watched him marry someone else. He was crying his eyes out in joy both times. So, no, I don't think that's how it works for everyone. But I think maybe that's how it's going to work for *me*."

"I'm glad that you had it," Samantha says.

"So am I," Bryan says. "It would have been nice to have it a little longer, is all." He sets down his wineglass, which he had been fiddling with this entire time. "Samantha, I'm sorry," he says. "I've just done that thing where I tell my date how much I love my wife. I don't mean to be a widower in front of you."

"I don't mind," Samantha says. "I get that a lot."

· · · · ·

"I can't believe you still have that camera," Margaret says to her husband, once again behind the lens. They are walking through the corridors of the *Intrepid*. They have just been assigned together to the ship.

"It was a wedding present," her husband says. "From Uncle Will. He'd kill me if I threw it out."

"You don't have to throw it out," Margaret says. "I could arrange an accident."

"I'm appalled at such a suggestion," her husband says.

Margaret stops. "Here we are," she says. "Our married quarters. Where we will spend our blissfully happy married life together on this ship."

"Try saying that without so much sarcasm next time," her husband says.

"Try learning not to snore," Margaret says, and opens the door, then sweeps her hand in a welcoming motion. "After you, Mr. Documentary."

Her husband walks through the door and pans around the room, which takes a very short amount of time. "It's larger than our berth on the *Viking*," he says.

"There are broom closets larger than our berth on the *Viking*," Margaret points out.

"Yes, but this is almost as large as *two* broom closets," her husband says.

Margaret closes the door and faces her husband. "When do you need to report to Xenobiology?" she asks.

"I should report immediately," her husband says.

"That's not what I asked," Margaret says.

"What do you have in mind?" her husband asks.

"Something you're not going to be able to document," Margaret says.

· · · · ·

"Did you want to make a confession?" Father Neil asks.

Samantha giggles despite herself. "I don't think I could confess to you with a straight face," she says.

"This is the problem of coming to a priest you used to date in high school," Father Neil says.

"You weren't a priest then," Samantha notes.

The two of them are sitting in one of the back pews of Saint Finbar's Church.

"Well, if you decide you need confession, you let me know," Neil says. "I promise not to tell. That's actually one of the requirements, in fact."

"I remember," Samantha says.

"So why did you want to see me?" Neil asks. "Not that it isn't nice to see you."

"Is it possible that we have other lives?" Samantha asks.

"What, like reincarnation?" Neil asks. "And are you asking about Catholic doctrine, or something else?"

"I'm not exactly sure how to describe it," Samantha says. "I don't think it's reincarnation exactly." She frowns. "I'm not sure there's any way to describe it that doesn't sound completely ridiculous."

"It's popularly believed theologians had great debates about how many angels could dance on a head of a pin," Neil says. "I don't think your question could be any more ridiculous."

"Did they ever find out how many angels could dance on the head of a pin?" Samantha asks.

"It was never actually seriously considered," Neil says. "It's kind of a myth. And even if it weren't, the answer would be: As many as God needed to. What's your question, Sam?"

"Imagine there's a woman who is like a fictional character, but she's real," Samantha says, and holds up her hand when she sees Neil about to ask a question. "Don't ask how, I don't know. Just accept that she's the way I've described her. Now suppose that woman is based on someone in our real world— looks the same, sounds the same, from all outward appearances they could be the same person. The first woman wouldn't exist without having the second woman as a model. Are they the same person? Are they the same soul?"

Neil furrows his brow and Samantha is reminded of him at age sixteen and has to suppress a giggle. "The first woman is based on the second woman, but she's not a clone?" he asks. "I mean, they don't take genetic material from one to make the other."

"I don't think so, no," Samantha says.

"But the first woman is definitely made from the second woman in some ineffable way?" Neil asks.

"Yes," Samantha says.

"I'm not going to ask for details of how that gets managed," Neil says. "I'm just going to take it on faith."

"Thank you," Samantha says.

"I can't speak for the entire Catholic Church on this, but my own take on it would be no, they're not," Neil says. "This is a gross oversimplification, but the Church teaches us that those things that have in themselves the potential to become a human being have their own souls. If you were to make a clone of yourself, that clone wouldn't be you, any more than identical twins are one person. Each has its own thoughts and personal experiences and are more than the sum of their genes. They're their own person, and have their own individual souls."

"You think it would be the same for her?" Samantha asks.

Neil looks at Samantha oddly but answers her question. "I'd think so. This other person has her own memories and experiences, yes?" Samantha nods. "If she has her own life, she has her own soul. The relationship you describe is somewhere between a child and an identical sibling—based on someone else but *only* based, not repeating them exactly."

"What if they're separated in time?" Samantha asks. "Would it be reincarnation then?"

"Not if you're a Catholic," Neil says. "Our doctrine doesn't allow for it. I can't speak to how other faiths would make the ruling. But the way you're describing it, it doesn't seem like reincarnation is strictly necessary anyway. The woman is her own person however you want to define it."

"Okay, good," Samantha says.

"Remember, this is just me talking," Neil says. "If you want an official ruling, I'd have to run it past the pope. That might take a while."

Samantha smiles. "That's all right," she says. "What you're saying makes sense to me. Thank you, Neil."

"You're welcome," Neil says. "Do you mind me asking what's this about?"

"It's complicated," Samantha says.

"Apparently," Neil says. "It sounds like you're researching a science fiction story."

"Something like that, yes," Samantha says.

· · · · ·

Sweetheart,

Welcome to Cirqueria! I know Collins has you cranking away on a project so I won't see you before we go to the surface for the negotiations. I'm part of the Captain's security detail; he expects things to proceed in boring and uneventful ways. Don't wait up any longer than Collins makes you. I'll see you tomorrow.

Kiss kiss love love,
M

P.S.: Kiss.
P.S.S.: Love.

· · · · ·

Samantha buys herself a printer and a couple hundred dollars' worth of ink and prints out letters and photographs from the collection that she was given a month previously. The original projector had disappeared mysteriously as promised, collapsing into a crumbling pile that evaporated over the space of an hour. Before that happened, Samantha took her little digital camera and took a picture of every document, and video capture of every movie, that she had been given. The digital files remained on the camera card and on her hard drive; she's printing documents for a different purpose entirely.

When she's done, she's printed out a ream of paper, each with a letter from or a picture of Margaret Jenkins. It's not Margaret's whole life, but it's a representation of the life that she lived with her husband; a representation of a life lived in love and with love.

Samantha picks up the ream of paper, walks over to the small portable shredder she's purchased and runs each sheet of paper through it, one piece at a time. She takes the shredded papers into her small backyard and places them into a small metal garbage can she has also purchased. She packs the paper down so that is loosely compacted, lights a kitchen match and places it into the trash can, making sure the paper catches. When it does, Samantha places the lid on top of the garbage can, set slightly askew to allow oxygen in while keeping wisps of burning paper from floating away.

The paper burns down to ashes. Samantha opens the lid and pours a bucket of beach sand into the trash can, smothering any remaining embers. Samantha goes back into her house to retrieve a wooden spoon from her kitchen and uses it to stir the sand, mixing it with the ashes. After a few minutes of this, Samantha upends the trash can and carefully pours the mixture of sand and ashes into the bucket. She covers the bucket, places it into her car and drives toward Santa Monica.

· · · · ·

Hello.

I don't know what to call you. I don't know if you will ever read this or if you will believe it even if you do. But I'm going to write like you will read it and believe it. There's no point in doing it otherwise.

You are the reason that my life has had joy. You didn't

know it, and you couldn't have known it. It doesn't mean it's not true. It's true because without you, the woman who was my wife would not have been who she was, and who she was to me. In your world, you played her, as an actress, for what I believe was only a brief amount of time—so brief that it's possible you don't even remember that you played her.

But in that brief time, you gave her life. And where I am, she shared that life with me, and gave me something to live for. When she stopped living, I stopped living too. I stopped living for years.

I want to start living again. I know she would want me to start living again. To do that I need to give her back to you. Here she is.

I wish you could have known her. I wish you could have talked to her, laughed with her and loved her as I did. It's impossible now. But at the very least I can show you what she meant to me, and how she lived with me and shared her life with me.

I don't know you; I will never know you. But I have to believe that a great part of who my wife was comes from you—lives in you even now. My wife is gone, but knowing that you are out there gives me some comfort. I hope that what was good in her, those things I loved in her, live in you too. I hope that in your life you have the love that she had in hers. I have to believe you do, or at the very least that you can.

I could say more, but I believe the best way to explain everything is simply to show you everything. So here it is. Here she is.

My wife's name was Margaret Elizabeth Jenkins. Thank you for giving her to me, for the time I had her. She's yours again.

With love,
Adam Jenkins

. . . . .

Samantha Martinez stands ankle deep in the ocean, not too far from the Santa Monica Pier, and sprinkles the remains of Margaret Jenkins' life in the place where she will have one day been on her honeymoon. She does not hurry in the task, taking time between each handful of ash and sand to remember Margaret's words, and her life, and her love, bringing them inside of her and letting them become part of her, whether for the first time or once again.

When she's done, she turns around to walk up the beach and notices a man standing there, watching her. She smiles and walks up to him.

"You were spreading ashes," he says, more of a statement than a question.

"I was," Samantha says.

"Whose were they?" he asks.

"They were my sister's," Samantha says. "In a way."

"In a way?" he asks.

"It's complicated," Samantha explains.

"I'm sorry for your loss," the man says.

"Thank you," Samantha says. "She lived a good life. I'm glad I got to be a part of it."

"This is probably the worst possible thing I could say to you right this moment," the man says, "but I *swear* you look familiar to me."

"You look familiar to me too," Samantha says.

"I swear to you this isn't a line, but are you an actress?" the man asks.

"I used to be," Samantha says.

"Were you ever on *The Chronicles of the Intrepid*?" the man asks.

"Once," Samantha says.

"You're not going to believe this," the man says. "I think I played your character's husband."

"I know," Samantha says.

"You remember?" the man asks.

"No," Samantha said. "But I know what her husband looks like."

The man holds out his hand. "I'm Nick Weinstein," he says.

"Hello, Nick," Samantha says, shaking it. "I'm Samantha."

"It's nice to meet you," Nick says. "Again, I mean."

"Yes," Samantha says. "Nick, I'm thinking of getting something to eat. Would you like to join me?"

Now it's Nick's turn to smile. "I would like that. Yes," he says.

The two of them head up the beach.

"It's kind of a coincidence," Nick says, after a few seconds. "The two of us being here like this."

Samantha smiles again and puts her arm around Nick as they walk.

I wrote this novel in the wake of having worked on a science fiction television show, so before I do anything else, let me make the following disclaimer: *Redshirts* is not even remotely based on the television show *Stargate: Universe*. Anyone hoping this is a thinly veiled satire of that particular experience of mine is going to have to be disappointed. Indeed, I would argue that *Stargate: Universe* was all the things that *The Chronicles of the Intrepid* wasn't—namely, smart, well-written and interested in having its science nod in the direction of plausibility.

I was really pleased to have worked on *SG:U* as its creative consultant; I also had a lot of fun with it. And of course I genuinely enjoyed *watching* it, both as a fan of the genre and as someone who worked on it and could see where my contributions showed up on the screen. *That* was cool. I've co-dedicated this book to Brad Wright and Joe Mallozzi, the *SG:U* producers who brought me into the show, but I'd also like to take a moment here to bow deeply to the cast, crew, writers and staff of *SG:U* as well. It's a shame it couldn't have lasted longer, but no good thing lasts forever.

I also wrote this novel while serving as president of the Science Fiction and Fantasy Writers of America, the largest organization of SF/F writers in the world (and possibly in the entire universe, although of course there's no way to confirm this, yet). Over the years, there's been a bit of received wisdom that if one serves as SFWA's president, one has to essentially lose a year of creative productivity to the gig, and possibly one's sanity as well. I'm happy to say I have not found this to be true—and the reason it was not true in my case was that I was fortunate to have an SFWA board of directors filled with very smart, dedicated people, who worked together for its members as well as or better than any board in recent memory.

So to Amy Sterling Casil, Jim Fiscus, Bob Howe, Lee Martindale, Bud Sparhawk, Sean Williams and in particular Mary Robinette Kowal, my sincere thanks, admiration and appreciation. It was an honor to serve with each of you. Thanks also to all those who volunteer for SFWA and make it a writers' organization I am proud to be a part of.

Every time I write a novel, I am amazed at how much *better* it is when it finally comes out in book form. It's because so many excellent people improve it along the way. This book was helped along by Patrick Nielsen Hayden, my editor; Irene Gallo, Tor's art director; cover artist Peter Lutjen; copyeditor Sona Vogel; text designer Heather Saunders and also production editor Rafal Gibek. Thanks are also due to Cassie Ammerman, my publicist at Tor, and of course to Tom Doherty, who continues to publish my work, for which I continue to be ridiculously pleased. Thanks are also due to my agent, Ethan Ellenberg, and to Evan Gregory, who keeps track of my foreign sales.

Redshirts was read by a small core of first-line readers who offered invaluable feedback and assured me that the thing was something more than just a piss-take on televised science fiction (although obviously it is that too). My appreciation, then, to Regan Avery (as always), Karen Meisner, Wil Wheaton, Doselle Young, Paul Sabourin, Greg DiCostanzo and my wife, Kristine Scalzi, who also deserves thanks for putting up with me in a general sense. I'm really glad she does.

And finally, thank you, dear reader. I'm glad you keep coming back for more. If you keep coming back, I'll keep writing them. That's a promise.

John Scalzi,
July 22, 2011

Divided West
European Security and the
Transatlantic Relationship

Tuomas Forsberg and
Graeme P. Herd

CHATHAM HOUSE

The Royal Institute of International Affairs
Chatham House
10 St James's Square
London SW1Y 4LE
http://www.chathamhouse.org.uk
(Charity Registration No: 208223)

Blackwell Publishing Ltd
350 Main Street, Malden, MA 02148-5018, USA
108 Cowley Road, Oxford OX4 1JF, UK
550 Swanston Street, Carlton South, Melbourne, Victoria 3053, Australia
Kurfürstendamm 57, 10707 Berlin, Germany

First published 2006 by Blackwell Publishing Ltd

Library of Congress Cataloging-in-Publication Data has been applied for.

ISBN 1-4051-3042-3 (hardback); ISBN 1-4051-3041-5 (paperback)

A catalogue record for this title is available from the British Library.

Set in 10.5 on 13 pt Caslon with Stone Sans display
by Koinonia, Manchester

For further information on
Blackwell Publishing, visit our website:
http://www.blackwellpublishing.com

For Birgit and Nora

Contents

Contents

Acknowledgments

The authors first collaborated in 2002 while working at the George C Marshall European Center for Security Studies (GCMC) in Garmisch-Partenkirchen, Germany. The experience of teaching young civilian and military professionals from the United States, Europe and Eurasia in a German–American institution, coupled with the expertise of a very diverse international faculty, created the perfect environment in which to think through the transatlantic themes and arguments contained in this Chatham House Paper. We would like to extend our warmest appreciation to all our former GCMC colleagues and course participants for discussing and debating these issues in lectures and seminars. In particular, we are very grateful to those who took the time to read individual chapters and provide valuable feedback. They include Denis Alekseev, Ambassador Grudzinski, John Kriendler, Detlef Puhl, Matthew Rhodes, Jiří Šedivý, Peter Schneider, Jack Treddenick and James Wither. We would also like to express our gratitude to Margie Gibson and all the staff of the Marshall Center Research Library (a veritable jewel), and in particular to Jill Golden for her hard work on the bibliography.

Without the support and encouragement of Chatham House, this book would not have seen the light of day. Our thanks go first to the two anonymous Chatham House referees for their instructive reports and especially to Margaret May, Editor at Chatham House, and Olivia Bosch, Senior Research Fellow of the International Security Programme there. We also thank Julie Smith, former Head of the European Programme, who encouraged us to submit the initial proposal for a book in late 2003. Lastly, we must acknowledge the excellent contributions of Kim Mitchell, the copy-editor, who managed to gather stray thoughts into coherent paragraphs and did much to clarify the text. Despite such help and encouragement, all errors of fact and weaknesses of interpretation remain ours alone.

Helsinki and Geneva, March 2006   *Tuomas Forsberg*
                                                             Graeme P. Herd

About the authors

Dr Tuomas Forsberg is Acting Professor of World Politics at the University of Helsinki and adjunct professor at the University of Lapland. Between 2002 and 2004 he was Professor of Western European Security Studies at the George C. Marshall European Center for Security Studies, Garmisch-Partenkirchen, Germany. Prior to that he worked as senior researcher and acting director at the Finnish Institute of International Affairs. His research has dealt primarily with European security issues, focusing on ESDP, Germany, Russia and Northern Europe, and he has published in journals including *Co-operation and Conflict, European Security, Geopolitics, Journal of Peace Research, Political Science Quarterly, Review of International Studies and Security Dialogue*. His most recent publication (as co-editor) is *Finland and Crises: From the Years of Danger to the Terrorist Attacks* (Helsinki: Gaudeamus, 2003).

Dr Graeme P. Herd is a resident Faculty Member at the Geneva Centre for Security Policy and is involved with expert training in comprehensive international peace and security policy for mid-career diplomats, military officers, and civil servants from foreign, defence, and other relevant ministries, as well as from international organizations. He is also an Associate Fellow of the International Security Programme at Chatham House. Between 2002 and 2005 he was Professor of Civil-Military Relations and Faculty Director of Research at the George C. Marshall European Center for Security Studies, Garmisch-Partenkirchen. He has published extensively on aspects of contemporary security politics, in journals including *Armed Forces & Society, Co-operation and Conflict, European Security, Journal of Peace Research, Journal of Slavic Military Studies, Mediterranean Politics, Political Science Quarterly, Security Dialogue* and *The World Today*. His books include *Russia and the Regions: Strength through Weakness* (London and New York: RoutledgeCurzon, 2003) and *Soft Security Threats and European Security* (Oxford and New York: Routledge 2005), co-edited with Anne Aldis. His latest book is forthcoming 2006 and focuses on countering ideological support for terrorism.

1

The divided West: challenges and obstacles

The deterioration in transatlantic relations during the presidency of George W. Bush and the exposure of latent cleavages within and between European states have serious consequences for global stability in the twenty-first century. Are these tensions enduring or temporary, deep-seated or personality-driven? What are their causes, and what are the consequences for transatlantic foreign and security policy-making on an individual, joint and collective basis? By 2006, strategic divorce had not materialized, but strategic realignment had yet to occur: 'After half a century of partnership, the "pillars of the free world" are too far apart to be reunited by an archway.'[1] The dynamic events before and after the US-led Iraq war of 2003 and the policy and power shifts that underpinned them appear to lack the constructive potential to generate a push for 'strategic renewal' or the destructive power to enforce a total 'strategic divorce'. If neither strategic divorce nor strategic renewal is likely to occur, then strategic dissonance and continued turbulence become the default transatlantic condition. In other words, the trauma that emerged as a result of the Iraq war remains unresolved. Its causes are still poorly understood, let alone managed, and the dynamics that generate its power still have the potential to resurface and further fragment and paralyse the unity of purpose and action of the transatlantic security community.

Strategic divorce suggests a transatlantic world in which duplication of functions and confusion over roles, missions and duties within and between NATO and the EU are rampant: doctrinal and institutional competition is predominant, with little or no coordination apparent. Strategic realignment suggests that a complementary division of labour, responsibility and resources has been brokered, allowing the most efficient and effective means to be deployed towards agreed strategic ends. Strategic dissonance falls between the two: the lasting and all-embracing solutions implied by strategic realignment fail to characterize the current transatlantic relationship, but the complete breakdown, chaos and confusion engendered by strategic

1

divorce do not do so either. Instead, a fluid transatlantic environment replete with uneasy compromises has emerged, one that more or less manages the contradictions and tensions between strategic means and ends. This alternative future has the appearance of an unstable and dysfunctional transatlantic half-way house where policy approaches are incomplete, initiatives are politically half-baked and operations are militarily half-cocked. But is such an appearance deceptive? Is constructive strategic dissonance a rhetorical fig leaf that cloaks a deeply divided West or is it set to become an effective, self-sustaining and enduring transatlantic approach to global security issues?

Before addressing these questions, the emergence of strategic dissonance as something more than a temporary transatlantic default position needs to be examined. How might such an outcome be accounted for? This book argues that just as it is difficult to envisage conditions under which strategic divorce would occur, so strategic realignment and reformation are unlikely in the short and medium term. Of the three possible transatlantic futures – divorce, realignment and dissonance – strategic dissonance best reflects and supports the foreign and security policies of the 'five Europes'– Atlantic Europe, Core Europe, New Europe, Non-aligned Europe and Periphery Europe – into which the continent appears to have become divided. The first three divisions describe a traditional Franco-German axis at Europe's core and, on the other hand, a 'New Europe' to the east (the new NATO and EU entrants) and those states in 'Atlantic Europe' (such as the UK, the Netherlands, Denmark and Portugal) that have always demonstrated a pro-US foreign and security policy perspective. 'Non-aligned Europe' (consisting of Finland, Sweden, Austria and Ireland) and, to a greater extent, 'Periphery Europe' (those European states that are not members of NATO or the EU, such as Belarus, Moldova, Russia and Ukraine) appear to be marginalized from the mainstream; Russia aside, they have little ability to shape the transatlantic relationship and the European security agenda. Strategic dissonance allows 'Non-aligned Europe' to maintain equidistance between 'Core Europe' and 'Atlantic Europe'; it lowers the risks and political trade-off costs for 'New Europe' and provides 'Periphery Europe' with an ideal strategic environment in which to pick and choose policy responses to particular issues and to float freely between coalitions. Given the financial costs or, more precisely, the absence of political will to finance strategic realignment and also a genuinely different strategic world view, realignment according to a US-imposed vision is not in the interests of 'Core Europe'.

At the same time, however, the high military and political consequences of strategic divorce also rule out that possibility. 'Managed dissonance' represents the line of least resistance for 'Core Europe'. Even 'Atlantic Europe' can make strategic dissonance pay dividends. The opposition of 'Core Europe' to US policies and influence increases the value of the United Kingdom in American eyes: its support provides the United States with legitimacy and multilateral cover when needed and its outreach and relations with 'New Europe' provide a European rationale for supporting the US that would otherwise be lacking. Thus strategic dissonance is not so much a condition brought about by temporary aberrations and disagreements within the transatlantic security community as it is a natural and instinctive default position that reflects the material interests and supports the policy preferences of all five Europes. Arguably, this is also in US interests: the challenges, obstacles and dilemmas of the global war on terrorism have created a weaker and more divided Europe, and this enables cherry-picking and coalition-building on US terms.

STRATEGIC DIVORCE, REALIGNMENT OR DISSONANCE?

The number and complexity of the issues on the post-9/11 global security agenda are growing. This agenda demands a sustained, comprehensive and unified transatlantic response if it is to be managed effectively. In 2002–3, the question of how to manage the perceived Iraqi threat seriously stressed the integrity and foundations of the transatlantic partnership. In 2005, the possible lifting of the EU arms embargo to China in the face of US opposition and also divergent US and European approaches to managing Iranian and North Korean nuclear ambitions and the Israeli–Palestinian conflict were outstanding challenges to international stability. In view of these present challenges and future threats, will the transatlantic community be able to act effectively in coping with these sources of insecurity? Or have the transatlantic trauma of 2002–3 and the causes and dynamics that underpin it essentially disabled a unified response and generated such tension and mistrust that the transatlantic relationship itself is now a source of insecurity for the United States and Europe?

There are few recent issues in international politics that have generated as much controversy and angst as the transatlantic rift; it was as traumatic as it was unexpected. As late as 2001, it was predicted that the 'EU–US relationship will evolve towards greater partnership than conflict'.[2] The crisis of 2002–3 threatened to divide the NATO alliance and split the 'West' into competing blocs and coalitions, fracturing it to such an extent that one might wonder whether the 'West' could still exist as a coherent and operative entity. How serious are the divergences in transatlantic relations in the early twenty-first century? Are the debates currently raging over military capabilities, an overabundance or lack of political will and the use of force as part of NATO's new collective security role merely the contemporary echo of the collective defence disputes of the Cold War such as the Suez crisis, the Skybolt affair or the intermediate nuclear missile crisis in Europe of the 1980s? Do these disputes reflect natural and inevitable growing pains within the alliance as it refocuses and adjusts its role, missions and duties from collective and territorial defence towards out-of-area expeditionary war fighting and peacekeeping? If so, will the strategic consensus within the alliance be reformed by an increase of military capabilities among European NATO partners and lead to strategic renewal? Or has a basic and fundamental disconnect emerged that will, with or without greater parity in military capabilities, lead to 'strategic divorce' and the demise of the transatlantic relationship as we know it?

Today, almost all analysts, policy-makers, practitioners, academics, and journalists argue that the Iraq crisis in 2003 was much more serious than any previous crisis in transatlantic relations. However, assessments differ as to the extent of the seriousness and the potential for managing its consequences. We consider that the future of the relationship will follow one of the three possible paths indicated above: renewal of the transatlantic partnership through strategic realignment, transformation and institutional reformation; irrevocable strategic divorce generated by a combination of intent and neglect; and continued strategic dissonance or turbulence in the near and medium term, driven by an inability either to summon the courage and political will to embrace an agreed realignment agenda or to accept the consequences and disruption to the international system of strategic divorce.

Those who warn of the possibilities of strategic divorce point to a growing strategic disjunction, highlighted by divergent responses to 9/11, that, they contend, undercuts efforts at renewal or reformation. This tendency could become a dominant trend and lead to a decoupling of US and European strategic cultures, policies and objectives. Robert Kagan's strategic formulation best captures the spirit informing this disjunction: Americans are from Mars and Europeans are from Venus; they do not inhabit the same planet.[3] Strategic divorce unfolds, and it offers few and only temporary and limited possibilities of rapprochement in some contested transatlantic security issues. The Bush administration no longer represents the same America that came to Europe's aid after the Second World War: the old world and the new world have simply grown apart, both conceptually and as a working reality.[4] As François Heisbourg has contended, 'in strategic terms, the Atlantic Alliance belongs to the past, along with the overall network of permanent defence alliances between the US and its European and Asian-Pacific allies established after World War II'.[5] Others have noted the growing gaps in perception and policy between Europe and the US[6] or the structural forces that pull them apart.[7] According to this variant, 'counterbalance' is perceived as 'equality': for the Europeans, the transatlantic partnership requires a strong and confident Europe; a counterweight Europe is essential for an effective and united alliance.[8]

The rise of anti-Americanism throughout Europe appears to be connected to an increase in US unilateralism in international affairs and a deep distrust, even fear, among its erstwhile allies of the United States' attempt to build an imperial 'world order' and 'the overall impact of American society (including [its] government) on the rest of the world'.[9] In turn, the United States' increased mistrust of Europe is reflected in its perceptions of Europe's weakness and lack of political will to address the post-9/11 world and deal decisively with global security threats. The inability or unwillingness of European NATO allies to undertake reform, in particular to tackle the agenda of the Prague Capabilities Commitment (PCC) (see below), points to a clear trend. The June 2003 NATO meeting to assess the allies' response to the PCC's five core functions noted very little progress. In 2005, the United States, with an all-volunteer force, spent over $420 billion on defence. NATO's European members combined only managed to stump up around half that amount between them, much of it on personnel costs, little on research and development. Germany, for example, as the second-largest ally in terms of population, spends only 1.2–1.3 per cent of GDP per annum on defence, admittedly with four per cent of GDP per annum (€80–90 billion) transferred to the former German Democratic Republic since unification. The US assumes the lion's share of the load, a politically unpopular and unsustainable definition of 'burden-sharing'. If the allies are unwilling to undertake serious defence reform, then NATO becomes a two-tier alliance that is increasingly dysfunctional and ripe for collapse.

Successful strategic realignment would prevent the possibility of strategic divorce. Salvation is possible through actively working to close the transatlantic strategic and military capabilities gap and making efforts to achieve strategic reformation and renewal. The alliance is in need of renewal in order to manage the threats of the twenty-first century: 'American and European policies no longer centre round the transatlantic alliance to the same overriding extent as in the past. As a result, it is no longer simply a question of adapting transatlantic institutions to new realities.'[10] According to this future possibility, the United States and its European partners forge a new strategic vision of world order, integrate their military and security structures more closely and, by addressing capability differences, create deployable, employable and sustainable forces that can counter threats to transatlantic stability. European NATO member states support the NATO Response Force (NRF); and at the same time, the EU members support a credible European security and defence policy in a collective security role that can operate outside Europe. The EU is providing Javier Solana, its foreign policy

5

head, with much greater powers, to allow his office to carry more weight. It is increasing its (in Solana's words) 'laughable budget' and its staff and is streamlining the decision-making process. It is also rectifying the obstacles that Solana has identified: 'Our system of external representation with constantly changing faces, an inflation of actors, and sometimes changing priorities is simply no longer adapted to the modern world and to our ambition to be a serious actor on the international scene.'[11]

In short, a cautiously optimistic approach to transatlantic relations can be embraced and supported by the realization that 'The United States and Europe do not constitute power-political and socioeconomic antagonism. It is the design of critical choices – that generates transatlantic disputes over a wide range of policy areas.'[12] According to this perspective, although the US–Europe relationship is 'uncertain and challenged', it 'is on a solid foundation'.[13] Flexibility and cooperation can overcome the transatlantic crisis because 'the crisis in the transatlantic relationship is a crisis of will and not of principle. And it will be overcome through action and not rhetoric. Looking beneath the rhetoric, there is some evidence to suggest that the will to overcome the crisis exists.'[14]

Despite the best intentions of the transatlantic partners, might not strategic dissonance – a continuation of the current level of transatlantic turbulence into the medium term – best characterize the transatlantic relationship?[15] Such an outcome rests on the realization of at least two key assumptions. First, the forces that might break the alliance asunder lack the power to do so. The United States has never rejected all multilateral frameworks or policy approaches. Even when it has acted unilaterally, multilateral overtones have been apparent, for example in allies' permission for overflights, basing rights and access to infrastructure and intelligence sharing. Its experience in Iraq has tempered faith in the efficacy of unrestrained US military power: the 'battle for Iran' is unlikely to replace Iraq as the new 'central front' in the global war on terrorism.

Secondly, the forces that might enable a reformation of the alliance lack the political strength and economic power to reforge the transatlantic relationship. Indeed, although many European states may be quietly congratulating themselves on their foresight in expressing scepticism about the weapons of mass destruction–al-Qaeda–Iraq nexus, it should be recalled that the EU could not agree a common approach to issues of good governance and human rights, for example in Chechnya.[16]

Despite the apparent convergence towards strategic consensus with the US through overlapping security strategies, there are important differences between the two sides. For the EU, pre-emptive action means diplomatic and economic pressure, the exercise of 'soft' power within multilateral frameworks. For the United States, it means the deployment of military force, unilaterally if need be, or through a 'coalition of the willing', if possible. In short, the EU lacks the finance, decision-making capacity and 'political will' to develop 'hard', military power outside NATO; and in the eyes of some, it has become Kagan's caricature of a participative supranational Kantian paradise: 'It is symptomatic of Europe's weakness that the dispatch of 1,400 troops to the Congo, where thousands are being massacred at present, is hailed as an important step in its military revival.'[17]

Let us now identify and review the nature of the dynamic events that have generated such divisions and mistrust within the transatlantic security community.

TRANSATLANTIC RELATIONS: DYNAMICS OF STRATEGIC DIVORCE OR RENEWAL?

There is no space here to reiterate all the crises that occurred in transatlantic relations during the Cold War. Historians disagree over their importance almost as much as policy analysts do about the crises of today. The dominant view, however, is that the United States was a benign hegemon that created what has been variously termed an 'empire by invitation'[18] or an 'empire by consent' based on multilateral institutions and practices, containment and deterrence.[19] Other historians, drawing on newly opened archival sources, have emphasized that there were more and deeper transatlantic disputes than appeared to be the case.[20] Nevertheless, disagreements among the allies during the Cold War were undoubtedly managed, and the fundamental basis of the alliance was not seriously contested.

What is relevant to this analysis is that a picture of harmonious transatlantic relations prevailed among political elites. This picture of the past was also projected on to the future. Accordingly, NATO was to remain the enduring central institution and anchor. It would unite the US and its European partners around a shared strategic vision of world order, and there was the political will to integrate their military and security structures more closely in order to counter threats to transatlantic stability. It is this vision, or illusion, that is now highly contested.

The change of vision is palpable if we compare the post-9/11 period to the immediate post-Cold War era. Then, transatlantic ties were strong: the US–EU Transatlantic Declaration of 1990 reflected a traditional internationalist US foreign policy, and US–EU goodwill was reinforced during the Clinton presidency by the publication of the New Atlantic Agenda in 1995, which promoted global and regional cooperation, as well as by an institutionalization of the transatlantic relationship through annual EU–US summits. NATO re-established itself as the central pillar of Europe's security architecture, and the presence of US military and political power in Europe continued to be appreciated.

Five dynamic events, reflecting and reinforcing underlying trends and processes, helped to undermine the certainties that had shaped transatlantic relations in the Cold War and the immediate post-Cold War era: the Kosovo campaign in 1999; the election of George W. Bush as president in 2000; 9/11; the NATO Prague Summit of 2002; and the Iraq war of 2003. The result has been greater ambiguity, ambivalence and unpredictability in transatlantic relations. Although these events begin with transatlantic disputes over how to approach and manage the war in Bosnia, the Kosovo campaign of 1999 highlights more clearly the serious differences in both strategic thinking and capabilities between Europe and America. Moreover, the lessons learned in that crisis acted as a catalyst in framing subsequent points of disagreement and conflict between the transatlantic allies. As John Ikenberry has noted, 'perhaps the NATO campaign in retrospect will be seen as a watershed moment when European allies begin to develop more independent military capabilities, setting the stage for future strategic rivalry'.[21]

When NATO launched its war against Yugoslavia over Kosovo in March 1999, the alliance looked healthier than ever. Operation Allied Force demonstrated that NATO was both able and willing to engage in a large-scale coercive collective security action – that is to operate outside the borders of its member states in a non-collective defence role – in accordance with its new security concept. The decision to intervene was difficult to agree upon, as it occurred without a UN mandate and thus was illegal under international law. But it was regarded as necessary, legitimate and justified by a humanitarian rationale (reinforced by the failure to prevent the 1995 Srebrenica massacre), and almost all NATO members (with the partial exception of Greece) and states in the immediate region supported it. In April 1999, the alliance also celebrated its fiftieth anniversary, and the Washington Summit of that month was simultaneously the first integration into NATO of former communist states, opening up the prospect that the transatlantic alliance would shift further eastward over the next decades. At the same time, the Kosovo war was sandwiched between the Franco-British St Malo Summit in 1998 and the EU's Cologne Summit in 2000, the former initiating the European Security and Defence Policy (ESDP) and the latter consolidating it.

However, the NATO alliance's conduct in fighting the Kosovo war received mixed and, in many cases, negative reviews by the US and European NATO members. In particular, the campaign embodied the weaknesses and limitations associated with 'war by committee'. As Lord Robertson, a former secretary general of NATO, has stated, '... in an age where threats give little warning before they strike, NATO suffered from the perception in some circles that its consensual decision-making culture was too slow and cumbersome to deliver in time'.[22] The parallel political review process that the US and NATO chains of command demanded, together with NATO's cumbersome decision-making structures, was detrimental to the achievement of 'closure'/victory in the campaign. This perception was particularly strong in the United States.[23] Britain, in turn, argued that the US lack of political will to consider the possible use of ground troops at the beginning of the air campaign undermined the deterrent effect of NATO. Perhaps more importantly, a capability and technology gap between the United States and all other allies was highlighted, with the former deploying 80 per cent of all precision weapons in the campaign. In all events, the Kosovo war led the French minister of foreign affairs Hubert Védrine to adopt the term 'hyper-power' to describe America's power and influence.[24] Open transatlantic political quarrels and structural disparities sparked an intense debate over 'drifting apart', which European nostalgia for the Clinton era should not obscure.[25]

The second event that profoundly affected transatlantic relations was George W. Bush's election as president of the United States in November 2000. His foreign policy proposals when a candidate suggested that transatlantic relations could be strengthened. His team was highly critical of President Clinton's foreign policy: it had no clear idea of US national interests; it was too idealistic and orientated towards humanitarianism; it was too reliant on multilateral institutions; and it was militarily over-extended and buttressed by the illusion that democracy could be exported through US politico-military intervention. Bush indicated that, if elected, his administration would offer a realistic, 'humble', pragmatic and limited engagement in world affairs based on a new hierarchy of national interests, the reinvigoration of the United States' military power and a diminution of the ideological component of its foreign policy. Once in office, the new Republican administration lowered its predecessor's focus on terrorism by non-state actors (including al-Qaeda); it stressed the danger of rogue states and put forward a state-centric agenda based on 'a clear and classical statement of deterrence'.[26]

Even before 9/11, it was clear that President Bush's foreign policy would represent a different kind of America from what had been suggested by his electoral rhetoric. The domestic values his administration projected did not resonate well in Europe, nor did his approach to international issues, despite the rhetoric of the presidential campaign. Bush's decision to ignore the Kyoto Protocol on climate change and not to ratify the treaty on the International Criminal Court (ICC) or to renew the Comprehensive Test Ban Treaty, the Landmine Treaty, the US–Soviet Strategic Arms Limitation Treaty and the Protocol on Biological Weapons were cases in point. In security issues, the domestic debate revolved around US plans to build a national missile defence system.[27] These decisions and plans evoked strong protests from the European allies: the stereotypical image of a simple-minded unilateralist, a 'toxic Texan' with a cowboy mentality who had little education and less understanding of international affairs, was forged in the pre-9/11 period.

The atrocities of 9/11 constituted the third dynamic in transatlantic relations. As Europeans spontaneously expressed their solidarity towards the Americans, a strong desire arose to strengthen the transatlantic relationship. The attacks were widely understood as threatening the whole of 'Western civilization' and thus international stability. As a result, the United States and Europe united more forcefully than ever, with the German chancellor Gerhard Schröder offering 'unlimited solidarity' and Le Monde declaring that 'We are all Americans now.'[28] For the first time in its history, NATO decided to invoke its Article 5 collective defence commitment. Also, 9/11 propelled the Bush administration to declare a global war on terrorism. According to this post-9/11 outlook, elaborated in the new American National Security Strategy (NSS) of September 2002, the nexus of terrorists, tyrants, 'terrible weapons' and failed states was deemed to pose imminent threats to the US; pre-emptive strikes against these foes could be justified. The NSS served as the basis of the Iraq war in 2003, and Operation Enduring Freedom of 7 October 2001 laid the framework by attacking Taliban–al-Qaeda links in Afghanistan. In response to the shocking impact of 9/11, the Bush administration determined that it would use force abroad in regions of critical strategic interest and that it 'would seek to dominate the international system to such an extent that no strategic challenge would ever again be posed'.[29]

The 'lessons learned' from 9/11 impacted heavily on the transatlantic response to the terrorist attacks (particularly the foreign policy reconstruction of the Bush administration), and to an extent they complemented the conclusions drawn during the Kosovo campaign about the utility of NATO. Operation Enduring Freedom was fully supported by European governments as a legitimate act of self-defence, although public support was weaker. But there was concern over the direction that the global war on terrorism might take, exacerbated by President Bush's 2002 State of the Union Address to the Congress. In it, he identified an 'axis of evil' consisting of Iraq, Iran and North Korea as the greatest threat to world peace. The Europeans were 'shocked and stunned and not to say a little amazed' by the way these three different rogue states were lumped together. Moreover, they were critical of the Manichaean world view that supported the US analysis and worried that they would not be consulted in the conduct of the war on terrorism.[30]

'Far from encouraging the emergence of a shared global vision', argues Peter Ludlow, 'the September 11th attacks highlighted the fact that most Europeans and most Americans tend to look at the world in very different ways.'[31]

The United States did little to engage its European NATO allies after 9/11, despite their offers of support. This diplomatic failure was partially driven by its perception that they had little to offer and even less to contribute quickly in response to the events of 9/11. This reaction both undermined NATO and highlighted its lack of relevance. Although its support proved to be politically useful, the US rejected its offer to conduct war-fighting operations in Afghanistan: 'The Bush administration viewed NATO's historic decision to aid the United States under Article 5 less as a boon than a booby trap.'[32] In this sense, although its collective defence concept was enacted, NATO failed to exercise it fully. Part of the explanation of why it did not do so is rooted in the US perception of NATO's failings and limitations in Operation Allied Force. In the words of the US secretary of defence, 'the mission defined the coalition, not the coalition the mission.'[33] The implications of the global war on terrorism and the US-led and -inspired 'coalitions of the willing' – à la carte multilateralism – were apparent to European NATO: the US would lead and other states would follow; opposition would only encourage the US to step outside the international system completely. NATO would be politically neutered and reduced to a military tool box from which coalitions could pick and choose assets to be deployed.

A fourth dynamic occurred with the November 2002 NATO summit in Prague. NATO heads of state and government met on 21–22 November for a 'transformation summit'. They invited seven countries to accession talks and committed themselves to equip the alliance with new capabilities to meet the security threats of the twenty-first century, including the creation of a NATO response force, and to enhance its existing military capabilities. As the secretary general Lord Robertson stated, 'This is not business as usual, but the emergence of a new and modernised NATO, fit for the challenges of the new century.'[34] As in the alliance's general response to 9/11, the debates that preceded the summit were informed by lessons learned from Kosovo but also by the imperatives that flowed from 9/11. The summit appeared to repair the alliance temporarily and to give it new direction, as will be discussed below.

NATO's deficiencies were exposed and addressed. The low defence expenditure of the European NATO member states and the largely static nature of their force structures were compounded by their lack of strategic mobility and their poor reconnaissance and surveillance capability. These shortcomings had been exposed in the Balkan wars, the experience of which again focused transatlantic debates on the optimum burden-sharing and division of labour within NATO.[35] In addition, the new NATO first-echelon members (those states – the Czech Republic, Hungary and Poland – that had joined NATO in the first new wave) were perceived to have performed poorly, with political elites unwilling to spend political capital in order to persuade their publics of the necessity and virtue of NATO intervention.

To solve these problems, the summit focused its attention on three issues. The first was a new mission. The 53-year-old alliance had at last to turn from collective security roles within the European theatre to supporting European and North American interests worldwide, especially in North Africa, the southern Caucasus, Central Asia and the Middle East. It had to become a strategic actor capable of projecting power globally. For the European allies (except France and the United Kingdom) to deploy and sustain expeditionary troops in war-fighting or peacekeeping roles globally, new capabilities and a new mindset were needed. The Prague Capabilities Commitment addressed this shortfall, focusing on the development of five core capabilities: strategic airlift (the US has 222 C-17s; the UK has four; and other allies have none); air-to-air refuelling; precision-guided munitions; and communications. The NATO Response Force, the fifth capability, was to be the catalyst and the most visible and useful objective of the PCC. It would consist of 20,000 troops and be technologically advanced, deployable, interoperable and sustainable by 2006. By October 2003, these troops were to be sustainable for operating in the field for 14–30 days. The NRF was understood to be a means of improving the NATO capabilities of European states that would, with no additional spending, help to keep NATO interoperable through intense periods of training and deployment on missions.

Secondly, a decision was taken to integrate seven new members (Bulgaria, Estonia, Latvia, Lithuania, Romania, Slovakia and Slovenia) into the alliance. However, this second-echelon enlargement was shaped by the first echelon's performance after integration. The lack of support for the Kosovo campaign from the public and elites of the Czech Republic, Slovakia and Poland, the poor rate of defence reform and force restructuring by these states since their integration into NATO and their low rates of defence expenditure were compounded by the fact that it was 'more difficult to gain compromise once the new allies were members'.[36] 'Once bitten twice shy' became NATO's watchword: it could exert reform pressure on candidate members only through the threat of exclusion; once they were integrated, leverage was lost. The new NATO members were also strongly encouraged to reform their internal security structures: the civil–military focus of the Membership Action Plan (MAP) process was extended to include more explicitly civil security sector reform in which security/intelligence services, ministries of the interior, emergency ministries, border guards, tax police etc. could all perform a role within the framework of the global war on terrorism. This emphasis on transforming NATO complemented 'defence transformation' in the US, an acceleration of the move to integrated high-technology-dependent, rapidly mobile and well-armed response forces with a global reach.

Thirdly, the establishment of the NATO–Russia Council (NRC) in May 2002 had created a 'new relationship' with Russia.[37] The Prague Summit welcomed what it termed 'the significant achievements' of the NRC, noting progress in areas such as peacekeeping, defence reform, WMD proliferation, search and rescue, civil emergency planning, theatre missile defence and the struggle against terrorism.[38] Relations between Russia and NATO were becoming 'routinized' under the NRC as a practical agenda of activities was developed and an administrative capacity and a shared institutionalized culture took root. The agenda included discussions on theatre missile defence and research and development collaboration, search and rescue for submarines, joint peacekeeping efforts and joint airspace initiatives. Despite President Putin's objections to the Iraq war, Russia continued to promote security cooperation with the United States in the global war on terrorism. However, the Iraq war was discussed not by the NRC forum but in bilateral discussions between Washington and Moscow. The framework of the Russian–US strategic partnership rather than NATO was favoured, and this further underscored NATO's increasingly limited relevance to transatlantic relations.

The latent tensions exposed by Kosovo had slowly but inexorably evolved into simmering disagreement and discontent, and this was expressed at the Prague Summit. The United States' declaration of a global war on terrorism and its intervention in Afghanistan had the potential to bind transatlantic ties, but its use of a 'coalition of the willing' for the intervention and also the implications that this held for US security policy did not allow these ties to be consolidated. Open disagreements within the transatlantic security community continued to surface. These were particularly evident in France, which had been preoccupied with the exercise of American 'hyper-power' since the Clinton era, and in Germany. Chancellor Schröder was engaged in a closely fought political election, and he politicized his Social Democratic Party's opposition to US 'adventurism' in order to capture critical floating voters and to bolster his Green Party coalition allies. The 'Bush Doctrine' of pre-emption (articulated, as noted above, in the US National Security Strategy of September 2002) against countries that threaten the United States or that might conceivably threaten its primacy was perceived by some alliance members as liable to lead to neo-imperial 'adventures'. This had to be opposed or counterbalanced by a greater emphasis on NATO or other multilateral institutions such as the UN.[39]

The Prague Summit and the electoral cycles that buttressed it found the European NATO allies caught between a desire to respond in a meaningful way to the post-9/11 security environment and an unwillingness to accept substantial increases in defence expenditure and reforms of decision-making or to spend political capital in support of US initiatives in the face of over-whelming opposition from their publics. This general unwillingness and/or inability was juxtaposed with an apparently contradictory determination to rejuvenate NATO's role so as to keep the United States engaged in the alli-ance. An unanswered question was left hanging: were the new members to focus on niche capabilities that they would offer to the NRF or were they to contribute to EU peacekeeping and peace support operations? Most of them (and the majority of old NATO members) could not do both.

The final and most important dynamic was the decision, principally by the United States with Britain, to invade Iraq in the face of an alleged immi-nent strategic threat posed by Iraqi missiles, WMD and operational links to al-Qaeda. Although many pre-emptive wars have occurred in history, Oper-ation Iraqi Freedom, initiated on 20 March 2003, was the first pre-emptive war in accordance with the new US national security strategy. It ushered in 'an era in which the US has thrown off the constraints and balances of the multi-lateral system and exercised its enormous political and military supremacy on its own terms'.[40]

UN Security Council (UNSC) Resolution 1441 was passed unanimously in November 2002. Its passage was highly contested, however, and brought fully into the open the divisions between a number of European coun-tries and the United States. The basic message of the resolution was clear – Saddam should disarm – but ambiguity as to the consequences should he not cooperate papered over disagreements between the allies. The permanent UNSC members France and Russia demanded that the Security Council pass another resolution before the war could be declared legal. Germany, a rotating member of the Security Council, stated that it would not support the war in any case. France, Russia and Germany argued, along with non-aligned European states, that more time should be given to the UN weapons inspec-tions and to other diplomatic efforts to achieve Iraqi disarmament, the stated goal of the US and the UK. The strategic partnership between the United States and Turkey was deemed to be 'in tatters' too.[41] By contrast, appar-ently Atlanticist European NATO members signed the 'Letter of Eight'[42] in support of the US position on Iraq, and days later a further 10 'New European' states (the 'Vilnius 10') joined this group of pro-American countries.[43]

Germany's and France's resistance in the UN to the US-led push for war against Iraq also had consequences for the cohesion of NATO. The alliance was seriously disrupted when these two countries did not support the decision to start defensive preparations in Turkey in anticipation of a war in Iraq, on the grounds that such preparations would signal that war was inevitable. Turkey, in turn, refused to allow US troops to operate from its territory. Both these events led to widespread pessimism about NATO's future. In the words of Sir Timothy Garden (now Lord Garden), a defence analyst with the Royal United Services Institute and a former assistant chief of defence staff, 'If NATO is to be the stick for the United States to beat the Europeans into submitting to an American view of the world, then the alliance really is doomed.'[44]

During this period, the European Union was elaborating a draft constitution and strengthening its security and defence policy. In April 2003, France, Germany, Belgium and Luxembourg held an extraordinary meeting in Brussels, which US commentators dismissed as a 'chocolate summit'. The agenda of the meeting included discussion on the creation of a separate military headquarters for EU forces and the inserting of a mutual defence clause in the EU constitution. This was grist to the mill to those who predicted the emergence of the EU as a counterweight and competitor to the United States, which would lead to a 'strategic divorce' in the transatlantic relationship. It appeared that this EU quartet advocated a common command structure in the form of a multinational HQ, a separate planning cell, something akin to NATO Article 5 commitments, a separate defence procurement institution and a new EU defence college. As many of these tasks are currently undertaken by NATO in order to ensure the integration of member states' military establishments and planning resources, the proposals were seen as duplication, promoting institutional competition and violating the 'Berlin Plus' principles. (The 'Berlin Plus' arrangements, adopted on 17 March 2003, provide the basis for NATO–EU cooperation in crisis management by allowing EU access to NATO's collective assets and capabilities for EU-led operations. In effect, they allow the alliance to support EU-led operations in which NATO as a whole is not engaged.[45])

These splits among the allies now appeared to be fundamental in nature and constituted a crisis for NATO, comparable in its history only to the Suez crisis of 1956, when the US opposed occupation of the Suez canal by a French- and British-led 'coalition of willing' to the point of forcing a humiliating retreat by its erstwhile allies. The transatlantic rift over Iraq undercut the appearance of enduring Western collective unity and suggested that 'the visions of Europe and America will end up defeating each other – a tragedy for the West and the world in general'.[46] In the words of the US secretary of defence Donald Rumsfeld, Europe could be divided in two, between 'Old Europe' and 'New Europe', between those who chose to deal with existential threats and those who did not.[47] The strategic formula attributed to

Condoleezza Rice when she was national security adviser encapsulated the trauma in transatlantic relations: 'Forgive the Russians, ignore the Germans and punish the French.'[48] The US had the means, opportunity and motive to capitalize on European disagreements and build coalitions to undermine Franco-German pretensions to European hegemony. A balance between US hegemony, deterrence and containment, and consent had sustained America's benign hegemony in the Cold War. This balance was broken by its use of military pre-emption without the legitimacy of support by an alliance against a state, Iraq, which was both deterred and contained.

These five dynamics straddled the Clinton and Bush presidencies and the shift from Clinton's model of an economic superpower to Bush's model of a military superpower. They both generated and illustrated tensions and cleavages that were cumulative in nature but driven in the short term by French, German and Russian opposition to US intervention in Iraq without a second UN resolution. This opposition reflected overwhelming popular European public sentiment (and perhaps the silent majority within their elites). It also highlighted the European powers' inability either to prevent the US-led intervention by political and diplomatic means or to emulate it with military power. It underscored the realization that Europe lacked sufficient military power and political determination to become a global strategic power through the exercise of military force. These dynamics signposted a major change in the history of US foreign policy. The strategic focus of the United States had shifted: 'Kurdistan matters more to the United States than Kosovo, and Mesopotamia means more to the US than Macedonia. And in American thinking, after the Middle East will not come Europe, but East Asia.'[49]

For some, the cumulative impact of these dynamic events and the disparities, tensions and stresses they embodied had fractured the balance of power within NATO. It was clear that NATO had become a habit, not a necessity.[50] As a result, progress on the ESDP was imperative, but the dynamics themselves underlined the challenges and obstacles that this project would have to overcome: poor military capability, weak 'political will', ineffective decision-making structures and a now traumatized (if not schizophrenic) transatlantic strategic culture. For others, the shock of the crisis over NATO's role in the face of a US-led Iraq war, the vigorous intervention of aspirant, and now new, NATO and EU member states in current transatlantic debates and the opportunity for alliance members to build bridges afforded by the postwar reconstruction efforts in Afghanistan and Iraq may all help to reform transatlantic relations in the twenty-first century.

What are the factors and dynamics that currently shape the relationship? Which of these dynamics appears to be enduring and which could be subject to change, and under what conditions? The answers to these questions provide clearer signposts for identifying the particular path or at least general direction which the transatlantic alliance is likely to take.

The post-9/11 environment reflected and reinforced transatlantic strategic dissonance. It fractured pre-existing fault lines and consolidated realignments around concepts of 'Atlantic Europe', 'Core Europe', 'New Europe', 'Non-aligned Europe' and 'Periphery' Europe. These are not coherent entities. They reflect a conceptual shorthand that seeks to suggest that European blocs are capable of formation, even if their memberships are somewhat fluid, determined as much by contingency, the nature of specific security challenges and different understandings of the utility of force as by binding interests. This book deploys these concepts to bring fresh perspectives and insights to the analysis of the impact of transatlantic dissonance on European foreign and security policy preferences. But how might this transatlantic relationship be theorized, allowing analysts to dive beneath the flotsam and jetsam of contemporary issues and to better understand the nature of the underlying dynamic links and ties that bind the West?

To address this question, Chapter 2 focuses on placing the transatlantic relationship in a more rigorous and systematic theoretical framework in order to present more clearly the explanations of the trauma of 2002–3. It examines middle-range explanations, such as a diverging or converging of values, interests, strategic culture and the role that 'othering' and anti-Americanism play in transatlantic relations, and locates them within the realist, liberalist and constructivist paradigms. This chapter provides the means to systematize and deepen our understanding of different explanations given to the crisis in transatlantic relations in the hope that 'nothing is as practical as a good theory'. This serves as a bridge towards more academic literature, and gives coherence to the analysis that follows. Acknowledging the existence of different theories enables us to discuss a wider range of explanations than would otherwise be the case. We are then in a position to examine the five case studies that focus on the security policy implications of this divide.

Chapter 3 ('Atlantic Europe') examines the Blair government's attempts to navigate between US unilateralism and 'Euro-Gaullism'. Sceptics and outright opponents of the 'special relationship' argue that beneath the rhetoric of shared cultures, history, traditions and close military and security cooperation, the sad reality entails Britain providing a bilateral fig leaf for unilateral US power. Such a diplomatic cover is, as the EU gathers strength as a security actor, unsustainable: fence-sitting becomes increasingly precarious and, in the words of Yeats, the centre cannot hold. The chapter argues that

9/11 and Afghanistan reinforced the bridging role of Europe's pre-eminent Atlanticist state but that the Iraq war has brought the utility of such a policy into question. It suggests that under George W. Bush's second term, the limits of Britain's brand of Atlanticist behaviour are being exposed further.

Chapter 4 focuses on 'Core Europe', and takes Germany as its case study. It argues that Germany's foreign policy is best explained by reference not to pacifism or anti-Americanism but to a new assertiveness that is associated with the normalization of its foreign policy. Germany is increasingly determined to be part of the West but also to define what the 'West' itself is and how it should be understood, and it wants to shape the implications of this reassessment for questions of war and peace on the global stage. It remains to be seen whether the normalization of German foreign policy will facilitate or exacerbate German–US cooperation in facing pressing global security concerns. Germany has so far been able to argue against security policy initiatives, but it is unable or unwilling to position its opposition within a coherent alternative strategic context that supports its national interest. For now, the *Sonderweg* (a distinctive German path or approach to international relations) is rooted in constructive ambiguity: Germany's national interest is not defined, and so there is little basis upon which it can build allies in support of its strategic initiatives.

Chapter 5 identifies the countries of 'New Europe', an entity we take to consist of the majority of the 'Vilnius 10' states, which have recently been integrated into the EU and NATO or will be in the near future. These states are prepared to integrate into a common Euro-Atlantic defence culture; but, for the most part, they lack the ability to contribute to the new collective security roles of NATO in a meaningful way. The chapter suggests that the strong Atlanticist attitude of 'New Europe' has a limited shelf life. Although 'New Europe' will not become openly hostile to Washington after the Iraq involvement, its members are increasingly prepared to criticize US leadership and US-sponsored foreign and security policy initiatives. At the fundamental level of world views, the new members do not differ radically from the old members in terms of perspective and approach to international relations. In short, they are likely to become 'European', that is to be prepared on occasion to disagree with the mainstream perspective but in most cases to support the strengthening of the EU's foreign and security policy. The 'small-state complex' may assert itself in other new members as they oscillate between inclusionist and disillusionist experiences of membership. The trade-offs and costs incurred by 'New Europe' in its support for European or US priorities become less complex the more divided Europe remains or the more that US and European policy initiatives overlap. The more united Europe becomes and the greater the gulf becomes between US and European policy responses to security threats, the more stressed 'New Europe' becomes.

Chapter 6 discusses the impact of these debates on the security strategies of 'Non-aligned Europe'. Through comparative case studies of Finnish and Swedish responses to 9/11, it demonstrates that the states in this group do not act as a cohesive bloc. For different reasons, both Finland and Sweden have adopted non-alignment as a security strategy, and thus they do not necessarily share the same strategic thinking. But although, like 'Core Europe', they opposed intervention in Iraq, they reframed their 'military neutrality' and adopted a policy of equidistance between 'Core Europe' and 'Atlantic Europe'. This policy will become increasingly hard to sustain unless strategic dissonance continues: convergence between 'Core Europe' and 'Atlantic Europe' on the role and function of NATO and on the ESDP and the divisions of labour within it leave non-aligned states with little room for manoeuvre.

In Chapter 7 ('Periphery Europe'), we examine Russia as an example of a state that has little or no prospect of integration into the EU and/or NATO but that still aims to strengthen its partnership and cooperation with these organizations. The chapter argues that Russia has the potential to become a disruptive actor, whether by default or design, in transatlantic relations. The possibility of Russia developing this approach is apparent, but it has yet to adopt such a policy in any systematic way. Paradoxically, the very divisions that characterize relationships between the 'new', 'core', 'non-aligned' and 'Atlantic' European states may make such a policy unfeasible: Russia's attempts to exploit rifts may serve only to heal them. Transatlantic relations can even be reinvigorated around support for nascent democracies in 'Periphery Europe'.

The book concludes in Chapter 8 by examining possible 'transatlantic futures'. It is suggested that the Euro-Atlantic security community may attempt to manage threats by strengthening global institutions, by increasing Euro-Atlantic institutional cooperation or, as appears most likely, by adopting a compartmentalized and differentiated approach over a range of issues that combines institutional cooperation, competition and ad hoc coalitions. This chapter argues that the dominant foreign and security policies of the five Europes push towards strategic dissonance and that this dissonance has the potential to be constructive rather than destructive when it comes to transatlantic management of key global security concerns.

2

Theory and the transatlantic crisis

The clash between the United States and the principal European states in 2002–3 surprised most scholars of international relations almost as much as the sudden end of the Cold War and the collapse of the Soviet Union had done more than 10 years earlier. Although theories can retrospectively account for the emergence of this transatlantic crisis, the dominant approaches to understanding the world order that emerged after the end of the Cold War had little to say on the prospect of such a clash. This predictive failure suggests that theories were unable to recognize or unwilling to account for the underlying schisms among the transatlantic partners.

Liberals, celebrating Francis Fukuyama's version of the 'end of the history', stressed the shared historical ties and democratic traditions that bound the US to Europe.[1] The West had won, and much credit could be attributed to the enduring strength of the transatlantic relationship. There was a strong belief in the continuity of liberal democratic political cultures and convictions, common interests and goals (for example liberty, human rights, democratization and stability), robust institutions and a shared security community – a community within which war between its members is, in Karl Deutsch's words, 'unthinkable'.[2]

Realists were more sanguine in their analysis of the end of the Cold War, but even those who predicted a future still dominated by the use of force and conflict did not predict the levels of tension, open division and distrust that emerged between America and Europe. John Mearsheimer envisaged renewed rivalry among the European powers themselves after the retreat of the United States from Europe following the end of the Cold War.[3] Samuel Huntington, in turn, put forward a new paradigm of emerging clashes between, not within, civilizations.[4] Kenneth Waltz and Christopher Layne predicted that other countries would try to bring American power into balance, but they both focused mainly on Japan, although they mentioned Germany and the EU, if it managed to achieve unity, as potential great powers too.[5] Owen

Harris was one of the few analysts who took note of President Gorbachev's spokesman for foreign affairs Gennadiy Gerasimov, who famously cautioned that 'We have done to you the most terrible thing we could have done. We have deprived you of an enemy.' Harris argued in 'Collapse of "the West"' that without a common external threat or enemy, the West would divide and then collapse. But despite the title of his article (it was published in *Foreign Affairs* in the issue after Huntington's 'clash of civilizations' thesis),[6] Harris's main arguments were directed at NATO's enlargement rather than at relations between the US and Europe. Additionally, it was perhaps only a few marginal scholars, such as the Marxist Warren Wagar, who, with reference to world systems analysis, noted the inevitability of conflict between capitalist power centres and thus argued that the US–Europe nexus would face growing stress and tension, leading to nuclear conflict.[7]

Of course, the transatlantic crisis is hardly of the same order as the clash between the West and radical Islamism that became manifest after 9/11 in 2001. As 'poisoned' as relations between some European capitals and Washington became in 2002–3, there is still no sign of a major rupture in relations, much less a military confrontation, between Europe and the United States.[8] In this sense, as war between the US and Europe has not become 'thinkable', the security community remains intact and Deutsch's assertion that pluralistic security communities have a high rate of survival holds true.[9] Nevertheless, this 'family quarrel' was so unexpected and of such significance that it cannot be characterized as a temporary transatlantic spat, a storm in the proverbial teacup. The scholarly community must provide a sustained account of why the disagreement took place, to highlight the root causes and to assess the foreign and security policy implications for future transatlantic relations and European security. A clearer analysis of the causes of this rupture provides a framework that can help to analyse the potential future consequences of this division.

A reading of various political commentaries, newspaper columns, think tank reports and scientific articles and books in preparation for this research project made clear that there are two basic approaches to explaining the transatlantic rift. Some attribute the split to structural factors, such as growing power and value asymmetries, that push the US and Europe apart; others believe that the crisis was more a result of circumstantial factors, such as diplomatic ineptness and poor personal relations between leaders.[10] Analysts and commentators who are generally optimistic about the prospects of the alliance's ability to reform gradually and remain the central anchor in transatlantic relations argue that the crisis was produced by circumstantial factors. These analysts contend that transatlantic disagreements are explained by some kind of irrational ideological deviation that runs counter to the rational interests of states and institutions on either side of the transatlantic divide, undermining attempts at closer and more coherent cooperation. Explanations of this sort refer to the 'cowboy mindset' of George W. Bush and his administration, the disruptive power of short-sighted tactical electoral politics or narrow economic interests, the miscommunication of aims and objectives or poor personal relations. By contrast, those who argue that the transatlantic alliance can be saved only through fundamental root-and-branch reform, imposed if need be, explain the trauma by reference to more fundamental structural factors, be they a gradual divergence of strategic interests owing to an enlarged power gap or a divergence of shared identities and societal values. The only question was when, not if, this divergence would surface.

Most analyses rely upon a mixture of these explanations. There is much to commend this 'third way' approach, as the transatlantic crisis cannot be accounted for by a single factor or one set of limited explanations. What have generally been absent from the debate about its causes are more systematic accounts that assess the relative importance of the various factors and a deeper analysis of the mechanisms and processes that generated the crisis. As we shall argue, there were different mechanisms and causal dynamics at work in different European countries. Also, any theory that purports to explain why the US and Europe collided should be able to explain why Europeans disagreed among themselves over the proper way to respond to US policies.

In this chapter, we shall examine the myriad explanations offered by the realist, liberal and constructivist theoretical frameworks.[11] This approach should provide a more systematic basis for an assessment of the causes of the rift than the simpler exposition in the first chapter. This then offers a framework, a reference point through which we can discuss the turbulence in transatlantic relations from the perspectives of the different Europes that appear to have been created.

DISTRIBUTION OF POWER AND THREAT

Realism is the dominant perspective in international relations, but it is hardly a single theory. It is based on a set of assumptions according to which states are rational and unitary actors; and as the central actors in international relations, they are inherently selfish. The goal of a state is to maximize its national interest, and the accumulation and exercise of power is the key to understanding international behaviour and state motivation. Archetypal realists define state interests in strictly material terms and explain policy change as a result of the shifting distribution of power, particularly military and economic power, rather than as a consequence of the histories and identities of states. For realists, military power remains the most effective means of ensuring national security and state survival. For this reason, the military distribution of power continues to be essential.[12]

In the Cold War, the US and (western) Europe were close partners because they faced a common enemy: communism and the Soviet Union. As Lord Robertson, a former NATO secretary general, has noted, the allies' common interest in avoiding 'the spectre of Soviet troops pouring through the Fulda Gap' suppressed the differences that existed among them.[13] NATO was the embodiment of American–European mutual dependence: European NATO needed US military power to guarantee security and the US needed European allies to stop Soviet expansion. When the existential threat to NATO's survival, the Soviet Union, collapsed in 1991, a neo-imperialist Russia did not emerge that would provide the glue to hold the alliance together.

Realists can argue that with the ending of the Cold War and the vanishing of the spectre of Soviet power, the disappearance of the common enemy undermined the rationale for a close transatlantic strategic partnership. Although realists disagree about the need for and likelihood of Europe balancing US power, they agree that the changes in the international distribution of power and perceived threats have made it less likely that Americans and Europeans will agree on policy issues. In 1993, Kenneth Waltz asserted that although the days of NATO were not yet numbered, its years certainly were.[14] Stephen Walt proposed that the US would increasingly look to the Middle East and the Asia-Pacific region and thus that its interest in and commitment to Europe would wane.[15]

Yet the basic realist understanding is, as Kagan has argued, that transatlantic strategic interests have diverged after the end of the Cold War because of the uneven distribution of capabilities.[16] America is strong and Europe is weak, thus either side thinks differently about the international order and the management of global problems. The weakness of European military power is reflected in states' 'strategies of weakness': multilateralism, foreign aid, the UN and diplomacy. The strength of US military power enables a resort to force when freedom is threatened and thus the effective management of threats to global peace. The United States is prepared and able to use raw political and military power to tackle perceived global threats, but Europeans lack that capability and instinctively prefer a rules-based system of international law whereby military action is legitimized only by multilateral institutions such as the EU, NATO and the UN. 'Europe ... is moving into a self-contained world of laws and rules and transnational negotiation and co-operation. ... Meanwhile, the United States remains mired in history, exercising power in an anarchic Hobbesian world where international laws and rules are unreliable.'[17] As a result, the US more readily adopts responses based on 'hard' – that is, coercive military – power; its European allies rely more on 'soft', non-military, power. As Kagan puts it, 'An assumption of conflict inevitability is implicit in US thinking, while Europeans far too often opt for a form of conflict myopia.'[18]

It is not difficult to find evidence for the realist claim about diverging strategic interests. Perceptions of the threat of WMD proliferation and terrorism, even after 9/11, were not the same on both sides of the Atlantic. As the leading global power, the US perceived the threat posed by Iraq and other rogue states in much stronger terms than did the Europeans.[19] After 9/11, the global war on terrorism and the formation of 'coalitions of the willing' only exposed the structural, strategic and political differences within the alliance rather than reinforcing and strengthening it. The shared strategic culture generated by the Cold War paradigm – common agreement within the alliance over when force should be used, where it should be used and how it should be used – had fractured.

Changes in threat perception and in the distribution of capabilities, the key variables of realist theory, thus seem to provide a fairly compelling explanation of the transatlantic crisis. But how might this theory explain the different reactions within Europe to US policy on Iraq? It would contend that there are two possible explanations that account for the differing levels of support for the US in Europe. First, larger states are more likely to oppose the US for fear of the consequences of global US hegemony, and smaller states are more likely to fear the hegemony of large states in Europe than the US and its global ambitions.[20] In Europe, countries that border on Germany or Russia and that have traditionally been threatened by them would be more eager to support US policies than countries that do not feel threatened by rising regional powers. Conversely, according to realist logic, current or aspiring regional powers, typically Germany, France and Russia, would thus have a greater incentive to oppose the US.

Secondly, as the major clash between the US and Europe occurred over the decision to pre-emptively invade Iraq in the face of a supposedly imminent threat (the self-fulfilling 'central front' in the global war on terrorism), we should also focus on the specific justifications of decisions related to that case. Here realists would expect that states that are either more threatened by global terrorism or are most dependent on the delivery of oil from the Middle East would support US policy, in particular concerning the war in Iraq. However, the practical application of these assumptions is more likely to lead to different outcomes than the first set of realist assumptions.

One assumption contends that the UK, France, Germany, Spain and also Russia should be more concerned about the global terrorist threat and that smaller countries with a small Arab migrant population or few, if any, significant potential terrorist targets should give the US-led war on terrorism less importance.[21] Alternatively, it can be argued that states with large Muslim populations would be more worried about the consequences of a military invasion in the Middle East. This is indeed the implication that analysts have more often drawn, and it is logical too because it is based more on a prudent than an offensive variant of realism. Another assumption would note that although most European countries are dependent on Middle Eastern oil, even more than the US is, they should have an interest in supporting the free flow of oil from the region. By contrast, according to the logic of material interests, oil-producing countries such as Russia and Norway should have fewer incentives to support the US policy of pre-emptive intervention in Iraq: intervention would increase oil production, thus breaking OPEC and causing the price of oil to collapse; and US companies would receive the lion's share of concessions. Paradoxically, irrespective of their support for US policy, all oil-producers were to benefit hugely from record oil prices in 2005: production in Iraq is still at pre-war levels, and the volatility of the insurgency and incipient civil war there ensures that this will remain the case for some time to come.

Realist theory thus does not offer a clear set of practical conclusions when applied to the transatlantic crisis. It is as indeterminate as it is a rich approach to international relations.[22] Although realist theory has its supporters, especially among American scholars,[23] many contemporary analysts have questioned the relevance of the realist perspective, noting the many inconsistencies that it fails to capture or account for. Šedivý and Zaborowski, for example, argue that

> a material argument could not explain why Ireland and Denmark, two states of a similar location and power potential, acted so differently during the conflict, with the former one distancing itself from the actions of the US and the latter acting as one of Washington's core supporters. After all, Ireland is strongly economically linked to the US and its neutral status has been at least partially possible due to its geographical proximity to the US. At the same time, Denmark has much more developed economic ties with 'Old Europe' than with the US.[24]

It is therefore imperative to look at alternative, non-realist theoretical explanations that might account for the transatlantic crisis.

VALUES, INSTITUTIONS AND DOMESTIC POLITICS

Liberalism is a theoretical perspective that rests on the assumption that all humans are rational beings and that as such they are able to articulate and pursue their interests, understand moral principles and live according to the rule of law. Liberals value individual liberty above all else and believe it is possible to achieve positive changes in international relations. Cooperation is a central feature of all human activity, including international relations. States are increasingly interdependent; and as the boundaries between them become more and more permeable, cooperation is promoted through the spread of democratic institutions, economic liberalization and the growing significance of international institutions. A state's use of military tools in achieving goals is important, but so too are political, economic and diplomatic instruments. There is much innovation in liberal theory, and a number of distinctive strands are relevant to understanding the transatlantic crisis, particularly in accounting for European perspectives. In this respect, the significance of common institutions, liberal internationalism as a world view and the emphasis on domestic politics and societal values are worthy of examination.[25]

Liberalism can easily account for the continuity of cooperation with and the lack of balancing behaviour against the US among European states. First, the transatlantic security community continued to survive after the end of the Cold War because its foundations were firm: it was built upon a dense network of institutional relationships, with NATO as the cornerstone of the institutional architecture. Celeste Wallander has argued that NATO was well developed as an institution, which is why it survived the end of the Cold War. Institutional theory, however, focuses mostly on exploring the effectiveness of state cooperation, and it failed to anticipate the transatlantic rift that would emerge as a result of the Iraq crisis.[26] Institutional theory has not provided a compelling explanation for turbulence and disruption in cooperative efforts; their causes lie outside its purview. Robert Keohane has argued that the source of the transatlantic cleavage was to be found not in the institutional failings of NATO but in the ideological character of the Bush administration.[27] However, if institutions underpin effective cooperative efforts between states, then it follows that a dearth of institutions or weak, ineffective and outdated ones explain crises and the absence of cooperation despite common interests. Indeed, if the institutional approach is used to explain the transatlantic divide, we should contend that NATO as an institution is ill-adapted to face and combat contemporary security challenges despite attempts at 'transformation'.[28]

Secondly, liberals can base their explanation of the past success of transatlantic relations on a set of shared values as well as on common institutions. NATO was premised not only on the existence of a common enemy but also on a common value base that included democracy and the liberal rule of law. Although many liberals are still optimistic about the future and believe that the common value base continues to exist, others have explained the transatlantic crisis as a reflection of diverging values during the 1990s. In other words, an emerging value gap could provide a better explanation of the crisis than diverging material interests or threat perceptions.[29] And Kagan, who has focused on power disparities as a source of transatlantic crises, notes that differences in strategic culture cannot be reduced to power disparities; they are also related to differing ideologies shaped by different histories on either side of the Atlantic.[30] Other realists, such as Walt, have also argued along liberal lines that a growing cultural distance between elites has resulted in an erosion of transatlantic ties.

Many studies bear out this contention about diverging values. It is a well-established insight that American and European socio-economic values are based on different ideologies.[31] Typically, these differences are reflected in attitudes towards gun ownership, patriotism and capital punishment, income inequalities and the propensity to sacrifice social capital for material gain.[32] Recent studies have shown that a value gap exists, particularly with regard to the predominance of the 'traditional values' of religion, family and patriotism in the US as opposed to 'secular-rational' and postmodern values in Europe.[33] For example, many Americans believe that it is necessary to believe in God in order to be moral while a majority of Europeans, the French in particular, reject that view.[34] These differences in values are detectable at the level of policy-makers too. In one interview, the EU's foreign policy spokesman Javier Solana stated that there was an increasing rift between the US and Europe because of the tug-of-war between religion and secularism: 'The US [is] increasingly viewing things in a religious context ... For us Europeans this is difficult to deal with because we are secular.' He argued that a religious society tends to perceive evil in terms of moral choice and free will; a secular society understands the causes of evil in political or psychological terms.[35]

The differences in values between the United States and Europe can be linked as well to more general foreign policy ideologies, which Kagan has characterized as Hobbesian and Kantian cultures and Michael Smith has ascribed to 'warrior states' and 'trading states'.[36] Americans still value sovereignty, but Europeans have moved into a postmodern conception of international relations.[37] Americans are said to be more Manichaean while Europeans tolerate difference. As Kalypso Nikolaidis notes, 'at its core, the European Union is about institutionalising tolerance between states.'[38] These basic models of international order are reflected in different attitudes towards the use of force, although opinion surveys caution not to exaggerate these differences.[39] Nevertheless, such world views can explain why Europeans are reluctant to invest in and use military force.

Applying these liberal theories to inter-European divergences, we can generate a number of working assumptions about levels of transatlantic cooperation and conflict. First, one could expect that the countries that are more closely tied to the US through institutional networks, NATO in particular, would be more willing to support its policies. By contrast, non-NATO European countries that lack this close institutional affiliation with the US would be less eager to lend support. Russia's position should depend in part on the functioning of the NATO–Russia Council.

Secondly, explanations based on values could account for the different reactions of the European states to the transatlantic crisis insofar as their values were similar to or different from those of the US. The World Values Survey, for example, indicates that Europeans in general, and the Scandinavian countries, Germany and the Baltic states in particular, have a much more postmodern value system, one that is less family-centred and less religious, than the more traditionalist United States; and only Ireland and Spain are closer to the US.[40] As for the willingness to use force in international affairs, the UK, France and Russia have typically been more willing to employ it with or without a UN mandate. Germany and smaller European countries have been more reluctant to support the use of force, at least if not sanctioned by the United Nations.[41]

Moreover, if values drive policies, then domestic politics should be an important factor in shaping transatlantic relations.[42] In general, one would expect the following tendency to be in play: a right-wing government ought to support the policies of a Republican US administration whereas a left-wing government ought to oppose it. There are two well-known cases that have made this explanation plausible and relevant: Germany and Spain. Many observers have argued that although Gerhard Schröder's Red–Green coalition opposed the US war on Iraq, a German government led by a CDU–CSU coalition would have backed it. The case of Spain is even clearer: the conservative Aznar government sent Spanish troops to Iraq and intended to maintain them there, but the socialist government led by José Luis Rodriguez Zapatero, who in the election campaign had criticized the war, decided immediately on gaining office to withdraw Spanish troops from the international coalition. However, these two examples cannot be taken to imply that domestic politics were a critical factor in other European states or that values explain the policy choices of governments. Indeed, what became clearly visible in Europe was that many conservative politicians and parties opposed the US-led war in Iraq and that ultra-right nationalist parties typically harbour a hostile view of the United States.

In the academic literature, there has been some debate over the relevance of these liberal explanations, notably those that rest on the assumption of common values.[43] Michael Cox argues that the transatlantic split 'not only casts doubt on the idea of the "West" but also brings into question various liberal theories of international politics that suggest that the two regions are so bound together by ideology, interest and institutions that a serious disagreement between them was, and presumably remains, unlikely'.[44] For his part, Michael Mihalka argues that common values are a poor predictor of participation in the Iraq war coalition: the majority of European states joined the 'coalition of the willing' despite the fact that their value systems were closer to those of Germany and France; but Ireland, a state that has a value system most similar to that of the US, did not even give it political support.[45] Furthermore, as American values hardly differ that much from European values when compared to the rest of the world, it can be asked why they would cause a transatlantic rift, particularly in the context of Middle Eastern policies.

PSYCHOLOGY AND IDENTITY CONSTRUCTION

Besides the realist and liberal perspectives, the transatlantic crisis can be explained by using constructivist insights about learning and identity construction. The basic view of constructivist theory is that international politics are socially constructed, shaped by different beliefs and cultures; and therefore neither material interests alone nor institutions or values can explain state behaviour completely. In addition, norms and rules shape international relations. They can be constructed by international organizations and NGOs as much as by states and national values. Material interests, institutions and values matter only if they are made to matter, and this in turn often depends on different and partly unconscious psychological mechanisms as well as on the nature of the interactions between states.[46]

Constructivists believe that interests and identities are not fixed or static; they are flexible and can change. Indeed, as ideas are the main drivers of history and identities are heavily shaped by ideas, radical changes in international relations are possible. Europe's identity is a case in point. What are the limits of Europe – geographical, cultural, religious and historical? Conceptions of what it is to be European are changing continually. To take another example, Cuba and Canada are medium powers, and both exist alongside the US. A simple realist assessment of the balance of military power cannot possibly explain why Canada is a close US ally and Cuba is a sworn enemy.

The strategic culture of a state shapes its approach to the use of force in international relations by predisposing it to a particular response and pattern of behaviour. A strategic culture is the composite of specific state-centric beliefs, attitudes and practices that have developed and evolved over time.[47] One principal way to understand differences in strategic cultures is to look at the conclusions that specific states have drawn from the lessons of history and how these conclusions shape their contemporary foreign and security policy decision-making. This decision-making is often driven by historical analogies and other lessons learned from the past. While Americans have adopted the view that the Cold War was won on the basis of superior US military power, Europeans tend to emphasize the importance of civil society and the revolutions from within in eastern Europe and the Soviet Union. By contrast, the lessons drawn from the Second World War may still divide Europe. Not only the US but also the UK, France and most east European states have been shaped by the Munich débâcle and the imperative to avoid its repetition: states must not give in to dictators; doing so only increases their power and encourages their appetite for further conquest. Germany and most of its allies or satellites in the war did not absorb this lesson. The lesson derived from the experience of defeat was understood as the need to avoid any extensive use of offensive force. And countries such as Sweden, neutral in the Second World War, and Finland, neutral in the Cold War, concluded that a policy of accommodation and avoidance of international conflict was an effective means of ensuring national survival.

The basic tenet of identity theories is that every identity is based on something that one does not want to be or represent.[48] In-group–out-group dynamism is a recurring element of human behaviour that is linked to different levels of identity building. We see it at work in transatlantic relations too (for example, Michael Smith suggests that in-group–out-group dynamism is more a structural than a contingent factor[49]). Although contemporary analysts focus mainly on European dynamics of identity formation, the impulses that drove colonists to America established a society and state created in contrast and even opposition to the old continent. For its part, Europe measured its identity in the early modern and modern periods against close neighbours on its periphery such as Russia and Turkey. In the postmodern era, according to Jürgen Habermas, the role of 'the other', of what Europe is not, has now been adopted by the US, and European unity is increasingly built around what he terms 'the transatlantic value gap'.[50] Peter van Ham is explicit when he argues that the 'EU is looking for a suitable other, which seems to present itself in the shape of "America", the long-standing comrade-in-arms which so many Europeans love to hate.' He contends that it is 'the narcissism of minor differences (as Sigmund Freud labelled it) that explains why Europe's emerging identity is striving to differentiate – and perhaps even emancipate – itself from the USA.'[51]

The perspective of identity theories can be linked to an assumption that became widespread especially after the mass demonstrations against the US-led war in Iraq. This was that Europe's reaction was based on irrational sentiments and ungrounded emotions that create an ideology of anti-

Americanism. Anti-Americanism can be understood as supportive of European identity formation, but very often it has a national origin and is shaped by local circumstances and historical experiences.[52] Although many commentaries on European anti-Americanism have a strong political bias – criticism of US policies is condemned as 'irrational' while irrational and obsessive elements of pro-Americanism are ignored – this explanation should not be rejected from the outset as pure political propaganda. Furthermore, it is also possible to identify the presence of American 'anti-Europeanism' and with it the corresponding tendency to dismiss Europe on the basis of prejudice rather than fact.

'Anti-Americanism' is thus not a product of any genuine interests or values; instead, it is seen as an obsession or prejudice that 'remains impervious to rational arguments or factual proof'.[53] It can perhaps be best explained through psychological and cultural factors. Some argue that 'it is based on the powerful but irrational impulse of envy – an envy of American wealth, power, success and determination. It is an envy made all the more poisonous because of a fearful European conviction that America's strength is rising while Europe's is falling.'[54] Others associate anti-Americanism more with the view that America is degenerating, that the American way of life and the US political system are inferior and that the society is soulless and consumerist.[55] Tony Judt notes:

> To a growing number of Europeans – it is America that is in trouble and the 'American way of life' that cannot be sustained. The American pursuit of wealth, size, and abundance – as material surrogates for happiness – is aesthetically unpleasing and ecologically catastrophic. The American economy is built on sand (or, more precisely, other people's money). For many Americans the promise of a better future is a fading hope. Contemporary mass culture in the US is squalid and meretricious. No wonder so many Americans turn to the church for solace.[56]

In the constructivist paradigm, whether or not value differences are deemed to be real is immaterial: they do not matter *per se*; they are made to matter by the nature of the interpretation placed upon them. For example, Europeans may simply project unwanted attributes of their own societies onto the United States. Most analysts of anti-Americanism believe that such irrational sentiments are generated more by intellectuals than ordinary people, but politicians and other opinion-makers can use them in order to solicit mass support.[57] Senator Richard Lugar, quoting Anthony Blinken, cautions that the transatlantic crisis has resulted because 'some politicians and members of the media in Europe and the United States have promoted caricatures and oversimplifications that appeal to the resentments and prejudices of their electorates.'[58] Under these circumstances, European states can be understood as 'free-riding appeasers' of states that threaten US global interests; Europeans can perceive Americans as 'simplistic crusaders who seek to assert their authority over their own allies'.[59] *The Economist* neatly captures all these perspectives, arguing that French anti-Americanism is not what it seems: 'First, because it is an elite doctrine that is often not shared by ordinary people. Second, because it is used by the political class more as a scapegoat for its own troubles than as a reasoned response to real threats. And, third, because it implies that the French clash with America out of antipathy. The real reason is rivalry, tinged with jealousy.'[60]

There are a number of corollaries that could be derived from these identity theories. First, we would expect that countries where dislike of America is embedded in deep cultural structures, which are formed and vary depending on the local context, would be more willing to oppose US policies simply on the basis of this cultural instinct rather than according to a rational calculus of interests and values. By contrast, countries that have defined their identity more on an enduring partnership with the US would be inclined to support its policies no matter how detrimental they would actually be to their national interests and core values. Secondly, deeper integration into EU structures and socialization towards Brussels' policies and decision-making culture, as well as adoption of a 'European' identity, would increase the likelihood of support for opposition to US policies on the basis of fostering an in-group–out-group distinction. The counter-hypothesis is that countries that tend to resist deeper European integration for fear of losing their national identity should be more pro-American in their foreign policy outlook.

THE LIMITS OF THEORETICAL PERSPECTIVES

Theories provide a context and are useful for helping us to understand specific events. But they do have their limits: realism ignores the world as it is becoming; liberalism sees the world as it never was; and constructivism insists on seeing an entirely different world. Realism is simple and understandable but appears to reduce the complexity of transatlantic relations to a few general Kaganian laws, which are hardly comprehensible. Its emphasis on the principles of power politics suggests a status quo theory that fails either to make specific predictions about the trauma in transatlantic relations or to account for the current turbulence. The realist approach assumes that a rational calculus can identify and quantify material interests. It also assumes that national elites are then willing and able to develop security policies according to an objective, rational decision-making process. Constructivism may be mistaken regarding the ideas, learning and identity not related to or driven by underlying material factors.

Theoretical perspectives need to catch up with the post-9/11 reality in transatlantic relations. This requires combining different perspectives in an effort to account for contemporary foreign and security policy choices: the United States uses realist means to achieve idealist ends against enemies whose identity is ever-changing, not static, as Condoleezza Rice has suggested.[61] Indeed, it is difficult to locate American neoconservatism within the theoretical boxes of realism or liberalism because of its value-laden and collectivist understanding of the United States' national interest.[62] Melvyn Leffler looks to the interplay among threat assessment, calculation of interest, articulation of values and mobilization of power to explain US foreign policy choices after 9/11, suggesting that 'At times of heightened threat perception the assertion of values mounts and subsumes careful calculation of interest ... [W]hen threat perception has been high, policy makers gravitate to rhetorical strategies emphasizing ideals and values. Conversely, when threat perception is low, officials tend to dwell on interests rather than ideals.'[63] But does this observation explain US policy choices after 9/11, and can different threats, interests, ideals and distributions of power account for the transatlantic gap?

It can be argued that the transatlantic security community moved to a different drumbeat following the shock of 9/11. That event can be theorized as a catalyst for the creation of an international coalition to promote justice and to wage a painstaking war over years or decades against the networks, groupings and states that sponsor 'global terror'. In an effort to legitimize this enterprise, political elites, initially in the US and the UK, fused together the assumptions in the paradigms of Fukuyama and Huntington in the context of discourse about globalization. President Bush explicitly addressed the issue of 9/11 in terms of mounting a defence of the values of 'freedom-loving peoples' in democratic states rather than in terms of a limited engagement or a return to isolationism.

The world was to be divided between a 'civilization' underpinned by global justice and a new moral order and its antithesis: violence, terror and 'evil'. Implicitly, those who were not 'for' Western liberalism and for embracing market democracy, modernization and the universal benefits for peace and stability that they promised were 'against us'. By extension (an implication Huntington avoided but President Berlusconi of Italy could not resist), non-market democratic modernization paradigms were uncivilized, 'beyond the pale' and in opposition to the West. At the British Labour Party conference in 2001, Prime Minister Blair extended this viewpoint by arguing that peace, justice, human rights, the environment, poverty and debt, the touchstones of the anti-globalist protesters, were now the legitimate focus of the 'civilized world'. Market democratic states were to utilize their power in an effort to achieve these ideals – the operating assumptions of realist means were to be harnessed to achieve idealist ends. In his State of the Union address in January 2002, President Bush underlined this commitment by stating that US policy would now be based on 'non-negotiable demands': human dignity, 'the rule of law ... respect for women ... private property ... free speech ... equal justice ... religious tolerance.'[64]

This Bush–Blair paradigm recreates a bipolar world view that is underpinned by two radically opposing views of how states should modernize. In essence, then, the two alternative modernity systems – radical Islamism and market democracy – are presented as opposing civilizations. In the Cold War, the US had built coalitions to contain communism and protect the 'free world', making it safe for democracy and capitalism. In the new century, the US and its allies are rebuilding 'coalitions of the willing' in order to protect market democratic states and to contain global terror. In Bush's words, there is to be no 'neutral ground' or non-aligned status: either states join the coalition of the 'good' market democratic civilization or they are, whether by default or design, construed to be 'sleeping with the enemy' and part of an 'evil' civilization. This coalition will wage war against Iraq, North Korea and Iran, the 'axis of evil', which supports global terror and thereby threatens peace in the world. This 'other' must be defeated in this new Manichaean struggle and consigned to the 'dustbin of history'. Indeed, the US National Security Strategy of 2006 explicitly sets 'the genius of democracy' in opposition to the 'terrorist tyranny' and directly compares this post-9/11 'battle of ideas' with the Cold War ideological contest between democracy and communism.[65]

As Brian Urquhart notes, the implications of this world view are evident in the rhetoric and actions of the Bush administration:

> The absolutes of Good and Evil, the references to God's will in relation to adventures like the Iraq war, the idea that those who are not with us are against us, impose a rigidity that dismisses criticism and makes it impossible to admit reverses publicly or to correct mistaken policies. Such trends are a serious hazard for such a powerful and important country.[66]

This is perhaps to overstate the case, although it certainly does appear that the relationship between religion and foreign policy is stronger in the US than in Europe. It is doubtful, for example, whether a US presidential candidate could succeed against the active opposition of the Christian right. Also, the rhetoric of religious language that so informs US foreign policy pronouncements and that resonates with US domestic audiences does tend to alienate European publics.

CONCLUSIONS: THEORY AND PRACTICE

The nature of the transatlantic crisis is generally explained by particular circumstances and contingencies and by deeper structural factors. Most accounts of the crisis are partial, because they are not located within a conceptual framework. The theoretical frameworks provided by realism, liberalism and constructivism are helpful in assessing the nature of its circumstantial and structural causes. They provide a framework that contributes to a more comprehensive and contextualized understanding of the transatlantic crisis. These theories consist of sets of ideas that are coherent and internally consistent and that rightly claim to have some purchase on the nature of the world and how it works.

Realism argues that disparities in power are paramount in explaining transatlantic discord and that we should expect European attempts to counterbalance US power, an effort impelled by diverging strategic interests and capabilities. Realist theory suggests that regional powers that fear US hegemony will oppose it and that states that are dependent on the US will support it. Does a more focused and detailed analysis of each of the five Europes support these contentions?

Liberalism generally suggests that there is more cooperation and continuity in transatlantic relations than counterbalancing. The transatlantic relationship remains fundamentally strong, supported by strong institutional links and networks as well as by shared values and a common strategic culture. But are these values diverging or converging? Are institutional bonds weakening or strengthening? Is this strategic culture more fragmented or more unified? Liberal perspectives assume that states which have close institutional links and shared values and which have the same political outlook as the US are far more likely to provide support than states without these commonalities. Is this so?

Constructivist theory suggests that beliefs and cultures shape relations and thus policies. Material (military and economic) interests and institutional links are not in themselves key determinants of the strength or weakness of relations; they are important only if elites and publics believe them to be so. Here 'othering', anti-Americanism and a gap in values are important. Thus support for the US would not be forthcoming in states where these three dynamics are strong, irrespective of rationally calculated material interests and actual rather than constructed value differentials. Similarly, levels of socialization in the EU and, conversely, attempts to maintain a balance between EU integration and a strong transatlantic partnership would also determine levels of support for the United States. Has this occurred?

The post-9/11 environment is a cause and catalyst of transatlantic strategic dissonance. It fractured pre-existing fault lines and consolidated realignments around concepts of 'Atlantic Europe', 'Core Europe', 'New Europe', 'Non-aligned Europe' and 'Periphery Europe'. Having theorized about the transatlantic relationship, let us now turn to the experience of these five Europes and examine their policy responses to the growing transatlantic rift. The use of these concepts and case studies should bring fresh perspectives and insights to the analysis of the impact of transatlantic dissonance on European foreign and security policy preferences. It will enable the final chapter to reflect upon the relationship between the theory and practice of transatlantic relations and, on that basis, to explore the likely future evolution of these relations and policy implications for European security.

3

'Atlantic Europe': the UK, the US and European security

The concepts of 'Atlantic Europe' and 'Euro-Atlanticism' suggest that there is a community of European NATO member states that assume an American perspective in foreign and security policy and tend to support US initiatives. Conversely, this community indicates that there is an interest and focus in the United States that favours strong and close relations with pro-US European states. Traditionally, no other country has represented 'Atlantic Europe' better than the United Kingdom – it is the quintessential and instinctive Atlanticist state.

Timothy Garton Ash suggests that the UK is a 'seismograph' or 'thermometer' of European–American relations.[1] For proponents of the 'special relationship', mid-Atlantic bridging policies allow the UK to embody Euro-Atlantic values and take the middle ground, a 'third way', and thus to navigate the British ship of state adroitly to a safe passage between the Scylla of US unilateralism and the Charybdis of 'Euro-Gaullism'. Sceptics and outright opponents of the 'special relationship' argue that beneath the rhetoric of shared cultures, histories, traditions and close military and security cooperation, the reality entails a UK bilateral fig leaf for unilateral US power. This diplomatic cover becomes less sustainable as the EU's Common Foreign and Security Policy (CFSP) and European Security and Defence Policy gather strength: fence-sitting becomes increasingly precarious.

William Wallace warned in 2005 that the UK's 'special but dependent relationship with the United States, and a closer but hesitant relationship with the European continent, have now collapsed'.[2] The United States under President Bush no longer combines what Strobe Talbott has termed 'American leadership with institutionalized, codified cooperation with other countries'.[3] This shift in the organizing principles of US foreign policy has reinforced the 'core European' focus and undermined the position of Atlanticists. James Rubin accepts that the cause of multilateral global governance will suffer more if the US acts alone than if it could be prevailed upon to lead a coalition but he notes that the UK, as a close ally, the 'special relationship' notwithstanding, has little ability to influence the US to calibrate force with diplomacy.[4]

'Atlantic Europe' has provided a reactive dynamic and an alternative vision to a French desire to 're-establish Franco-German leadership of the EU'[5] and to an instinctive tendency throughout Europe to think in terms of narrow national interest. Indeed, Germany's determination to normalize its foreign policy by reasserting the primacy of its national interest underscores this dynamic. The UK, as an island off continental Europe with an Atlantic shoreline and a history of relations with the US dating back to the foundation of the American colonies in the seventeenth century, is the pre-eminent example of a strong and committed Atlanticist European power. As Walter Russell Mead elegantly observes, the relationship is long-standing and profound:

> Historically, the United States originated as part of the British world system of empire and commerce, and for most of our history our relationship to that system was the greatest foreign policy question we faced … We had more in common with Britain than we did with any other country, and only the British shared our interest in world order; at the same time, however, there was no other power so dangerous to us or so able to frustrate our territorial or commercial abilities.[6]

And then there was Iraq. As Tim Dunne notes, 'Of all Blair's wars the decision to join the US mission to disarm Iraq by force will have the most lasting impact.'[7] Can the 'special relationship' be sustained after the Iraq intervention? If so, what does this tell us about the nature of that relationship and the viability of Atlanticism in Europe? In particular, how dependent is 'Atlantic Europe' upon the transatlantic strategic environment? It appears that strategic dissonance most effectively supports and sustains the UK's 'special relationship' and thus the Atlanticist orientation within Europe.

THE 'SPECIAL RELATIONSHIP'

The 'special relationship' between the UK and the US helps to shape transatlantic relations, but it has always been questioned as an effective and enduring tool of cooperation even though there is little analysis of the consequences for transatlantic relations if it proves to be unsustainable. As the decolonization process took root in the post-Second World War period, Britain orientated its foreign policy towards three circles: the British Commonwealth and the fast-diminishing empire, the transatlantic partnership and continental Europe.[8] With the end of empire, Britain then focused its foreign policy and national interest on balancing its US relations with those with Europe. Its foreign policy was based on the assumption that it is in the British national interest – indeed it is an obligation – for the prime minister to have a close relationship with the United States.[9] The relationship cannot be characterized as automatic or seamless, and its utility is asymmetrical: for the UK to retain global influence, US support for its policy initiatives is 'virtually indispensable'; UK support for the US is 'useful and sometimes valuable'.[10]

Close economic ties bind the US to Europe, and in particular to the UK. EU investment in Texas is greater than US investment in Japan; US investment in the Netherlands is greater than in Mexico. The US is by far the largest foreign direct investor in the UK and vice versa: 43 per cent of British investment goes to the US and nearly 15 per cent of US investment goes to the UK (35 per cent of US investment goes to the EU, two-fifths of which is invested in the UK).[11] The UK has developed a trusted and moderating influence on the US and enjoys a 'special relationship' that is both instinctive and intellectual. It is underpinned by outward-looking global aspirations, self-confidence and shared interventionist instincts. Typically, President Bush and Prime Minister Blair reaffirmed the 'special relationship' as 'the unique alliance of common values and common purpose that binds the United States and the United Kingdom'.[12]

As well as the cultural, linguistic and economic aspects of the 'special relationship', there is the uniquely close Anglo-American bilateral military security cooperation, which existed before European integration and independently of NATO. It can be said to rest on three pillars: nuclear, military and intelligence. This cooperation promotes political and diplomatic unity at the operational and strategic levels. The effectiveness of the UK's nuclear deterrence, from Polaris to Trident, depends largely on cooperation with the US, and it has resulted in common strategies, procedures and equipment. The UK's conventional military has the closest cooperation with the US of all European states; and although it cannot attain US 'network-centric' status (that is, the ability to use technology to ensure a seamless connectivity of information, allowing high-quality situational awareness, self-synchronization and thus increased mission effectiveness), it plans to be 'network-enabled', which allows for continuity in military cooperation in the future.[13] An ingrained habit of cooperation at 'desk level' in the nuclear, military and intelligence spheres has weathered not infrequent crises between the two governments, including Suez, Vietnam, the Yom Kippur war, Grenada, Bosnia and Northern Ireland (in the early 1990s); the relationship is self-sustaining.[14] The UK response to 9/11 helped to consolidate the relationship, which is strengthened by friendship between Blair and Bush.[15] The warmth of the personal relations between Blair and Bush can transcend traditional

Labour Party suspicion of US intentions. This close cooperation can further the UK national interest; and as a useful by-product for a Labour government, it pays domestic political dividends: being seen to stand shoulder to shoulder with a Republican president deprives the opposition Conservative Party leadership of political space.

It is also argued that this solid UK–US nexus helps to consolidate the transatlantic partnership between Europe and the US. To this end, the UK adopts a broker status intended to help repair the rift between the US and 'Core Europe'. On 25 March 2005, for example, Prime Minister Blair pointed out that the alternative to partnership between the US and Europe was an 'extremely dangerous polarization between the powers of the two continents', and noted that 'if Europe and America split apart from each other, [the loser is] not going to be Britain'.[16] 'Atlantic Europe' would not suffer from the political fallout of such disputes, as it has adopted a strategic formula that allows for 'win–win' outcomes.

The US–UK axis is sustained by an understanding that on economic issues, the UK, as part of the EU, faces the US on a basis of equality and can disagree and hold independent positions; on defence issues, the US leads and Europe, however reluctantly, should follow. The UK still upholds this post-Cold War understanding of the transatlantic relationship, and so it was prepared to support the United States when it attacked Iraq against the wishes of much of the EU, including the most powerful 'Core European' states France and Germany. This strategic clarity (economic interdependence, military and security dependence), it is argued, prevents divergent transatlantic policy preferences from spilling over into and thus endangering the critical UK–US geopolitical relationship. However, through the 1990s it became increasingly clear that Europe's strategic importance in US global strategy was being downgraded in favour of the Middle East and Asia-Pacific regions. Under President George W. Bush in particular, the organizing principles of the Atlantic community have shifted away from the use of collaborative, consensual arrangements that had hitherto been considered 'appropriate and effective means of advancing American interests and values'.[17] What was once crystal clear has fast become opaque and indistinct; and with it, the preconditions for Atlanticist solidarity have become weaker.

The 'special relationship' was placed under immense strain by the twin interventions in Afghanistan and Iraq. As the stated strategic objective for those places was to eliminate rogue and failed states and thereby combat WMD proliferation and the nexus between tyrants, terrible weapons, terrorists and failed states, the prospect of a return to the past (to regimes that are as rogue or failed as the ones that were 'changed') would entail

strategic failure. By April 2004, President Bush argued that 'The consequences of failure in Iraq would be unthinkable. Every friend of America
and Iraq would be betrayed to prison and murder as a new tyranny arose.
Every enemy of America and the world would celebrate, proclaiming our
weakness and decadence, and using that victory to recruit a new generation
of killers.'[18] Thinking the unthinkable following NATO's Istanbul Summit
in June 2004, its secretary general Jaap de Hoop Scheffer raised the spectre
of Afghanistan and Iraq emerging as failed states unless the United States
and the international community found ways to work together to save them:
'Can we afford two failed states in pivotal regions?' he asked. 'It is both unde-
sirable and unacceptable if either Afghanistan or Iraq were lost. The international community can't afford to see those countries going up in flames.
There would be enormous repercussions for stability, and not only in those
regions.'[19] Under these conditions, the transatlantic relationship would be
stressed to the breaking point; and for many, the UK–US special relationship
would become untenable – the UK would cease to provide even an illusory
transatlantic bridge under conditions of strategic failure out of area. This
failure would lead to transatlantic strategic divorce.

9/11 AND AFGHANISTAN ('WE ARE ALL ATLANTICISTS NOW')

Being instinctively Atlanticist does not preclude the UK from elaborating a
coherent European policy: indeed, it engenders a policy that places Britain
at the 'heart of Europe'. A basic tenet of Britain's foreign policy is that it
can sustain a strong bridging relationship between the US and Europe.[20]
As Robin Cook, former Labour foreign secretary (1997–2002), argued, it
is 'an anti-European myth' to suggest that the UK must ultimately choose
between a close relationship with Europe and an intimate relationship with
the US. He maintained that this is a false dichotomy because the UK must
stay close to both Europe and the US: 'any loss of influence in Europe would
damage our economic relations with the US and our strategic relations'.[21]
Prime Minister Blair informed Britain's ambassadors and senior diplomats
in 2003 that in order to influence the US in private, the UK had to stand
with it in public: 'We should remain the closest ally of the US, and as allies
influence them to continue broadening their agenda. The price of influence
is that we do not leave the US to face the tricky issues alone.'[22]

Following 9/11, the US National Security Strategy of September 2002
identified a dangerous nexus, noted above, between terrible weapons, terrorists, tyrants and failed states as the greatest threat to US national security. The
EU Security Strategy paper of December 2003 also identified failed states,
WMD proliferation, terrorism and regional conflicts as key strategic threats

to the stability of the international system and to states. In the first draft of this strategy, written in June 2003 by Robert Cooper, Director General for External and Politico-Military Affairs at the Council of the European Union and a foreign policy adviser to Blair, pre-emptive engagement was preferred, clearly echoing the US NSS. In the final draft, at the request of the French and Germans, the concept of preventive engagement prevailed.[23]

The challenge was to counter these emergent or actual threats using all means, including military intervention if necessary, to avoid direct threats to US territory and national interests. Such interventions would ultimately aim to reduce and manage the underlying causes that had generated terrorists and tyranny: endemic despotism, corruption, poverty and economic stagnation. In this way, failed states (Afghanistan) and rogue states (Iraq) would no longer be able to threaten other regional states or the US and, by extension, transatlantic strategic interests.

In Afghanistan, the Taliban regime supported the al-Qaeda terrorists who had been directly responsible for the 9/11 attacks. Without intervention to kill or capture members of al-Qaeda or its associates and supporters within the Taliban regime, Afghanistan would continue to pose a threat to the US, its friends and allies. On 7 October 2001, Operation Enduring Freedom was initiated. A US-led 'coalition of the willing' attacked Afghanistan after the Taliban had proved to be 'unwilling or unable' to detain and extradite Osama bin Laden and other members of al-Qaeda for their part in the planning and implementation of the attacks in New York and Washington, DC. Only the UK had the means to join the initial strikes by air and cruise missile against Taliban targets. This illustrated a central foundation of the 'special relationship', the long-standing close operational cooperation between the armed forces of the two states.

By November, the Taliban had capitulated and al-Qaeda training camps and assets were overrun as Kabul fell to primarily US Special Forces and Northern Alliance troops. By late 2001, the legal basis for the Bonn Agreement (which was the result of the UN-sponsored conference on post-Taliban Afghanistan) was in place. The Bonn process began in January 2002 with the creation of an interim government of Afghanistan, which resulted in the holding of national elections in late 2004 and the election of Hamid Karzai, a Pashtun leader from Kandahar, as president of the Transitional Islamic State of Afghanistan.

The transatlantic relationship was reinforced by European participation in Operation Enduring Freedom. The UK and other Atlanticist states supported the operation, as did the 'Core European' states that were to oppose the Iraq war. Germany, for example, supposedly disabled by a powerful combination of pacifism and anti-Americanism and a determination to use a Franco-German axis to counterbalance the US and its Atlanticist values, took co-command of the International Security Assistance Force (ISAF) operation in February 2003. ISAF consisted of 6,500 troops, and a further 2,000 were added after the June 2004 NATO Istanbul Summit.[24] ISAF–US Combined Joint Task Force 76 cooperation has continued to 2006. It operates with the full support of 'Atlantic Europe', 'Core Europe', 'New Europe', 'Non-aligned Europe' and even 'Periphery Europe' under US direction. The partnership between Germany and the US has been instrumental in pushing forward this effort.

However, the stabilization and reconstruction effort in Afghanistan has also highlighted underlying transatlantic points of tension, even between the US and the UK.[25] According to critics of the Afghan operation, ISAF has had a record of poor planning and coordination mechanisms and failure to staff the mission adequately.[26] It took NATO six months to deploy three helicopters to Afghanistan for the support of ISAF operations. The 'S' in both Secretary General and Supreme Allied Commander Europe has become identified more with 'supplicant' than 'supreme' or 'secretary', as each has had to beg member states to align political promises with force deployments and resource commitments: 'I have felt like a beggar sometimes, and if the secretary general of NATO feels like a beggar, the system is wrong.'[27] Systemic NATO weaknesses that have still to be addressed include a lack of contingency funding, a long-term planning capability and force deployments. Even when forces have been generated, national caveats (restrictions by member states on the role and mission of their contributions) are cited as a key factor that undermines ISAF's operational effectiveness. The cancer of national caveats is perceived as symptomatic of the failure of member states to trust NATO and ISAF commanders. Although ISAF has been promoted as a 'model' to be emulated elsewhere, the operation itself has highlighted ongoing debates regarding NATO's transformation and Europe's military capability and defence expenditure.

IRAQ AND THE 'SPECIAL RELATIONSHIP': ATLANTICISM UNDERMINED?

Realists such as Richard Harvey and Robert Cooper have argued that when it comes to questions of security and the use of force, every state pursues its own interests.[28] Unlike Operation Enduring Freedom, Operation Iraqi Freedom highlighted the demands of Atlanticism and the difficulties of maintaining a distinction between US and UK national interests. Ultimately, as it was in Britain's national interest to support the 'special relationship', it followed that it was in its national interest to support the United States' determination to intervene in Iraq. To have actively opposed or even offered only passive support for its pre-emptive military intervention would have been to leave the US–UK strategic partnership in tatters and thus to damage the British national interest. Iraq highlighted the unqualified and unconditional nature of this strategic formula: it is in the UK national interest not to have the US act unilaterally, irrespective of the wisdom or merits of the action. A pro-war Labour government demonstrated that the 'special relationship' has become more of an end in itself than a means to an end.[29] The attainment of UK national interests through a balanced US and European policy has been severely destabilized, barely able to survive the transatlantic storm.

The stated strategic objective of intervention in Iraq derived from the need to address three overriding threats of a strategic nature that made the Iraq regime, in the words of President Bush, 'a threat of unique urgency'.[30] The Iraqi regime possessed a chemical and biological WMD capability. According to the US secretary of defence Donald Rumsfeld, 'He has at this moment stockpiles of chemical and biological weapons.'[31] Vice President Dick Cheney highlighted a nuclear threat: 'we believe he has ... reconstituted nuclear weapons'.[32] The urgency of this threat was reinforced by President Bush. 'Facing clear evidence of peril, we cannot wait for the final proof – the smoking gun – that could come in the form of a mushroom cloud.'[33] Saddam Hussein was also a threat, he informed the world, 'because he is dealing with Al Qaida'.[34] Cheney was equally sure of this: Saddam Hussein 'had an established relationship with al Qaeda'.[35] At the cessation of 'major combat operations' in Iraq, Bush again linked al-Qaeda to the events of 9/11: 'The battle of Iraq is one victory in a war on terror that began on September the 11, 2001 – and still goes on ... [T]he liberation of Iraq ... removed an ally of al Qaeda.'[36]

The way in which the US- and British-led operation was conducted has been heavily criticized, and the imminence and actual existence of a discernible threat has been convincingly discredited. Intervention by the 'coalition of the willing' has been understood to have undermined NATO cohesion. NATO's secretary general, in a comment sharply critical of the Bush administration for abandoning NATO as an alliance, has already noted that 'If the mission defines the coalition, then you don't need NATO. You will then see the Europeans falling into each other's arms.'[37] The debate over the Iraq operation's strategic errors, led by General Zinni, a former US Central Command combatant commander, has been well aired. It is important because the errors it has highlighted help to explain the failure of the operations to bring stability and security, and the plethora of strategic compromises and ambiguities, the security vacuum and legitimacy deficits that have characterized the 'post-major combat operations' stabilization or Phase IV period from May 2003.[38]

Atlanticist support for the US began to weaken when the *casus belli* evaporated in the heat of the Iraqi summer. In the 9/11 Commission Report, the US Senate Intelligence Committee found no link between Saddam and 9/11, and collaborative links in the 1990s between his regime and al-Qaeda were characterized as not of an operational nature, a conclusion supported by the American commission investigating 9/11.[39] The fact that no WMD stockpiles had been uncovered undermined the case for the imminence of the threat and supported the argument that this was not a 'war of necessity' but a 'war of choice'.[40] The Senate Intelligence Committee's report concludes that 'Most of the key judgments in the Intelligence Community's October 2002 National Intelligence Estimate (NIE), Iraq's Continuing Programs for Weapons of Mass Destruction, either overstated, or were not supported by, the underlying intelligence reporting. A series of failures, particularly in analytic trade craft, led to the mischaracterization of the intelligence.'[41] The US quietly stood down the Iraq Survey Group in November 2004, after the presidential elections. In the wake of the US Senate Intelligence Committee report, it appears that at best the Iraq campaign represents a 'strategic diversion' in the global war on terrorism and that at worst it has been a recruiting ground and source of ideological and financial support for al-Qaeda and its affiliates.[42]

In March 2005, the head of Britain's foreign intelligence agency Richard Dearlove admitted that MI6's 'facts and intelligence' were 'fixed round policy' in April 2002 to suit the United States' determination to invade and occupy Iraq.[43] Robin Cook, who resigned as leader of the House of Commons over Iraq, claimed that the WMD threat was the stated rather than the true reason for supporting the war:

> What was propelling the prime minister was a determination that he would be the closest ally to George Bush and they would prove to the United States administration that Britain was their closest ally. His problem is that George Bush's motivation was regime change. It was not disarmament. Tony Blair knew perfectly well what he was doing. His problem was that he could not be honest about that with either the British people or Labour MPs, hence the stress on disarmament.[44]

The positive view of the 'special relationship' as useful, which Operation Enduring Freedom had reinforced, was undermined by Britain's support for the US in Operation Iraqi Freedom. Even before the Iraq war, the wisdom of adopting a mid-Atlantic balancing act with no clear safety net had been questioned. It was the key line of attack of those who question the utility of the 'special relationship': it neither advances UK interests in Europe nor influences the US. Instead, a different and more damaging strategic formula is enacted: Britain gives; the US takes; Europe suffers.

In the build-up to and aftermath of the Iraq war, many former senior political and diplomatic figures have questioned, with increasing bluntness, the utility of the 'special relationship'. Sir Geoffrey Howe, a former (Conservative) British foreign secretary, in reviewing US–UK relations, stated that 'It is hard now to identify any decision of substance, as opposed to process, on which Britain's prime ministers [have] secured any real change in American plans. By contrast … we have seen serious damage to the effectiveness and credibility of NATO, United Nations and the European Union.'[45] One former Labour Foreign Office minister, in discussing the Bush–Blair meetings, commented, 'I hope there is an opportunity for some very straight talking by Mr. Blair to Mr. Bush. The president has benefited from very close support and co-operation from Mr. Blair and he is entitled to be able to say some very straightforward things.'[46] Sir Christopher Meyer, a former British ambassador to Washington, has suggested that such hopes are unfounded and that it is in fact wrong to present the UK approach to the Bush administration under Blair as 'public loyalty and private candour': in reality, candour has been lacking in both private and public.[47] A further 52 former British ambassadors and heads of mission criticized Blair for abandoning his principles over the road map to peace in the Middle East and over his failure to plan for the post-Saddam reconstruction and stabilization effort. They called for a 'fundamental reassessment' of UK policy towards the US 'as a matter of urgency' and warned: 'If that is unacceptable or unwelcome there is no case for supporting policies which are doomed to failure.'[48]

In addition, it is argued that the US takes the UK's diplomatic and political support for granted and judges its utility as a transatlantic partner primarily by its ability to influence European foreign and security policy decision-making. The US State Department has consistently asserted that the United States' relationship with Britain requires a strong British engagement with continental Europe. However, to be ignored in Europe may be worse than being taken for granted in Washington. The UK's traditional and unconditional support for the US has undermined its commitment to EU unity. As the German foreign minister Joschka Fischer put it, 'We all know that this is about the question of Iraq, but it is also about the question of Europe.'[49] Europe does not need the UK to act as a cultural intermediary; and if the UK draws political weight and significance from its special relationship with Washington, then this is eroded each time France or Germany approaches the US directly. Indeed, Chancellor Angela Merkel's positioning of Germany as a transatlantic honest broker suggests that in 2006 Germany will adopt this role.[50] Far from upholding the British national interest, this empty function further undermines it by detracting focus and attention from Europe: 'In the EU, Britain often punches well below its weight, for lack of sustained political engagement at the highest level.'[51]

Many critics already contend that this policy has been poorly sustained and that it is ultimately self-defeating: 'But his [Blair's] international adventures have alienated Britain from many of its fellow EU members without gaining any influence over Washington, where the British prime minister's visits are exercises in futility and humiliation.'[52] William Wallace has also noted that the 'special relationship' has passed its sell-by date owing to a combination of longer-term trends in both US domestic politics and world politics that 'have left British governments without either the levers [on] US administrations or appeals to shared values that resonate with the US electorate'.[53] President Bush had a five-day 'Europe tour' in February 2005. He visited Brussels, Mainz and Bratislava, but not London: 'Bush's visit to Europe makes life a lot easier for Prime Minister Blair. Bush has had his re-election; Blair's is yet to come. I'm sure people in No. 10 Downing Street breathed a sigh of relief when they realized President Bush was bypassing Britain and going straight to Brussels.'[54] The jarring juxtaposition of US foreign policy dogmatism and European empiricism was noted by one serving UK diplomat, who suggested – albeit in jest – that 'outposts of tyranny' was an improvement on 'axis of evil' because 'it denotes an element of European rationalism in that at least tyranny is an objective term whereas evil is a biblical subjective one'.[55]

BUSH, ATLANTICISM AND MANAGING POST-IRAQ TRANSATLANTIC RELATIONS

Despite the fallout from Britain's support for the United States over Iraq and the complexity of the current global security agenda, which is best addressed by a rebalanced transatlantic relationship, the Blair government can argue that the UK's European policy has placed it at the heart of Europe, at least in military and security matters. The Anglo-French St Malo initiative of 1998 on European defence, which saw the establishment of the ESDP, was driven by French–British security cooperation, and it placed the UK at the heart of European military reformation. As one senior EU official noted, 'You can't have a common foreign and defence policy without Britain's army any more than you could have had a common currency without the Germans.'[56]

To acknowledge that the Euro-Atlantic zone is a 'security community' does not necessarily mean that it shares a common strategic culture, and it should not gloss over the divergences in values between Americans and Europeans. As Julian Lindley-French notes, 'be it steel protectionism, environmentalism, capital punishment, agriculture or a host of other issues, it is clear that the two sides are not only partners but competitors of sorts, with two very different world views in which partnership cannot be taken for granted.'[57] Indeed, in President Bush's first term, the UK supported a range of European policy positions that were at variance with and, in some cases, in opposition to US policy preferences. The list included support for the Kyoto Protocol on global warming, the International Criminal Court and steel tariffs. In Bush's second term, Britain's support for the lifting of the EU arms embargo to China, its role within the big three EU states (alongside the Franco-German axis, no less) and its support for further EU political, economic and military integration all appear in opposition to US policy preferences. However, it remains an unanswered question as to whether an Atlanticist state, especially one with a 'special relationship', can sustain its European credentials during the second term of the Bush administration.

The United States has made 'One persistent and accurate criticism of Europe – that it wants to have it both ways, rejecting America's leadership while refusing to take responsibility for its own defence and international policy.'[58] Although Operation Iraqi Freedom was not a NATO operation, as the alliance's secretary general noted, 16 of the 26 NATO countries have participated, not least the US, the UK and Poland (whose multinational division NATO supports and within which contingents from Bulgaria, Romania, Slovakia and Lithuania, for example, have operated). Indeed, NATO, at its June 2004 Istanbul Summit, offered to train Iraqi military and security personnel after the appointment on 28 June 2004 of Iyad Allawi to be the prime minister of the post-occupation interim government.[59] The Afghanistan and Iraq operations have demonstrated the extent (and limits) of transatlantic military cooperation in terms of agreed strategic threats and functional operational cohesiveness.

The European NATO allies of the United States must be able to advance on two fronts: they must develop niche capabilities/specialized roles for a war-fighting NATO response force (NRF) and they must train troops for lower-intensity ESDP crisis management missions. Both types of missions are demanding, and resources are scarce. Given the unwillingness of some NATO allies to fulfil the Prague Capabilities Commitment agenda, it is doubtful whether they will mobilize resources for developing the NRF and then develop the political consensus to deploy it under US leadership.

Even if a division of labour is agreed, however, are the European allies prepared to spend money on a force whose destination they cannot agree on?[60] In 2003, NATO's secretary general Lord Robertson highlighted the implications of the transformation agenda in NATO: 'if the forty percent of the US defence budget that Europe currently spends produced forty percent, or even thirty percent, of the American capability, I doubt there would be nearly so many grumbles from across the water. The reality is that in a host of key areas we are usually closer to ten percent, and often worse.'[61] By 2005, Nicholas Burns, the outgoing US ambassador to NATO, indicated that this gap was growing, not receding: 'Europe needs to reflect on the low level of defence spending, which has left most European militaries in a state of despair.'[62]

It can be argued that Washington supports 'Atlantic Europe' in order to undermine the Franco-German axis and thereby undercut the assertive multilateralism of the EU. There are indications that in his second term, President Bush has placed Europe on probation: its standing in Washington depends on its behaviour. Observers on either side of the Atlantic have contended that transatlantic differences are fundamental and exist at the level of basic perceptions, strategy and policy. US commentators, particularly those in conservative think tanks, lobby against an international EU security presence. They express alarm at progress in Europe's effort to achieve closer integration through a new European Union constitution and greater coordination of foreign and defence policy, 'all of which are seen as evidence that Europe is going its own way in world affairs – or worse, following the French recipe of "balancing" the United States.'[63]

Jeffrey Cimbalo suggests that by structure and inclination, the EU, with the ratification of the Treaty Establishing a Constitution for Europe, would focus on aggrandizing its power at the expense of NATO. The alliance should be saved from Europe: the US should 'end its uncritical support of European integration' and aim to 'divide and conquer' Europe by forcing a blunt choice between the EU and NATO. To that end, it should encourage the public in Britain, Poland and Denmark to reject the new European constitution until its security clauses have been renegotiated to allow a permanent 'opt out' of NATO. The US should then decouple EU and NATO security arrangements and seek 'bilateral or multilateral strategic arrangements ... to replicate NATO's core of close supporters'.[64] Such thinking is also consistent with that of some right-wing conservatives in the UK: 'the EU adventure is hostile to many Anglo-Saxon values. The leading English-speaking countries believe in free trade, democracy, free speech, liberty, freedom of association, religious tolerance, competition, enterprise and choice. The EU for its part has rather different values. It believes in solidarity, cooperation, partnership, corporate solutions, European champions, some limitations upon the freedom of speech [sic] and the support of good order and consensus values above liberty.'[65]

This interpretation is at variance with support for the transatlantic relationship within the EU that comes not just from 'Atlantic Europe' but from the EU itself. The EU Commission's president, José Manuel Barroso of Portugal, has stated that 'Europe and America have reconnected'.[66] Both he and the high representative of the CFSP, Spain's Javier Solana, are Atlanticists, as is the EU ambassador to Washington, former Irish prime minister

John Bruton. Solana is able to engage in genuine EU–US strategic discussions, and the EU is much more pro-US and a useful partner than neoconservative hostility might suggest. Andrew Moravcsik argues that with respect to regional integration and 'peacekeeping, trade, aid, monitoring, multilateralism, and the use of non-military instruments of policy – Europe is already a superpower equal to or stronger than the United States. For institutional and ideological reasons – from supermajoritarian ratification rules for treaties and conservative opposition to foreign aid to the lack of a social democratic tradition – the United States seems quite incapable of matching European achievements.'[67] The stronger and more assertive the EU, the more effective a partner it is for the US; the more cohesive and capable of burden- and responsibility-sharing it is, the greater is the EU's contribution to partnership with the US in terms of political legitimacy, reconstruction and stabilization efforts and its utility as a military ally.[68]

CONCLUSIONS: 'ATLANTIC EUROPE' REDUX?

If NATO fails to transform, then the US will continue to prefer ad hoc US-led 'coalitions of the willing' over the alliance and to seek to make a virtue of this vice by pushing for a functional division of labour within NATO. It will strive to reduce European NATO to a peacekeeping or stabilization and reconstruction role and to preserve the high-intensity combat role for itself. This would reinforce the trend towards the marginalization of NATO to nothing but a militarily useful toolbox in support of coalitions. Given that the UK and other 'Atlantic European' states promote NATO as the anchor of transatlantic cooperation, a functional decoupling of the US from European NATO suggests that only through coalition partnership could close military cooperation with the US continue. The acceptance of this logic would, in turn, further undermine the effectiveness of NATO, so promoting coalitions and the ESDP. Already these dynamics have begun to impact on the role and function of the ESDP and its 'hard-power' relations with the US. In the divisive diplomatic build-up to the war in Iraq, the divisions and tensions between 'Atlantic Europe' and 'Core Europe' and their respective camps had the unintended consequence of breaking the paralysis and logjam in the EU over the scope, nature and role of the ESDP and how it was best to be realized. Both the increase in the ESDP's operational tempo and intense diplomatic discussions over possible intervention in Iraq made explicit hitherto tacitly competing agendas and ambitions that had hindered progress, including the balance between civil and military elements in the ESDP, the US–EU divide and the scope of the ESDP.[69] As the UK is the only power that has remained more or less interoperable with US forces through 'network-enabled' capability, it follows that its 'pivotal power' role in US–EU relations becomes more important the more the EU becomes a 'hard-security' player. This trend, in turn, further undermines NATO.

Afghanistan reinforced the UK's transatlantic bridging or balancing act; Iraq caused it to collapse. For the UK, the 'special relationship' faces short- and medium-term turbulence. If in US eyes Europe continues to lack the desire, commitment or capacity to align itself with a Bush global security agenda, then the organizing principles of UK foreign policy will be weakened to the point of incoherence. The make-up and composition of 'Atlantic Europe' will also become more fluid, not least as 'new European' members exhibit a complex brand of Atlanticism – 'repeated calls for NATO to be comprehensively involved on the ground in Iraq can be read both ways: as just more evidence of their deep-rooted "Atlanticism", but also as an indirect demand for a less unilateral approach to post-war reconstruction and peace-building in the region'.[70] But although Iraq demonstrated that the UK's Atlanticism and 'special relationship' had little impact and meagre influence on US policy, what of the alternative on offer? The heady brew of Gaullism (livened up by the German *Sonderweg* to taste) had little to recommend it and proved to be equally flat as an alternative approach to influencing the US.

The laconic Nye Bevan, a Welsh Labour politician and political foe of Churchill, noted, 'We know what happens to people who stay in the middle of the road. They get run over.'[71] The more robust the EU becomes militarily and the stronger its political will to use 'hard-' and 'soft-power' instruments to effectively manage the global security agenda, the less willing it will be to adopt the subordinate, camp follower role but the more able it will be to 'share responsibility as well as burden'.[72] Under these conditions, the UK's role as transatlantic broker will become more ambiguous and pivotal, and the risks of becoming a continual casualty in transatlantic traffic will only increase. On the US side, the more it shifts from the foreign policy of 1990s characterized by selective engagement, continuity in the tradition of self-restrained diplomacy and a realization of the institutionalized nature of US power (the multilateral and self-binding nature of its foreign policy underpinned by deep interdependence and shared values), the harder it will be for Britain to straddle the transatlantic divide.

4

'Core Europe': Germany's national interest, transatlantic relations and European security

The annual Munich Conference on Security Policy is a useful barometer of transatlantic relations. In February 2005, at the 41st conference, a speech written for German Chancellor Gerhard Schröder (but delivered by Defence Minister Peter Struck) lamented the fact that NATO 'is no longer the primary venue where transatlantic partners discuss and coordinate strategies' and that global issues now transcend the strategic partnership. NATO was rebuffed on Afghanistan; the Iraq war was not discussed within NATO, nor were Iranian and North Korean nuclear ambitions, restarting the Middle East peace process or maintaining the EU's arms embargo against China. NATO was a military alliance that did not face military threats, and as an institution automatically dominated by the US, it had reached an impasse. He proposed a 'high ranking panel of independent figures from both sides of the Atlantic to help find a solution'. A new strategic consensus was necessary in order to recast NATO for the new century, and 'This panel should submit a report to the heads of state and government of NATO and the European Union by the beginning of 2006 on the basis of its analysis and proposals. The necessary conclusions could then be drawn.'[1]

For many inattentive commentators, Schröder's arguments indicated that at best the goodwill generated by the US during the Cold War had been expended and that at worst Germany, with French acquiescence, was attempting to emasculate NATO. In response, the US defence secretary Donald Rumsfeld praised NATO and bluntly questioned the need for a new panel proposed by Chancellor Schröder: 'We are already reviewing NATO's structures. There is an enormous value in NATO for big countries to talk in front of little ones, and for little ones to be able to give an opinion has a certain magic. I would think twice about another high-level thing. We would have to pause and be careful.'[2] NATO's secretary general Jaap de Hoop Scheffer stated that the alliance was in good shape, despite the Iraq crisis, and he doubted whether the review suggested by Schröder would produce anything new: 'I'm not denying the rifts of course over Iraq were deep, but if I look at Iraq, Afghanistan, our partnerships ... I think quite honestly NATO is alive and kicking. The transatlantic link and transatlantic relations are in good condition. I think the result of a high-level panel might well be that the advice would be to re-invent NATO.'[3]

Why had US–'Core Europe' relations deteriorated so badly?[4] This latest transatlantic disagreement suggests that tensions and mistrust are deep-seated rather than specific and temporary. Germany's vehement opposition to the US-led war to oust Saddam Hussein in 2003 (Operation Iraqi Freedom) and its determination to join the 'axis of unwilling' with France and Russia appeared to the US to be a dramatic assertion of 'Core Europe's' desire to exercise a voice and, if possible, a veto over an American foreign and security policy. This policy was perceived by Berlin and Paris as hegemonic unilateralism, and they would not allow the US to define alone the nature of NATO's policy. An analysis of the security politics of Germany's policy response to Iraq helps to determine the nature of 'Core Europe's' cohesion, integrity and salience and provides a framework or prism through which we can better understand current and future 'Core Europe'–US relations. The relationship has improved lately, not least because of the change of German government in autumn 2005, but the underlying tensions are likely to remain, independent of the coalition or the leaders in power.

Attempts to explain Germany's behaviour have focused mostly on the power of its anti-Americanism or the potency of postwar pacifism within German society, reinforced by a culture of restraint and an ingrained strategy-based preference for multilateral institutional responses.[5] Although these arguments have some merit, a more comprehensive account ought to explain the timing of the volte-face and why it centred on the issue of Iraq rather than Afghanistan or US Middle Eastern policy in general. The political emancipation of Germany and the nature of the transatlantic storm have shaped Germany's role in 'Core Europe' as much as hitherto latent anti-Americanism and a tradition of pacifism. As a result of the Iraq crisis, Germany is now more determined to adopt the mantle of a leading European power and to assume greater international responsibility for shaping an international world order in which it is a key player. Germany, buttressed by its 'Core European' power base, has global ambitions and is determined to promote a world order based on multilateralism and global institutions.[6]

Many analysts expected Germany's foreign policy to change after unification. Yet Chancellor Helmut Kohl guaranteed its continuity until the end of the 1990s. In 1998, the *'Bonner Republik'* became the *'Berliner Republik'* as the capital shifted eastwards and a new generation of political leadership led by Gerhard Schröder and Joschka Fischer took the reins of power. Again, a change of policy was expected, but the transition to new leadership did little to alter its focus and direction: a pragmatic pro-Americanism continued to be one of the basic pillars and least-challenged doctrines of German foreign policy. In particular, Foreign Minister Fischer advocated a strong commitment to traditional doctrines and the continuity of Atlanticism. His background is considered to be radical but 'his political roots lie with the Greens of Frankfurt – who generally liked American culture and counter-culture more than left-wingers of Berlin did.'[7] Fischer went so far as to argue that not only were good relations with the US essential to German security, they also underpinned the legitimacy of German democracy itself.[8] Indeed, Max Otte concluded that 'under Schröder, Germany was even more ready to demonstrate solidarity with the United States than under Kohl.'[9]

Under the Red–Green government, the idea that Germany is a civilian power that can use military force only according to international law in a multinational context continued to inform German foreign policy discourse. Its ideological wellsprings lay deep within pacifist doctrines that had supporters among the governing Social Democrats and the Greens. But the peace movement had lost much of its influence since the 1980s, and the dominant discourse had started to emphasize Germany's need to participate in multilateral military operations rather than to abstain from them. Thus in 1999, Germany delivered active support for Operation Allied Force in Kosovo (in the face of the clearly illegal, non-UN-sanctioned intervention) and continued to engage its military in peace support operations abroad.

While Atlanticism continued and pacifism was being eroded, Germany's foreign policy moved towards 'normalization'.[10] However, the content (and indeed timing) of 'normalization' was contested. German assertiveness had been signposted before and after the Iraq war by a host of unilateral actions and declarations, starting with the unilateral recognition of Croatia and Slovenia under Kohl in 1991. Such actions seemed to multiply under Schröder, who, from the very beginning, had professed to support enlightened self-interest as the organizing principle of German foreign policy.[11] The willingness to exclude any possibility of support for military action in Iraq, even were it to have been mandated by the UN, can be compared to the U-turn on the reform of the Common Agricultural Policy in 2002 and the renunciation of the fiscal balance obligation under the so-called stability pact in 2003.[12] But Peter Rudolf argues that attempts to revive the myth of special German assertiveness should be treated with caution. For example, Germany's recognition of Slovenia and Croatia 'was more a sign of helplessness than assertiveness, a symbolic act to defuse domestic political pressure rather than the beginning of a new geopolitical assertiveness'.[13] The terrorist attacks of 9/11 at first confirmed Germany's position as a major partner and loyal ally of the United States: the day after the attacks, Schröder promised 'unlimited solidarity'.[14] This declaration obscured the fact that Germany perceived the nature of the terrorist attacks very differently from America and drew its own conclusions from the event. Most Germans regarded the terrorist attacks as horrific crimes that necessitated international law-enforcement action rather than a global war on terrorists and rogue states. Germans emphasized the root causes, such as poverty and the regional conflicts that spread terrorism, rather than an incompatible value system of a radicalized Islam.[15] Indeed, Schröder qualified his promise of solidarity by explaining that Germany would be willing to share risks with the US but that it was not prepared to undertake 'adventures'. He also reminded it of the importance of information and consultation as a part of alliance obligations.[16]

Such reservations notwithstanding, Schröder supported the US-led war on terrorism, and Germany participated in Operation Enduring Freedom in Afghanistan. The willingness to use military force 'out of area' in defence of freedom and human rights suggested that the culture of pacifism and self-imposed constraints that had hitherto shaped Germany's engagement in foreign military operations was eroding further. Although a number of Social Democrats and Greens opposed what they understood to be the further militarization of the country's foreign policy and demanded a pause in the bombing campaign in Afghanistan for humanitarian reasons, Schröder 'stuck to his guns' and was able to reinforce his pre-eminence in foreign policy.[17]

Throughout 2002, the prospect of a war against Iraq gathered momentum, initiated by President Bush's State of the Union address in which he declared that Iraq was part of an 'axis of evil'. Germans, as most other Europeans, considered the 'axis' concept to be weak and were critical of the idea of invading Iraq. They were also increasingly concerned that the views of allies were being given short shrift in Washington. Fischer highlighted this concern when he warned the Bush administration that European allies did not want to be treated like satellite states.[18] The Christian Democrats reinforced this message with a warning of their own: 'it cannot be that you act on your own and we trot along afterwards.'[19] Despite these misgivings, Schröder remained accommodating, and argued that 'we should not slip back into the old mistrust of the superpower and the Bush administration.'[20] Karsten Voigt, the Foreign Ministry's coordinator of German–US relations, argued that Bush was 'no cowboy' and that Washington would take European perspectives into account.[21] When Bush visited Germany in May 2002, he stressed the United States' belief that Iraq posed a strategic threat to regional and global stability, but he also took the time to reassure allies that the US would not act without first consulting with them. A compromise was reached: President Bush would not begin overt preparations for war before the German elections and Chancellor Schröder would not run on an anti-war platform during his election campaign.[22]

However, this uneasy agreement began to unravel in summer 2002 as the American press circulated stories of war planning. These stories were encouraged by the bolder rhetoric of President Bush, who, at West Point military academy in June, declared that 'we must take the battle to the enemy' and 'be ready for pre-emptive action'.[23] Schröder's campaign team immediately capitalized on the speculation. The possibility of an Iraqi war was identified as an issue that could mobilize popular support and so provide the chancellor with an opportunity to defy the projected result of opinion polls (his defeat) and carry the election. German public opinion surveys indicated that an overwhelming majority opposed the war, particularly in former East Germany, where the SDP had to compete with the former GDR socialist party the PDS. When US Vice President Dick Cheney delivered a strong appeal for pre-emptive regime change in August, the Iraq war was promoted to the central theme of the Bundestag elections.[24]

As soon as the German election campaign began in August 2002, Schröder stated explicitly that he would not support a war against Iraq. He argued that it was a mistake to consider military intervention and, reiterating his warnings voiced in September 2001, he declared that Germany was unwilling to participate in US 'military adventures'.[25] In an unusually patriotic declaration, Schröder declared his faith in German society and propagated the vision of a 'German way' that echoed in the minds of many the old German *Sonderweg* between East and West.[26] Fischer too was critical of the possibility of war but was careful to formulate his position with greater diplomatic finesse.

Both the rhetoric and reality of Schröder's political opposition to the war were of course noted in Washington, but it was Justice Minister Hertha Däubler-Gmelin's gaffe, delivered at a small local campaign event, that caused an immediate crisis in German–American relations. She suggested that Bush's preparation for war was instrumental, and could thus be compared to Hitler's deliberate attempts in the 1930s to shift the German public's attention from domestic issues, which would only exacerbate internal divisions, to those at the international level. This in turn served to consolidate support for his regime.[27] In response, the White House announced that German–American relations were poisoned. Condoleezza Rice was furious, and asked, 'How can you use the name of Hitler and the president in the same sentence?' Although Schröder wrote to Bush that the minister's words had been misreported, he did not apologize. Bush felt offended; he did not extend congratulations to Schröder on his election victory and he refused to talk to him at international meetings.

Although the German government refrained from actively aggravating this dispute, it continued to oppose the gathering US-led momentum towards war against Iraq. In December 2002, Fischer did not rule out the possibility of Germany's eventual political support for the war, but he left its actual policy deliberately ambiguous so that no state could predict with certainty how it would vote in the Security Council.[28] This policy of ambiguity was torpedoed in early 2003 when Schröder, at a regional election rally, declared that Germany would not support a UN resolution legitimizing war on Iraq.[29] His statement came as a surprise to Fischer, who disagreed with a categorical 'no' to the war (just as the 2005 Munich Conference speech came as a surprise to Defence Minister Struck despite the fact that he himself read the text that Schröder had prepared).

Schröder's statement initiated a further frisson in the transatlantic drama when Rumsfeld labelled Germany together with France as 'a problem', arguing that the Franco-German position did not represent a pan-European sentiment; rather, it was confined to 'old Europe'. Rumsfeld, in a crass and gratuitous diplomatic snub, named Germany alongside Libya and Cuba as countries unwilling to help the US in the global war against terrorism. This discounted Germany's deployment of troops to Afghanistan and Kuwait, as well as the continuous support extended to US bases in Germany.[30] Although the Schröder government dismissed Rumsfeld's comments, they helped to foster feelings of irritation and also alienated traditionally pro-US circles in Germany. Fischer defended the German stance against the war in an emotional speech delivered at the annual Munich Security Conference in 2003. In the presence of Rumsfeld, he declared that he was not convinced about the case for war against Iraq. 'Why now?', he queried. He reiterated that diplomatic means had not been exhausted and argued that the situation should not automatically lead to the use of military force. In his view, the more important task in the Middle East was to promote Israeli–Palestinian reconciliation.[31] At the same time, Schröder placed the issue of war in Iraq within the framework of world order paradigms: would decisions relating to world order be made multilaterally or not?[32]

Exacerbating already frayed relations, Germany together with France and Belgium blocked a US request to allow contingency planning for assistance to Turkey in the context of a war against Iraq. This opposition was designed to avoid the impression that NATO had begun preparations for war.

Although Germany promised to support Turkey bilaterally and was ready to end a week-long deadlock and paralysis in NATO, the net result was its further estrangement from the United States. In April 2003, it participated with France, Belgium and Luxembourg in a mini-summit of 'Core Europe' convened to consider proposals for further elaborating an autonomous European defence capability. Washington was critical of this summit; and for some it seemed anti-US in intent, suggesting that an ESDP was needed to counterbalance the US. Schröder also aligned himself with the French and Russian presidents Chirac and Putin and issued a common statement on the eve of the war pleading for the continuation of the UN weapons inspections in Iraq. The active phase of the Iraq war was over in late April 2003 when US forces occupied Baghdad. Germany did not congratulate the US and the coalition on the victory, but it did acknowledge that it favoured the defeat of Saddam Hussein's regime. Its concern about the Arab world's reaction and the difficulties inherent in managing the occupation were apparent, but criticism was muted, and it announced that it was willing to participate in the reconstruction.[33] In May 2003, Schröder stressed the importance of strong transatlantic relations and the existence of common values and interests despite the disagreements over Iraq.[34] Germany pushed for a greater UN role in postwar Iraq and a clear timetable for restoring Iraqi sovereignty; it was ready to support Bush and Blair's plan for the Security Council to lift sanctions against Iraq.

Although some American officials had threatened Germany with sanctions were it not to support the war in Iraq, the US started to reduce its military presence in Germany for military rather than political reasons. The war had necessitated the reconfiguration of the US military 'footprint' throughout Europe, but especially in Germany. Some 'enduring-value' bases will be maintained, such as the airbases at Ramstein in Germany and Aviano in Italy, and the overall number of US troops in Europe will remain stable at approximately 112,000 (with 84 per cent in Germany), but the location of these troops will change. For example, the two US divisions (each with 15,000 troops) in Germany, the 1st Armored Division near Heidelberg and the 1st Infantry Division, currently in Iraq, will have only a brigade (3,000–5,000 troops) redeployed to Germany after the Iraq operation. The balance will be sent back to the US or will be deployed to new US forward bases in 'New Europe', where equipment and a skeleton staff are pre-positioned, allowing for a lighter US military 'footprint'.

The absence of political support from some 'Core European' allies, which contrasted sharply with the Vilnius 10's support, had operational consequences for US military effectiveness. There was a delay of several days before the Pentagon obtained permission to deploy the US Army's

173rd Airborne Brigade, stationed in northern Italy, for parachuting into northern Iraq. Austria did not make its rail network available for US forces, and German, French and Turkish opposition to the war provided a reason to decrease future dependence.

On the other hand, public support in Bulgaria, Romania, Poland and Hungary for America's military presence, aims and objectives in Europe is greater than in 'Old Europe', and this lessens possible threats to deny access to infrastructure on their territory. Moreover, the economic benefits of America's use of these bases, even the lower-cost 'lily pads', will be likely to maintain or increase public support in those states. The US European Command HQ at Stuttgart puts an estimated $150–175 million into the local economy; the cost would be considerably less in 'New Europe'.[35] The eastward and southward tread of the lighter US military 'footprint' might have been expected to have security policy implications, but they have not emerged: Germany does not feel diplomatically snubbed or resentful of the economic (and cultural) impact of the move and the 'strategic seam' in the transatlantic fabric has not been weakened, let alone broken, by this new approach.

After the occupation of Iraq and a year of frozen personal relations between Bush and Schröder, tensions and mistrust between Berlin and Washington began to thaw. The two presidents met in September 2003 in New York and assured each other that mutual disagreements were now behind them.[36] In a conciliatory spirit, President Bush assured Chancellor Schröder that he understood the dynamics of the German electoral cycle and campaign before the war and the impact of pacifism on German foreign policy.[37] In turn, Germany expressed a willingness to restore relations with Washington: at the February 2004 Munich Security Conference, Fischer argued that he had yet to be convinced of the war's strategic rationale but he assured the audience that the debate was over tactics rather than goals. He emphasized the need to reconcile differences and to focus on future cooperative efforts rather than the problems of the past.[38] By 2004, transatlantic tensions had been reduced, but fundamental policy dilemmas remained. These surfaced at the NATO June 2004 Istanbul Summit, where Germany did not support a US proposal to expand NATO's role in Iraq, and again at the February 2005 Munich Security Conference. Although it was possible to talk of a normalization of German–US relations, 'normality' was no longer represented by the pre-war default position that had characterized the two sides' relations in the post-Cold War era.[39]

FOREIGN POLICY COUNTERBALANCE OR NORMALIZATION?

Many political commentators and analysts have argued that Germany's unwillingness to support the war in Iraq was based on a strong anti-American sentiment.[40] 'Anti-Americanism' is, of course, a contested and politically loaded concept insofar as it can be defined as a prejudice and bias derived from ignorance rather than a reasoned critique. What is undisputable is that the image of the United States deteriorated radically after 9/11 in Germany. Nearly 80 per cent of Germans rated the United States positively in 1999; but in summer 2002, the figure was down to 61 per cent; and in spring 2003, only 23 per cent of Germans took a favourable view. America's image had improved somewhat by spring 2004 but it remained more negative than positive. And even though a majority of Germans supported the US-led war on terrorism, the extent of support had declined from 70 per cent in 2002 to 55 per cent in 2004.[41]

However, public opinion ratings do not identify the causes of anti-Americanism or its consequences. America's decision to go to war in Iraq could explain the increase in negative feelings towards it in Germany just as much as an ingrained anti-Americanism could explain German opposition to the war.[42] A more critical assessment suggests that the swing in public opinion reflected dissatisfaction with the Bush administration and its policies, not anti-Americanism *per se*. Indeed, public opinion polls indicated that Americans were not hated as a country or people.[43] Moreover, as Elizabeth Pond has argued, 'to an American who lived in Germany during the massive anti-missile demonstrations in the 1980s what was new about the brief German antiwar marches of 2003 was precisely the effort of protesters to differentiate between their opposition to the Iraq war and their affection for the United States.' In her view, Schröder's opposition to the war did not initiate a tsunami of popular anti-Americanism in Germany; the chancellor's policy was widely criticized as isolating Germany.[44]

There are many who suggest that anti-Americanism is a persistent part of German culture. Dan Diner, for example, has argued that German anti-Americanism has long roots in history and is a reflection of German anti-Semitism. However, his evidence for contemporary anti-Americanism in Germany remains fragmentary.[45] Moreover, the fact that parts of Germany's cultural elite were vocally 'anti-American' fails to explain the policy shift: these same groups frequently expressed anti-American views *before* the war in Iraq. Furthermore, ignorant and offensive anti-Americanism (as with the advocacy of 9/11 conspiracy theories), which was supported by a considerable number of Germans, was firmly resisted by opinion leaders, who otherwise were critical of Bush's determination and decision to invade and occupy Iraq.[46] The widespread condemnation of the Däubler-Gmelin's *faux pas* spoke more about the attitudes of the political elite than the remarks themselves.

It is equally difficult to interpret Germany's participation in the strengthening of the European Security and Defence Policy as a sign of its supposed anti-American orientation. Plans for the ESDP were initiated long before the Bush administration came to office, let alone the 2003 war. The timing of the mini-summit, April 2003, during the war, was more an unfortunate coincidence than a deliberate protest or snub: Schröder was keen to assure the US that a stronger ESDP would not emerge at the expense of a weakened NATO. Both the chancellor and his foreign minister repeatedly claimed that there was not 'too much of America but too little of Europe in NATO'.[47] As Rudolf notes, 'from the prevailing German perspective, a strong Europe cannot be built on the basis of opposition of the United States.'[48] Indeed, the most vociferous of Germany's critics of the US have not been the most vocal proponents of the ESDP. Attempts to reinforce the ESDP through 'enhanced cooperation' were championed by, among others, the CDU's Wolfgang Schäuble, who supported the war in Iraq and continuously stressed the importance of the transatlantic relationship: in his view, every attempt to unify Europe against the United States would fail.[49]

German behaviour and policy responses over the Iraq war have also been explained by reference to a second pillar of German political culture, namely pacifism or a general reluctance to use force and support offensive warfare. As Thomas Risse has suggested, the disagreements with the United States can be explained by Germany's commitment to be a civilian power.[50] Public opinion in Germany has remained war-averse: in 2003, only two in five Germans agreed that under some conditions war is necessary to obtain justice; in the United States, more than four in five agreed with this statement.[51] Although it is undeniable that German public opinion strongly supported Schröder's decision not to participate in the Iraq war, the main reason that drove opposition was the issue of legality. Four out of five Germans thought that states should have UN approval before using military force to deal with an international threat. German public opinion was more willing to support a war sanctioned by the United Nations. It did not support a unilateral German 'no' to the war, made independently of the UN decision, as such a stance would both weaken the UN and isolate Germany.

The anti-war platform undoubtedly helped Schröder to win the election in September 2002, but did inherent and ingrained German pacifism shape his decision-making? In the Bundestag before the war, he defended his Iraq policy by reminding MPs that 'No realpolitik and no security doctrine could lead surreptitiously to our coming to regard war as a normal instrument of politics.'[52] But at the same time, Schröder admitted in an interview that

German participation in the war was not a legal or moral issue but a political question: he simply believed that the threat posed by Iraq was not of sufficient immediacy or salience to provide a convincing reason for military intervention.[53] In March 2003, he reiterated this argument: the extent of the Iraqi threat did not justify a war in which thousands of innocent people would die.[54] The German government never clarified its position on the question of the war's legality.

Following the Bonn Agreement of December 2001, the international community pledged support for the stabilization and post-conflict reconstruction of Afghanistan; and for six-month periods each, an international stabilization assistance force, under UK, Turkish, German–Dutch and, in late 2003, NATO command, monitored and aided this effort.[55] For the six months beginning on 9 August 2004, the Eurocorps assumed command of ISAF, thereby taking the lead in NATO operations in Afghanistan. Its mission was to protect the Karzai government, to enable presidential elections to be held on 9 October 2004 (which were completed successfully) and to facilitate parliamentary elections planned for spring 2005 (but delayed until September 2005).[56] Germany also supported, but with a very small military contribution, the ESDP's Operation Artemis in the Congo in July 2004. Indeed, it was engaged in many military operations abroad, deploying almost 10,000 men in total.[57] Therefore, it is difficult to believe that 'pacifism' or anti-war sentiment as such would have led to a strong opposition by the German government to the war in Iraq although there were different perceptions about the utility of the war.

For these reasons, other explanations of Germany's behaviour must be examined. The country's political emancipation provides a more convincing explanation for its action and policy as part of 'Core Europe' during this period. Its growing self-identity and great-power self-perception and its resistance to the US vision of a unipolar world are key. The underlying dynamic in the transatlantic relationship was not so much a widespread and pervasive dislike of America and its values as a defensive reaction to its neglect of its allies. The increasing emancipation of German foreign policy was manifested in Chancellor Schröder's conviction that support for the US would be conditional.

In Mainz in 1989, President George Bush Sr 'stooped to conquer' when he declared America and Germany to be 'partners in leadership', a winning formulation.[58] German political elites made a distinction between US leadership, which in principle Germany did not oppose, and US hegemony, which it did. Leadership suggested a tendency to consult with allies first and persuade them through reasoned argument to adopt particular policy choices within a framework of shared democratic values. In the 1930s, a hegemony-seeking Germany had destroyed the existing balance of power, and German elites were all too aware of the dangers of failure to consult allies, of an instinctive desire to embrace unilateral action and of the inherently destabilizing influence of unilateralism on stability.

At the outset of the George W. Bush Jr presidency, Chancellor Schröder did not view the US administration as particularly unilateralist in its approach to foreign and security policy matters; rather, it was self-confident and open to dialogue.[59] Indeed, before his inauguration Bush had characterized his foreign policy as humble. But in summer 2002, Schröder changed his opinion about the US and its willingness to listen to its allies. It became a mantra for him that the Europeans should be able to discuss issues of strategic importance eye to eye – '*auf gleiche Augenhöhe*' – with the Americans.[60] This expression did not suggest that Germany considered itself the politico-military equivalent of the US but that it was determined to be treated as a moral equal, not a subordinate. It needed to be recognized, consulted, respected and taken seriously as a partner. With reference to the August 2002 speech of Vice President Cheney that strongly advocated regime change in Iraq, Schröder complained 'that is why it is just not good enough if I learn from the American press about a speech which clearly states: We are going to do it, no matter what the world or our allies think. That is no way to treat others.' He argued that 'the duty of friends is not just to agree with everything, but to say: We disagree on this point.'[61] Other criticisms of the United States that have been attributed to German anti-Americanism – such as the SPD politician Ludwig Stiegler's remark that the US ambassador Daniel Coats behaved like the Soviet ambassador to the German Democratic Republic – often focused on arrogance in US foreign policy. Even ex-Chancellor Kohl, who has criticized Schröder and Fischer for their anti-Americanism, agreed that Washington had paid too little attention to European sensibilities and had acted like a 'new Rome'.[62]

When Schröder began to articulate his anti-war position, he did not expect that it would cause a major rift and then trauma in German–American relations; he believed that good friends could disagree upon occasion. His promise of 'unrestrained solidarity' after 9/11 did not give Washington carte blanche over all foreign and security policy decisions with global impact and significance. Schröder believed that he could afford, after already risking the popularity of his government in support of the Kosovo campaign and the Afghanistan operation, to disagree with Washington over the question of intervention in Iraq.[63] The need to disagree was perhaps even more pointed given Germany's support in the past: a demonstration of its independence in the present would bolster his credibility and allow for future consensus. In addition, Germany remained unconvinced of the strategic necessity of pre-emptive intervention in Iraq. Instead of viewing Iraq as the 'central front' in the global war on terrorism, elite and public opinion viewed the intervention as a strategic diversion from tackling al-Qaeda.

The German anti-liberal political scientist Carl Schmitt had accurately captured the dilemma the German state now faced: 'if it [the state] no longer has the ability or the will to distinguish between friends and foes, it ceases to exist politically.'[64] Indeed, in a major speech at the Bundestag during the election campaign, Schröder declared that 'the existential questions for the nation would be decided in Berlin and nowhere else'.[65] The more the US tried to constrain Germany's freedom of action, the more important it was for him to maintain Germany's position and defend its interests. He believed that he would be able to do so without personalizing the dispute or allowing it to spill over into other transatlantic policy issues.

Schröder's effort to redefine Germany's foreign policy identity in transatlantic relations was underpinned by German public opinion, which clearly supported a more assertive and active German role in international affairs, especially within a European framework.[66] Even before the Iraq war, a majority of Germans rejected the US concept of a unipolar world order and believed that the United States had failed to take into account the interests of Germany when formulating and implementing international policy decisions.[67] In an opinion poll survey in 2005, two-thirds of Germans said that they no longer needed to be thankful for US support in the post-1945 period, and 29 per cent thought that Putin was more trustworthy than Bush (24 per cent considered that Bush was more trustworthy than Putin).[68] This data reveals a strong desire for emancipation from the past, and this desire found voice in German foreign and security policy during the Iraq crisis.

CONCLUSIONS: GERMANY AS A SECURITY PARTNER

The clash between Berlin and Washington in 2002–3 surprised the community of scholars and analysts charting German foreign policy developments and the evolution of transatlantic relations. Following unification and the end of the Cold War, German foreign policy was characterized more by continuity than change, despite the dramatic transformation of power relations in Europe, the subsequent move of the capital to Berlin and the election of a Red–Green coalition run by the postwar generation. Most attempts to explain Germany's behaviour concerning the war in Iraq have focused either on the anti-American or the pacifist nature of German society. These explanations do not account for the timing of the change, its sudden emergence and its focus on the Iraq issue.

Throughout the 1980s, West Germany before unification had gradually grown into its role as a leading power in Europe. In the 1990s, reunified Germany began to show increasing signs of willingness to assume greater international responsibility; and in return, it expected other states, particularly the US, to listen to German concerns when making crucial decisions about peace and war. When Berlin felt that it was not consulted in the decision-making process, it reacted strongly. Germany refused to automatically follow an American policy decision, particularly when it had not had the opportunity to shape that decision and it had domestic support for its position. In other words, German foreign policy changed under Schröder's chancellorship, and thus the decision not to follow the US in the critical decisions regarding the war in Iraq was more than pure 'opportunism' connected to the election campaign. Germany was not prepared to support a US policy that it regarded as strategically inept and morally flawed. But although Germany is more assertive than before, it cannot be assumed that it follows a strategic blueprint or master plan.

Germany's position on Iraq emerged more through a combination of default and design than as an ad hoc response resulting from conscious strategic rethinking. An important contingent factor was the timing of the Bundestag elections. Without the election campaign, Schröder might have tried to steer a course closer to the US, or at least he might have refrained from strong criticism and rigid postures that gained votes but frayed transatlantic ties. Once the disagreements started, they were self-sustaining and escalated owing to the dynamics of mutual distrust, frustration and misunderstandings. Fractiousness now predominated, as elite communication was allowed to break down and partisanship prevailed. The Bush administration appeared to have adopted a policy of divide and rule – and the division of Europe into pro- and anti-US groups was effective: 'the Bush administration did more in three years to divide Germany into an anti-American bloc with France than Charles de Gaulle accomplished through a long and brilliant career.'[69]

Yet, for all that, it would be a mistake to conclude that the dispute over Iraq was purely accidental. The elements of a German–US rift were present before the war, and were only muted by the terrorist attacks of 9/11. A growing divergence in expectations became evident between Washington's demands for loyalty and support and the new '*Berliner Republik*'s' requirement for recognition and consultation. The split was one of style and substance. The question was not whether a dispute would occur but rather which particular issue would force the crisis, its timing and how strongly each party would press its position.

In Germany, there was a genuine sense (both in government and among the public) that the United States' rationale for war in Iraq lacked legitimacy and prudence. Joschka Fischer was not convinced that Iraq was linked to the events of 9/11 and al-Qaeda and thus that the war could be justified as part of the global war on terrorism. The WMD rationale was undercut by the United States' refusal to allow UN weapons inspectors more time to verify their existence. Germany's decision not to support the US-led 'coalition of the willing' over Iraq received overwhelming public support, but was founded more on a sharp, almost visceral, distrust of the Bush administration's post-Afghanistan strategic response to 9/11 than on a wholesale rejection of partnership with the US. Pacifism and anti-war sentiment prior to the Iraq war were stronger and more influential in Germany because of the weakness of the premise that supported pre-emption against an immediate threat: the lack of concrete evidence to suggest operational Iraqi links to al-Qaeda in general, Iraq's responsibility for the events of 9/11 in particular and that it had an active WMD capability, let alone that it possessed weapons that could pose a strategic threat. Germany and France opposed a war that was directed not against fighting terrorism but at securing America's hegemony in accordance with its national security strategy.

Germany had not become more anti-American or more pacifist, but had it become more self-conscious about the role it should adopt in international politics? To a certain degree, German foreign policy exhibited a 'new assertiveness', 'emancipation' or 'normalization', a new sense of self-esteem and independence. Yet this new assertiveness did not entail a return to its historical *Sonderweg*, nor did it signal an end to Germany's *Westbindung*. Instead, it underscored a new determination not only to be part of the West but also to define what 'the West' itself was and how it should be understood and to shape the implications of this reassessment for questions of war and peace on the global stage. In short, Germany wanted the ability to determine which strategic threats demanded a response and to shape its response in a manner that is compatible with the notion of a 'civilian power' that has repudiated unilateral military options in favour of respecting international law and cooperation.

There is no doubt that by 2005, this geopolitical assertiveness was in evidence. Karsten Voigt, the Foreign Ministry's special envoy to the US, has suggested that normalization will improve US–German relations: 'If one speaks of a new beginning, then one speaks of a positive start with a goal. ... Germany was against the [Iraq] war, but we have an interest in the success of the United States in Iraq. More stability and more democracy in Iraq are in European interests, too.' On the other hand, he has cautioned against a US–German relationship that mirrors the two countries' ties during the Cold War: 'It is a very traditional close partnership which is changing, and will improve if we recognize that this partnership needs to be more and more relevant in view of new challenges, and new opportunities and new threats'.[70] He has also noted that 'Germany's security culture is changing. Germany was traditionally a global player in terms of the economy but not in terms of security. Until recently, global security was not on the horizon. The US will have to engage us on the security issues.'[71]

The nature of the impact of Angela Merkel's new government on transatlantic relations is open, and the reality behind the rhetoric of 'honest broker' remains to be seen. Merkel promises to improve the relationship between Germany and the United States, but the most noticeable change so far has occurred only on the level of personal relationship between the Chancellor ('she's plenty capable') and the President ('I completely share your assessment' [of the terrorist threat]).[72] The new government has not been willing to commit German troops to Iraq, and it is concerned that Washington should listen to its allies before making crucial decisions. When visiting NATO, Merkel asserted that the alliance 'should be the place where people turn first with member states to discuss political issues of common concern'.[73] Yet there is no guarantee that the normalization of German foreign policy (a process that is likely to continue) will facilitate German–US cooperation in addressing pressing global security concerns.[74] Germany has so far been able to argue against policies, but it is unable or unwilling to position its opposition within a coherent strategic context (a German strategy for Iraq) that supports its national interest. For now, the *Sonderweg* is mired in constructive ambiguity: the national interest is not defined in a clear-cut way, and so there is little basis upon which Germany can build alliances in support of its strategic initiatives. It still finds it easier to articulate and advocate interests and policies from a European rather than a German position. Moreover, when Europe is divided, Germany has lacked the ability to become the linchpin and anchor of a unified European approach to strategic issues.

5

'New Europe' and transatlantic relations

'OLD EUROPE', 'NEW EUROPE'

The US Secretary of Defense Donald Rumsfeld, in response to a press conference question on his attitude towards French and German criticism of America's Iraq policy, answered, 'That's old Europe ... if you look at the entire NATO Europe today, the centre of gravity is shifting to the east.'[1] 'Old Europe', a Franco-German axis resistant to the necessity of rapid change, wedded to inflexible Cold War structures and sclerotic institutional mindsets, and antagonistic to US policy initiatives, was counterposed by the younger, fresher, more optimistic dynamism of 'New Europe', at least in the imagination. This construct was given form in the 'Letter of Eight' and the declaration by the 'Vilnius 10' in which 13 post-communist states and five EU/NATO members rallied in support of the United States' Iraq policy. What motives lay behind the decision of central and east European (CEE) leaders to place loyalty to the US above their commitment to core EU states? And, as a result, to what extent might this 'New Europe' power bloc impact on the EU's Common Foreign and Security Policy, how might it relate to NATO and how might it shape the quality of transatlantic relations?

US policy initiatives implemented in response to 9/11 served to polarize opinion in Europe and to exacerbate political divisions there. The post-9/11 climate transformed the strategic context and helped to renationalize foreign policies by reinforcing pre-existing national beliefs, traditions, attitudes and practices that hitherto had remained dormant or muted. It thereby led to the reshaping of historically conditioned perceptions as to the strategic utility of the transatlantic relationship: 'the French banter about "Anglo-Saxons" became noisier, German pacifism more pronounced and British as well as Polish Atlanticism more apparent'.[2] In particular, America's apparent unwillingness to utilize NATO as a key policy instrument in its response to the 9/11 attack alienated elite opinion in Europe. Simultaneously, the slow drum beat in the build-up to the Iraq war alienated these very same elites from their publics, which overwhelmingly opposed the use of force on this occasion, as demonstrated by huge anti-war rallies and the catastrophic decline in Europe of public expressions of support for the US.

As the EU and NATO enlarge and integrate more countries, diversity increases within those organizations and the gap between members and non-members widens.[3] Romania and Bulgaria have also achieved NATO membership, and, despite the French and Dutch failure to ratify the European constitution, they are still expected to become members of the EU in the period 2007–10. It is a possibility that by the end of 2006 both the State Union of Serbia and Montenegro and the international protectorate of Bosnia and Herzegovina will have joined the Partnership for Peace (PfP) process, and the EU–Balkan Summit of June 2003 endorsed the belief and aspiration that the entire region could be integrated into the EU over the next decade.

The 'Old Europe'–'New Europe' dichotomy has become a popular catch-phrase but it has its problems too. It obscures the fault lines of 'New Europe', its points of tension and cleavages and also its inability to be wholly Atlanticist or to remain uncritical of the US. As Dominic Moïsi has argued, 'The categorization of "old" and "new" Europe is not only intellectually false, but also politically offensive.' The assumption that 'a country's degree of modernity is determined by its standing with Washington is misguided and narcissistic in the extreme'.[4] As these issues are focused on, it becomes apparent at once that 'New Europe' embraces both Atlanticist and 'Core European' tendencies and sensibilities. There is no single European strategic strait-jacket, and even the political identity and the foreign and security policies, preferences and interests of the states of 'New Europe' are and will remain fluid. The notion of 'New Europe' as a monolithic Atlanticist bloc within an enlarged EU and as representing first- and second-echelon NATO members conditioned to support US foreign policy appears compelling, but it is in fact an illusion.

'NEW EUROPE'S' ATLANTICISM AND ITS IMPACT ON THE CFSP

How might we characterize the impact of the enlargement of the EU by 10 states on the CFSP in general and the European Security and Defence Policy (ESDP) in particular? This question is not easily answered because the behaviour of the new EU states has evolved through the accession process and because the CFSP is also in a process of development. Although predictions are necessarily open-ended, it is clear that a bloc of an 'EU-10' has not emerged. The new members exhibit different priorities and give importance to a variety of issues, and this in itself will change over time.[5]

These caveats aside, two views are often advanced in an effort to characterize the impact of EU integration on the commonality of interests and the foreign and security policy objectives of the accession states. First, new members from among the CEE countries (rather than Cyprus and Malta) are much keener in supporting the US in world politics. They are orientated towards NATO on questions of security rather than being active participants in the construction of an autonomous ESDP. In other words, they strengthen the Atlanticist character of the Union: 'the new members are likely to be strongly Atlanticist, wanting Europe to be partner to the US, not a counterweight in world affairs'.[6] Secondly, prior to accession, it was often argued that enlargement would complicate decision-making in the Union: 'a Europe of 25 members is going to find it even more difficult than a Europe of 15 nations to agree on a common diplomacy and defence'.[7] Christopher Hill has contended that 'it is difficult to see how the transformation of the EU into a 25-member system with at least eight states still enjoying ... recovery of their national independence, can in the short run avoid making foreign policy co-ordination a looser and more competitive process'.[8]

Although these arguments have some validity, they are misleading as solid guides to future preferences and 'New European' security policy decision-making; the reality is more complex.[9] Thus, Matthew Rhodes identifies multiple motivations and distinguishes between three types of explanation for the Atlanticism of 'New Europe'. First, there is 'bandwagoning' for profit. Secondly, there is balancing against the residual threat of Russia or preserving 'voice opportunities' in Europe. Thirdly, there are difficulties in bridging the divisions among transatlantic partners in order 'to preserve and sustain a viable membership within NATO and the broader Euro Atlantic community and so fulfil their primary foreign and security policy goal of the 1990s that they have worked so hard [for] over the past decade'.[10] In short, the Atlanticism of 'New Europe' is pursued for different ends and by multiple means.

The new member states do not have an in-built propensity to prefer the US/Atlantic Europe over 'Old Europe' led by France and Germany. Rather, they prefer to prioritize their security interests within the EU, and these may coincide or oscillate more or less equally between those of 'Old Europe' and America/Atlantic Europe. Their post-accession experience demonstrates that on most occasions and issues, the new members have continued to support EU policies and that over time, they will be increasingly influenced by the EU socialization process. They are eager to be considered constructive members of the Union, and seek to strengthen their voices concerning the CFSP and the ESDP. Indeed, the key obstacles associated with EU decision-making are not generated by the small EU member states but by the inability of the larger states to elaborate and agree upon a common position.

The assumption that the new members of the EU will import an Atlanticist leaning (some might call it a bias) into the Union is supported by their orientation towards the US and NATO in the post-Cold War period, and in particular by the political and some military support they rendered to the US as part of a 'coalition of the willing' in Iraq in the face of Franco-German opposition. How might we account for this Atlanticism? Three main reasons have been offered: a historical debt of gratitude; a calculation that national interest is best served by active US engagement in Europe; and general disillusionment generated by the perception of Franco-German missteps and policy failure. Each rationale was buttressed, it is commonly argued, by shared values as well as, in some cases, a shared strategic culture. Poland, for example, demonstrates a concern for territorial defence, a preference for pro-active engagement and a sceptical and utilitarian attitude to security institutions (apart from NATO).[11]

First, 'New Europe' was grateful to the US for its support for their liberation from the communist yoke during the Cold War. Here the contention is that the US acted in a manner that was more forceful (as befits a superpower), consistent and articulate than European states. The widespread perception in the CEE states of the US as a benign hegemon had its origins in the Wilsonian idealism of the 1920s. President Truman's doctrine of deterrence and containment beginning in the late 1940s reinforced this perception, as did President Carter's support for human rights and democracy in the 1970s. Finally, President Reagan's active de-legitimization of Soviet power (the 'evil empire') in the 1980s further strengthened this image. In the post-Cold War environment, President Clinton's 'enlargement and engagement' strategy was widely perceived to be the driving dynamic of NATO's enlargement, and the appeal of US leadership finds contemporary expression in President George W. Bush's commitment to the idea of 'freedom from tyranny' and support for the 'Rose', 'Orange', 'Purple' and now 'Cedar' and 'Tulip' revolutions in Georgia, Ukraine, Iraq, Lebanon and Kyrgyzstan respectively. The US was understood by the CEE states to have played a critical role in undermining communism, promoting independence, supporting market democratic modernization and, ultimately, fostering NATO's enlargement. The new member states were acutely aware that in return for US support in the past, they could now repay and reciprocate such efforts in the post-9/11 strategic context of the global war on terrorism.

Secondly, it was clear to 'New Europe' throughout the 1990s that on any rational calculus, the US remained the world's only superpower, the key guarantor of their security and the most important player with regard to achieving CEE security policy goals and shaping the international security agenda. In particular, it was considered critical on the eve of their admission to NATO to be close to Washington in order to secure accession. By contrast, the EU as a military actor was still considered to be (and indeed was) nascent, a work-in-progress. European powers in general were incapable of projecting force, even if they had the political will to do so, which they did not.

Thirdly, there was a widespread perception that French and German diplomacy disregarded (either through negligence or disdain) the foreign policy perspectives of the candidate countries, blithely assuming that they would simply follow the lead of the EU 'core'. This perception rankled. The prime minister of Hungary, Peter Medgyessy, stated that he had signed the 'Letter of Eight' supporting Bush's policy because Paris and Berlin had not bothered even to solicit, let alone consider, his opinion. In other words, the CEE countries supported the United States less as an expression of policy agreement than as a protest against the strongly held perception of Franco-German condescension, not to say outright arrogance.

Indeed, the pro-Americanism of the new members is often explained by the power of the perception that 'New Europe' was more afraid of German–French hegemony on the continent than of US hegemony in the world: 'Our countries understand the dangers posed by tyranny and the special responsibility of democracies to defend our shared values.'[12] They are therefore more likely to support the US than an EU dominated by a Franco-German core. The poor image that France and Germany suffer from in 'New Europe' has been compounded by their post-Cold War reluctance to promote NATO's enlargement and their apparent willingness to negotiate compromises with the Russian Federation on issues that greatly concern the CEE states without consulting their 'near abroad'. Needless to add, President Jacques Chirac's caustic remarks after the Vilnius-10's pro-Atlanticist declaration that applicant countries had lost a good opportunity to 'shut up' provided bitter icing on this particularly unappetizing cake.

Before accession, the three factors above played a powerful role in shaping the policy responses of states in 'New Europe', but they had less influence once EU membership had been attained. The strong levels of support for the US exhibited through participation in the 'coalition of the willing' that formed Operation Iraqi Freedom have faded, with the countries of 'New Europe' indicating that they will not automatically contribute militarily to future US wars. How might this be explained?

First of all, insofar as gratitude can ever account for security policies that are driven by national interests, there is a perception that the debt of gratitude to the US has now been paid by the CEE states, partly or in full.[13] Gratitude to the US may also have led to disappointment when this repayment went unacknowledged or even unreciprocated. Antonio Missiroli has reported that Poland, for example, which has been described as one of the United

States' closest allies, an emerging regional leader and America's protégé in the east, expected returns from Washington for its military contribution in Iraq. As an adviser to the Polish prime minister put it, 'We are America's true friends and we have shown it many times, and there should be ... concrete steps from the US to back that up.'[14] In October 2004, the Poles announced that they would withdraw their forces from Iraq by the end of 2005. This 'surprised Poland's allies inside NATO and even its own diplomats'.[15]

Secondly, it is possible that the perception of power relations will change and that the EU will become a more important player in the eyes of 'New Europe'. It may gradually evolve from a 'moral superpower' with 'soft power' to an entity that can project 'hard power' regionally in support of its interests and then perhaps globally. In this way, the EU can begin to frame a policy for the international security agenda and play a leading role in shaping approaches to it rather than responding largely as a reluctant and recalcitrant US partner. Although leading EU politicians are keen to preserve the strong transatlantic relationship and foster friendly bilateral relations with Washington, other elite voices in key opposition parties or respected independent analysts in the new member states warn that historical and geographical realities will make the EU the centre of geostrategic aspiration. This is doubly true because America's interests are global and it seeks global partnerships and coalitions to fulfil its national security objectives. As a result of the growth of EU power and the global reach of US strategic interests, the reliability of American security guarantees to Europe have become eroded, and Europe's reliance on US power looks increasingly fragile and hard to sustain. By contrast, the EU's interests will remain orientated primarily towards Europe and its near neighbourhood; and if attempts to promote its security and defence policy are realized, it will soon become a much more relevant player even in issues related to military security. As one Estonian diplomat has reportedly stated, 'our attitude towards NATO might change if the EU could ever provide a security guarantee. If it did, it would fundamentally alter the transatlantic relationship by making NATO weaker if not irrelevant to our security.'[16]

Another factor in flux is the European perception of Russia as a main source of threat. This is not to suggest that Putin's foreign policy will align Russia appreciably closer to the EU and that Russia's military resources and its policies towards post-Soviet space and beyond will remain moderate. However, even slight improvements in the quality of Russia's cooperative engagement with members of 'New Europe' would decrease the perception of it as a latent threat. Moreover, this perception may lessen over time: historical memories lose their significance and power as generations change. Were Russia to be perceived as a reduced and ever-diminishing threat, the importance of the US security guarantee would lose salience and the role of the EU as a regional and global actor would be enhanced. Conversely, the EU's resistance to Poland's version of Ostpolitik, its 'Eastern Dimension' project, 'could estrange Warsaw from Europe and enhance Poland's ties with Washington'.[17]

Finally, the countries of 'New Europe', as full members of the EU, are now more actively involved in EU decision-making. Germany and France's active engagement with them, especially Poland, has demonstrated their intention to make a special effort to mend fences with CEE states. It is useful to note that in the course of the interview in which President Chirac criticized the new members for their irresponsible behaviour, he also said that 'When you're in the family, you have more rights than when you're knocking on the door.'[18] In turn, the perception of 'New Europe' that a real danger of Franco-German hegemony exists within the EU has also proved to be relative. This perception is especially strong in Poland and the Czech Republic, reinforced by historical experience; but in many of the other new members, such as the Baltic states, Slovakia and Hungary, there is no national memory of having suffered under German or French hegemony. Although the new members do not want to be given second-class treatment, most of them have no historical reflex that prompts or inhibits close cooperation with Germany and France. Therefore, clear opportunities exist for the new members to overcome psychological hurdles. Indeed, France and Germany are making additional efforts to emphasize their benign intentions and their commitment to upholding the national interests of the new member states. For example, a particular effort has been made to engage Poland. The establishment of a 'Weimar triangle' aims to intensify Franco-German-Polish consultation on how the institutional design of Europe should evolve and how to address key international issues.

Furthermore, some commentators in 'New Europe' and elsewhere have suggested that the leaders of ex-communist states have a deeper understanding of the value of freedom and the necessity of military action because they have recently overthrown dictatorships. However, an explanation such as this, accounting for the behaviour of CEE countries with reference to their internalization of 'American' values, is misleading. 'New Europe' did not back the US over Iraq because they shared a common value system or world view. Extensive opinion poll surveys in the CEE countries have demonstrated that commonality and a commitment to the same set of values did not lead their publics to support the US. Nor does evidence suggest that CEE leaders justified their states' membership in US-led coalitions on the grounds of shared values. As Ivan Krastev argues, ex-communist leaders currently govern the former communist states that now constitute 'New Europe', and their defining characteristic is hardly a 'commitment to freedom'.[19] For many states in 'New Europe', terrorism is not the main strategic threat. That is a central concern of Russia. Strategic partnership with the US consolidated through active membership in the global anti-terror (and now anti-tyranny) coalition mitigates Russian influence over their foreign and security policies. In any case, public opinion in 'New Europe' and 'Atlantic' Europe has tended to mirror that in 'Core Europe', 'Non-aligned Europe' and indeed 'Periphery Europe'. The populations of the CEE states proved to be as pacifist as those in the rest of Europe, and did not support the US-led war in Iraq by overwhelming margins. Nor was the view of the US necessarily more positive among the new members than in the EU-15. For example, 43 per cent of the citizens in the then candidate countries believed that the role of the United States in maintaining peace in the world was negative; only 34 per cent considered it to be positive. In the old member states, the pattern was similar: 41 per cent had a positive perception of the US role in maintaining global peace while 39 per cent held a negative view.[20]

Perhaps too much attention has been paid to Iraq in understanding current CEE state behaviour and, on that basis, attempting to predict future trends. On most issues of less importance than Iraq, the new members have aligned themselves with the old EU-15. 'New Europe' has supported the common EU trade policy in transatlantic disputes and its members have also backed the EU's position on more sensitive political issues, such as support for the International Criminal Court. Also, they voted in the UN General Assembly or in the Organization for Security and Cooperation in Europe (OSCE) with the EU rather than the US.

Finally, the continuing instability in Iraq even after the referendum of 15 October 2005 approved of the new constitution and after the December 2005 national elections, and the failure to find proof of the existence of weapons of mass destruction or operational Iraqi links to transnational terrorism (particularly al-Qaeda), have made it much more difficult for CEE elites to support potential US pre-emptive military intervention in Iran or Syria, for example, were an imminent threat alleged. The implosion of the US-led coalition's strategic rationale for pre-emptive military intervention in Iraq has damaged America's credibility and the reputation of its intelligence-gathering capability. It has also raised the suspicion that its intelligence-gathering process is vulnerable to politicization. Thus it will probably be harder for the US to persuade other countries to support the logic of its national security strategy in the future.

In sum, the impact of 'New Europe' on the EU has not radically transformed the latter's approach to transatlantic relations. Some of the new member states do demonstrate a greater understanding of and sympathy for US positions, but this does not translate into a unified Atlanticist bloc.

Underlying historical, geographical and cultural factors, as well as the particularities of each state's domestic political agenda, all promote floating coalitions within the EU. Indeed, 'New Europe's' integration into the Union has reinforced existing tensions between the EU and the US rather than realigned EU policy with that of the US: the views of 'New Europe', 'Core Europe' and 'Atlantic Europe' as expressed through reference to the EU are fundamentally similar.

The claim that enlargement will complicate decision-making in foreign and security policy was often heard on the eve of enlargement. Many argued that if decision-making in foreign and security policy is based on unanimity, then it is logical that increasing the number of EU member states by 10 would create further obstacles to and dilemmas about agreeing on anything but the lowest common denominator. The parliaments in the 'New European' states that had only recently regained their freedom and, in some cases, independence could prove to be unwilling to relinquish control over key foreign and security policy decisions. These sovereignty dilemmas would paralyse the EU's ability to formulate coherent policy. This reasoning was put forward in the European convention that drafted the new constitutional treaty. In the course of the debate, arguments were voiced that supported leadership groups of big states and promoted qualified majority voting. Although both proposals were rejected, many believed that a policy based on the lowest common denominator of 25 or more countries would lead to stagnation in foreign and security policy-making and damage the EU's ability to shape and influence the transatlantic security agenda.

Despite initial concerns, events have demonstrated that enlargement has not handicapped decision-making. To begin with, neither the number of states nor the tendency of small states to disagree with the majority position has constituted the most serious problem. The essential difficulty has been that the big three to five member states have not been able to agree on a common position on a number of issues. If the large states form a common position, then the small states are likely to follow them. This dynamic exists independently of whether there are 10 or 20 small states in the Union.

This consideration is illustrated both by the actual observable behaviour of the EU states and by public opinion polls. First, the small states vote with the majority of the EU in the UN General Assembly more often than do some of the old members, most notably France and the UK.[21] Even before accession to the EU, 'New Europe' aligned itself with the vast majority of the EU's policy statements.[22] Secondly, public opinion in the new member states supports the strengthening of EU institutions. In the view of the citizens of those countries, decision-making on defence and security should be conducted increasingly on the EU level rather than at the national or NATO level.[23]

Of course, there is a kernel of truth in the assumption that decision-making would become more cumbersome after enlargement, because it is undoubtedly more difficult to find compromises in a larger group of countries. There is also an increased likelihood that individual problem countries will emerge and block compromises over particular issues. One example from the 1980s is Malta's role in blocking for several months the closing of the Madrid follow-up meeting of the OSCE. Another possible source of difficulty is Cyprus. It is divided and has delicate relations with Turkey. The dispute between them may block further development of EU–NATO relations.

For the most part, the new member states play a constructive role in the EU, and their political positions have aligned with the majority view. The new members want the EU to be effective, and have not assumed a spoiler's role. The policies of the small member states have also been influenced by the socialization effects of membership and by their desire not to be marginalized in the process.[24] If we examine the experience of the previous round of enlargement, it is evident how the Europeanization process works in practice. Finland and Sweden provide good examples that demonstrate the extent to which EU membership has gradually influenced policy positions on security and defence that were believed to be fundamental and fixed (see Chapter 6). Their understanding of 'neutrality' or, more accurately, 'military non-alignment' has slowly expanded and has enabled them to support the initiation of the ESDP, to participate in its operations and to make a commitment to build military capabilities and participate in a rapid reaction force with, in theory at least, a global geostrategic role.[25]

To summarize, although the enlargement of the EU from 15 to 25 states has marginally further complicated achieving rapid and timely decisions, it has not led to calls for a formal '*directoire*' of the larger member states. When the big EU states have reached agreement, the smaller states have followed suit. Indeed, if EU decision-making in security and defence issues is in real need of streamlining, then more majority decision-making should be introduced. In reality there is a tradition to avoid voting on issues where the unanimity principle holds, but rather to take decisions on a consensus basis. Voting as a last resort provides the incentive to find a consensus. In practice, even new member states are able to shape the EU agenda on initiatives in which it is recognized they have a regional or functional interest: Poland's special relationship with Ukraine is one example, and when Romania and Bulgaria join the EU it is likely that they will play a major role in shaping its relations towards the western Balkans, Moldova and the South Caucasus. But even though 'New Europe' has not had a discernible impact on the approach of the EU towards foreign and security policy decision-making about transatlantic relations and the transatlantic security agenda, can the same be said of its members' role in NATO?

In the post-Cold War era, enlargement has generated asymmetrical and differentiated responses from the EU and NATO. This has been reflected in the security debates on minimizing competition and maximizing complementarity and cooperation in terms of the roles, missions and duties of these organizations. Enlargement has also generated tensions between current EU and NATO members and those in the process of integration, as well as between states that have the ability to integrate and those that either cannot integrate or whose elites and publics perceive integration as a long-term generational strategic objective.

It might have been argued, half in jest, that the best interests of the southeast European states and the Baltic states within a transatlantic security alliance would be to join any emerging consensus. This would maximize their influence. However, the events of the past few years have shown that such a policy is now untenable. As Secretary of Defense Rumsfeld himself has noted, 'The distinction between old and new Europe today is not really a matter of age or size or even geography. It is a matter of attitude, of the vision that countries bring to the trans-Atlantic relationship.'[26] Bluntly put, which is more important to the Baltic and southeast European NATO states: European NATO priorities or American NATO priorities?

Along with NATO membership comes the duty to effectively fulfil the responsibilities of membership. The US in particular asks two key questions of its new allies in 'New Europe': will their commitment to democracy strengthen the alliance's ability to protect and promote its security, value and interests? Can NATO be confident that a new member's commitment to democracy and the alliance's values will endure? In military terms, these questions translate more practically into the challenge for members of the EU and NATO to balance a need to develop both niche capabilities and specialized roles in the NATO Reaction Force (NRF) with a responsibility to develop peacekeepers to support the European Rapid Reaction Force and the EU's battle group concept. Can the Baltic and southeast European states advance on two fronts at once or is their choice constrained because of financial, personnel, administrative and institutional capacity shortfalls and limitations? Both tasks have the potential to unbalance their militaries and create tensions in defence planning, in responding to contingencies and in tasking.

On the one hand, role specialization for the NRF enhances the 'strategic partnership' with the US and opens the possibility of integration into 'coalitions of the willing'. But this participation would be symbolic at best – the 'New European' states' contribution is not needed militarily – and it could be unpopular at home depending on casualties and the gap between the perceived necessity for pre-emption and the perceived imminence of the threat. On the other hand, preparing with the EU for peace support operations could be more popular domestically, but it is far from clear whether the EU has the decision-making capacity and the financial and political will to operate in an effective way. These doubts have increased since it expanded to 25. To take Estonia as an example, it currently concentrates on professionalizing its military and training a light infantry quick reaction battalion for the NRF; it has no capacity to contribute military units to ESDP operations. Other states such as Slovakia and Hungary are developing forces that could be used either by NATO or by the EU, but their commitment to NATO is to be given priority. Lithuania hopes to avoid these choices by adopting a 'three Ss policy': a single set of forces, planning for a single kind of contingency and a single decision-making base.

Another issue that has already raised the question of priorities is the US rejection of the EU-supported International Criminal Court (ICC). On 1 July 2003, the United States froze military aid programmes for many allies in Europe and Latin America in response to their refusal to sign bilateral agreements granting immunity to all US citizens from war crimes prosecution by the ICC. Waivers had been given to Albania, Bosnia-Herzegovina, Macedonia, Romania and Tajikistan, but diplomats and analysts were surprised that the US did not exempt the European countries that were due to join NATO in 2004 (Bulgaria, Estonia, Latvia, Lithuania, Slovakia and Slovenia) as well as the aspirant and existing PfP members – the State Union of Serbia and Montenegro and Croatia respectively.[27] Romania, in particular, supported the US position on the ICC; but in doing so, it undermined an EU-supported institution and thus strained its relations with the Union. The US position towards the ICC has not changed substantially since 2003; and in late 2005, the issue of 'extraordinary renditions' refocused attention both on differing US and European legal interpretations and approaches to international law, and on US illegality and European hypocrisy.

The decision to integrate seven new NATO members into the second-echelon enlargement process was shaped by the performance of the first-echelon states after their integration. A number of 'lessons learned' had been identified, which have suggested security policy implications for the second-echelon integration states. Based on the experience of the Czech Republic, Hungary and Poland, it became clear that the force structure of prospective NATO member states would need to change after accession. All new members face budgetary constraints as they attempt to restructure their militaries. Inadequacies in their constitutional and legal systems persist and must be addressed, along with changes to national security doctrines, and military concepts and doctrines. Emerging incompatibilities between national and NATO defence planning have to be resolved. Whether their publics and elites will continue to support membership of NATO to the same extent after accession as in the pre-accession period remains to be seen.

NATO's enlargement opened the possibility that the US would reconfigure the posture of its military forces in Europe. The changing US military presence reflects the necessity of policing the 'new American perimeter'.[28] Three principles will ensure that the interests of the United States and of its allies are upheld in this process. First, the reconfiguration must advance US strategic interests; it must allow the US to respond more effectively to the asymmetrical challenges (that is, threats which conventional forces configured for conventional warfare find hard to counter) of the twenty-first century. Secondly, a military reconfiguration should have an operational impact that increases the United States' ability to respond to current threats and to facilitate and enhance its transformation from the industrial to the digital age. As NATO extends east, so does its centre of gravity, and the US reconfiguration is reflecting this reality. At the same time, a balance between 'lightness' and 'lethality' must be maintained. Thirdly, reconfiguration should not be driven only by political or economic considerations, although economic prudence and political ties can and do enter the equation in decisions on maintaining bases or creating new ones.[29]

These principles entail a switch in emphasis from building large, heavily staffed garrisons to a more modern style of basing. General James L. Jones, from 2003 Supreme Allied Commander, Europe and Commander of the United States European Command, has spoken of the creation of 'bare bones bases' or 'lily pads', jumping-off points for pre-positioned equipment rather than Okinawa-style American mini-garrisons, noting that a Pentagon study in 2002 determined that 20 per cent of the 499 bases in Germany are no longer 'terribly usable'.[30] Instead, he favours these smaller, lighter, more scattered bases in which such pre-positioned equipment and six-month rotating skeleton staff (without dependants) can respond with greater speed and flexibility to deployments out of area. Discussions continue to determine where these 'bare bones' bases might be located. In Poland, Krzesinsky airbase near Poznan has been mentioned; in Hungary, Taszar airbase is a possibility. In Romania, Mihail Kogalniceanu airbase near Constanta, the Babadag training ground and Mangalia port are all under consideration. In Bulgaria, the airfields of Dobrich in the northeast, Kroumovo in the south and Graf Ignatievo near Plovdiv have been discussed, as have the ports of

Burgas and Varna and the training grounds of Koren and Novo Selo.

The military benefits of these bases are clear: locating bases closer to areas of conflict increases geostrategic flexibility (for example, mid-air refuelling for tactical-range F-16s becomes less of an issue). Positioning bases in states with less restrictive environmental legislation allows more live-fire exercises, training manoeuvres in heavily tracked vehicles and helicopter night flights. This contributes to maintaining a higher level of military readiness and conducting joint exercises with host-nation militaries and to increasing the interoperability of new NATO member states. In addition to consolidating political ties, basing US military forces in Bulgaria and Romania will relieve the basing burden on Turkey and give Turkish politicians some diplomatic cover because actions will be regional initiatives rather than solely US–Turkish efforts.

Will 'New Europe' generate unrealistic expectations about the military, economic and political benefits that will accrue from opening up new bases or restoring and extending existing Soviet-era ones? Will the NATO–Russia Council allow the issue of new bases on former Soviet borders and of even extending US bases from Central Asia to the southern Caucasus (e.g. Georgia and Azerbaijan) to be managed or will Russia begin to object to this increased US presence?[31] Given the US bases already in Turkey, Armenia is unlikely to argue that it is concerned with the proximity of new NATO bases. But if the US presence at these bases should impact negatively on Russia–NATO relations, it would be concerned.[32] One can also argue that the minimal nature of these 'lily pads' helps to immunize them against negative perceptions of an overbearing US presence.

However, two processes might occur that would blur this positive interpretation. First, bureaucratic, institutional and political considerations might lead to the padding of the 'bare bones' bases. They would thus negate the benefits of the lighter presence and increase Russian antagonism. Secondly, with the greater possibility that the EU will deploy peacekeepers to the Dniestr region of Moldova (as part of its growing efforts to increase stability in its neighbourhood), it is highly likely that in conformity with the 'Berlin Plus' agreement (on which, see Chapter 1), the EU will want to use America's NATO assets (such as airfields) in Romania.[33] This may also generate concern on the part of neighbouring states, particularly Russia. A clear understanding of the hidden costs of such a move might also undermine the US Department of Defense's determination to carry it through. Moreover, there is an air of unreality about the notion of forward-basing troops and particularly equipment in 'New Europe' rather than in 'Old Europe'. Deploying from Romania to the Middle East as opposed to from Germany saves a day. Presumably, if the transit time of heavy forces is critical, then they are deployed a day earlier from Germany. If not, then light forces are sent with no time delay.

Enlargement into northeastern and southeastern Europe has strained NATO Europe's and the EU's relations with both traditional regional partners and near neighbours. After the accession of the Baltic states to NATO and the EU, the attitudes and choices of their elites put pressure on the ability of their foreign and defence establishments to maintain cohesion in foreign and security policy formation and implementation. Foreign policy coordination among the states of the Baltic in the military security sector is widely perceived as the jewel in the crown of that region's cooperation. It is the most active, interoperable (in terms of personnel, materiel and infrastructure) and effective example of practical and meaningful collaboration.

In southeastern Europe similar dynamics are at work. Slovenia, Romania and Bulgaria, all new NATO members, have argued that PfP membership for all states in the western Balkans is critical to stability in the region. They have praised the role of the Southeast European Stability Pact, which Macedonia, Serbia and Montenegro, Bosnia and Herzegovina, Bulgaria, Croatia, Romania and Albania joined in 1999: 'Initiated by the EU with strong US support and placed under the auspices of the Organization for Security and Cooperation in Europe ..., the Stability Pact aims to strengthen democracy, economic development and security throughout the region.'[34] The Adriatic Charter, modelled on the 1997 Baltic Charter that was developed as a compensatory alternative to first-echelon NATO membership, has been offered to Albania, Croatia, and Macedonia as compensation for failure to gain integration into the second echelon of NATO. Similar to the Baltic Charter, the Adriatic Charter encourages new and intensifies existing cooperation among these states. In addition, it demonstrates a significant cooperative capacity, thereby strengthening the possibility of third-echelon membership. The June 2003 EU–Balkan Summit reaffirmed the EU's desire eventually to integrate all Balkan states into the Union. As the Slovene Prime Minister Anton Rop stated, 'The EU has shown that the integration of the Balkan states is one of the priority tasks.'[35] Lord Robertson too has emphasized the necessity for integration. He has argued that border controls need to be strengthened in order to fight organized crime, a prominent threat to regional stability: 'Either the region takes control of its borders or the criminals will take control of the region.'[36]

However, there are a number of challenges that must be overcome. Some are relatively straightforward. Although 90 per cent of Albania's population supports membership of NATO, the state has low democratic standards; however, the process of gradual integration into the EU will enhance democratization efforts and the support of near neighbours will lead to improvements. Bosnia-Herzegovina (BiH) represents another challenge that poses tough policy questions for the EU and neighbouring states. It has low internal cohesion: there have been 13 prime ministers, 180 ministers and 760 legislators within three entities (Respublika Srpska and the Bosnian and Croat parts of the Federation); and these are led by nationalist leaders with a zero-sum mentality – if one entity benefits, it can only be at the expense of the other two.[37] BiH can be governed only through an international supervisory administration. Central to the emergence of a sustainable and efficient state will be comprehensive, unified support by neighbouring states and the unity of the international community in forcing reforms (including the non-toleration of anti-Dayton factions). But the power and credibility of the international community, particularly of the EU, is weak: security promises and actions by the EU have little effect in BiH more than 10 years after the massacres at Srebrenica on 11 July 1995. Trust will be hard to rebuild.[38] Also, near neighbours lack comprehensive policies towards BiH. Although in 2003 the new Croatian government withdrew outright support for integrating Croats in BiH into Croatia, it has not found a substitute for the policy for the break-up of BiH.

The State Union of Serbia and Montenegro faced implementing a huge reform process after the assassination of Prime Minister Djinjic in February 2003, with few allies, few resources and the continued influence of privatized security services, organized crime groups and ultra-nationalist political and religious leaders. Its difficulties were compounded by the ever-present possibility of the independence of Montenegro following the election in early 2003 of a pro-independence president. Indeed, a referendum is set for 21 May 2006. The final status of Kosovo will also be determined in 2006, with a decision by the international community that the status quo is not sustainable. It is highly likely that by the end of 2006 some sort of qualified sovereignty will have been agreed, with the international community in a supervisory role for the next 10–15 years. Will independence for Kosovo and perhaps Montenegro break the logjam by overcoming the expectation, development and integration gaps in the Western Balkans?[39] Will the international community be able to guarantee viable autonomy for minorities, or will such an outcome reinforce the current trend of indirect ethnic cleansing in the province and serve as a precedent to other secessionist movements in the region, not least Abkhazia and South Ossetia in Georgia? Panacea or Pandora's box: either outcome will affect stability in Serbia, Montenegro, Kosovo and Macedonia and hence relations between the five Europes and the United States at least until the centenary of the assassination of Archduke Ferdinand in Sarajevo in June 1914.

The Bush administration has progressively been turning over America's

Balkan responsibilities to the EU, including short-term crisis management and the long-term development of the region. Its funding and military presence are being reduced. For its part, the EU is assuming a greater role through a number of instruments: a region-wide stability pact to provide a framework for concrete projects, a stabilization and association process for mapping steps towards association and eventual membership of the EU, and an assistance programme for reconstruction, development and stabilization. However, current EU member states' policies appear to be split: the ESDP's coherence is losing out to the national policies of individual governments, and the appearance of unity is dispelled further each time policy reform issues are brought to the table. For example, some EU member states argue for the early integration of BiH into the PfP, despite the absence of a functioning ministry of defence in BiH. The Union's inability to develop a consensus towards BiH poses an additional major challenge for state consolidation, and is further compounded by a difference in approach between it and the US.

Dual enlargement has also strengthened the perception that the Baltic and southeast European states are on the front line, at the interface between a European core and periphery, and that they need to engage and interact with states that have little or no prospect of integration into NATO or the EU. This outreach function will constitute their contribution to producing security.[40] Nevertheless, this responsibility is a burden too, and must be managed. During the first decade of the post-Soviet period, the Baltic states successfully undertook democratization efforts to achieve stability and security, and as a result they integrated into the EU and NATO in 2004. Their success has raised expectations that they can effectively export their civil and military transformation to neighbours. The Baltic military establishments have 'conceptual expertise' in modernization and 'change management', experiences that existing NATO countries by definition do not share. As small post-Soviet states, they could contribute valuable lessons and experiences that will help to stabilize the military reform projects in the southern Caucasus states of Georgia, Armenia and Azerbaijan. Their contribution could be graduated and directed, beginning with the 'soft' end of civil and military reform and continuing into the 'harder' end, by identifying elements that require stabilization and then reforming the specific institutions that will take part in the stabilization role. This policy appears attractive. If the Baltic states were able to export security successfully, their value would increase in NATO's eyes. This process has already started: the Central Asian Battalion and the Sarajevo Military Academy are using the Baltic Battalion and Baltic Defence College experiences as templates for their own development.[41]

However, this prospect also raises possibilities that could strain the defence establishments of the Baltic countries. The needs of the southern

Caucasus states are great; and even though the Baltic region has made enormous progress in the past 15 years, it still needs to focus on maintaining its own momentum. The Baltic states should not have to bear the major part of the burden of civil and military reform outreach simply because of geography, their new role in NATO and their common history and experience as former components of the USSR. Having joined NATO and the EU, they must juggle many balls as good members of those organizations, as effective interlocutors with Russia, Ukraine and Belarus, as participants in US-led 'coalitions of the willing' in the global war on terrorism and as mentors sharing their experience in the southern Caucasus. Their civil and military elites must coordinate their limited assistance so as to make its impact as effective as possible.

CONCLUSIONS: DYNAMICS OF INCLUSION OR DISILLUSION?

As of 1 May 2004, the EU's membership was 25 countries. This enlargement created fears that the Union's ability to make unanimous decisions in the field of foreign and security policy would be disrupted or compromised. Some states feared and others hoped that the centre of gravity would shift away from a 'Gaullist' continental foreign and security policy towards a more Atlanticist, pro-US direction. Consequently, attempts to strengthen the ESDP would be seriously handicapped.

Neither contention has yet to be proved entirely false, and each represents a simplification that fails to account clearly for the effects of both EU and NATO enlargement on the foreign and security policies of these states. In addition, such contentions ignore the more idealistic and values-based perspectives new members have brought to the EU and NATO, which contrast with the more pragmatic and realpolitik approaches of old members. For this reason, neither should be regarded as a major point of reference for policy recommendations. This chapter has suggested that the strong Atlanticist attitude in 'New Europe' has a limited shelf life. Although CEE states will not become openly hostile to Washington, they are increasingly prepared to criticize America's leadership and foreign and security policy initiatives within the context of the global war on terrorism. At the fundamental level of world views, the new members do not differ radically from the old members in terms of their perspective on and approach to international relations. In short, the new members are likely to become 'European' – that is, to be prepared on occasion to disagree with the mainstream perspective but in most cases to support the strengthening of the CFSP and the ESDP.

As a security strategy, 'bandwagoning' by 'New Europe' may well prove to be most effective in the context of current transatlantic relations. This

allows the new entrants to maximize their gains, particularly strategic partnership with the US, which will be supported by greater American military
assistance. However, the role of balancer may well recommend itself to the
larger CEE states. Poland, a member of NATO, has a geopolitical weight
that can shape the strategic balance between European members of NATO
and the US. The deployment of a Polish division to Iraq illustrates this.
But as Adam Daniel Rotfeld, the Polish deputy minister of foreign affairs,
has stated, 'Let me note here that the unfortunate statement by Donald
Rumsfeld about "old" and "new" Europe doesn't reflect properly the new
realities, and, in fact does not make things easier for those allies, who – as
Poland – demonstrate their solidarity with the United States. Such differ-
entiation does not correspond to the very logic of the on-going process of
European integration.'[42]

Romania, as a new member of NATO, may well wish to lead a sub-
regional political and economic system in southeastern Europe. But because
it seeks EU membership by 2007, its priorities may not stray too far (at least
publicly) from the EU consensus, at least until it secures membership. This is
particularly likely to give the EU pause for dialogue and debate following the
rejection of the constitutional treaty in May 2005. A 'small-state complex'
may assert itself among other new members as they oscillate between inclusionist and disillusionist experiences of membership. The trade-offs and
costs incurred by 'New Europe' in its support of European or US priorities
becomes less complex the more divided Europe remains or the more US and
European policy initiatives overlap. The more united Europe becomes and
the greater the gulf between American and European policy responses to
security threats, the greater the obstacles, challenges and dilemmas will be
that confront the foreign and security policy-making of 'New Europe', and
the more fragmented it will become.

6

'Non-aligned Europe' and transatlantic relations

The transatlantic turmoil and the US-led global war on terrorism affected not just 'Core Europe', 'Atlantic Europe' and 'New Europe' but also states that were members of the EU but not NATO. This group, much overlooked in discussions of the transatlantic trauma and European security, consisted of those countries that had adopted military non-alignment as the organizing principle of their foreign and security policy: Sweden, Finland, Austria and Ireland. President Bush's clear-cut, black-and-white challenge to the global community presented policy dilemmas to all non-aligned states – the very integrity of that concept was called into question: 'each nation, each region has to make a choice. Either you are with us or you are with the terrorists' and 'Against such an enemy, there is no immunity, and there can be no neutrality.'[1] It is therefore instructive to examine how the European 'post-neutrals' have reacted to the post-9/11 world and in particular to the trans-atlantic trauma that split Europe into opposing camps and soured relations between and among states in the transatlantic security community. How and in what ways were the material interests, the values and the identities of these states challenged by the transatlantic crisis?

Austria, Finland, Ireland and Sweden are often lumped together as coun-tries belonging to the category of European 'post-neutral' states.[2] As EU member states, they have chosen to remain militarily non-aligned in that they are not members of any military organization, such as NATO, although they do actively participate in NATO's Partnership for Peace programme. Malta and Cyprus became EU members in 2004 and are now militarily non-aligned, but Malta's neutrality was defined within the Mediterranean context, and Cyprus's primary foreign and security goal is to secure unification of the island and to improve Greek–Turkish relations. For its part, Switzerland has retained a more traditional or classical neutrality-based foreign and security policy: it stands outside both the EU and NATO.

There are a number of states in 'Periphery Europe' that are also neither EU nor NATO members. Some of them do have a tradition of non-alignment – Albania with its Cold War isolationist foreign policy springs to mind, although it now seeks NATO membership. (Former) Yugoslavia also declared its non-alignment policy when it broke from the Soviet camp in 1948, but now Slovenia is a NATO member and all other of its former republics seek membership, with varying degrees of success. Some post-Soviet republics, such as Moldova and Belarus, are now officially non-aligned, but only Turkmenistan declares itself to be neutral.

Thus states that either traditionally or currently are non-aligned or neutral do not form a distinct and homogeneous group.[3] Even Finland, Sweden, Austria and Ireland, which were neutral during the Cold War, have considerable differences in their traditional understanding of neutrality: the origins of neutrality differ in each state, as does the legal status of their neutrality (Austria's, for example, is based on a treaty). Despite these differences, there are important commonalities in their historical experiences and development. They are all small states with no significant recent colonial heritage, although the Swedish and Austro-Hungarian empires certainly share imperial pasts. As a result of their Cold War neutrality, they also lack a history of strong and active cooperation with the US and principal 'Atlantic European' states in the NATO framework. Currently, they are all EU members, and all face the policy dilemmas posed by the further militarization of the ESDP. It is primarily in this context that they can play a role in narrowing or widening the transatlantic rift and in exacerbating or ameliorating the trauma in European security that followed it.

This chapter will focus on the Finnish and Swedish experience of transatlantic relations before and after 9/11. In the post-9/11 period, these states had to decide where their primary loyalties lay. This loyalty could be orientated towards the US, the EU or their commitment to the traditional principles of 'neutrality' and their small-states doctrine, which was based on strong support of the UN and international law. This doctrine includes an emphasis on the peaceful solution of all disputes and a strong aversion to military intervention. We argue that the small-states doctrine remained paramount in the post-9/11 period but that neutrality ceased to have what little practical meaning it had inherited from the Cold War. Non-alignment did, however, hold symbolic meaning and was central to identity-building in these former neutral countries. They have been unwilling to abandon their non-aligned status, as it is powerfully connected to their positive self-image: it is not considered a strategy of the weak and powerless or a means of unscrupulous and selfish free-riding but seen as an active and consistent policy that is appropriate in a globalizing world. All the same, they have readjusted and recast the meaning of non-alignment for the era of the global war on terrorism. Instead of occupying a middle ground between Islamist terrorists and the 'West', they have positioned themselves between the US and 'Atlantic Europe', on the one hand, and 'New Europe', 'Core Europe' and 'Periphery Europe', on the other. They seek to remain non-aligned from these power blocs and interests by recourse to what might be understood as a policy of non-alignment through equidistance.

9/11 AND AFGHANISTAN: 'FOR US OR AGAINST US?'

Sweden and Finland displayed different attitudes towards the US and NATO in the Cold War. Sweden preferred to remain outside NATO because it already had a strongly established tradition of neutrality. Finland, having narrowly missed being incorporated into the Soviet Union by conquest during the Second World War, did not see NATO membership as an alternative to neutrality. Neutrality was the preferred option to full and forcible integration into the Soviet bloc.[4] For Sweden, the choice to adopt a security strategy based on 'non-alignment in peace time, shifting to neutrality in war' reflected a viable and effective strategy that would protect its national interest even in wartime.[5] In the context of an East–West conflict, Finland, unlike Sweden, had little hope of remaining neutral. But in peacetime, neutrality had a dual function in protecting the Finnish national interest: it created some distance between Helsinki and Moscow and it positioned Finland's identity and policies firmly within a Nordic context.

During the Cold War, Finland's foreign policy was based on preserving 'good-neighbourly relations' with the Soviet Union. As a result, Finland was careful to restrain its criticism of the USSR. By the 1970s, this was characterized as 'Finlandization'. Not only did the Soviet Union and the mutual cooperation treaty with it pose restrictions on Finland's integration into the West but also Finnish society was unable to discuss honestly the reality of socialism in the Soviet Union. But owing to its neutral status, Finland was equally reluctant to criticize the US. In this sense, its relationship with and attitude towards the US clearly differed from that of Sweden.

Sweden's self-image was historically centred on the notion of the 'moral superpower'; and in the Cold War, this translated into a desire to act as the world's conscience, freely criticizing the Soviet Union and the United States for their imperialist ambitions.[6] The former Finnish diplomat Max Jakobson noted that there was some truth in the observation that 'Finland tried to maintain good relations with both sides in the Cold War, while Sweden insulted both even-handedly'.[7] Yet in practice, Sweden as a 'silent partner' of NATO aligned with the alliance: it both counted on NATO assistance in the case of a Soviet attack and secretly planned for it.[8] These two policy postures coexisted in Sweden under the umbrella of neutrality; and as a result, historians have often sought to make a distinction between 'political Sweden' and 'military Sweden' when discussing its neutrality.[9]

When the Cold War ended, Finland, with its closer and imposed Soviet ties, was quicker to demonstrate its Atlanticist orientation. It did so, for example, through the purchase of Hornet F-18 fighters rather than Swedish JAS fighters. With regard to NATO, both countries simultaneously developed a relationship based on closer cooperation. They joined the Euro-Atlantic Partnership Council and the PfP programme, and in both countries the foreign policy elites actively debated about the real content of neutrality or military non-alignment and its significance in the post-Cold War world. The possibility of NATO membership was also discussed (the 'not if but when?' debate), particularly after the accession of Sweden and Finland to the EU in 1995, but neither the leading politicians and parties nor public opinion embraced the idea of abandoning military non-alignment. Both states formally supported the Kosovo campaign of 1999, but public opinion was divided and the war appeared to strengthen rather than erode the policy of military non-alignment.[10]

The terrorist attacks of 9/11 brought 'political Sweden' closer to the US. President Bush's visit to Sweden during the Swedish presidency of the EU in June 2001 had already swept the remnants of Cold War tensions aside.[11] Sweden's reactions to 9/11 expressed solidarity rather than historical anti-Americanism. Prime Minister Göran Persson, together with Foreign Minister Anna Lindh, forcefully condemned the terrorist attacks in New York and Washington from the outset. In Persson's view, the US had a right as well as an obligation to defend itself. He argued that Sweden must support America's right to self-defence, a right enshrined in Article 51 of the UN Charter, the UN being an institution Sweden wholeheartedly supported. At the Social Democratic Party Congress in November 2001, he used strong language in describing the Taliban regime as 'Satan's murderers' and 'a creature of a dictatorship'. This language evoked resonant historical parallels: the expressions were those of former prime minister Olof Palme when he had referred to Franco's Spain and post-1968 Czechoslovakia.[12] Persson's visit to Washington in December 2001 was understood as a clear demonstration of Sweden's strong partnership with the US.[13] Sweden deployed special forces units in support of Operation Enduring Freedom, and it also decided to participate in ISAF's operations in Afghanistan, committing a small intelligence unit and two transport aircraft.

Sweden's institutional support for the US-led global war on terrorism did not undermine its security strategy of military non-alignment. Political parties in Sweden did continue to debate the merits and costs of possible NATO integration. But in the Social Democratic Party, the debate was lukewarm. The conservative party Moderaterna, as well as the Christian Democrats, were willing to consider Sweden's membership in NATO at a future date but it did not think that it was propitious to discuss the question of membership in the immediate post-9/11 context. The small liberal Folkpartiet remained the only party that openly supported Sweden's integration into NATO. The Green Party and the Left Party, traditionally the strongest opponents of NATO membership, argued that 9/11 only underscored the necessity and virtue of holding close to a security strategy of military non-alignment.[14]

These differences of opinion became very clear in a parliamentary debate in mid-October 2001. Critics from the Left Party and the Greens did not support the concept of a US-led global war on terrorism and argued that the use of military force in Afghanistan would only lead to a 'spiral of violence without end'. Prime Minister Persson and the representatives of the parties on the right responded by stressing the necessity of combating terrorism and arguing that counter-terrorist initiatives and anti-terrorist cooperation had achieved a broad level of international support. A critical voice in the public debate from within the Social Democratic Party was provided by former prime minister Ingvar Carlsson, who, together with the former minister for education Carl Tham, argued that the terrorist attacks could be understood as a legitimate attack on an unjust global order supported by the US. The fight against terrorism should therefore focus on the root causes of terrorism.[15] Also, the 'grand old man' of Sweden's neutrality policy, Sverker Åström, argued that Sweden and the EU should take responsibility for fighting terrorism and refrain from continuing as providers of transport for the US effort.[16] According to this thinking, non-alignment could realistically offer room for impartiality even in the context of the war on terrorism.

In opinion polls, a majority of Swedes backed Prime Minister Persson's policy towards the US and the US-led Operation Enduring Freedom in Afghanistan.[17] But support for Sweden's membership in NATO decreased as Operation Enduring Freedom unfolded, as it had done two years earlier during the NATO campaign in Kosovo, and only 25 per cent supported military alignment with the alliance.[18] The longer the war in Afghanistan continued, the more critical of it public opinion became.[19]

Some observers were ready to contend that Sweden was more willing than Finland to join the US-led coalition against international terrorism.[20] Finland's leaders had immediately condemned the terrorist strikes; and in the EU, it supported the formula 'each according to his capabilities', the

organizing principle of EU–US solidarity. However, reservations and caveats
were apparent. Finland was concerned that the US should maintain propor-
tionate and appropriate strategies to fight terrorism. There was much uncer-
tainty about the future but no urgent sense of threat posed by international
terrorism.[21] According to Tomas Ries, the general position of the foreign
policy leadership was to maintain a low profile and a cautious and reserved
attitude, indicating a desire to avoid raising the prominence of this issue as
far as possible.[22] Ries's judgment was based on a number of incidents. The
Finnish environment minister drew a causal connection between the terrorist
strikes and US unwillingness to sign the Kyoto Protocol on carbon emis-
sions. Foreign Minister Erkki Tuomioja claimed that the great powers had
pressured the EU ahead of its declaration in support of the US campaign,
and President Tarja Halonen made a point of emphasizing that Finland
would not be involved at all in any NATO military response to the terrorist
attacks.[23] Moreover, the government was divided on the issue of a potential
US need for overflight rights, and its eventual decision that Finland would
open its air space only to humanitarian flights appeared to be a half-hearted
commitment to the fight against terrorism.[24] Finally, there was also widespread scepticism as to whether the military strikes in Afghanistan would be
effective, and Tuomioja suggested that the legitimacy of the military operation should be understood only in terms of international law enforcement
and that it would be weakened as humanitarian costs mounted.[25]

The perception that Finland had failed to provide the US with its full
support in the campaign against international terrorism was realized when
some US-produced maps depicted Finland as a 'grey' country, indicating
that it was not part of the coalition. This perception stimulated a debate to
identify and overcome the challenges, obstacles and dilemmas in improving
Finnish–US relations. Max Jakobson argued that Finland should not take
good relations with the US for granted.[26] The government was quick to
deny vigorously that substantive problems existed, and President Halonen's
visit to the US in spring 2002 appeared to draw a line under the debate
about whether Finland's relationship with the US had deteriorated during
the winter. At the same time, Finland decided to send a small contingent to
Afghanistan in support of the ISAF operation.

Finnish public opinion clearly supported the government's 'moderate'
policy, and the mood of the public as evidenced by opinion surveys revealed a
fairly widespread perception that the US had somehow deserved the terrorist
attacks and that the threat posed by global terrorism should not be Finland's
concern. It was not of Finnish making, and the dangers, if they existed at all,
lay elsewhere. Support for any kind of military participation by Finland was
very low, as in Sweden. Furthermore, the Finns were close to the bottom of

the list of 15 EU states when it came to humanitarian assistance, economic reconstruction and other soft means of combating terrorism, in contrast to the Swedes, who widely supported such measures.[27] In an opinion poll conducted before the US began its military action, only 23 per cent of the Finns surveyed supported the strikes.[28] Although 50 per cent later approved of the US military action in Afghanistan, support for sending Finnish troops to Afghanistan remained very low.[29] Just as during Operation Allied Force, popular support for NATO membership now collapsed as a consequence of the terrorist attacks and their countermeasures. Only 11 per cent of the population supported it while more than three-quarters were in favour of preserving military non-alignment.[30]

IRAQ: NON-ALIGNMENT AND PREVENTIVE WAR

In 2002–3, Iraq became prominent as an issue of strategic importance in transatlantic relations. Finland attempted to improve its relations with the US while the US expressed determination to invade and occupy Iraq as part of the global war on terrorism, causing the disruption of transatlantic relations. Paradoxically, US support for 'coalitions of the willing' undermined the utility of NATO and provided an ideal mechanism by which Finland could both preserve the centrepiece of its security strategy (military non-alignment) and at the same time establish a strategic partnership with the US. The underlying principle of neutrality, which had been replaced by formal non-alignment, translated into a determination to remain equidistant between 'Atlantic Europe' and 'Core Europe'.

After 9/11, Prime Minister Lipponen became more supportive of the US both unilaterally and through EU initiatives; he also defended Operation Enduring Freedom against critical voices from within his own government. Further, he took pains to remain equidistant between Germany and France, on the one hand, and 'Atlantic Europe', on the other, despite his well-known sympathy towards Germany and personal friendship with Chancellor Schröder. It therefore came as no surprise that he used his visit to Washington in December 2002 as an attempt to maintain and improve relations with the US. The Finnish government had decided to support the Iraqi reconstruction and stabilization effort and to deliver humanitarian assistance, but its support was tied explicitly to UN approval. At a meeting in the White House, Prime Minister Lipponen exchanged platitudes with President Bush: Finland appreciated Bush's leadership and his decision to bring the matter before the UN. The US thanked Finland for joining the coalition. In February 2003, Finland, in contrast to Sweden, also attended a meeting at the State Department held to brief coalition partners and discuss the situation in Iraq, but the government continued to back the UN line supporting the weapons inspections and the necessity of deciding upon the use of force in the Security Council.[31]

Subsequently, the issue of Iraq became one of the main themes of the parliamentary elections held in March 2003. The Centre Party opposition candidate Anneli Jäätteenmäki accused Prime Minister Lipponen of undermining the effective functioning of the Finnish government: it had unilaterally decided about Finland's coalition membership and thus undermined the principles of collective cabinet accountability and transparency in government decision-making. Chancellor Schröder's success in Germany had convinced Jäätteenmäki and her team that the contentious Iraq issue could mobilize public support in her favour and raise her foreign policy profile, thereby compensating for her relative lack of experience in this area. According to Finnish opinion polls, nearly half the population opposed the war and would do so even if the intervention received a UN mandate; almost no one supported intervention without a UN mandate. Jäätteenmäki based her accusations on the classified documents about the meeting between Lipponen and Bush that she had received through a leak from the President's office. Her ploy proved to be successful: she won the elections and became the first female prime minister of Finland.[32]

Jäätteenmäki's 'reign' was very short, however: she stepped down in June, having lost the confidence of parliament after lying about how the classified documents about the Washington meeting had come into her possession. The media exposed the truth just as the police were launching their own investigation. Her unpopularity was compounded by the fact that Lipponen's supporters had never forgiven what they considered to be her blatantly populist election tactics. In addition, there was the unfavourable perception that Jäätteenmäki had created in the minds of the wider foreign policy elite, including leading media commentators, who feared that she would have a catastrophic effect on Finland's foreign policy. Although Jäättenmäki's election campaign implied changes in foreign policy, she was not in office long enough to implement a new Finnish policy on Iraq. When the war began, the outgoing government issued a statement to the effect that Finland regretted its initiation and emphasized that resorting to war without UN approval was and remained unacceptable. This formulation reflected past statements on similar issues, but critics, for example a group of international law scholars, argued that the statement was pusillanimous because it failed to condemn the war on the basis of its clear illegality.

The new prime minister, Matti Vanhanen of the Centre Party, adopted a very low profile on this issue, but he was vocal in his defence of the importance of building a common front against terrorists with countries that shared the same values. The Finnish public remained vehemently anti-war – only 18 per cent supported the war in Iraq in April 2003 – but the foreign policy establishment, including three former prime ministers who were publicly worried about 'anti-Americanism' in Finland, emphasized the importance of strong US ties with Finland and Europe and the need to preserve good relations with Washington. Lipponen, for example, urged the government to express positive views about the partnership with the US and to avoid squabbling.[33] The unremitting official focus on the future rather than the past was broken only when President Halonen stated that the war was illegal in a speech to the UN General Assembly in 2004.[34] The government's White Book on Security Policy, delivered to parliament in September 2004, was laconic in the extreme on the nature of transatlantic disputes and the contested US-led war in Iraq. It noted merely that Finland 'considers it important that transatlantic cooperation be conducted in a spirit of global responsibility and shared basic values and respect for international law'.[35] Instead, it stressed the continuing significance of the US presence in Europe and the volume and density of existing transatlantic links that Finland sought to foster. On the issue of Finland's possible membership of NATO, the White Book stayed true to the traditional policy of stating that this remained a future option.[36]

Sweden, by contrast, started to voice more and stronger criticism of the US as the war in Iraq rose on the global security agenda. Finland and Sweden had strongly backed the UN track as the preferred option for managing the Iraq crisis. During the winter of 2002, Persson did not exclude the use of military force as such – indeed, he went so far as to say that it could have positive effects – and was even willing to commit Sweden to participate in the war effort, as it had done in the Gulf war of 1991. Yet his primary policy was to press for a UN-brokered solution, and he emphasized the importance of continuing with the IAEA-backed weapons inspection and monitoring regime. Foreign Minister Lindh was more outspoken in her rhetoric, calling Bush 'the lone ranger', which did not amuse the White House.[37] Both Persson and Lindh indicated that they would have used the veto in the UN Security Council if Sweden had been a permanent member.[38]

When the war began, Persson condemned it clearly, stating that 'The attack on Iraq is in contravention of international law and threatens the lives of thousands of people. The disarming of the terrorist regime in Iraq must take place within the framework of international law and must therefore be returned to the United Nations Security Council.'[39] Persson also described the 'Letter of Eight' from Atlanticist EU members as ill-considered and a mistake, arguing that it was 'a strange situation, when the pressure which should be on Saddam Hussein is moved to a discussion between parties within NATO and countries in the EU. It is a bad and dangerous development.' But, like Finland, he was careful not to align Sweden with German and French opposition to the war; he hoped that a rapprochement between Chirac and Bush would clear the air. A policy of non-alignment through equidistance emerged.[40]

During the war, Prime Minister Persson continued to criticize the US for its decision to abandon the UN approach, and warned that the costs of liberating Iraq would be high because of the lack of political legitimacy. He stressed, however, that it was in Sweden's interest to look to the future and to participate in the reconstruction and stabilization of Iraq as part of a broader, UN-mandated role that could be implemented in the aftermath of the war.[41] Persson did not criticize the US occupation of Iraq and he tried to improve relations with the United States: President Bush was described as a 'nice' and 'intelligent' person, one who was well informed about details.[42] Washington was also delighted see the new Swedish foreign minister Laila Freivalds being less critical towards the US (Lindh was murdered in September 2003).[43] Persson did nonetheless take issue with the United States' handling of the prisoners at Guantánamo Bay, where one Swedish citizen was imprisoned.[44]

As in Finland, the rationale for Sweden's Iraq policy derived from the principles of its well-established policy of military non-alignment. The government could choose to voice criticism of the US or to try to mute anti-American sentiments among its public, but it could not shift from the position of supporting war only with a UN mandate. Although Swedish public opinion did become more supportive of the war, the majority remained critical: only 17 per cent had been in favour of the war when it started; after the war ended, support had risen to 41 per cent.[45] Public opinion remained strongly in favour of preserving military non-alignment, and hoped for more UN involvement in Iraq.[46]

THE EU, THE ESDP AND 'NON-ALIGNED EUROPE': DEATH BY A THOUSAND CUTS?

Even more than NATO and the US-led global war on terrorism, the militarization of the EU has brought into question the viability of a non-alignment strategy on the part of the 'post-neutral' states.[47] Before Sweden and Finland joined the EU in 1995, they had already narrowed the meaning of 'neutrality' and then deleted the word in descriptions of their status because it raised concern in Brussels and leading EU capitals as to where their primary loyalties and commitments lay. Rather than the formula 'non-aligned in peace and neutral in war', the new watchword 'military non-alignment' was officially adopted, with the expectation that the peoples or parliaments would then decide whether to be neutral in time of war – this option remained open. This more technical term had two advantages: it expressed the fact that Sweden and Finland were not formally members of a military alliance and it was flexible enough to transmit to domestic audiences that the governments would continue the tradition of neutrality.

During the 10 years of their membership of the EU, Finland appears to have reorientated itself westward further and faster than Sweden. The most visible example of this has been its integration into the European Economic and Monetary Union (EMU), in contrast to Sweden's decision to remain outside it. But at the same time, the security policy approaches of the two non-aligned states have been strikingly similar. Both were in favour of enhancing the EU's security role in crisis management, particularly civilian crisis management, and both have resisted moves towards building a collective defence system. Their respective publics have broadly supported these policy approaches: yes to crisis management but no to common defence; but it is noteworthy that there are higher levels of support in these states for joining a common European defence system than for joining NATO.

The two states supported all the major policy initiatives that led to the establishment of the ESDP. The militarization of the EU has not been their primary foreign policy goal; but rather than attempting to block this development, they have tried to render it compatible with their policy of military non-alignment. They have been in favour of strengthening the EU's role as a global actor but not as a counterweight to the US, nor do they want the EU to develop into a military alliance that would compete with NATO. Also, they have resisted the idea of a core group of a few EU states that would push forward the Union's independent defence planning but have argued in favour of policy coherence. Before the Amsterdam Summit in 1997, Sweden and Finland initiated a debate on the inclusion of the Petersberg tasks ('humanitarian and rescuer tasks; peacekeeping tasks; tasks of combat forces in crisis management, including peacemaking'[48]) within the CFSP, thereby countering and neutralizing a Franco-German idea to fuse the Western European Union (which provided for collective self-defence and for economic, social and cultural collaboration between its signatories) and the EU. They accepted the EU's Cologne Summit formulations on security and defence in 1999, and the ESDP was strengthened further during Finland's presidency of the EU. Because the EU's crisis management policy is understood as a continuation of their traditional non-aligned peacekeeping role, the two governments have consistently emphasized that a clear distinction between crisis management and territorial defence must be upheld.[49]

Sweden and Finland, and also Austria and Ireland, had difficulty in accepting the idea of 'closer cooperation' through the establishment of collective defence as called for in the EU's new constitutional treaty. They believed that the UK would block any mutual defence clause. However, once the UK was satisfied with a formulation that stressed the continuance of NATO's primary role in European security, it withdrew its threatened opposition. Only on the eve of the EU summit of December 2003 did these states realize that the binding nature of the EU's military mutual assistance pact would be inconsistent with their national security policies: they would cease to be 'militarily non-aligned' states. In response, the four 'post-neutral' states, spearheaded by Finland, proposed a watered down version of the 'all-for-one' clause in the constitution (this would have obliged them to provide military aid to a fellow EU member when it was attacked). Finland proposed that an attacked country 'may request that other member states give it aid' by all means possible: EU member states would have a right to ask for assistance on the basis of Article 51 of the UN Charter but other EU members would not be obliged to give it. Swedish Foreign Minister Laila Freivalds held that this was acceptable because it would give 'us the freedom which being non-aligned demands'.[50] But this counter-proposal was unacceptable to leading EU powers, and the compromise that resulted was in the best traditions of decision-making by committee: an obscure statement emerged according to which the article 'shall not prejudice that specific character of the security and defence policy of certain member states'.[51]

Indeed, the debate in Finland and Sweden over the EU's collective security appeared to be driven more by identity than by rational interest. For one, it could hardly be feasible for militarily non-aligned states, fully integrated with the EU politically and economically, not to assist fellow European countries should they be attacked by a third power, as Lindh had suggested.[52] Furthermore, the military in the two countries highlighted the lack of clarity in the political separation of crisis management and collective defence. For example, Johan Hederstedt, Sweden's Supreme Commander of the Armed Forces, acknowledged that there was a thin line between crisis management and warfare, as Operation Allied Force had so recently demonstrated. He asked, 'If we participate in crisis management that develops into war, what do we do then? We haven't worked that out yet.'[53] Against this background, it is understandable that former Finnish prime minister Paavo Lipponen characterized the whole debate over non-alignment as 'theological'.[54]

In November 2004, EU defence ministers decided to boost the EU's military crisis management capability further by agreeing to set up 13 rapid reaction 'battle groups', each with 1,500 troops, by 2007. The EU battle group concept did not place a strain on the non-aligned states' commitment to the ESDP, unlike the proposal for collective defence guarantees, although it did seem to shift the EU's role further away from traditional peacekeeping tasks and towards possible interventions. The Finnish president was concerned about the heavy responsibility when it came to the use of the rapid reaction forces, but she was eventually willing to endorse the concept and the possible use of the forces without a UN mandate.[55] Emphasizing the Nordic tradition of cooperative security, Sweden and Finland formed a common battle group together with the EU outsider Norway. Additionally, Finland decided to contribute to another EU battle group alongside Germany and the Netherlands, illustrating a continued determination to maintain a bridging role between 'Atlantic Europe' and 'Core Europe'.

'NON-ALIGNED EUROPE' AND TRANSATLANTIC RELATIONS

Sweden's and Finland's critical stance on the US-led war in Iraq can be explained by reference to their policy of military non-alignment, which was buttressed by their long tradition of supporting the primacy of international law and multilateral international institutions in international relations. Although the scope of 'neutrality' had been narrowed radically in both countries after the end of the Cold War, it was still an important foreign policy legacy, and it strongly informed public opinion in the two states even though neutrality was formally abandoned in the early 1990s. During the Cold War, Finland had understood neutrality in terms of avoiding taking sides in international conflicts, especially when the superpowers disagreed, as they usually did. Sweden understood neutrality to mean an impartiality that allowed it to approach international conflicts on the basis of a disinterested and moral basis. When Sweden and Finland joined the EU, they had to make a commitment to the principles of its common foreign and security policy, and both countries now regarded the EU's principled stances in international affairs as being compatible with their foreign policy of non-alignment.

It is unlikely that either Finland or Sweden would have condemned the Iraq war had the EU states been unified in their approach. But when the EU's guidance was weak, their traditional foreign policy principles and preferences gained traction and became more relevant. The chief European division between 'Core Europe' and 'Atlantic Europe' allowed for, and even encouraged, a pragmatic reinterpretation of the principles that had underpinned their security policies in the Cold War. Prime Minister Persson adopted those principles in his approach to the US. Finland, however, returned to the old policy of avoiding strong stances and participation in a crisis. Its Cold War default positions proved to be powerful, as conceptions of what might be termed 'positive' and 'negative' neutrality remained in play even though both states were non-aligned.

It was within this basic and traditional framework of neutrality that we can understand the approaches of these non-aligned northern states to the transatlantic crisis. For both countries, the principles of international and humanitarian law were important yardsticks against which to measure their policy responses towards the wars in Afghanistan and Iraq. And, as suggested above, the strong traditions and memories of neutrality were revived in the lead-up to and during the transatlantic trauma. Neither Sweden nor Finland was willing to join any of the competing European groupings – 'New Europe', 'Atlantic Europe' and especially 'Core Europe' – despite the fact that there was very little daylight between their principled stances and those of France and Germany.

As is typical in crises, and perhaps particularly so in the case of smaller states, personality as well as policy factors shaped attitudes. In Finland, the main dividing lines in the domestic debate were to be found not between the parties but within the governing Social Democratic Party. Both the president and the foreign minister were seen as more committed to the idealism of their youth; but Prime Minister Lipponen had reorientated his foreign policy thinking during the 1980s and was one of the first politicians to suggest that Finland should join the EU.

After 9/11, Persson saw the opportunity to become a real statesman with a strong foreign policy profile, but he resisted this temptation and returned to more traditional principles before Operation Iraqi Freedom was initiated. Part of the explanation as to why he adopted such a determined and strong policy on this issue was that Hans Blix, the chief IAEA weapons inspector, was a Swede. Not only did Persson know and trust Blix personally but he was also expected to support a fellow countryman in this important international task. Further, an attack on the integrity of Blix was widely perceived as an attack on the integrity and trustworthiness of Sweden itself.

Public opinion in both countries remained critical of the US-led wars in Afghanistan and Iraq, but particularly in Finland some responses to those wars and also to 9/11 revealed the presence of anti-American sentiments. For example, 63 per cent of Finns (54 per cent in Sweden) believed that the US represented a threat to world peace.[56] Arguments about the difficulty of distinguishing justified criticism and principled pacifism from 'irrational' anti-Americanism notwithstanding, it is difficult to explain why criticism of the US surfaced in such a pronounced manner. Traditionally, Finland had enjoyed a warm relationship with the US; and although it fought on the side of the Germans in the Second World War, America never declared war on it, in honour of its democratic character and absence of anti-Semitic state policies. Finland was neither liberated by US troops nor helped by the US diplomatically in peace negotiations, but it did receive substantial US financial assistance outside the Marshall Plan framework. This was essential in preventing it from falling completely within the Soviet sphere of influence. Furthermore, as was acknowledged after but not during the Cold War, the Finns benefited from the United States' strategic balancing of the Soviet Union in northern Europe.

Nonetheless, there were at least three different but interlinked historical sources that account for Finland's critical attitude towards the US. One source was simply ingrained Finnish suspicion of the behaviour of any hegemonic power, be it Russia in the former Soviet Union, Germany in the EU or the US in the world, or even Helsinki within Finland. This attitude was based on a free peasant mentality and on Finland's historical experience of domination by Tsarist Russia and then the Soviet Union. Another source of mistrust was more directly derived from the legacy of Cold War neutrality, which suggested that there was some kind of moral equivalence between the superpowers. The positive value of neutrality would have proved illusionary had the Cold War been defined in terms of evil East against good West. Last and least, there was undoubtedly politically motivated anti-Americanism that was typically expressed by supporters of the leftist parties. Viewing US foreign policy as driven by exploitative capitalism echoed not only some myths of Soviet propaganda but also larger Western socialist ideology, which remained prevalent in parts of the leftist parties and gained new ground in the anti-globalization movement. The first source of anti-Americanism was typical in Finland; the two latter were detectable in Sweden.

However, it is clear that the foreign policy elites of Finland and Sweden maintained deep blue water between themselves and the anti-American sentiments of the population. Those elites felt that anti-Americanism was out of proportion to the accusations levelled against the US; and particularly in Finland, factors of realpolitik dictated that it was always prudent to preserve good relations with the US because of the potential if latent Russian threat. For the Finnish elite, the United States' military 'footprint' in Europe and its interest in northern Europe were understood as vital to the preservation of regional and continental stability. In the agrarian Centre Party, this attitude was coupled with a general distrust of European great powers and the process of ever-deepening European integration. Within the EU, militarily non-aligned Finland has been and continues to be more 'Atlanticist' than 'Core' European in its security policy. It could be argued that in emphasizing the importance of US commitments to Europe and NATO, Finland also strengthened its own policy of non-alignment by making it more unlikely that a European common defence policy would emerge that would force it to abandon its military neutrality. And instead of being undermined by a strengthened NATO, its non-alignment was underpinned by the global war on terrorism, which resorted to coalitions rather than military alliances.

CONCLUSIONS: POST-IRAQ NON-ALIGNMENT AND EUROPEAN SECURITY

Both Sweden and Finland were willing to condemn the terrorist attacks forcefully and to express their solidarity with the US. They were also ready to support the US-led war against terrorism, but only with a number of reservations. They placed greater emphasis on legal approaches to the war, on threat management through common institutions (be they the UN or the EU) and on the humanitarian costs of the campaign than they did on military responses, particularly those by alliances. There were also small but significant differences between Sweden and Finland. Although it may have been more a question of style than substance, Finland appeared at first to be more reserved and cautious in its support of the US than did Sweden; but with regard to the war in Iraq, Sweden began to voice clear criticism earlier than did Finland. The US-led war on terrorism and the transatlantic crisis only appeared to strengthen the Swedish and Finnish security strategy of non-alignment.

Regarding the debate between the optimists and the pessimists on the future of the transatlantic relationship, the reactions in Sweden and Finland discredit claims of an automatic and seamless top-down dynamic in accounting for criticism of the US and reluctance to support the military operations of the war on terrorism. In both states, the foreign policy elites adopted a much more friendly attitude towards the US than did public opinion. In the case of Sweden and Finland at least, it cannot be argued that the leaders manipulated public opinion in order to adopt an anti-American stance that could then be exploited at the polls. On the contrary, they had to explain to the public why they should support the US in the context of 9/11 and why they should support self-defence and then military pre-emption. Public opinion mostly tracked the opinion of the political elites, but only after some months' delay.

The case of the non-aligned countries demonstrates that critical grass-roots views of the US in Europe have different sources. This finding should not be exaggerated, but its existence cannot be ignored. In Sweden and Finland, the need to assert distance from the US partly reflects domestic political views shaped by social democratic ideology. However, it is also an outcome of the need to justify neutrality in moral terms and a reflection of a small-state ideology that is sceptical about the hegemonic tendency of all great powers regardless of their political ideology and values.

It is interesting to consider whether Finland and Sweden can continue to give expression to their non-alignment in an age of terror by maintaining a policy of positioning or equidistance between 'Atlantic Europe' and 'Core Europe'. The militarization of the EU has made it more difficult to preserve this identity niche, and this explains why the two governments perceived the rejection of the European constitution and its mutual defence guarantees with some relief. As in Finland and Sweden, heated debates over the politically sensitive status and meaning of non-alignment and neutrality have taken place in Dublin and Vienna.[57] The more fragmented European security remains, the easier it is to maintain equidistance; the greater the convergence between 'Atlantic Europe' and 'Core Europe', the harder it is for non-aligned states to reformulate the utility of such a policy. If NATO, undercut by 'coalitions of the willing', becomes more of a military toolbox than a political actor, then non-aligned states' cooperation with its members within coalitions is facilitated. But if the EU militarizes further, in intelligence cooperation for example, then non-alignment is harder to sustain and the non-aligned countries may need to abandon the rest of their 'post-neutral' legacy. Paradoxically, for states that provide models of consensus-based politics and security cooperation, continued transatlantic strategic dissonance best supports, promotes and protects the viability of non-alignment; convergence, realignment and reformation only serve to undercut it.

7

'Periphery Europe': Russia and transatlantic security

The terrorist attacks of 9/11 and the US-led global war on terrorism created a paradox for Russia: the war on terrorism agenda made it easier for Russia to join the West but the split within the NATO alliance complicated its decision about which West to join. The dilemmas it faces in its relations with the West are exemplified by its engagement with the EU and NATO. During the latter half of the 1990s, it appeared that Russia's relationship with the EU was evolving rapidly and would include a military dimension but that its relations with NATO would continue to be fractious and sour. Russia endorsed the EU's enlargement but vehemently opposed NATO's 'expansion'. Although Putin joined the 'coalition of the unwilling' alongside France and Germany in opposition to the Iraq war, the trends that characterized Russia's general engagement with the West in the 1990s have now reversed: relations with NATO and the US now appear stronger than those with the EU.

Russia's policy towards Europe and the US is driven by a combination of contemporary state interests and psychological elements embedded in the legacies of the past, including the Cold War experience. The ultimate goal of Soviet foreign policy was to drive a wedge between the US and its NATO European allies – to divide and rule. With the West no longer the principal adversary, Russia's policy towards the Euro-Atlantic world has become more complex and ambiguous. There is no possibility that Russia will become a member of either the EU or NATO in the short to medium term. Nevertheless, as Europe's largest state, its relations with both organizations shape transatlantic relations and European security: it could exacerbate strategic divorce or facilitate strategic realignment, and in all events it must manage the current strategic dissonance. Clearly, a weak and divided West would promote the status of Russia as a great power, and so it is a Russian interest to exacerbate the transatlantic rift. However, closer Russia–NATO relations after 9/11 may suggest that a more political, fragmented and less cohesive

NATO is emerging. Similarly, stronger Russia–EU relations may bolster a move to counterbalance the US and promote a preferred Russian view of global order based on multipolarity, or these integrative impulses may indicate that the EU remains in Russia's eyes an attractive but limited 'soft' power.

This chapter argues that the nature and quality of Russia's relationship with NATO, the US and the EU, and also the issues that secure closer integration and those that generate isolation, provide a litmus test of the level and nature of transatlantic cooperation and conflict. It begins by examining Russia's relationship with NATO and argues that under President Putin, by contrast to President Yeltsin, Russia has developed a stronger institutional basis for managing its relationship with NATO. The creation of the NATO–Russia Council (NRC) has facilitated greater cooperation, but the integrative capacity of this institutional link is limited by Russia's inability to undertake defence reform and, ultimately, by the values gap between Russia and NATO member states. However, after the events of 9/11 the Russia–NATO nexus was undercut, but to an extent compensated for, by Russia's membership of and cooperation with US-led 'coalitions of the willing' in the global war on terrorism. When combating terrorism internationally became the United States' primary strategic objective, that global war provided Putin with the opportunity to establish a direct and effective strategic partnership with the US, and it has strengthened Russia's great-power status. This partnership is centred on shared interests rather than values. Russia is therefore able to influence the transatlantic relationship and European security through two mechanisms, both formal and informal: the quality of its participation in NATO-related activities provides an institutional anchor that binds it to the transatlantic world; close bilateral relations with the US and participation in US-led coalitions that include Atlanticist NATO member states allow Russia the flexibility to pick and choose missions and control the levels of cooperation. As yet, these two mechanisms of cooperation have not raised significant challenges, obstacles or dilemmas for Russia, NATO or the US.

The chapter will then focus on Russia–EU relations and the dynamics that drive this relationship forward. The policy issues and dilemmas raised by the EU's enlargement eastward are much more profound, deep-seated and far-reaching for Russia's security and stability than those arising from NATO's enlargement. However, Russia is constrained in its ability to cooperate with the EU by disagreements over a range of political and economic issues that prevent the emergence of a viable European bloc to counterbalance the US. In addition, with its participation in the global war on terrorism and a functioning NRC, Russia's security relationship with the EU has lacked urgency, significance and rationale. Russia has not given priority to ESDP cooperation over NATO or its commitment to the war on terrorism, and this reduces the likelihood that in military and security matters Europe could counterbalance the United States.

In the early 1990s, the Russia—NATO 'mood music' was in sharp contrast to the discordant klaxon Cold War sounds of 'evil empire' and 'aggressive bloc'. As early as July 1990, NATO's Secretary General Manfred Wörner declared that the confrontation, distrust and hostility of the past must be buried.[1] Russia's early post-Soviet foreign policy was characterized by perhaps the most pro-Western rhetoric since the era of Catherine the Great or even Peter the Great. Russian Foreign Minister Alexander Kozyrev advocated a partnership strategy with a more political NATO, arguing that cooperation would serve as an effective mechanism for overcoming the division of Europe: 'We see NATO nations as our natural friends and in future as allies.'[2] However, this optimistic and open perception of Russia's national interest was undercut by rising nationalism and disillusionment with democratic reforms in the early and middle 1990s.

As a result, Russia supported the Partnership for Peace programme half-heartedly. The PfP concept was unsatisfactory in that it failed to grant Russia a specific status in its relations with NATO. The PfP encouraged democratic defence reform efforts; and although Russia supported the process in principle, it has yet to adopt reform in a systematic manner. Russia's strongly stated opposition to NATO's enlargement affected national debates in Europe and the US. Nevertheless, President Clinton was determined to drive that policy forward after Yeltsin was re-elected as president in 1996. When Russia realized that its vehement opposition to NATO's enlargement was futile, it sought to cut its losses through damage limitation, demanding a legally binding treaty that would limit NATO's presence on the territory of the new members of the alliance.[3] NATO helped to reduce tensions with Russia by establishing the Founding Act of March 1997 and the Permanent Joint Council (PJC). The Founding Act signified 'an enduring political commitment undertaken at the highest political level ... [to] build together a lasting and inclusive peace in the Euro-Atlantic area on the principles of democracy and cooperative security'.[4]

However, this partnership was paper-thin, and at almost every turn the commitment to transparency proved to be illusional. Neither Yeltsin nor Foreign Minister Yevgeny Primakov attended NATO's 1997 summit in Madrid when the first-echelon entrants were named; NATO was refused permission to open an office in Moscow; and the NATO—Russia brigade initiative was stillborn. Russia declined to establish a full mission at NATO headquarters (its NATO representatives worked as an adjunct to the Russian embassy in Brussels rather than at NATO headquarters). Indeed, for Russia the PJC and participation in the PfP held only instrumental value: it could demonstrate dissatisfaction with NATO by threatening to end cooperation.[5] Russia objected to NATO's enlargement, its new strategic doctrine and its out-of-area military operations, all of which were deemed to threaten Russian security. NATO's Kosovo campaign underscored the dangers for Russia of NATO military operations and the fallacy that a 'new NATO' was more political than military.[6] Russia's relationship with NATO was thus in constant crisis during the 1990s.

Political cooperation between NATO and Russia in the framework of the PJC ultimately failed. The PJC consultation process was fragile, functioning as a forum in which Russia was informed about NATO's decisions but had little ability to influence them. In addition, NATO argued that Russia had not explored all possibilities and avenues of cooperation with its programmes. As a result, when Russia froze cooperation with NATO during the Kosovo campaign, many informed analysts predicted that it would take a long time to mend broken Russia–NATO relations.[7]

POST-9/11: REAL STRATEGIC PARTNERSHIP?

The main impetus for an improved relationship between NATO and Russia was the election of Vladimir Putin as president in 2000 and his readiness to readjust Russia's strategic interests and orientation. Even prior to 9/11, he had decided that the core of his foreign policy programme was to use improved relations with the West as a means to another end, the strengthening of the Russian state.[8] To this end, he quickly relaunched the relationship with NATO: Secretary General George Robertson visited Moscow on 16 February 2000. In 2001, practical cooperation was signalled by the inauguration of NATO's information office in Moscow, illustrating the extent to which the alliance's enlargement was no longer considered a strategic threat by Russia.[9]

The events of 9/11 further consolidated strategic realignment with the West, providing it with substance in the form of partnership in the global anti-terror coalition.[10] Famously, President Putin was the first statesman to deliver his condolences to President Bush. A new non-Western enemy allowed for greater levels of cooperation: Putin became not only an acceptable but also an indispensable partner of the West. The renewed partnership was further evidenced by the PJC meeting of 13 September 2001, which resulted in a statement condemning the terrorist attacks and supporting a joint fight against terrorism.[11]

Although post-9/11 solidarity had revitalized the importance of the PJC, Russia's participation in the global war on terrorism and the prospect of second-echelon states' integration into NATO demanded a fundamental institutional readjustment of the relationship. In November 2001, Prime Minister Blair proposed a new forum for NATO–Russia relations. This was to be based on a framework of round-table discussions that reflected the idea of 'equality': Russia would have voting rights in certain issue areas that concerned common interests. Although conservatives in the US administration were still suspicious of Russia's sincerity and reliability as a partner, President Bush, who professed to have formed a personal friendship with President Putin, supported this initiative.[12]

The NATO–Russia Rome Declaration on a 'New Quality of Relations' (approved on 28 May 2002) established the NRC. It was designed to hold monthly meetings at the ambassadorial level under the chairmanship of the NATO secretary general, and aimed, in nine areas of cooperation, to 'work out common positions, taking common decisions and carrying common or coordinated actions whenever possible'.[13] NRC decisions would no longer be 'pre-cooked' by the 19 NATO members. This allowed Russia to participate in the discussions on an equal basis: the format was to be 'NATO at 20' rather than '19+1'. A functioning institutional mechanism for cooperation was created, underpinned by conceptual rapprochement and practical cooperation.[14] In reality, however, the difference between the PJC and the NRC was more symbolic than real. When asked what really had changed, Lord Robertson explained that 'the answer is more in chemistry than in arithmetic'.[15]

Russia's policy of rapprochement with NATO is likely to continue because President Putin has made a clear commitment to cooperation with NATO. In his view, 'the choice made in favour of dialogue and cooperation with NATO was the right one and has proved fruitful. In just a very short time we have taken a gigantic step from past confrontation to working together and from mutual accusations and stereotypes to creating modern instruments for cooperation such as the Russia-NATO Council.'[16] He also declared that 'my firm conviction [that Russia is a reliable partner] is based on the fact that I see the national interests of Russia and the United States coincide to large extent'.[17]

Putin also initiated personnel and structural changes in the Russian Ministry of Defence (MoD) in order to facilitate this cooperation. Russia has strengthened its mission to NATO by appointing an ambassador and increasing the staff. A Russian liaison office was established at SHAPE (Supreme Headquarters Allied Powers Europe), and parts of the Russian mission have moved to NATO HQ; daily cooperation has become much more natural and flexible.[18] Putin replaced the defence minister Igor

Sergeyev, a NATO sceptic, with a loyalist, Sergei Ivanov, and dismissed the most vocal critic of NATO, Colonel-General Leonid Ivashov, head of the MoD's international cooperation department. In summer 2004, he also resolved the paralysis and duplication of function between the MoD and the General Staff: Yuri Baluyevskiy replaced Anatoly Kvashnin and the General Staff was again subordinated to the MoD.

Maintaining strong relations with Russia has many supporters in NATO member states and structures: Bush, Blair, Chirac, Schröder and Berlusconi formed good personal relations with Putin. Although the interests of these European leaders and Putin can differ, European pressure to halt cooperation within the NATO framework and thus isolate Russia is not a factor. Even when Bush met Putin in Bratislava in February 2005 to deplore the rollback of Russian democracy and to encourage democratic reform, he continued to engage Russia positively.[19] This willingness is supported by a large part of the foreign policy elites and their militaries.[20]

Indeed, from the outset the NRC has performed on a qualitatively different basis than the PJC: contested issues are not allowed to infect broader cooperative efforts, as illustrated by the continued functioning of the NRC through the Iraq war. The main areas of cooperation have consisted of anti-terrorism, military interoperability and civil emergencies. In December 2004, the parties approved a comprehensive action plan on terrorism.[21] Russia also decided to join the NATO anti-terrorist operation Active Endeavour in the Mediterranean, and discussions on a joint missile defence system continue. Military-to-military cooperation has a much more intensive training and exercise programme than previously.[22] Russia demonstrates increased interest in creating a NATO-compatible Russian peace-keeping brigade; it conducted a 'lessons learned' study of their joint crisis management operations and designed a document outlining the political aspects of a generic concept of such operations. The legal framework of all military-to-military cooperation was enhanced substantially when Russia's accession to the PfP's Status of Forces Agreement was finalized in 2005. Post-9/11 cooperative progress is facilitated by greater political commitment and trust and by 'increasing understanding in both NATO and Russia about practical benefits which NRC cooperation brings to both sides'.[23]

For all this positive account, a number of problems exist. First of all, sceptics can argue that levels of trust have not increased significantly: Russia's wider national political and military security apparatus and strategic establishment still perceive NATO as more aggressive than defensive. Public opinion polls measuring Russian attitudes towards NATO have changed little and are still more negative than in 1997.[24] Russian MoD documents released in October 2003 indicated that Moscow would rethink its nuclear strategy if NATO failed to remove its 'anti-Russian components and maintains its current "offensive" doctrine'.[25] As Sergei Ivanov noted in early 2004, 'Russia may still question NATO's right to exist and wonder why an organization that was designed to oppose the Soviet Union and its allies in Eastern Europe is still necessary in today's world?'[26]

Secondly, practical cooperation within the NRC has not progressed much beyond agenda setting, feasibility studies and preliminary consultations.[27] Although interoperability has been the main focus of cooperation, very little joint action has resulted; and Russia's withdrawal for economic and strategic reasons from SFOR and KFOR operations in 2003 removed the practical *raison d'être* for giving priority to interoperability for the time being.

The most contentious Russia–NATO disputes have been about arms control. After NATO's enlargement of 2004, it was unclear whether the Baltic states would join the Treaty on Conventional Armed Forces in Europe (CFE), which set equal limits for east and west in Europe from the Atlantic Ocean to the Ural Mountains 'on key conventional armaments essential for conducting surprise attacks or initiating large-scale offensive operations'.[28] Plans for a new US 'military footprint' or basing paradigm had become a major source of concern for Russia. For example, Putin's foreign policy envoy Sergei Yastrzhembsky argued that it would be 'very negative' if the alliance had 'any footprint regardless of the size' in Estonia, Latvia or Lithuania.[29] Ivanov demanded that Russia have monitoring facilities at NATO bases in order to verify that they do not threaten Russia.[30] NATO air patrols over the Baltic states and NATO's contention that those countries would join the CFE treaty only after Russia had fulfilled its own commitments to withdraw troops from Georgia and Moldova have drawn strong Russian protests.

Although some analysts argue that 'the present day formation and feature of Russia's go-West course may not be sustainable',[31] there are few signs that its current foreign policy towards the transatlantic security community will change radically. Confusion, ambiguity and schizophrenia may all characterize Russian attitudes towards NATO, but ultimately Russia has a clear preference for cooperation over confrontation.[32] While public opinion in Russia views NATO negatively, it has a much more positive view of the key members of NATO. Paradoxically, Russia's perception of the US is more positive than that of the other NATO allies: 86 per cent of Russians have expressed a favourable opinion of Americans. Together with Israel, Russia was one of the few countries in the world that preferred George Bush to John Kerry in the 2004 US presidential election.[33]

RUSSIA–EU RELATIONS BEFORE 9/11

Historically, Russia's relationship with Europe has been characterized by ambiguity as to its status and identity.[34] After the collapse of the Soviet Union, the desire to 'return to Europe' and Westernize according to the prevailing Euro-Atlantic model of market democratic transition and then consolidation was strong, but so too were historical impulses towards Eurasianism in Russia. Both Europe and Asia have represented existential threats to the opposing Westernizing and Slavophile camps, with most prepared to argue that Russia was both a part of Europe and apart from Europe.[35] At the end of the twentieth century, the Europeanization tendency in Russia became predominant, driven by Russian reliance on Western capital, technology and security and by the EU's growing energy dependence on Russia – by 2005, 60 per cent of the energy it consumed was generated in Russia.

In the early 1990s, Russia's relations with the EU were primarily economic, but it slowly began to develop a broader agenda with the signing of a partnership and cooperation agreement with the EU in June 1994 (ratified December 1997). The EU's Northern Dimension concept was adopted at the European Council in Vienna in December 1998. In May 1999, at the Cologne Summit, the EU unveiled the 'Common Strategy of the European Union on Russia', with the aim of promoting 'a stable, democratic and prosperous Russia, firmly anchored in a united Europe, free of dividing lines'.[36] Russia then elaborated a 'Medium Term Strategy for the Development of Relations between the Russian Federation and the European Union (2000–2010)'.[37] The year 1999 also marked the launch of the ESDP and the beginning of a military relationship between Russia and the EU. Russia's mid-term strategy on relations with the EU argues that increased cooperation with the ESDP would help to diminish 'NATO-centrism in Europe'.[38]

For Russians, the EU has had a much more positive image than NATO. According to one poll taken in 2002, the EU evoked mostly positive feelings in 60 per cent of respondents; NATO was viewed negatively by 69 per cent of respondents and positively by only 20 per cent. Since the early 1990s, Russia's EU policy and its relations with the Union have reflected this pattern.[39] Whereas Russia objected to NATO's 'expansion', it welcomed the enlargement of the EU, even when the former Soviet Baltic republics were integrated in 2004. The positive image of the EU was driven in part by the perception that it was primarily a civilian power, and on balance its growing security role has been evaluated favourably in Moscow. Even the nomination of NATO's secretary general Javier Solana as the high representative of the Common Foreign and Security Policy of the Union did not change Russia's basically positive view of the EU.[40] For Russia, promotion of the ESDP was instrumental in its attempt to balance the United States and to fragment

NATO's 'hegemony' in security policy. It reflected the continuity of Soviet and post-Soviet Russian foreign policy goals.[41]

However, this policy was unsustainable, and the evolution of the ESDP has been a disappointment for those in Moscow who advocated it as a counterbalance to a US-led NATO. The EU summit in Nice in December 2000 underlined the close linkage between the ESDP and NATO rather than the autonomous role of the former that had been more apparent in the Cologne Declaration following the EU summit of 1999. Russia concluded that European states would ultimately side with the US on most security-related issues. As one Russian analyst noted, 'Attempts to view cooperation between Russia and the European Union as an alternative or a counterbalance to the policy of NATO and the United States may be described as wishful thinking. Such attempts would have an opposite effect, i.e. increase the Atlantic accent of the European policy and diminish the interest of the European Union in the development of a partnership with Russia.'[42] Prior to 9/11, Russia had concluded that stronger US–NATO military and security relations would best increase its influence in Europe. A pragmatic Putin realized that with or without Russian support, the ESDP would remain in the shadow of NATO for some time and therefore that for Russia, it was more important to influence NATO than the ESDP.[43] Consequently, Russia's policy towards the ESDP was now to be understood as a means of consolidating its relations with Washington rather than as a way to encourage the potential establishment of a powerful bloc that could counterbalance the US.[44]

RUSSIA–EU RELATIONS POST-9/11: DYNAMICS OF TRANSATLANTIC CONFLICT?

Closer Russia–EU political and economic integration would constitute a necessary precondition for Russia to provide Europe with a serious counterbalance to the US. However, a number of sources of tension and disagreement between Russia and the EU present obstacles to this outcome. The EU's concern at growing authoritarianism in Russia, unstable Russia–EU cooperation (particularly in the energy sector), EU criticism of Russian human rights abuses in Chechnya and divergences in the two sides' understanding of the 'Colour Revolutions' in the post-Soviet space all currently characterize and impact on the quality of the relationship. These points of conflict are symptomatic of a deeper divergence in Russia–EU relations concerning which values, norms and rules should predominate in what is increasingly becoming a shared neighbourhood. Indeed, the EU has developed a European Neighbourhood Policy, and Russia strongly contested its inclusion as one of 13 states, indicating its need for special status and its desire to reduce direct competition in what was formerly its own sphere of influence. These tensions continue to work against the possibility of establishing a wider European bloc, as opposed to simply an EU one, that exerts even a political and economic counterbalance. An examination of Russia's policy towards the ESDP after 9/11 indicates that the possibility of stronger and more developed military and security cooperation with the EU was undercut by the primacy of the US in its foreign policy orientation. For these reasons, the Russia–EU relationship has not made a significant impact on the quality and nature of the transatlantic relationship.

In the early 1990s, Russia's interaction with the EU was characterized simultaneously by a lack of interest in and understanding of the nature and power of the EU and by the declaratory and aspirational framework of 'closer cooperation', 'mutual understanding' and a 'balance of interests'. The Cologne Summit of 1999 began gradually to align the rhetoric of the abstract benefits of 'partnership' with a much greater awareness of the reality of EU policy-making and the implications of its enlargement strategy on Russia's relations with other former Soviet republics, particularly Belarus, Ukraine and the Baltic states.[45] This resulted in the channelling of greater Russian resources, both human and capital, into its engagement with the EU and an apparent willingness to switch emphasis from bilateral relations between Russia and individual EU states to Russian–EU negotiations. As President Putin noted, 'It is impossible to view the relations between Russia and Germany now beyond the context of Moscow's relations with the European Union. Germany is one of the centres of European integration.'[46] Despite this acknowledgment, Russia still favours bilateralism, a preference EU member states reciprocate by utilizing EU fora to deliver unpopular messages, thus preserving their 'special relationship' with Russia.

Political and economic interests are the central planks in the Russia–EU relationship, but it was not until the events of 9/11 and the first round of enlargement, in 2004, that they began to exercise a significant impact on transatlantic relations. Russia's trade turnover with EU countries amounted to 40 per cent of its total in 2001; and this rose to 55 per cent when Poland and the three Baltic states joined the EU in 2004, outstripping intra-CIS economic relations. Russia was becoming a priority track for the EU's economic policy, particularly given the EU's energy dependency. For this reason, Putin's attempts to modernize and renovate the Russian state are of particular significance to the Russia–EU relationship.

However, political reform within Russia is currently perceived by the EU as detrimental to the preservation and consolidation of democratic values, structures and institutions. Putin is reversing the process of decentralization under Yeltsin, which had been characterized by regional bloc formation on an incremental ad hoc basis rather than elite policy choices or strategy. In its place, Putin has instituted a new, vertical hierarchy of power, with himself at the apex and power flowing through structures he has created and staffed by personnel he has appointed. Many of these appointees now embedded in the bureaucracy are, like Putin himself, recruited directly from the opaque and less transparent military or security services (*siloviki*), and this has a negative impact on the democratization of Russia's political culture.[47]

Putin has abandoned the triangulation politics of the Yeltsin years in which the president stood as arbiter between competing factions within an enclosed elite. In September 2004, he announced that regional governors were now to be appointed, and it was clear that the independent power bases of oligarchs within the media or industry (revealed by the 'Yukos affair') had effectively been curtailed. From the outset, he argued that the 'federative package' would provide greater economic and political stability for inward investment, increasing the efficiency of the federal state administration and consolidating the growth of a single unified legal space within the Federation – all necessary precursors for strong, integrative and cooperative relations with the EU. He explicitly denied that these changes would enforce a 'dictatorship of the centre', arguing that the 'methods of controlling everything from Moscow have already failed'.[48]

In addition, obstacles to functional integration with Russia abound. As befits a 'postmodern community', the EU is subject to supranational and sub-national governance dynamics. This creates a functional challenge for the Russian Federation. EU decisions can be made and implemented at the sub-state and/or trans-state regional levels, but Russia is wedded to exercising political decision-making in Moscow and to traditional bilateral or interstate relations. The EU's regional policy allows national governments to increase central control over regions in a number of ways: by tightening border accords; by encouraging regional sub-components (such as cities) to become involved in the centralization process (thus undercutting the primary position of the region); and by creating rapprochement between Russia and the EU. The Russian and EU systems of governance are at variance in terms of their decision-making process and political culture and also at a conceptual level, with no commonly held definitions of such basic political concepts as 'regions', 'regionalism', 'federalism', 'subsidiarity' and 'sovereignty'. Modern concepts of state sovereignty and territorial integrity are much more important in Russia and the US than in the EU.

A more contentious issue, which has damaged EU–Russia political relations, has been the EU's response to Russian human rights abuses in Chechnya.[49] Despite its occasional vociferous condemnation and its threatened and actual use of sanctions against Russia, the impact on Russian decision-making appears to have been meagre and to have generated little positive change in its approach to and behaviour in the conflict. The EU's policy failure has been due to its lack of power resources, will and skill. It simply does not have any leverage or 'stick' that would be big enough to beat Russia into order, nor are its 'carrots' sweet enough to tempt Russia to constrain its behaviour and risk the realization of *de facto* Chechen independence. When the EU had to determine its order of priorities, realpolitik interests trumped the normative agenda. Because the EU wanted to prevent the Chechen issue from spilling over and 'contaminating' the rest of the EU–Russia policy agenda, which would disrupt or stall cooperation, all leeway was extended to Russia. This approach was driven forward in ways that have generated short-term political capital for particular member states at the expense of undercutting the role, function and integrity of key EU institutions over the longer term. Indeed, the willingness of EU member states to give priority to their bilateral relations and strategic interests in Russia over the integrity of a unified and common approach is a core reason for the ineffectiveness of Union policy towards Russia. Paradoxically, the very ineffectiveness of the EU's policy recommends itself to national leaders. They can continue to promote it for domestic political reasons safe in the knowledge that their bilateral strategic partnership with Russia will be preserved. In response to domestic pressure and criticism to react to human rights abuses in Chechnya, individual EU member states have been able to refer their publics to EU statements of condemnation and concern. These declarations have provided them with a 'safe haven': they can criticize Russia without damaging bilateral relations. Indeed, these same member states can ignore reference to such 'condemnation' and 'concern' in bilateral relations with Russia.[50]

On this issue, the EU has clearly been understood in Russia to be a more difficult partner than the United States. As one Russian analyst has noted, 'While the US leaders appear to understand that the Chechen situation is rather complex and multi-dimensional and that Russia indeed has been compelled to deal with confirmed terrorists, West European politicians and analysts have often seen the Chechen problem as a violation of human rights on the part of the federal forces, with the terrorist activities of the Chechen separatists being completely overlooked.'[51] The EU's actions and initiatives with regard to Chechnya have also been a reflection of its wider inability to coordinate joint policy responses with the US. Particularly after 9/11, EU representatives have felt unsupported in pushing the normative agenda.

Following the 'Rose Revolution' in Georgia (November 2003) and then the 'Orange Revolution' in Ukraine (November 2004), Russian analysts and politicians have accused the US and the EU (through support for NGOs and the activities of their embassies) as well as the OSCE and the Council of Europe of 'manufacturing' and 'marketing' or 'exporting' democracy and revolution to the CIS. At the 25 November 2004 Russia–EU summit, it was apparent that the two sides did not share the same interpretation of the validity of the electoral process for choosing the president in Ukraine. Visits by Javier Solana and two presidents of new EU member states, Alexander Kwasniewski of Poland and Valdas Adamskus of Lithuania, helped to persuade President Leonid Kuchma of Ukraine to allow an unprecedented second-round run-off in December 2004. In this election, the Russian-backed Yanukovych conceded defeat to Yushchenko.[52]

The implications of these events for Russia's power, prestige and image are not contested. The Ukrainian presidential election has been interpreted in the Russian media in terms of a foreign policy Waterloo, a 'political Stalingrad', Russia's worst foreign policy defeat in the post-Soviet period.[53] In early 2005, the Russian defence minister Ivanov clearly stated that the CIS and the post-Soviet space was Russia's top foreign policy priority. And Russia also subsidizes the majority of the CIS through energy supplies. 'These are precisely the reasons why we react and will react the way we do to exports of revolution to the CIS states, no matter ... what colour – pink, blue, you name it – though of course we recognize that Russia ... has no monopoly on CIS states.' He noted further: 'Yet someone has not abandoned stereotypes of the past, which is proven by the reaction of certain circles in Europe and the USA to the political crisis in Ukraine.' Even before the presidential election in Ukraine, 'there had been clear signals that the West would not recognize the ballot results if the wrong candidate won the elections.'[54] Gennadiy Seleznev, a former Russian State Duma speaker, has described the situation in Ukraine as 'extremely alarming', arguing that 'We have the impression that what is taking place on Kiev's streets is not happening spontaneously – it is a well-prepared action. You can even tell from the emblems that this is a revolution for export. These oranges, which do not grow in Ukraine, have suddenly become a symbol of liberals.'[55] Sergei Mironov, the Russian Federation Council chairman, has stated that it was possible to detect 'a producer's hand' in the Ukrainian revolution, just as in Yugoslavia.[56]

Russia's fear of Western-imported revolution, which gathered pace after the 'Orange Revolution' and then the 'Tulip Revolution' in Kyrgyzstan in March 2005, may herald a new crackdown and help to justify and accelerate current policies towards opposition groups in some CIS states, including Russia itself. NGOs, international organizations, diplomatic missions and independent trade unions are increasingly perceived to constitute threats to internal security. In response, laws on protest and referendums are being strengthened and independent trade unions, NGOs, opposition leaders and their political parties are being circumscribed.

Russia's foreign and security policy is also influenced by this perception, and it is likely that US, NATO and PfP military-to-military contacts will be scrutinized to a greater degree than hitherto, that Russia will take steps to isolate some states more from Western influence and that the image of the West as an external enemy may well be strengthened. The various revolutions along its periphery have reinforced Russia's criticism of the OSCE, in particular its 'human dimension' of activities. Russia refuses to pay its share of the OSCE budget, has closed the OSCE assistance group to Chechnya and has broken the OSCE Istanbul Summit commitments agreed in 1999.[57] Its integration, based on shared values, into the Euro-Atlantic security community is thus put into doubt by its responses to regime change, which are at variance with those of central and west European members of the OSCE.

Such perceptions are sure to influence negatively Russia's attitudes towards the EU's evolving ESDP and its own desire to have security issues in Europe resolved by European structures rather than within the framework of NATO. As we have noted, the ESDP was initially perceived in Russia as a means of counterbalancing the US by diminishing the importance of NATO. However, Russia's improved relationship with the US after 9/11 has decreased its interest in the ESDP: it is far simpler to deal with NATO and Washington than 'with individual European nations and politicians, some of whom are openly anti-Russian', and 'it is becoming convenient for Russia and NATO to be friends against the uncooperative European Union'.[58] Putin's orientation towards Washington has been more pragmatic than ideological: Russia joined the 'coalition of unwilling' with France and Germany during the war in Iraq, but its membership did not indicate the formation of a permanent Moscow–Berlin–Paris axis. Moscow's desire to decouple Europe from America was no longer a priority.

As with NATO, Russia cooperates with the EU on a range of issues that encompasses the 'hard' and 'soft' security agenda. Cooperation in the nonproliferation and disarmament sector includes the chemical weapons destruction programme and the utilization of arms-grade plutonium programme. Russia ratified the 1990 convention on money laundering and thus participates in EU anti-corruption programmes. Environmental security cooperation occurs within ecological programmes, which include water purification efforts in St Petersburg. The October 2001 Russia–EU summit in Paris has been considered a 'breakthrough' in the two parties' security cooperation: Russia became the first non-member state 'to gain monthly consultations with the EU's Political and Security Committee (COPS), the main decision-making body of the ESDP'.[59]

But what of the Russia–EU and Russia–NATO dynamics that both underpin and undermine security cooperation over the medium and longer term? It is variously argued that Russia and the EU or NATO do not share the same fundamental strategic culture and value system that have underpinned the Euro-Atlantic security community over the past half-century. It is also said that there is a basic incompatibility between Russia and the EU and NATO member states in the military and technology sector and that this capabilities gap precludes effective cooperation in the military and security sphere. For example, Russia would never contribute peacekeepers to an EU-led peacekeeping mission, let alone sanction a NATO operation, in the post-Soviet space. For these reasons, Russia's military and security cooperation with the EU or NATO is not likely to widen or deepen transatlantic rifts.

Some argue that a capabilities gap and problems with interoperability between Russia and EU states preclude effective cooperation in the military and security sphere, but it is equally true that gaps in technology, defence spending and collective security capability between the US and its European allies in NATO are large and, in some instances, growing.[60] But these gaps do not rule out Russian contributions to US-led 'coalitions of the willing' or to EU missions. There is a real basis for interaction in the military and technical sphere, particularly in the US Global Orbiting Navigation Satellite System and the EU's Galileo global satellite navigation systems and other aspects of the defence and space complex, as well as in the managing of crises and emergencies.[61] Although satellite reconnaissance and navigation programmes and heavy airlift are two obvious areas of military security cooperation that plug existing gaps in the EU's Rapid Reaction Force (ERRF) capability profile, Russian satellites have poor reliability records and the EU has already rejected, in 2002, Russia's offer of heavy airlift for ERRF operations.

It is ironic that as Russia has become less prepared to play its European card, the transatlantic relationship has weakened as a result of cleavages, stresses and mistrust. For all that, however, the rift in the transatlantic relationship has yet to make Russia more attractive to the EU. Nicole Gnesotto argues that an EU–Russia alliance directed against the US would be both profoundly mistaken and absurd.[62] Even though Europeans have begun to be increasingly concerned about US unilateralism, they have not been willing to adopt a counterbalancing strategy against Washington: Russia has neither the push nor pull factors that could stimulate this.[63]

CONCLUSIONS: VALUES, INTERESTS AND REALPOLITIK

Russia has imported, assimilated and Russified the French and German traditions of *raison d'état* and realpolitik, allowing for a cold-blooded calculus of national interest to organize its foreign policy. Under Putin, this calculation suggests that despite its traditional great-power status, Russia faces systemic pressures that propel it to long-term cooperation with strategic partners. Russia's integration into the global economy, its ability to develop its technological base and demographic pressures, to name but a few of the key dynamics set to shape the international politics of the new century, all suggest that its future lies to the west and that it could be anchored by closer strategic cooperation with the EU, NATO or the US. However, the dual enlargement process of May 2004 has brought the EU and NATO ever closer to Russia's borders. This has highlighted basic differences in approaches to conflicts (particularly 'frozen conflicts') in the shared neighbourhood and different understandings of security cooperation and has exacerbated as much as ameliorated residual fears of and rivalries with NATO. In late 2005 Sergei Ivanov, Russia's Defence Minister, was still able to highlight differences over civilian and military transit access to Kaliningrad, interpretations of the CFE Treaty, and shortfalls in anti-terrorist cooperation as areas that need to be addressed.[64] The deterrence–cooperation dichotomy continues to characterize Russia's relationship with NATO, and its strategic partnership with the EU is a triumph of form over substance.

Although Russia's membership of NATO would certainly splinter transatlantic relations further, this prospect is too long-term to disrupt the current transatlantic security discourse. The question itself is much less relevant in the transformed post-9/11 strategic context, which has so effectively reframed the nature and basis of Russia's partnership with the US. The NRC has diminished in importance as a bridge between Russia and NATO in the face of ad hoc US-led 'coalitions of the willing', which have undercut the very utility of NATO. Indeed, Russian–US strategic partnership in the global war on terrorism appeared to be stronger in 2003 than US relations with the Franco-German axis in NATO.

A paradox emerges. The very weakness of the concept of a 'global war against terror' becomes its greatest strength. As far as Russia is concerned, the inherent ambiguities and ambivalence of this 'war' provide it with an ideological pretext for strategic realignment. At the same time, the disparities and fractures within the Euro-Atlantic security community secure the opportunity for President Putin to pick and choose which of the core values and interests of a divided transatlantic community Russia shares.[65] This cherry-picking is facilitated by systemic weaknesses in the EU's foreign policy-making process: 'National egoism, distinctly divergent foreign policy interests of the individual members and an inefficient decision-making system in CFSP, along with far reaching retention of sovereignty by individual states, all led to a lack of coherence in collective action and was thus a great handicap to the conduct of European foreign affairs.'[66] Thus Putin's differentiated strategic engagement with the divided West tells us as much about Russia's foreign policy preferences as it does about the nature of the distribution of power, political will and state capability in the West.

Perhaps because of the very indefinite and weakly rooted nature of these strategic partnerships, Russia does have the ability to become a disruptive actor, whether by default or design, in transatlantic relations. Sergei Karaganov has argued that Russia's relationship with the EU has become an instrumental object of EU–US tensions and differences: 'The EU has sought alternatively to involve Russia in "anti-American triangles" or to "punish" it for "excessive closeness" to Washington by toughening the EU position on Russian accession to the World Trade Organization.'[67] Equally, however, a Russian Federation well versed in its near neighbourhood in the dark arts of divide and rule may itself begin in a pragmatic and rational way to seek to exploit existing transatlantic rifts in order to maximize its own legitimate state interests. The potential for Russia to develop such an approach is apparent, but it has yet to adopt such a policy in any systematic way and it may not be willing to do so as it realizes that attempts to exploit rifts may serve only to heal them.

8

Transatlantic futures in an age of strategic dissonance

The revolutions of 1989 and the collapse of the Soviet Union in 1991 signalled for many that 'the West had won' the Cold War. In this period, transatlantic ties were strong: the US–EU Transatlantic Declaration of 1990 reflected a traditional internationalist US foreign policy, and US–EU goodwill was reinforced during the Clinton presidency by the publication of the 'New Atlantic Agenda' in 1995. This promoted global and regional cooperation and an institutionalization of the transatlantic relationship through annual US–EU summits. The relationship rested on many pillars. Strong trade links and shared common values such as democracy, the rule of law and free markets were understood to unite the transatlantic world despite a growing public perception that there were increasing differences between the US and Europe over social issues, in particular religion, the death penalty and abortion. Common interests, for example the promotion of democracy and free trade, and also a desire to combat the proliferation of WMD, cooperation to promote regional stability (in the Balkans, the Middle East and Africa) and a web of regulatory economic cooperation appeared to create durable transatlantic ties.

But, as noted in Chapter 1, these ties did not bind the transatlantic community together after 9/11. As Ronald Asmus has put it, 'Somewhere between Kabul and Baghdad, then, the United States and Europe lost each other.'[1] The transatlantic trauma of 2002–3 stood in stark contrast to the relative transatlantic harmony of the 1990s and so gave rise to intense analysis and speculation as to its causes and consequences. Many analysts and commentators suggested strategic divorce as a possible future; others predicted strategic realignment; and still others resigned themselves to continued strategic dissonance. Almost all those who analysed trends and trajectories stressed the negative consequences for transatlantic and global stability and security that would result from the fragmentation of NATO into competing blocs and coalitions. Would the dynamics that could split

121

the alliance into competing blocs be powerful enough to do so? Alternatively, would the political, economic and military factors prevail that might enable a transatlantic reformation, or would the trauma remain unresolved?

In order to address these questions effectively, Chapter 1 sought to give a short narrative and description of the dynamic events that signposted the deterioration of transatlantic relations. This provided a basis upon which we could theorize in Chapter 2 about the transatlantic relationship, highlighting explanations that accounted for divergent or convergent trends within and between 'Atlantic Europe', 'Core Europe', 'New Europe', 'Non-aligned Europe' and 'Periphery Europe'.

The theoretical approaches offered by realism, liberalism and constructivism provided a framework through which we were able to arrive at a more comprehensive and systematic understanding of the transatlantic crisis. We first examined realist theory and the key elements of its explanation of the transatlantic division. These rested on growing disparities in 'hard' and 'soft' power and material interests across the Atlantic. Realist theory suggests that states which fear the consequences of US hegemony would be more likely to oppose it while states which are to a greater degree dependent on the US would tend to support it. Realist explanations could thus account for the crisis as a 'Core European' attempt to counterbalance US power in the context of diverging strategic interests and capabilities. Liberalism suggests that the strength of the transatlantic relationship relates to the degree to which institutional links and networks are strong and to the extent to which values are shared and a common strategic culture is held. The liberal perspective assumes that states which enjoy close institutional links and shared values and which have the same political outlook as the Bush administration are much more likely to support the US than states that do not. It argues that NATO countries ('Core Europe', 'Atlantic Europe' and 'New Europe') would be more inclined to support the US position and that 'Non-aligned Europe' and 'Periphery Europe' would not. Constructivist theory contends that beliefs and cultures shape relations and thus foreign and security policies. It supposes that support for the US would remain low in states where the dynamic of 'othering' or other cultural factors lead to an anti-American reaction to US foreign and security policy. This would therefore indicate that 'Core Europe's' building of a new European identity would occur in opposition to the United States whereas 'Atlantic Europe' and 'New Europe' would be more supportive of it and 'Non-aligned Europe' and 'Periphery Europe' would be found somewhere between these two camps.

FIVE EUROPES: THEORY AND PRACTICE

Chapter 3 focused on the United Kingdom as an example of 'Atlantic Europe', and it examined the nature of the US–UK 'special relationship' and its utility in the twenty-first century. The UK is an example of an Atlanticist state that fears unbridled and unilateral US hegemony; but rather than uniting with 'Core Europe' in opposition, it has supported the US in order to provide it with a multilateral fig leaf for its actions and to avert US isolationism. The working assumptions of realism are undermined by this response. The chapter argued that 9/11 and Afghanistan reinforced the bridging role of Europe's pre-eminent Atlanticist state but that the Iraq war has brought the utility of this policy into question. The *modus operandi* of the global war on terrorism (the use of coalitions to fit missions) undercuts the utility of NATO. This damages a prime institution that binds the UK to the US and underpins the special relationship. At the same time, a weaker NATO supports a stronger ESDP and promotes a greater British commitment to European military development.

The chapter suggested that under George W. Bush, the limits of the UK's brand of Atlanticist behaviour will be exposed further but that the UK–US relationship will prove to be durable despite the turbulence, not least for lack of a compelling alternative that secures the British national interest. The UK's Atlanticism has had little influence on US policy, but in Britain's view French Gaullism and the German *Sonderweg* have been equally ineffective as means of influencing the US. As a result, the UK's role as transatlantic broker will become more ambiguous and harder to sustain. In the context of the global war on terrorism, the United States' tradition of self-restrained diplomacy has largely been abandoned, and its promotion of the multilateral and self-binding nature of its foreign policy underpinned by deep interdependence and shared values is fading as well.

Chapter 4 took Germany as an example of 'Core Europe' or 'Old Europe' both because Germany articulated its anti-war position earlier than France and because it had traditionally aligned itself with the Atlanticist camp in transatlantic security relations. The state of German–US relations has also been understood to set the tone of EU–US relations.[2] The chapter suggested that constructivist explanations that account for changes in German foreign policy through the simplistic prism of pacifism, anti-Americanism or 'othering' were weak. Nevertheless, a change in beliefs and values has allowed for a new assertiveness to enter German foreign policy. This underscores the 'de-Europeanization' and renationalization of German foreign policy – that is, its normalization on the assumption that Germany can no longer be side-lined in transatlantic relations. Karsten Voigt, the foreign ministry's special envoy to the US, has argued, perhaps somewhat plaintively, that 'The US will have to engage us on the security issues.'[3]

However, Germany's emancipation has made it harder for it to provide bedrock support for a truly European foreign policy. Its response to the US intention to overthrow Saddam Hussein was reactive rather than proactive. Germany has been able so far to argue against the inclusion of Iraq in the global war on terrorism, reinforcing the contention that Iraq is a strategic diversion from that campaign, but it appears to be unable or unwilling to position its foreign policy within a coherent European strategic context in which the German national interest can be advanced. Any *Sonderweg* is mired in constructive ambiguity as long as its national interest is not defined, and thus there is little basis upon which Germany can build allies in support of its strategic initiatives. Germany's commitment to transatlantic institutional links will continue to be strained by this fundamental lack of strategic clarity in its foreign policy. Chancellor Angela Merkel has begun to forge a new strategic partnership with Russia in which both the tone and the substance of the relationship have changed, as she addresses several controversial issues Chancellor Schröder was reluctant to air. At the 2006 Munich Security Conference she signalled to the French, among others, that Germany considers NATO to be the primary security organization.[4] Despite the reaffirmation of NATO in German security policy, the transatlantic relationship between Germany and the US appears to have changed in tone only.

After the rejection of the constitutional treaty by the referenda in France and the Netherlands in May and June 2005 and a subsequent period of introspection, the real test for the EU's largest state will be the direction it takes on further enlargement and the nature of the Franco-German axis. Germany has a pivotal role to play with regard to both the integration of Romania and Bulgaria into the EU in 2007 and the nature of the accession discussions with Turkey that began in October 2005. Much will depend on the nature of the 'new honesty' that the CDU-led coalition headed by Chancellor Merkel will bring to German foreign policy. But given the economic constraints on the defence budget, 'full honesty' can translate only into stylistic rather than substantive changes in 'hard' security issues.[5]

Chapter 5 identified the main security policy dynamics among those states that have been termed 'New Europe'. Their experience and motivations underpin realist understandings of the transatlantic division in that they supported the US primarily because they felt greater dependence on rather than fear of US hegemony. Undoubtedly, the trade-offs and costs incurred by 'New Europe' in its support for European or US priorities become less complex and lower the more divided Europe remains or the more US and European policy initiatives overlap. On occasions in which the United States, France, Germany and the United Kingdom agree on policies and/or priorities, the cost of 'New Europe's' opposition would be much higher. The greater the gulf between US and European policy responses to security threats, the harder it is to sustain Atlanticist policies.

For these reasons, the strong Atlanticist attitude in 'New Europe' has a limited shelf life, and support for the US on the Iraq issue will be the exception rather than the rule. By 2005, there was a fracturing among the 'coalition of the willing' partners and their support for maintaining troops in Iraq, and this fragmentation was also evident over arms procurement policies among the 'New European' states. 'Small-state complex' may assert itself as 'New Europe' oscillates between inclusionist and disillusionist experiences of EU membership, but the trend will be towards socialization into the EU and, with that, support for strengthening the Common Foreign and Security Policy and the European Security and Defence Policy. Indeed, as 'New Europe' is unwilling to accept automatic 'Core European' leadership in the EU and rejects the scapegoating of former communist states (on the basis of their lower economic and social costs), divisions between EU member states are set to continue. This trend can be balanced by another: increased EU profile and attention to stability in the western Balkans and Southeast Europe, from Pristina to Tiraspol. In 2006 the EU is set to increase its engagement with the Transdniestria frozen conflict, and the realization that the post-conflict status quo in Kosovo is unsustainable will further EU integrative efforts in the heart of 'New Europe'. This, coupled with the EU decision to begin EU association agreements with Bosnia-Herzegovina, Serbia and Montenegro and start accession talks with Macedonia (with Croatia to follow in short order), all suggest that the EU will become a more dominant security actor than NATO in the region.

Chapter 6 examined the experience of 'Non-aligned Europe' through a comparative analysis of Finnish and Swedish responses to the terrorist attacks of 9/11. It suggested that non-alignment as a viable and useful security strategy was questioned after 9/11. Even between Finland and Sweden we can note variations in approach to the transatlantic rift, which demonstrate the relatively fluid nature of this 'bloc'. Their opposition to the Iraq war and unwillingness to support the US and 'Atlantic Europe' cannot be explained entirely by 'othering', anti-Americanism or a growing values gap; nor can it be explained by a desire to counterbalance US power, because the non-aligned states did not support 'Core Europe'. Indeed, political elites in Finland and Sweden were more positive in their attitudes to the US than was their public opinion.

Realist and liberal theories do not offer a full account, though material interests and institutional bonds can help in understanding Finnish and Swedish behaviour. Realist theories can explain why preserving good relations with the US was more important to Finland than to Sweden given the perception of a latent Russian threat. However, they can also explain why Finnish support to the US was, at least in the immediate aftermath of 9/11, more reserved than Sweden's in view of the low perception of a terrorist threat to Finland. Institutions and values do account for why 'Non-aligned Europe' responded differently from 'Atlantic' Europe, but they do not appear to explain the small differences between Swedish and Finish reactions to the crisis. Finland was, for example, more reserved in its support for the US during the first stages of the campaign against terrorism than was Sweden, but it was more willing to consider NATO membership. Nevertheless, European institutions were important in soliciting support from both countries, especially Finland, for the campaign against terrorism. What emerges, therefore, as important in this analysis is the national discursive context and leadership through which the two states' positions were defined. In Sweden, neutrality was never defined in terms of abstaining from taking a stance on international conflicts; but in Finland, that was a crucial part of its Cold War neutrality doctrine.

Although these two states shared material interests and some institutional bonds with 'Atlantic Europe' and, to a lesser extent, the US, their societal values were probably further from the US than those of any of the other Europes. The necessity to keep the US at arm's length partly reflected domestic political views shaped by social democratic ideology, but it is also explained in terms of small-state ideology, which harbours suspicion of all great powers and is still mentally attached to, if not dependent upon, a policy of military non-alignment.

Thus, a policy of equidistance between 'Atlantic Europe' and 'Core Europe' was developed to give contemporary expression to the concept of non-alignment in an age of terror. However, such a policy can be sustained only if European security policies and orientations remain fragmented and polarized. Continued divergence between 'Core Europe' and the US still allows non-aligned states room for manoeuvre, whereas growing transatlantic convergence makes it difficult to sustain a policy of non-alignment. The weakening of NATO and the strengthening of the ESDP also poses difficult policy dilemmas for non-aligned states: whether to support the strengthening of a military alliance in order to maintain the transatlantic link without joining it, or to promote the ESDP to an extent that rules out the possibility of continued non-aligned status.

In Chapter 7, we examined Russia as a case study of 'Periphery Europe', that is European states that have little or no prospect of integration into the EU and/or NATO but still aim to strengthen partnerships and cooperation with those organizations. We would therefore expect realist-based accounts to have the greatest purchase in explaining Russia's response to the transatlantic crisis: a significant overlap of material interests rather than shared values explains why cooperative patterns of behaviour rather than competition would predominate. Institutional links have been developed, but so far they reflect the general pattern of the relationship rather than its nature. However, Russia's traditional role as a great power and the legacy of the Soviet period suggest that old psychological factors create obstacles to full cooperation.

Although *raison d'état* is part and parcel of Russia's foreign policy tool box, under President Putin the realization that Russia faces systemic pressures that propel it to long-term cooperation with strategic partners has shaped its Euro-Atlantic policy and has calmed competitive impulses. Despite this long-term trend, the deterrence–cooperation dichotomy continues to characterize Russia's relationship with NATO, and its strategic partnership with the EU is a triumph of form over substance. A paradox was noted in which the very weakness of the concept of a 'global war against terror' becomes its greatest strength as far as Russia is concerned: the inherent ambiguities and ambivalence embodied by this 'war' provide Russia with an ideological pretext for strategic realignment. At the same time, the disparities and fractures within the Euro-Atlantic security community allow Putin to pick and choose which of the core values and interests of a divided transatlantic community Russia shares. The very divisions that characterize the relationships between the 'New Europe', 'Core Europe', 'Non-aligned Europe' and 'Atlantic Europe' make a policy of divide and rule unfeasible: Russia's attempts to exploit rifts, it was noted, may serve only to heal them.

Nevertheless, over the longer term the co-dependence of Russia and the EU (energy in exchange for goods, capital and technology) is set to move to greater EU dependence on Russia than Russian dependence on the EU. Russian energy reserves change the balance of power as the EU finds it increasingly difficult to diversify away from Russia. This gives Russia a freer hand in bending or leveraging geo-economic power towards its own geo-political ends, particularly in its near neighbourhood. As Anatol Lieven noted following Russia's gas price hike in December 2005, such a trend exposes the 'bizarre illusion' upon which 'the West's strategy toward Ukraine has been founded: that Ukraine would leave Russia's orbit and "join the West", and that Russia would pay for this [through a] de facto annual energy subsidy estimated by independent experts at somewhere between $3 billion and $5 billion a year'.[6] With presidential elections in Russia set for March 2008, the price hikes of late 2005 served as a well-timed if poorly aimed shot across the EU's bows. The potential for EU criticism of 'Operation Successor 2008' – the name given to the aim of President Putin and the Kremlin to name a successor to the presidency (much in the manner in which Putin himself assumed power) – will as a result be much more muted and circumspect. As the reality of the EU's energy dependency on Russia sinks in around EU capitals, Russia will be increasingly able to maintain its European relationship on its own terms. However, economic dependency will serve only to further highlight divergent values and norms between the EU and Russia.

TRANSATLANTIC TRENDS: THE 'HARD' AND 'SOFT' POWER CALCULUS

It was clear from the narrative of Chapter 1 that 'New Europe' and 'Atlantic Europe' broadly supported the US position on the global war on terrorism and on Afghanistan and Iraq. For their part, 'Core Europe', 'Non-aligned Europe' and 'Periphery Europe' supported Operation Enduring Freedom but expressed reservations over the nature of the war on terrorism and the necessity of pre-emption, and they registered strong opposition to Operation Iraqi Freedom. When we examined in some detail explanations for the behaviour of the UK, Germany, a range of 'New European' states, Finland and Sweden, and Russia, we discovered little overlap between security policy decisions and the realist, liberal and constructivist theoretical explanations that purport to explain those choices. The foreign and security policy approaches of those states could not be understood in terms of a clear-cut application of any one theory: no overarching theoretical framework or set of explanations emerged that accounted for the transatlantic rift or the policy responses of the five Europes that have been identified and analysed. Different factors have been shown to have different kinds of importance in different countries in Europe.

What does this analysis indicate to be the principal current determinants of state behaviour? Are these likely to shape key future trends in transatlantic security relations, and how will these shape the quality of transatlantic security cooperation and policy responses to issues of outstanding strategic importance, in particular China, Iran and North Korea? Let us examine key current trends before addressing the principal strategic issues that face the transatlantic security community.

As theories and practice appear to be at odds, what can be asserted with some certainty about the strategic cultures, values, material interests and institutional links that tie the transatlantic security community together? There are two factors in transatlantic security cooperation, and they shape the texture and patterns of cooperation. First, the US possesses 'hard', military, power, and this will remain a constant. As Lawrence Freedman notes, the collapse of the Soviet Union dissolved Cold War strategic imperatives: 'The United States was left in a class of its own, not even *primus inter pares* among Great Powers but the lone superpower – a super-duper power, a hyper-power.'[7] Disparities between the United States and Europe in 'hard' power and 'soft' power shape the willingness of states within the transatlantic security community to cooperate actively in the international arena. The exercise of US military power has the potential to make others resentful, fearful and suspicious, particularly when the US is prepared to use this power unilaterally, proactively and pre-emptively at a time when the transatlantic gap in military capabilities is widening. America's exercise of its 'hard' power after 9/11 has diminished its 'soft' power.[8]

A second factor is the EU's increasing ability to act as an attractive 'soft', economic and political, power and provide a gold standard of liberalized markets and democratic governance which post-communist states could aspire to emulate. The development of this power was exemplified by the integration of 10 new member states into its institutional and normative framework on 1 May 2004. The EU enjoys three-quarters of 'New Europe's' trade and is Russia's largest single trade partner. It looks to integrate the Balkan region, southeastern Europe and Turkey and to strengthen polit-ical and economic links with Russia and Ukraine. However, rejection of the constitutional treaty has serious implications for its further enlargement. Carl Bildt has argued that the 'no' vote has weakened the EU's 'soft' power and created greater instability in the wider region by reducing the prospects of 'European reformation of Turkey and also reconciliation and reintegration of the war-torn societies of the Balkans'.[9] As François Heisbourg concludes, 'No matter which way you look at it, after the French and Dutch vote against the Constitution, there is a big, deep political crisis. Even though we should be looking outward, there is no way of escaping a period of introspection. It will take a few years before we start looking outwards.'[10] As a result of this vote, latent fault lines, whose source is different conceptions of domestic political governance and divergent foreign policy orientations, have emerged in Europe. Broadly, the UK, 'Non-aligned Europe' and 'New Europe' push for an economically liberal (Anglo-Saxon capitalism) and wider Europe; France, Germany and Belgium ('Core Europe'), and also Spain and possibly Italy, support a 'social Europe' (Rhineland capitalism) and oppose further enlargement.[11] This suggests that foreign policy paralysis and turbulence in Europe are distinct possibilities.

But does the EU's 'soft' power influence the global application of US 'hard' power? Is there the political will in Europe to spend political capital in a period of economic downturn, to spend three per cent or more of GDP on defence (as do the US, France, the UK, Bulgaria, Romania, Greece and Turkey) and to direct that spending to force restructuring and 'war-training' (mobility, employability and sustainability) in order to have the military

129

capability to make a meaningful contribution to the NATO Response Force (NRF)? Are European elites prepared to finance and participate in robust peace support operations beyond Europe and to act pre-emptively with niche capabilities alongside the US? The answer to these questions is a qualified 'no'. Cornish and Edwards argue that when examining progress towards the emergence of a EU strategic culture, it is apparent that despite marked development, there are still substantial intra-EU differences in capabilities, in understandings of the legitimacy of autonomous EU action, in levels of civil–military integration necessary to sustain such action and in attitudes towards cooperation with NATO.[12] A larger common budget has not been created, nor has an agreement between NATO and the EU on a division of labour been reached. Germany in particular has fallen short in developing military power. The spending, capability and usability gaps between it and other large EU members, France and the UK if not Italy and Spain, are stark.[13]

There are three possibilities for transatlantic military cooperation; but they are contentious, and there is little intra-European or transatlantic consensus on the way forward. First, a functional division of labour within NATO might be adopted whereby the US agrees to undertake war fighting, European NATO handles the immediate phase after major combat (phase IV operations) and the EU members of NATO concentrate on post-conflict prevention and rehabilitation operations (as, for example, in the Balkans). Secondly, a regional distribution of labour might be agreed: NATO's NRF goes global; the EU polices the Balkans and Africa.[14] The 1.4 million American and 2.4 million European NATO forces are still not 'transformed'. European NATO forces remain largely passive, linear and static and little new emphasis has been placed on identifying forces, capabilities and assets that can undertake stabilization and reconstruction efforts. NATO members appear more willing to choose their own degree of commitment to the organization and quite prepared to resist peer pressure to fulfil their obligations. Thirdly, a functional rather than geographical division of labour between NATO and the EU might be agreed, with NATO having first right of refusal before the EU intervenes (this would be sequential in terms of the 'Berlin Plus' agreement that specifies the EU can gain access to NATO planning, logistics and intelligence for missions in which NATO is not involved).

But although some European states may not support US policies, they cannot effectively oppose them: they lack the means to offer alternative military-based solutions when 'soft' power options have been exhausted. The 2005 Darfur operation is of interest in this respect. NATO agreed to provide military, transport, logistic and planning support for the African Union, which is prepared to assume a greater role in ending violence in the Darfur region in western Sudan. At the same time, France and Belgium pushed for the EU to take the lead. NATO's secretary general commented that 'NATO and the EU are entering into a very good example of what I would say is practical and pragmatic cooperation. Let's not have theology. Let's do it. There is no room for competition. There is plenty of work to be done.'[15] Another way to interpret Euro-Atlantic responses to Darfur would be through the prism of unresolved competition between the EU and NATO. France's objection to the proposal to hold the NRF's first full operational capability (FOC) test, essentially its first major and visible training exercise, in Mauritania in spring 2005 forced it to be moved to Cape Verde. In addition, the French questioned the nature of the FOC, insisting that it should replicate a high-intensity operation rather than follow a humanitarian aid scenario. This points to a determination to have a functional and geographical division of labour that suits France's conception of EU interests: all medium- and low-intensity Petersberg tasks (humanitarian and rescue operations and peace-keeping rather than tasks of combat forces in crisis management, including peace-making) are to be addressed by the EU, and Africa falls within the EU's area of responsibility.[16] At the same time, the NRF is to be used not as an end in itself for limited high-intensity Petersberg combat operations but as a means to another, more limited end, the transformation of NATO European militaries. Indeed, France's insistence that the NRF performs only high-intensity Petersberg tasks makes it unlikely that the NRF will actually be utilized in this role and thus at all.

Just as the EU is pausing for reflection after the rejection of the constitutional treaty, so too is there an increased tendency in the US to question the integrity and rationale of the global war on terrorism. Jeffrey Record has argued that the justification for intervention in Iraq has not been sustained, that the Iraq war was a 'war of choice, not necessity' and that, as such, it constituted a strategic diversion.[17] Stephen Biddle contends that the United States' grand strategy after 9/11 has two fatal flaws: it fails to define the enemy and it does not explain what constitutes success and what constitutes failure. Without clarity, the United States' strategic responses lack coherence and integrity.[18]

In addition, US public support for the war is fading; and this is of critical importance because the domestic front represents, according to US Army General George Casey, commander of the multinational forces in Iraq, the US military's 'friendly strategic centre of gravity'. Opinion polls in June 2005 indicated lowest-ever levels of domestic support for the intervention: 75 per cent of respondents believed that the number of US casualties was too high; 6 in 10 believed that the war was not worth fighting; two-thirds believed that the US military was bogged down in Iraq; and 52 per cent considered that the war does not contribute to long-term US stability.[19] There is a vocal policy debate over whether to stay for the long haul and 'victory' or to 'cut and run', speed up the 'Iraqification' process and withdraw US troops so as to deny insurgents a rallying cause. The former president Jimmy Carter, as well as some Republican internationalists in the Senate, suggested that the Guantánamo Bay detainee interrogation centre, which an Amnesty International report referred to as 'a gulag of our time', should be shut down. Zbigniew Brzezinski, President Carter's national security adviser, has argued that the 'minimum metrics' for stabilizing and democratizing Iraq would involve deploying 500,000 US troops, spending $500 billion and instituting a military draft and wartime tax and that the operation would take 10 years.[20]

More generally, Brent Scowcroft, President George H.W. Bush's national security adviser and a proponent of the 'realist' school of foreign policy thinking, has voiced his opposition to the 'transformationalist', neoconservative or liberal interventionist approach of President George W. Bush.[21] Lawrence B. Wilkerson, who served as chief of staff to Secretary of State Colin Powell from 2002 to 2005, has characterized US foreign and security policy decision-making as dysfunctional: 'insular and secret' although 'efficient and swift'. He argues that 'the secret process was ultimately a failure. It produced a series of disastrous decisions and virtually ensured that the agencies charged with implementing them would not or could not execute them well.'[22] Rather than demonstrating US strategic coherence, the military intervention in Iraq has brought into question the United States' global war on terrorism strategy and its military doctrine in an age of 'fourth-generation warfare'.[23]

Moreover, the freedom and democracy agenda, the cornerstone of George W. Bush's foreign policy, has further undermined the coherence of the global war on terrorism and raised questions about the nature of 'democratic realism', 'preventive democracy' and the prospect of 'democratic imperialism' in US foreign policy.[24] In order to invade Afghanistan and Iraq, the US forged or strengthened strategic partnerships with a number of authoritarian and semi-authoritarian states, not least Saudi Arabia, Pakistan, Uzbekistan and Russia. The rhetoric of democratization and the promotion of democratic values have raised expectations that in reality the US may find are hard to meet, particularly those pertaining to national interests and the elimination of terrorists. Cynics may argue that the US cannot 'do democracy and oil', that dependence on the 'axis of oil' to defeat an 'axis of evil' places too much strain on clarity of purpose and coherent policy. It is not clear whether the US has now made democratization a higher strategic priority than the concerns of realpolitik. The massacre in Andijon, Uzbekistan in May 2005 highlighted a growing perception of a tension in US foreign policy between the need to secure strategic partners for the global war on terrorism – partners which act as bulwarks against neo-Taliban forces, provide military bases and overflight rights and support 'extraordinary rendition' – and the freedom and democracy agenda.[25] The US NSS of 2006 states that democratization efforts will be 'balanced' by 'other interests that are also vital to the security and well-being of the American people'.[26]

While the global war on terror is open to claims of incoherence on the analytical level, the growing US domestic political and popular backlash against the perception and reality of an imperial executive and the poor quality of the President's performance are likely to have a dramatic impact on the substance of US strategy. Congressional financial and policy support for the President is waning, and there appears an increasing willingness in both the judiciary and the legislature to hold the executive to account. Hurricane Katrina, torture and domestic wire-tapping without court approval are just some of the issues that fuel the backlash. With corruption scandals tying a Republican Congress to lobbyists, the growing problem of the deficit and other assorted financial issues, Iraq slipping towards civil war, and less money for defence spending, the last three years of the Bush presidency may well be characterized by policy paralysis, scandal and Democratic Party control of the House of Representatives, if not the Senate, in the November 2006 mid-term elections.

Looking further forward towards the 2008 US presidential elections and the likely Democratic and Republican Party candidates who will stand, the perennial orientation between the two models of US foreign policy will move centre-stage and be debated. One model argues that the US should interact with the world only to defend direct and specific US geo-strategic interests. Alliances should be abandoned, as should permanent allies and permanent US military bases outside the US, but not the pursuit of permanent US interests. Essentially this model suggests a return to the isolationist foreign policy the US adopted prior to the Second World War. The second model, and the one currently embraced by the Bush administration in its second term, is that of US engagement with the world in order to create a world order in the US image. The 'Freedom Agenda' is reflective of US values and practice and needs the application of US 'hard' and 'soft' power and the cooperation of US partners, allies and friends to achieve its ends. Over the longer term such engagement holds open the possibilities of transatlantic strategic realignment, and disengagement adds powerfully to the drift into transatlantic strategic divorce. But is it possible that extreme short-term events could hasten the process either way by tipping the transatlantic security community towards divorce or realignment?

EXTREME SCENARIOS: DIVORCE OR REALIGNMENT?

It is within the post-9/11 strategic environment that strategic dissonance between and among states, their institutions and strategic cultures has flourished. The apparent necessities of the global war on terrorism demand useful and deployable assets. NATO is viewed by the US as a useful tool box: its assets are militarily useful for coalitions against particular targets, but politically it is a liability. NATO will become politically useful to the US only if its basic consensus principle is amended to allow some form of qualified majority voting to give sanction for NATO operations. According to the premises of the war on terrorism, military expediency and efficiency outweigh political legitimacy.

In addition, although the US and Europe may agree in general terms on what constitutes a threat, their common strategic culture is undermined by three fundamental differences. The US and European states disagree over which means are necessary and appropriate to counter threats, particularly with regard to the legitimacy of using military force as opposed to political and economic instruments of policy. This is partly explained because each side of the Atlantic assesses differently the risks of action against the costs of inaction. Some European allies appear more risk-averse than the US; and the US, at least according to some European states, has proved itself incapable of overcoming self-imposed obstacles and barriers (ideology, ignorance and incompetence) to effective enactment of such a strategy based primarily on the use of force. Niall Fergusson has argued that US power can be understood as imperial. It has over 750 bases in more than 130 countries around the world. However, structural reasons preclude the effective establishment of a global pax Americana: the US has large foreign debts and a negative domestic dependency ratio; there is a lack of will among the public and political class for sustaining 'democratic imperialism'; and there is an attention deficit that may lead to a rapid withdrawal from Iraq.[27] Transatlantic disagreement also results from what is identified in Europe as a means–ends dichotomy: all agree about the ends but there is divergence over means, and there is a normative clash between means used and the outcome achieved.

As a result, Europe and the US have different approaches to securing world order. The basic cleavage within the alliance springs from a difference in approach, unilateral versus multilateral, rather than simply from the United States' possession of overwhelming force and its willingness to use it. The Bush administration believes that US unilateral efforts or ad hoc US-led 'coalitions of the willing' better achieve the objective of global stability and security. Indeed, this point was reinforced in early January 2006 by a senior US State Department official: though NATO would remain a 'bedrock alliance, a model and framework', it was also unreliable. As a result the US was 'focused on the enduring dynamics of coalition warfare'.[28] By contrast, US internationalists and European elites and publics argue that world order is best secured by involving and cultivating allies within institutions (the UN, NATO) and through international negotiation. The use of military force is a last resort, and then it is applied only to counter clear military threats.

Lawrence F. Kaplan and William Kristol argued in 2003 that American pre-eminence must be utilized and that 'if the US leads strongly enough, others, however reluctantly, will follow'.[29] However, this was never a certainty, and, indeed, how can the US lead if no other states are inclined to follow? Under what conditions might the US act unilaterally, and would this unilateralism reflect a total lack of support from potential allies? The WMD and al-Qaeda nexus would need to be much stronger than the hopelessly deficient case made against Iraq. In addition, the strenuous assertion by Europeans that multilateral deterrence and containment would gain the same objectives at less political, economic and military cost and with a smaller destabilizing spillover effect would have to be ignored by the US. In other words, if the US were unilaterally to mount a pre-emptive invasion of Iran, Syria or North Korea as part of the global war on terrorism, strategic divorce would be far more likely. It would be more likely not because North Korea and Iran do not possess nuclear ambitions but because the costs and benefits of pre-emption after Iraq would be viewed differently on either side of the Atlantic. French warnings about the dangers of the exercise of US 'hyper-power' would generally be accepted by most EU member states as a given – US primacy would now be perceived as outright hegemony, a bold bid to accumulate a monopoly of power and diplomatic initiative come what may.

Under these extreme circumstances, many realists would argue that European states would unite to counterbalance the unilateral exercise of US power. This would propel the EU to develop its ESDP, the military capability, decision-making structures and political will to project a significant independent military force beyond Europe and become a global strategic player. The application of the ESDP to states and regions outside Europe would influence the manner of US intervention, if not in all cases the actual decision to intervene. Under such extreme conditions NATO's common defence and security culture would be undermined on two fronts. The US would continue to take a very functional approach to security by utilizing ever-smaller 'coalitions of the willing', and those European NATO allies that were 'unwilling or unable' to participate in them would look more to the ESDP as the way in which to exercise military power and regain some influence over the global strategic agenda. US power would then be counterbalanced by a combination of EU political and economic power and, to a more limited extent, military power.

Alternatively, strategic realignment would presuppose a much more commonly perceived actual threat. Mass casualty terrorist attacks (modelled on the Madrid railway bombing of 9 March 2004, the 'Black Dawn' in Brussels on 3 May 2004[30] or the London bombings of 7 July 2005), in which Amsterdam, Berlin, Boston, Bucharest, Geneva, Paris, Stockholm and St Petersburg were targeted simultaneously in a concerted and bloody campaign, could create a context in which European elites and publics would be much more likely to accept unconditionally the urgent necessity of realignment with the US in opposition to terrorists. Current counter-terrorist cooperation and growing coordination in the 'homeland security' arena between the US and Europe, which already occur in the context of the global war on terrorism, would be strengthened. Shared responses to common strategic threats would be consolidated. As Senator Richard Lugar has argued, external threats are shared by the US and Europe, and they unite both sides of the Atlantic: 'The bottom line is this: for the foreseeable future, the nations of the Transatlantic Alliance will face an existential threat from the intersection of terrorism and weapons of mass destruction.'[31] Although it is true that the US 'over-militarizes' foreign and security policy and the EU 'over-civilianizes' it, the realization that transnational terrorists can be best countered through a combination of 90 per cent non-military (political, diplomatic, economic and financial strategies) efforts and only 10 per cent military efforts would bring the focus back to combining and consolidating the 'soft' power–'hard' power nexus and financing each element accordingly. A dynamic and framework for strategic realignment would be in place.

Both the prospect of US military pre-emption bereft of any European support and the possibility of simultaneous WMD mass casualty attacks throughout Europe are admittedly extreme circumstances. If it can be argued that it is difficult to envisage conditions under which such strategic divorce would occur, so can it also be contended about strategic realignment and reformation, since there is no certainty that even a massive terrorist attack in Europe would impel a common transatlantic approach in support of US policies.

We find, therefore, that of the three possible transatlantic futures, stra-tegic dissonance best supports the foreign and security policies of the five Europes. Strategic dissonance allows 'Non-aligned Europe' to maintain equi-distance between 'Core Europe' and 'Atlantic Europe'; it lowers the risks and political trade-off costs for 'New Europe' and provides 'Periphery Europe' with an ideal strategic environment in which it can pick and choose policy responses to particular issues and float freely between coalitions. Given the financial costs (more precisely, the absence of political will to finance stra-tegic realignment) as well as a genuinely different strategic world view and threat assessment, realignment according to a US-imposed vision is not in 'Core Europe's' interest.

At the same time, however, the high military and political costs and consequences of strategic divorce rule out this possibility as a likely outcome. With Iraq, transatlantic elites glimpsed the future and moved back from the precipice. In this period leaders and perhaps even publics grasped the vulnerability of European and transatlantic security institutions and realized that the pain of divorce would be higher than any conceivable gain.

To exaggerate and simplify our argument, 'managed dissonance' represents the line of least resistance for 'Core Europe'. Even 'Atlantic Europe' can make strategic dissonance pay dividends. 'Core Europe's' opposition to US policies and influence increases the value of the UK in US eyes: its support provides the US with legitimacy and multilateral cover when needed, and its outreach and relations with 'New Europe' provide a European rationale for US support that would otherwise be lacking. Thus strategic dissonance is not so much a condition brought about by temporary aberrations and disagreements within the transatlantic security community as a natural and instinctive default position that reflects the material interests, shifting values and identities, and supports the policy and institutional preferences of all five Europes. Arguably, this is in the United States' interests too: a weaker and more divided Europe allows cherry-picking and coalition-building, which the challenges, obstacles and dilemmas of the global war on terrorism create. It also minimizes the prospect of unified European criticism of US strategic blunders and imperial hubris, criticism that could slip towards coordinated counterbalance.

MANAGING THE GLOBAL SECURITY AGENDA:
IS GREY THE COLOUR OF HOPE?

How will a transatlantic security community fragmented by strategic disson-ance manage current and future issues of outstanding strategic importance, in particular those related to China, Iran and North Korea? It was only Presi-dent Bush's election in 2004 to a second term that began what appears to be a deliberate process of normalizing the transatlantic relationship. Although the majority of Europeans supported the Kerry candidacy, they have responded pragmatically to the reality of a second Bush administration. President Bush responded in turn when, on his European tour of February 2005, he stated that 'no temporary debates can permanently damage tranatlantic ties, no power on earth will ever divide us' and that 'in the new century, the alliance of America and Europe is the main pillar of our security.'[32] He declared emphatically that NATO was to remain the cornerstone of the transatlantic relationship.[33] In January 2005, Secretary of State Condoleezza Rice had signalled the new 'mood music' of the second Bush administration by welcoming a new era of transatlantic unity.

Despite these warm words, many European states are still bruised by the experience of the transatlantic trauma of 2002–3 and are unsure as to how the US will seek to cooperate in its foreign and security policy with Europe. Moreover, intra-European splits are still not healed, and the integrity and orientation of 'Atlantic Europe', 'New Europe', 'Core Europe' and 'Non-aligned Europe' towards a wider regional and global security agenda appear highly ambiguous. Chancellor Schröder's speech at the February 2005 Munich Security Conference in which he argued that NATO was no longer central to transatlantic relations prompted accusations of counterbalance and extended 'punishment'.[34] Similarly, on the other side of the Atlantic questions were raised about the relationship between the rhetoric of partnership and the reality of US policy by a number of appointments that rewarded the architects and vehement supporters of the war in Iraq with important governmental and international positions. Condoleezza Rice replaced Colin Powell as Secretary of State; John R. Bolton became the new US ambassador to the UN, albeit as 'damaged goods' and via a recess appointment; and Paul Wolfowitz, the intellectual architect of the Iraq war, was appointed as the director of the World Bank. From a European perspective, these appointments were accepted but not applauded. Substantive transatlantic cooperation continues, but a good three years after the invasion of Iraq, a combination of sullen accommodation in some quarters, a realization, reinforced by Afghanistan, that NATO weakness strengthens the utility of coalitions in US eyes and an improvement in tone and atmosphere characterizes transatlantic relations.[35]

'Regime change' has already occurred in Germany, with Chancellor Angela Merkel leading a coalition; and it is likely that Nicholas Sarkozy will be the president of France by 2007 and that Gordon Brown will be Britain's prime minister in 2008, when the US and Russian presidential elections take place. Can these three leaders agree a common European response to tackle the global security agenda and thereby relaunch the European project? How will the new US, and to a much lesser extent Russian administrations, shape strategic transatlantic thinking? Even if a common European approach were to be brokered, how the US implements its wider defence 'transformation agenda' involving strategy, capabilities, global posture and basing abroad will still continue to have significant consequences for transatlantic relations.[36]

To take one example of the complexity of issues facing these prospective leaders and their inability to agree a common strategic approach, Condoleezza Rice has stated that the 'organizing principle of the 21st century' is the expansion of freedom all over the world.[37] President Bush has reinforced this message: 'by bringing progress and hope to nations in need, we can improve many lives, and lift up failing states, and remove the causes and sanctuaries of terror.'[38] Although European states cannot oppose this principle and 'support' tyranny, they would certainly disagree that freedom can be imposed from without, particularly through émigré-based, exported democratic revolution or as a consequence of military intervention. Democracy cannot be spread by force of arms; it needs to be internally generated, negotiated and gradual in order to be sustainable. But without the prospect of further enlargement of the EU, how will the Union balance its own democratization efforts (and support the normative agenda of the CFSP) with its strategic economic interests in near neighbourhood states in the Balkans and in Belarus, Moldova and Ukraine? Can the EU both press ahead with democratization and be dependent for energy on the Russian Federation?

Strategic dissonance is here to stay. It can be argued that the transatlantic allies have little real interest in resolving it and that they are more resigned to managing it. They can work within the framework of choices and action that disagreement imposes, and from that limited base they can seek to identify, manage and address security threats that are current and emergent. Strategic dissonance is reinforced now by the strategic pause or 'holding pattern' that has followed the failure to ratify the constitutional treaty and the largely self-imposed travails that have beset the second Bush administration.

In retrospect, strategic dissonance was always bound to resurface with the end of the transatlantic alliance's Cold War unity. When James Woolsey, the then director of the Central Intelligence Agency, appeared before the Senate in 1992, he stated that 'We have slain the dragon but now live in a jungle full of poisonous snakes.'[39] In an age of the US-led global war on terrorism where the management of global security issues touches so many moral and legal grey areas, perhaps only the tension of transatlantic strategic dissonance can initiate and implement sustainable and effective security policies. In 2006 might a 'divided West' begin to manage the complexity of these dynamic events more effectively than would appear possible? Is there a hidden and constructive utility to strategic dissonance?

Even by 2003 the fantasy was ending that clear-cut definitions and moral clarity could provide unity of purpose, circumvent or, better still, slice cleanly through the challenges, obstacles and dilemmas that are integral to contemporary security policy. Although post-9/11 policy-makers acknowledge a new threat paradigm in which non-state actors can threaten states with WMD, the world view in Washington and European capitals, not least Brussels, is still primarily based on the Westphalian state order and international system. In reality, the multiplicity of institutions and cultural identities, the interpenetration of diverse political units and loyalties, and different types of solidarity between various transnational networks and organizations, all suggest an evolution towards a post-modern or neo-medieval international system, rather than one based on the primacy of states. As the certainties and false distinctions of the post-9/11 period blur and as priorities distort and threat assessment becomes even more complex, strategic dissonance can allow for the construction of a strategic template upon which to launch calibrated and differentiated transatlantic responses that address, and hopefully manage, contemporary security threats.

Transatlantic strategic dissonance does not undermine areas of ongoing active cooperation and it does not preclude the management of some crises. It lowers unrealistic transatlantic expectations and allows current transatlantic leaders room to raise and air honest policy disagreement. At the same time it provides a new generation of European leaders the encouragement to discuss fundamental differences of view about the utility of force, to consider future transatlantic options and to arrive at a better understanding of Europe's changing strategic personality. Paradoxically, it is a latent transatlantic strength that economic, political, ideological and military disparities and divergences, institutional weaknesses and identity conflicts are so prevalent. These points of conflict carry with them the potential to generate a workable pathway between military efficiency and effectiveness, and especially between both of these and political (and moral) legitimacy in the management of the global security agenda. There are few uniform answers to global security problems. For example, even if democracy is the answer to global instability, which model of democracy is to be promoted globally? Strategic dissonance suggests that a divided West can engage the world in a manner that better reflects and mirrors the complexity and dynamic changes that world experiences, not least caused by a fundamental global shift in the balance of power towards India and China in Asia. This shift in power distribution, as much as the rise of non-state and transnational actors, will dominate the security politics of our century.

In short, dissonance reaches those parts of the world that divorce or realignment never could; transatlantic strategic dissonance carries with it the potential for constructive transatlantic strategic engagement with the wider world. In a world where black and white have become opaque, grey really is the colour of hope.

Notes

1 THE DIVIDED WEST: CHALLENGES AND OBSTACLES

1 Jo Biddle, 'Bush-Europe Love Fest Papered Over Cracks', Agence France Presse, 23 February 2005, citing an editorial in the left-wing daily *Frankfurter Rundschau*.

2 Schwok (2001: 385).

3 Kagan (2003: 102). See also Kagan (2002) and Kagan (2002–3).

4 van Ham (2001). See also Smith (2004) and Allin (2004).

5 Heisbourg (2004). See also Heisbourg (2002–3).

6 Mahncke, Rees and Thompson (2004).

7 Walt (2004: 29).

8 Asmus (2003); Asmus and Pollack (2002); Gordon (2003); Albright et al. (2003); Garton Ash (2004); Habermas and Derrida (2005); and Kriendler (2005).

9 Mead (2004:18).

10 Daalder (2003).

11 'Solana Seeks More Power for the EU Foreign Policy Chief', Reuters, 15 October 2002. See Lindley-French (2002) for the scale of the task; and for solutions, see Grant (2003).

12 Weidenfeld et al. (eds) (2004: 72).

13 Papp (2002: 246) and Kissinger, Summers and Kupchan (2004).

14 Jones (2004: 612) and Hunter (2004).

15 Nye (2000) and Nelson (2003).

16 Forsberg and Herd (2005).

17 Skidelsky (2003: 30–5).

18 Lundestad (1998).

19 Gaddis (2004: 64).

20 Trachtenberg (2003).

21 Ikenberry (2002: 23).

22 Robertson (2004: 28). See also Michel (2003).

23 Clark (2001: 427).

24 Védrine (2003).

25 Rodman (1999).

26 Rice (2000: 61) and Zoellick (2001).

27 Gordon (2001).

28 Jean-Marie Colombani, 'We are All Americans', *Le Monde*, 12 September 2001 (*World Press Review*, Vol. 48, No. 11, November 2001).

29 Lindley-French (2002: 802).

30 Andrew Murray, 'The Axis of Nonsense', *The Guardian*, 15 May 2002.

31 Ludlow (2002).

32 Kagan (2003: 102). See also Kagan (2002).

33 DoD News Briefing – Secretary Rumsfeld and Gen. Myers, 18 October 2001, *http://www.dod.mil/news/Oct2001/t10182001_t018sdmy.html*, accessed 4 June 2003.

34 NATO Update, *http://www.nato.int/docu/update/2002/11-november/e1121e.htm*, accessed 21 December 2005.

35 Chalmers (2001).

36 Keith B. Richburg, 'NATO Tells Hungary to Modernize Its Military', *Washington Post*, 3 November 2002, p. A22.

37 Kay (2003).

38 Prague Summit Declaration, *http://www.nato.int/docu/pr/2002/p02-127e.htm*, accessed 21 December 2005.

39 Constanza Stelzenmüller, 'Hymn for Fortress America: The Last Superpower Writes a Security Policy Doctrine', *Die Zeit*, 26 September 2002, p. 9.

40 Gerard Baker, Judy Dempsey, Robert Graham, Quentin Peel and Mark Turner, 'The US has come to see the status quo as inherently dangerous', *Financial Times*, 30 May 2003, p. 17.

41 Gunter (2005).

42 The eight NATO members were Britain, Italy, Portugal, Spain, Denmark, Poland, the Czech Republic and Hungary.

43 The 'Vilnius 10' group consisted of Albania, Bulgaria, Croatia, Estonia, Latvia, Lithuania, Macedonia, Romania, Slovakia and Slovenia.

44 Judy Dempsey, 'New NATO force to be launched in October', *Financial Times*, 25 April 2003, p. 6.

45 Brzezinski (2003).

46 Calleo (2004: 32).

47 Gerard Baker, Judy Dempsey, Robert Graham, Quentin Peel and Mark Turner, 'The Rift Turns Nasty: the plot that split the old and new Europe asunder', *Financial Times*, 28 May 2003, p. 19.

48 Reuters, 25 May 2003. If this remark did reflect official US policy, it undermined any attempts to generate 'credibility, cohesion, convergence, commitment and candour', the prerequisites for transatlantic recoupling. Lindley-French (2002: 76). See also Hulsman (2003).

49 Mead (2004: 122).

50 Doug Bereuter, 'NATO Failure in Afghanistan Possible Unless Allies Provide Fair Share', 15 June 2004, *http://wwwc.house.gov/international_relations/108/news061504.htm*.

2 THEORY AND THE TRANSATLANTIC CRISIS

1 Fukuyama (1989).

2 Deutsch (1957).

3 Mearsheimer (1990).

4 Huntington (1993) and Huntington (1996).

5 Waltz (1993) and Layne (1993).

6 Harris (1993).

7 Wagar (1992).

8 Jervis (2005: Ch. 1).

9 Deutsch (1957: 66).

10 Asmus (2003); Andrews (2005): see especially comments by Geir Lundestad, Marc Trachtenberg and Miles Kahler.

11 For a similar theoretical framework for explaining transatlantic disputes, see Mowle (2004).

12 The standard realist works are Morgenthau (1948) and Waltz (1979). For an overview of realism, see Guzzini (1998).

13 Hamilton (2004: 25).

14 Waltz (1993).

15 Walt (1998–9).

16 Kagan (2002) and (2003: 3)

17 Kagan (2003: 3).

18 Lindley-French (2002: 802).

19 Gordon and Shapiro (2004: 83).

20 Joffe (1984).

21 Public opinion polls demonstrate that after 9/11, there was a correlation between one's perception of the likelihood of a terrorist threat and the size of one's country. See 'International Crisis', *Flash Eurobarometer*, No. 114, December 2001 [Question no. 4], *http://europa.eu.int/comm/public_opinion/flash/fl114_en.pdf*.

22 Guzzini (2004).

23 See, for example, Mowle (2004).

24 Šedivý and Zaborowski (2004: 192).

25 For liberal theory, see Keohane (1989) and Doyle (1986).

26 Wallander (2000).

27 Keohane (2005: x).

28 Rumsfeld (2002); Cornish (2004); Kriendler (2005); and Cordesman (2005).

29 Ackermann (2003).

30 Kagan (2003: 4).

31 Kaase and Kohut (1996).

32 Kupchan (2002) and Pei (2003).

33 'Living with a Superpower', *The Economist*, 2 January 2003. See also 'America's Image Further Erodes, Europeans Want Weaker Ties'; Pew Research Center for the People and the Press, 18 March 2003; and 'Among Wealthy Nations ... US Stands Alone in its Embrace of Religion', Pew Research Center for the People and the Press, 19 December 2002; and Bertram (2003).

34 Kohut (2003).

35 Judy Dempsey, 'Solana Fears Widening Gulf Between EU and US', *Financial Times*, 7 January 2003.

36 Smith (2004).

37 Rabkin (2004).

38 Nikolaidis (2005: 103).

39 Chicago Council on Foreign Relations and German Marshall Fund, 'Worldviews 2002. American and European Public Opinion and Foreign Policy', *http://www. worldviews.org/detailreports/compreport/html/summary.html*.

40 Inglehart and Baker (2000). On the World Values Survey, see *http://www.world-valuessurvey.org/*. The results were also reported in 'Living with a Superpower', *The Economist*, 2 January 2003.

41 'America's Image Further Erodes, Europeans Want Weaker Ties', The Pew Research Center for the People and the Press, 18 March 2003, *http://people-press. org/reports/display.php3?PageID=681*.

42 Kahler (2004).

43 Danchev (2005: 422).

44 Cox (2005: 203).

45 Mihalka (2005).

46 On constructivism, see Wendt (1999).

47 Johnston (1995) and Neumann and Heikka (2005).

48 Neumann (1999).

49 Smith (2004: 102).

50 Jacques Derrida and Jürgen Habermas, 'Unsere Erneuerung. Nach dem Krieg: Die Wiedergeburt Europas' [Our Renewal. After the War: The Rebirth of Europe], *Frankfurter Allgemeine Zeitung*, 31 May 2003 and Habermas and Derrida (2005).

51 van Ham (2001).

52 Hollander (2004) and Ross and Ross (eds) (2004).

53 Berman (2004: xiv).

54 Johnson (2003).

55 Ceaser (2003).

56 Judt (2005).

57 Revel (2003).

58 Blinken (2001). 'Lugar Speech for CSIS Conference on Transatlantic Efforts for Peace and Security on Norway's Centennial Anniversary', States News Service, 9 March 2005.

59 Burwell and Daalder (1999: 110).

60 'French anti-Americanism', *The Economist*, 24 December 2005–6 January 2006, p. 42.

61 Condoleezza Rice, 'America Has the Muscle, but It Has Benevolent Values, Too', *Daily Telegraph*, 17 October 2002.

62 Williams (2005).

63 Leffler (2005: 396).

64 Herd and Weber (2001).

65 US NSS (2006).

66 Urquhart (2005).

3 'ATLANTIC EUROPE': THE UK, THE US AND EUROPEAN SECURITY

1 Garton Ash (2004).
2 Wallace (2005: 67); Gray (2004); and Braithwaite (2003).
3 Talbott (2003: 1039).
4 Rubin (2003).
5 Gordon and Shapiro (2004: 127).
6 Mead (2004: 22).
7 Dunne (2004: 811).
8 Hoffman (2003).
9 Dunne (2004: 826).
10 Dockrill (2000: 110–11), citing a Foreign Office paper on Anglo-American relations prepared by the incoming Labour government in 1964. We are grateful to James Wither for drawing this source to our attention.
11 Gardiner and Hulsman (2003).
12 'Effective Multilateralism to Build a Better World: Joint Statement by President George W. Bush and Prime Minister Tony Blair', Public Papers of the President, 24 November 2004.
13 JSP 777 (2005).
14 James Wither, '"Uniquely Close"?: The Anglo-American Special Security Relationship', unpublished manuscript, April 2005.
15 Naughtie (2005).
16 Capell (2003: 38).
17 Talbott (2003: 1039) and Hoffman (2003: 1031).
18 Press Conference of the President, 13 April 2004, *http://www.multied.com/Documents/Bush/Bushpress413.html*.
19 Elaine Sciolino, 'NATO Chief Offers a Bleak Analysis', *New York Times*, 3–4 July 2004; and Herd (2004).
20 Bogdanor (2005: 689).
21 'Keeping Friends', *The Economist* (US edition), 10 February 2003.
22 'We Must Take Stand on Weapons of Mass Destruction', speech by Tony Blair at the Foreign and Commonwealth Office leadership conference, London, 7 January 2003, *http://www.labour.org.uk/news/tbleadershipspeech*.
23 Tardy (2006).
24 Germany, with 1,909 troops, and Canada, with 1,576, are the most generous of the NATO contributors. France ranks next with 565. The remaining 23 NATO countries, plus 11 outside NATO, have contributed about 2,500 combined. George Gedda, 'Disillusionment Widespread in NATO Role', AP, 14 July 2004. Afghanistan has the lowest troop-to-population ratio of recent interventions – 1:1,115 as compared to 1:161 in Iraq.
25 Julian Lindley-French, 'Saying Thank You is in America's Interest', *International Herald Tribune*, 2 July 2002.
26 A communiqué issued at the NATO Istanbul Summit asserted that 'Contributing to peace and stability in Afghanistan is NATO's key priority. NATO's leadership of the U.N.-mandated International Security Assistance Force demonstrates the readiness of the North Atlantic Council to decide to launch operations to ensure

our common security.' *http://www.nato.int/docu/pr/2004/p04-096e.htm*. For an assessment of mission deficiencies, see McCallum (2003).

27 Sciolino, 'NATO Chief Offers a Bleak Analysis' (see note 19 above).

28 Harvey (2003: 74) and Cooper (2003: 150–1).

29 Meyer (2005: 247–8).

30 White House, 'President, House Leadership Agree on Iraq Resolution', 2 October 2002.

31 Testimony by US Secretary of Defense Donald Rumsfeld, House Armed Services Committee, 18 September 2002. See also 'We know they have chemical and biological weapons', White House, Press Conference by Vice President Dick Cheney and His Highness Salman bin Hamad Al Khalifa, Crown Prince of Bahrain, at Shaik Hamat Palace, 17 March 2003.

32 'Meet the Press', NBC, 16 March 2003; 'We said they [Iraq] had a nuclear program. There was never any debate', US Department of Defense, 'Secretary Rumsfeld Live Interview with Infinity CBS Radio', 14 November 2002.

33 White House, 'President Bush Outlines Iraqi Threat; Remarks by the President', 7 October 2002.

34 White House, 'President Outlines Priorities', 7 November 2002; '[A]cting pursuant to the Constitution and [the Authorization for Use of Military Force Against Iraq Resolution of 2002] is consistent with the United States and other countries continuing to take the necessary actions against international terrorists and terrorist organizations, including those nations, organizations, or persons who planned, authorized, committed, or aided the terrorist attacks that occurred on September 11, 2001.' President Bush, in a letter to Congress outlining the legal justification for commencing war against Iraq, 18 March 2003, *http://www. whitehouse.gov/news/releases/2003/03/20030319-1.html*.

35 White House, 'Remarks by the Vice President to the Heritage Foundation', 10 October 2003.

36 White House, 'President Bush Announces Major Combat Operations in Iraq Have Ended', 1 May 2003.

37 Sciolino, 'NATO Chief Offers a Bleak Analysis' (see note 19 above).

38 Gen. Zinni cites 10 failures: abandoning the existing policy of containment; promoting a flawed regional strategy; creating a false rationale for war in order to maximize public support; failing to internationalize the effort; underestimating the task; propping up and trusting the Iraqi exiles; overall lack of planning; allocating insufficient military forces; installing an inadequate and ad hoc government; and enacting a series of bad decisions on the ground. Zinni (2004) and Metz (2003–4). See also Fallows (2004); Diamond (2005); Etherington (2005); and Packer (2005).

39 The 9/11 Commission Report (2004).

40 According to 'Statement by David Kay on the Interim Progress Report on the Activities of the Iraq Survey Group (ISG)', 'We have discovered dozens of WMD-related program activities and significant amounts of equipment that Iraq concealed from the United Nations during the inspections that began in late 2002.', *http://www.cia.gov/cia/public_affairs/speeches/2003/david_kay_10022003. html*. In February 2004, David Kay stated that 'We probably all got it wrong.' Prime Minister Tony Blair admitted in July 2004 that WMD would probably not

be found in Iraq.

41 United States Senate, Select Committee On Intelligence, 'Report On The U.S. Intelligence Community's Pre-war Intelligence Assessments On Iraq', *http://intelligence.senate.gov/iraqreport2.pdf.* See also Corn (2004).

42 Record (2003). Record argues that the global war on terrorism, as opposed to the campaign against al-Qaeda, lacks strategic clarity, embraces unrealistic objectives and may not be sustainable over the long haul.

43 Downing Street Memos (2002).

44 Agence France Presse, 20 March 2005. See also Henry Porter, 'Trust is Still the Crucial Issue', *The Observer*, 27 March 2005: 'The Hutton inquiry and Lord Butler's review of Intelligence on Weapons of Mass Destruction established beyond doubt that in the year before the invasion a tightly knit group at Downing Street controlled, finessed and manipulated the advice and information supplied by the executive to the Prime Minister, ostensibly so that he could decide whether to go to war.'

45 Short (2004).

46 Marie Woolf, Ben Russell and Andrew Buncombe, 'Now Is the Time for Mr. Blair to Prove the Special Relationship is Worth the Effort', *The Independent*, 16 April 2004.

47 Meyer (2005: 262) and Steve Richards, 'Review of the Year 2004: Iraq: Special Relationship: Britain as the Bridge over Troubled Waters? Hardly', *The Independent*, 27 December 2004.

48 Ben Russell, 'Diplomats' Revolt: Blair's Woes Deepen as Mutiny Staged over Iraq and Israel', *The Independent*, 27 April 2004.

49 Natapoff (2004).

50 Gunther Hellmann, 'Merkel Wants to be an Honest Broker', *International Herald Tribune*, 1 December 2005.

51 Wallace (2005: 62). See also Smith (2005).

52 Judt (2005).

53 Wallace (2005: 55).

54 Richard Tomkins, 'Bush Faces European Critics', UPI, 18 February 2005. He cites Claire Healey, a former head of policy for Britain's Labour Party, at a forum for the German Marshall Fund of the US.

55 Kampfner (2005: 8).

56 'Presidential Peak', *The Economist* (US edition), 2 May 2004.

57 Lindley-French (2002: 7).

58 Adrian Hamilton, 'The Transatlantic Gap Remains As Wide As Ever', *Financial Times*, 24 February 2005.

59 NATO troops will be deployed as trainers in August 2004, but not as part of the multinational force that the US leads. The relationship between NATO and the MNF will be decided on 15 September 2004. Daniel Dombey, 'Compromise by NATO Opens the Way to Iraq Training Mission', *Financial Times*, 31 July/1 August 2004, p. 5.

60 Barry Posen, 'Europe Cannot Advance on Two Fronts', *Financial Times*, 25 April 2003, p. 13.

61 Robertson (2003: 12).

62 In 2003, NATO European members spent $221 billion (€168 billion/£116 billion)

on defence, 1.9 per cent of GDP. By contrast, the US spent $405 billion, 3.7 per cent of GDP. By 2005, this spending gap had increased. Daniel Dombey, 'Europe Must Spend More on Defence', *Financial Times*, 3 March 2005.

63 Moravcsik (2005); Fredrick Studemann, 'US Conservatives Cast Wary Eye on EU Treaty', *Financial Times*, 5 November 2004; Miller and Molesky (2004); and Thomas Friedman, 'Our War with France', *New York Times*, 18 September 2003: 'France is not just our annoying ally. It is not just our jealous rival. France is becoming our enemy.'

64 Cimbalo (2004).

65 Redwood (2001: 125).

66 Daniel Dombey, James Harding and George Parker, 'Bush Charms Brussels Yet Divide with Europe Remains', *Financial Times*, 23 February 2005, p. 5.

67 Moravcsik (2005).

68 Asmus, Blinken and Gordon (2005).

69 Menon (2004).

70 Missiroli (2004–5: 130).

71 Aneurin Bevan (1897–1960), quoted in *The Observer* (London, 6 December 1953): *http://www.bartleby.com/66/29/7129.html*.

72 Crowe (2003: 537).

4 'CORE EUROPE': GERMANY'S NATIONAL INTEREST, TRANSATLANTIC RELATIONS AND EUROPEAN SECURITY

1 'German press mauls Schroeder over NATO reform demand', Agence France Presse, 14 February 2005.

2 Judy Dempsey, 'US brushes off German NATO Plan', *International Herald Tribune*, 14 February 2005, p. 1. Secretary of Defence Rumsfeld also noted that 'Our Atlantic alliance relationship has navigated through some choppy seas over the years. But we have always been able to resolve the toughest issues. That is because there is so much to unite us: common values, shared histories, and an abiding faith in democracy.' John J. Lumkin, 'Rumsfeld Defends Nato as Vital Link for Atlantic Nations', Associated Press, 12 February 2005.

3 'Germany Urges Nato Reform and Rethink of Transatlantic Ties', Agence France Presse, 13 February 2005.

4 Lamers and Schäuble (1994).

5 Hacke (2003); Harnisch (2004); and Szabo (2004).

6 Tewes (2002: 50).

7 'A Friend of America in Need; Germany's Foreign Minister', *The Economist* (US edition), 19 February 2005.

8 Fischer (1994).

9 Otte (2000: 218).

10 Hellmann et al. (2005) and Schwarz (2005).

11 Schröder (1999: 70).

12 Šedivý (2005).

13 Rudolf (2005: 134).

14 Gerhard Schröder, 'Der Gestrige 11. September wird als ein schwarzer Tag für

uns alle in die Geschichte eingehen' [Yesterday, September 11, Will Mark a Black Day in History for All of Us], Government Position, 12 September 2001.

15 Katzenstein (2002).

16 Gerhard Schröder, 'Die Anschläge in den USA' [The Attacks in the USA], Government Declaration, 19 September 2001.

17 Steven Erlanger, 'Fissures in German Support for U.S. Attacks', *New York Times*, 16 October 2001.

18 'Wir sind keine Satelliten' [We are no Satellites], An Interview with Joschka Fischer, *Die Welt*, 12 February 2002; Karp (2005-06: 68).

19 Steven Erlanger, 'U.S. Officials Try to Assure Europeans on NATO', *New York Times*, 3 February 2002.

20 Peter Ford, 'United against Terror, Divided on Trade, Coalition Strains', *Christian Science Monitor*, 8 March 2002.

21 Karsten Voigt, 'George Bush ist kein Cowboy' [George Bush Is No Cowboy], An Interview with Karsten Voigt, *Tageszeitung*, 19 February 2002.

22 Gordon and Shapiro (2004: 109).

23 George W. Bush, 'Graduation Speech', United States Military Academy, West Point, 1 June 2002.

24 Chandler (2003).

25 'Gerhard Schröder auf Anti-Amerika Kurs' [Gerhard Schröder on an Anti-American Course], *Tageszeitung*, 6 August 2002.

26 Gerhard Schröder, 'Meine Vision von Deutschland' [My Vision of Germany], *Die Bild-Zeitung*, 8 August 2002.

27 Tony Paterson, 'Schröder Clings on to Lead Despite Fury over "Hitler" Jibe', *Daily Telegraph*, 22 September 2002, *http://www.telegraph.co.uk/news/main.jhtml? xml=/news/2002/09/22/wger22.xml*.

28 'Die Hoffnung wird immer kleiner' [Hope is Becoming Smaller All the Time], An Interview with Joschka Fischer, *Der Spiegel*, 30 December 2002.

29 'Schröder schließt erstmals Ja zu Irak-Krieg im Sicherheitsrat aus' [For the First Time Schröder Rules Out a Yes to the Iraqi War in the Security Council], *Die Welt*, 21 January 2003.

30 Peter Ford, 'United against Terror, Divided on Trade, Coalition Strains', *Christian Science Monitor*, 8 March 2003.

31 Joschka Fischer, 'Struggling Hard to Find Solutions to the Conflict in Iraq', speech at the 39th Munich Conference on Security Policy, Munich, 8 February 2003, *http://www.securityconference.de/konferenzen/2003/*, accessed 1 February 2004.

32 Gerhard Schröder, 'Unsere Verantwortung für den Frieden' [Our Responsibility for Peace], Government Declaration, 13 February 2003.

33 'Irak-Krieg: Schröder warnt USA vor Wiederholungen' [The Iraq War: Schröder Warns the USA Not to Repeat], *Die Welt*, 11 April 2003.

34 'Schröder betont gute Beziehungen trotz Irak-Streits' [Schröder Emphasizes Good Relations despite the Dispute over Iraq], *Handelsblatt*, 9 May 2003.

35 Thomas Fuller, 'Romania Dangles Use of Sea Base to Woo US', *International Herald Tribune*, 18 June 2003, p. 1.

36 'Irak-Krieg: Schröder warnt USA vor Wiederholungen'.

37 'Bush: Die Deutschen sind Pazifisten' [Bush: The Germans Are Pacifists], *Die Welt*, 24 September 2003.

38 Joschka Fischer, 'Prospects of Transatlantic Relations', speech at the 40th Munich Conference on Security Policy, Munich, 7 February 2004, *http://www.security-conference.de/konferenzen/2004/.*

39 Richard Bernstein, 'The German Question', *New York Times*, 2 May 2004.

40 Berman (2004); Berendse (2003); Markovits (2004); and Nolan (2004).

41 'A Year After Iraq War. Mistrust of America in Europe Ever Higher, Muslim Anger Persists', *The Pew Global Attitudes Project*, Pew Research Center, Washington, DC, 16 March 2004.

42 Elizabeth Noelle, 'Die Entfremdung. Deutschland und Amerika entfernen sich voneinander' [Alienation. Germany and America are Diverging from Each Other], *Frankfurter Allgemeine Zeitung*, 23 July 2003.

43 Mertes (2004).

44 Pond (2004: 40).

45 Diner (2002).

46 'Verschwörung 11. September. Wie Konspirationstheorien die Wirklichkeit auf den Kopf stellen' [9/11 Plot. How Conspiracy Theories Turn Reality Upside Down], *Die Spiegel*, 8 September 2003.

47 'Vierergipfel plant europäischen Militärstab' [The Four Nations Summit Plans European Military Headquarters], *Financial Times Deutschland*, 29 April 2003.

48 Rudolf (2005: 137).

49 Wolfgang Schäuble, 'Amerika braucht uns' [America Needs Us], interview with Wolfgang Schäuble, *Die Zeit*, 15 May 2003.

50 Risse (2004: 24–31).

51 *Transatlantic Trends 2003* (Washington and Turin: German Marshall Fund and Compagnia di San Paolo, 2004).

52 Schröder, 'Unsere Verantwortung für den Frieden' (see note 32 above).

53 Gerhard Schröder, 'Rücktritt wäre Flucht, dazu neige ich nicht' [To Step Down Would Be Flight, That Is Not My Inclination]. interview with Gerhard Schröder, *Der Stern*, 13 February 2003.

54 'Ausmaß der Bedrohung rechtfertigt keinen Krieg' [The Magnitude of the Threat Does Not Justify War], *Die Welt*, 19 March 2003.

55 Friborg (2004–5).

56 'Eurocorps takes on command of NATO-led Afghanistan force', *http://www.afnorth.nato.int/ISAF/Update/Press_Releases/Release_09Aug04.htm.*

57 Becher (2004).

58 'Into the Lion's Den; George Bush in Europe', *The Economist* (US edition), 20 February 2005; and Gunther Hellmann, 'American Needs Meet German Ambitions', *International Herald Tribune*, 23 February 2005, p. 8.

59 Gerhard Schröder, 'German Chancellor Delicately Strives Not to Get in the Middle', An Interview with Gerhard Schröder, *Los Angeles Times*, 1 April 2001.

60 Nikolaus Blome, '"Operation Augenhöhe" des Bundeskanzlers' [Chancellor's Operation 'Eye-level'], *Die Welt*, 25 September 2002.

61 'No One Has a Clear Idea About What the Effects Would Be', interview with Gerhard Schröder, *New York Times*, 5 September 2002.

62 Helmut Kohl, 'Schröder ist ein Anti-Amerikaner' [Schröder is an Anti-American], interview with Helmut Kohl, *Die Welt*, 3 April 2003.

63 Interview with Gerhard Schröder, *Berlin Direkt*, ZDF, 11 August 2002.

64 Schmitt (1996 [1932]: 60).
65 Gerhard Schröder, 'Finanzplan des Bundes 2002 bis 2006' [Financial Plan of the Federation 2002 to 2006], Speech at the German Parliament, 13 September 2002.
66 Hellmann and Enskat (2004).
67 'A Year After Iraq War' (see note 41 above).
68 'Thin Pickings for Bush's Transatlantic Foray', *Daily Telegraph*, 25 February 2005, p. 25.
69 Mead (2004: 144).
70 David McHugh, 'On eve of Bush visit, German diplomat says relations with U.S. improving, speaks of "new beginning"', AP, Berlin, 19 February 2005.
71 Judy Dempsey, 'Newly confident Germany defends its interests', *International Herald Tribune*, 24 February 2005, p. 5.
72 Brian Knowlton, 'Merkel and Bush in "spirited" and friendly talks', *International Herald Tribune*, 14-15 January 2006, p. 1.
73 'New German Chancellor Calls for "Political" NATO', NATO Update, 23 November 2005, *http://www.nato.int/docu/update/2005/11-november/e1123a.htm*; Karp (2005-06: 78).
74 Janes and Sandschneider (2004); John Vincour, 'Schröder Unresponsive to American Advances', *International Herald Tribune*, 15 February 2005; and Gunther Hellman, 'American Needs Meet German Ambitions', *International Herald Tribune*, 23 February 2005.

5 'NEW EUROPE' AND TRANSATLANTIC RELATIONS

1 Baker (2003) and Graham E. Fuller, 'Old Europe – or Old America', *International Herald Tribune*, 12 February 2003.
2 Šedivý and Zaborowski (2004: 191) and Missiroli (2004–5).
3 NATO at 26 members and the EU at 25 members differ from NATO at 19 and the EU at 15. The EU's population has increased by 20 per cent and its GDP has grown by 5–9 per cent. The number of small-state members of the EU grew from 10 to 19. Batt et al. (2003: 17).
4 Moïsi (2003).
5 Elfriede Regelsberger, 'Are There Problems Arising from Enlargement and the Draft Treaty Leading to Paralysis Instead of Synergy?', paper presented at the FORNET meeting, Brussels, 23 April 2004.
6 Grabbe (2004).
7 Hoffman (2000).
8 Hill (2004).
9 Missiroli (2003); Lang (2004); and Zielonka (2004).
10 Rhodes (2004); Layne (2003); Szamuely (2003); Radu (2003); and Joffe (2003).
11 Zaborowski and Longhurst (2003).
12 'Statement of the Vilnius Group Countries', For the Record: 5 February 2003.
13 Missiroli (2004).
14 Edward Alden and Jan Ciencki, 'Poland Angered at US Failure to Waive Visas', *Financial Times*, 28 February 2004; and Zaborowski and Longhurst (2003).
15 Judy Dempsey, 'Poland Sets Pullout from Iraq in 2005', *International Herald Tribune*, 5 October 2004.

16 Judy Dempsey, 'We Used to be Sandwiched between the Big Powers', *Financial Times*, 29 April 2004.

17 Bagajski and Teleki (2005: 100).

18 Stephen Castle, 'Threat of War: Divided Europe – Chirac Attacks Eastern Block Backing for Bush', *The Independent*, 18 February 2003.

19 Krastev (2004).

20 'Public Opinion in the Candidate Countries', *Eurobarometer 2003*, 3 September 2003, p. 27. See also *Transatlantic Trends 2003* (Washington, DC and Turin: German Marshall Fund and Compagnia Di San Paolo, 2004), *http://www.trans-atlantictrends.org/*; Inglehart and Baker (2000); and World Values Survey (2003), *http://www.worldvaluessurvey.com*.

21 Luif (2003).

22 Regelsberger (2004:2).

23 'Public Opinion in the Candidate Countries', *Eurobarometer 2003*, 3 September 2003.

24 Smith, Michael E. (2004).

25 Ojanen et al. (2000).

26 Donald Rumsfeld, 'Address to 10th Anniversary Celebration', George C. Marshall European Center for Security Studies, Garmisch-Partenkirchen, Germany, 11 June 2003.

27 The suspension covered international military education and training funds, used primarily to pay for the cost of educating foreign officers at US institutions, and foreign military funding, which paid for US weapons and other aid. See Linden (2004).

28 Thomas Donnelly, 'Statement of Thomas Donnelly, Resident Fellow, American Enterprise Institute, before 108th Congress House Armed Services Committee', 26 February 2003.

29 Spence and Hulsman (2003).

30 Bradley Graham, 'US military Plans New Bases in Eastern Europe', *Washington Post*, 29 April 2003.

31 After all, this very scenario is identified as a threat in Russia's National Security Concept of 2000, which is still in operation.

32 Interview with Ronald D. Asmus, Mediamax News Agency, Yerevan, in English, 18 October 2004.

33 Herd (2005a).

34 *http://www.stabilitypact.org/about/default.asp*.

35 STA News Agency, Ljubljana, 21 June 2003.

36 Agence France Presse, 22 May 2003.

37 Herd and Tracy (2005).

38 Abramovich and Hurbunt (2002: 2).

39 International Commission on the Balkans (2005: 11–12); Batt (2005).

40 For an analysis of Poland's role as 'security provider', see Zaborowski and Long-hurst (2003).

41 Conference Report (2005).

42 'The "Old" and "New" Europe: New Dilemma of the Transatlantic Relation', lecture delivered at the Danish Institute of International Affairs, Copenhagen, 24 April 2003.

6 'NON-ALIGNED EUROPE' AND TRANSATLANTIC RELATIONS

1 President Bush, 'Message to the World', The White House, 11 March 2002, *http://www.whitehouse.gov/911/presidential_message.html*.

2 The Hague Conventions, 18 October 1907: Rights and Duties of Neutral Powers and Persons in Case of War on Land (Hague V); 'War on Sea' (Hague XIII). Although the rights and duties of neutral states are defined, the definition of neutrality itself remained unclear.

3 Ojanen (2004).

4 Arter (1996).

5 Hilary Barnes, 'Survey – Sweden', *Financial Times*, 4 December 2000, p. 4.

6 Nilsson (1991).

7 Jakobson (1998: 96).

8 Commission on Neutrality Policy (1994) and Mastny (2002: 73).

9 Kronvall and Petersson (2005).

10 Forsberg and Vaahtoranta (2001).

11 Rudberg, Ring and Jeppsson (2002).

12 Göran Persson, 'Inledningsanförande' [Opening Speech], Social Democratic Party Congress, 5 November 2001.

13 Andersson (2001).

14 'Nato splittrar de svenska partierna' [NATO Splits the Swedish Parties], *Göteborgs-Posten*, 23 September 2001.

15 Ingvar Carlsson and Carl Tham, 'USA styr med maktens arrogans' [The US Leads with the Arrogance of Power], *Dagens Nyheter*, 22 September 2001.

16 Sverker Åström, 'Sluta vara USAs transportkompani' [Stop Being the US Transport Provider], *Dagens Nyheter*, 12 February 2002.

17 'Varannan stöder Persson' [Every Second Person Supports Persson], *Göteborgs-Posten*, 7 November 2001. 'Två av tre svenskar stödjer USAs bombningar' [Two out of Three Swedes Support the US Bombing Campaign], *Aftonbladet*, 11 October 2001.

18 'Minskat stöd för Nato-anslutning' [Diminished Support NATO Integration], *Göteborgs-Posten*, 22 September 2001.

19 'Nej till kriget' [No to War], *Svenska Dagbladet*, 8 November 2001.

20 Robert von Lucius, 'Im Norden bröckeln die Fronten' [In the North the Fronts are Crumbling], *Frankfurter Allgemeine Zeitung*, 1 October 2001.

21 Hellenberg and Pursiainen (2004).

22 Ries (2002).

23 'Nato-maat painostivat EU:ta USA:n rintamaan' [NATO Countries Caused the EU to be Part of the US Coalition], *Helsingin Sanomat*, 25 September 2001; and 'President Halonen in Radio Interview: Finland not Taking Part in NATO Anti-terrorist Action', *Helsingin Sanomat*, international edition, *http://www.helsinki-hs.net/news*, 28 September 2001.

24 On potential policy differences within the government, see Forsberg (2001).

25 'Tuomioja pelkää sodan epäonnistuvan' [Tuomioja Fears that the War is Failing], *Kaleva*, 6 November 2001.

26 'Max Jakobson Criticizes Finnish Leaders for Soft Stances on Major Events', *Helsingin Sanomat*, international edition, *http://www.helsinki-hs.net/news*, 7

February 2002.

27 'International Crisis', *Flash Eurobarometer* no. 114 European Commission, Brussels 2001, *http://europa.eu.int/comm/public_opinion/flash/fl114_en.pdf.*

28 'Suomalaiset vastustavat iskua Afganistaniin' [Finns Oppose the Strike in Afghanistan], *Seura*, no. 39, 28 September 2001.

29 'Kokoomuslaisilta selvin tuki USA:n ilmaiskuille' [The Conservatives Give Strongest Support to US Air Strikes], *Helsingin Sanomat*, 21 October 2001.

30 Unto Hämäläinen, 'Naton vastustus kasvanut syksyn aikana' [Opposition to NATO Has Grown During the Autumn], *Helsingin Sanomat*, 21 October 2001.

31 Ervasti (2004).

32 Ibid.

33 Paavo Lipponen, Speech at the National Defence Training Association, Helsinki, 6 May 2004, *http://www.paavolipponen.org/cgi-bin/puheet.php?key=109.*

34 'Halonen at the United Nations: Iraq War as Illegal', *Helsingin Sanomat*, international edition, 22 September 2004, *http://www.helsinginsanomat.fi/english/article/1076154009154.*

35 *Finnish Security and Defence Policy* (2004: 81).

36 *Finnish Security and Defence Policy* (2004: 82).

37 'Sweden's Lindh calls Bush Lone Ranger on Iraq', Reuters, 7 June 2003.

38 'Högt pris om USA går vidare utan FN's stöd' [High Price if the US Goes Further Without UN Support], *Göteborgs-Posten*, 12 March 2003.

39 Göran Persson, 'First Comments on the Outbreak of War in Iraq', press release (unofficial translation), Ministry of Foreign Affairs, 20 March 2003, *http://www.sweden.gov.se/sb/d/911/a/8693;jsessionid=aALZHq2kJoL8.*

40 Granholm (2003).

41 Göran Persson, 'Utrikes-och säkerhetspolitiskt tal' [Speech on Foreign and Security Policy], Swedish Defence College, Stockholm, 25 March 2003, *http://www.regeringen.se/sb/d/1198/a/7151.*

42 'Statsministern försvarar Bush' [Prime Minister Defends Bush], *Aftonbladet*, 28 April 2004.

43 'Relationerna mellan USA och Sverige har tinats upp sedan Anna Lindh's död' [Relations Between the US and Sweden Thaw After Anna Lindh's Death], *Svenska Dagbladet*, 27 April 2004.

44 'Guantanamo-svensken högst uppe på dagordningen. Persson och Bush samtalade en timme' [The Guantanamo Swede High Up on Agenda. Bush and Persson Speak for an Hour], *Göteborgs-Posten*, 29 April 2004.

45 'Fler svenskar stödjer Irakkriget' [More Swedes Support the Iraq War], *Sydsvenskan*, 23 June 2003, *http://w1.sydsvenskan.se/Article.jsp?article=10048493.*

46 Bjereld (2004).

47 For this reason, Switzerland has refused to join the EU.

48 Petersberg Declaration, June 1992, Section II, *On Strengthening WEU's Operational Role*, para. 4.

49 Forsberg and Vaahtoranta (2001).

50 Sveriges Radio Ekot, 10 December 2003 and 'Finnish PM gives thumbs up to Italian proposal on EU Security', Agence France Presse, 10 December 2003.

51 Article I-41(7) of the Treaty Establishing the Constitution for Europe, *http://europa.eu.int/constitution/en/lstoc1_en.htm.*

52 Dick Ljungberg, 'Doktrinen kvar i Lindhs besked. Utrikesministern ville avdramatisera frågan i riksdagens utrikesutskott' [The doctrine remains in Lindh's announcement. The Foreign Minister wanted to play down the issue in the foreign affairs committee of the Parliament], *Dagens Nyheter*, 10 February 2000.

53 'Military Chief Wants Sweden's Neutrality Redefined', Agence France Presse, 21 November 2000.

54 Paavo Lipponen, Speech at the Finnish Institute of International Affairs, Helsinki, 10 December 2003, *http://www.paavolipponen.org/cgi-bin/puheet.php?key=65*.

55 'Finnish President Says Decision on EU Forces Will Be Hers', *Helsinki Hufvudstadsbladet* website, 5 December 2004.

56 'Iraq and the Peace in the World', *Flash Eurobarometer*, No. 151, European Commission, Brussels, 2003, *http://europa.eu.int/comm/public_opinion/flash/fl151_iraq_full_report.pdf*.

57 'Scheibner: Not Neutral, but Non-aligned', *Der Standard*, Vienna, in German, 23 January 2001, p. 8. See also 'Neutrality is a sham. We are non-aligned and Fine Gael is suggesting we end that non-aligned status', *Irish Independent*, 31 May 2003; and Jim Cusack, 'The enemy during a war will not see Ireland as being militarily neutral. Are we prepared for conflict now that the Government has aligned itself with the United States?', *The Irish Times*, 17 September 2001, p. 10.

7 'PERIPHERY EUROPE': RUSSIA AND TRANSATLANTIC SECURITY

1 Wörner (1990); Baker (1995: 572); and Light (1996).

2 Kozyrev (1993).

3 Sergounin (1997) and Black (1999).

4 'Founding Act' (1997). See also Carr (1999) and Matser (2001).

5 Primakov (1999).

6 Kazantsev (1999) and Brovkin (1999).

7 Antonenko (1999–2000) and Arbatova (2000).

8 Zevelev (2002).

9 Kosals (2001).

10 Bosworth (2002) and Hunter (2003).

11 'Meeting in Extraordinary Session of the NATO-Russia Permanent Joint Council at Ambassadorial Level', NATO press release, 13 September 2001, *http://www.nato.int/docu/pr/2001/p010913e.htm*.

12 NATO established its Military Liaison Mission in Moscow to support the contacts between NATO and the Russian military.

13 Danilov (2005: 80) and Grushko (2002).

14 Jamie Shea, 'U Rossii i NATO obschie problemy', *Rossiiskaya Gazeta*, No. 39, 26 February 2005.

15 'Remarks by the Secretary General of NATO Lord Robertson at the Joint Press Conference with the Foreign Minister of Russia, Mr. Igor Ivanov and the Foreign Minister of Belgium Mr. Louis Michel', Brussels, 7 December 2001, *http://www.nato.int/docu/speech/2001/s011207b.htm*.

16 Vladimir Putin, 'Speech at the Meeting of the Security Council', Moscow, 28 January 2005, available at *http://www.ln.mid.ru/brp_4.nsf/e78a48070f128a7b4325699*

9005bcbb3/ 854cb2ebb38d7704c3256f970049179f?OpenDocument, accessed 2 February 2005.

17 'Interview with President Putin', *New York Times*, 5 October 2003.

18 Baluyevskiy (2003).

19 'Candid Words on Russia's Drift From Democracy', *The Economist*, 24 February 2005, *http://www.economist.com/finance/displayStory.cfm?Story_ID=3688592*.

20 Hunter and Rogov (2004).

21 'NATO-Russia Action Plan on Terrorism', Brussels, 9 December 2004, http://*www.nato.int/docu/basictxt/b041209a-e.htm*. An important part of this plan is the cooperative airspace initiative to enhance air safety and counter the potential use of civilian aircraft for terrorist purposes. See also 'NATO-Russia. Forging Deeper Relations', *http://www.nato.int/docu/nato-russia/nato-russia-e.pdf*.

22 Harald Kujat, 'Enhancing Interoperability', article first published in *Krasnaya Zvezda*, 26 February 2004, *http://www.nato.int/docu/articles/2004/a040226a.htm*.

23 Oksana Antonenko, 'The NATO-Russia Council: Challenges and Opportunities', paper presented at the Conference on 'Dual Enlargement and the Baltic States: Security Policy Implications', Tallinn, 11–13 February 2004; and Zwack (2004).

24 The percentages that held NATO to be an aggressive/defensive alliance were 38/24 in 1997, 56/17 in 2000, 50/26 in 2001 and both 54/24 and 48/26 in 2002, *Fond Obshestvennoe Mnenie*, *http://www.fom.ru*.

25 'Putin Says Russian Military Still Mighty', Associated Press, 2 October 2003; Dmitriy Suslov, 'Russia Declares Cold War on NATO', *Nezavisimaya Gazeta*, 10 October 2003; David Holley, 'Russia Sees U.S., NATO Actions as Reasons to Watch Its Back', *Los Angeles Times*, 26 March 2004; 'Genshtab RF: rashirenie NATO na Vostok – ugroza dlya RF' [Russian General Staff: NATO Expansion Eastwards a Threat to the Russian Federation], RIA Novosti, 14 January 2004; and Vadim Soloyev, 'Russian General Staff Indicates Opposition to Joint Russian-NATO Exercises', *Nezavisimoye Voyennoye Obozreniye*, No. 43 (367), 5 December 2003.

26 Sergei Ivanov, 'As NATO Grows, So Do Russia's Worries', *New York Times*, 7 April 2004.

27 Viktor Litovkin, 'NATO-Russia: More Words than Real Action for Now', *Moscow Gudok*, 14 November 2003. This is not to argue that NATO–Russia cooperation has diluted NATO. See Yost (1998).

28 'Conventional Armed Forces in Europe Treaty', Fact Sheet, Arms Control Bureau, Washington, DC, US Department of State, 18 June 2002, *http://www.state.gov/t/ac/rls/fs/11243.htm*.

29 Judy Dempsey, 'Moscow Warns NATO Away from the Baltics: Envoy Says Alliance Troops or Equipment in New Member Countries Would not be Acceptable', *Financial Times*, 1 March 2004.

30 Sergei Ivanov, 'International Security in the Context of The Russia-NATO Relationship', speech at the 40th Munich Conference on Security Policy, Munich, 7 February 2004.

31 Bukvoll (2003); Baev (2003); and O'Loughlin et al. (2004).

32 Forsberg (2005).

33 'Survey: What the World Thinks of America', *The Guardian*, 27 October 2004.

34 Bassin (1991) and Neumann (1996).

35 Baranovsky (2001).

36 Stent (2002: 2) and Haukkala (2000).

37 'Medium Term Strategy' (1999: 20–8).

38 Ibid., p. 21.

39 Andreyev (2003).

40 Mahncke (2001).

41 Dmitri Danilov, 'Potentsialnyi soyuznik Moskvy: Militarizatsia Evropeiskogo Soyuza ob'ektivno vygodna dlya Moskvy' [The Potential Ally of Moscow: Militarization of the EU is Objectively Advantageous to Moscow], *Nezavisimoe Voennoye Obozreniye*, No. 47, 1999.

42 Zhurkin (2001).

43 Rontoyanni (2002).

44 Triantaphyllou (2002).

45 'A Common Strategy' (1999) and Bordachev (2001).

46 ITAR-TASS News Agency, Moscow, 10 April 2002.

47 Baev (2004).

48 Interfax News Agency, Moscow, 16 July 2000.

49 Forsberg and Herd (2005).

50 Haukkala (2003).

51 Khudoley (2003:18).

52 Herd (2005b).

53 Recent events in Ukraine 'can be seen as a planned strike against Russia aimed at creating ongoing instability on its southern borders. If this is pulled off, Russia will come up against a whole range of very complex problems - financial (the place of our capital in Ukraine), economic (linked to oil and gas pipelines to the West), political (questions of integration), military (the status of our fleet in Sevastopol) and demographic.' Vyacheslav Kostikov, *Argumenty i Fakty*, Moscow, 30 November 2004; Conference on Ukraine with Effective Policy Fund President Gleb Pavlovsky, RIA Novosti, 3 December 2004; and Natalya Galimova, 'Political predictions. Russia under the axe. Gleb Pavlovsky: Any moment, even the street cleaners in the capital will become revolutionaries', *Moskovskiy Komsomolets*, 21 December 2004.

54 Sergei B. Ivanov, Minister of Defence Russian Federation at the Council on Foreign Relations, New York, Inaugural Annual Lecture on Russia and Russian-American Relations, 'The World in the 21st Century: Addressing New Threats and Challenges', 13 January 2005.

55 RIA Novosti News Agency (in Russian), Moscow, 3 December 2004.

56 ITAR-TASS News Agency (in Russian), Moscow, 27 December 2004.

57 Judy Dempsey, 'U.S. Tries to Break Deadlock over OSCE: Americans and Europeans Coax Russia', *International Herald Tribune*, 30 March 2005, p. 3.

58 Valeria Sycheva, 'The Axis of Good', *Itogi*, 26 November 2002.

59 Rontoyanni (2002: 821) for quote, and Danilov (2005: 87).

60 Lindley-French (2002).

61 'Russia may also provide technology for the EU's satellite centre in Torrejon (Spain), and a cooperation agreement is pending between the European Space Agency and Russia's Rosaviakosmos'. Rontoyanni (2002: 824).

62 Gnesotto (2005: 6).

63 Forsberg (2004).
64 Ivanov (2005).
65 For a fuller elaboration of this argument, see Herd and Akerman (2002).
66 Müller-Braneck-Bocquet (2002).
67 Karaganov (2005: 28).

8 TRANSATLANTIC FUTURES IN AN AGE OF STRATEGIC DISSONANCE

1 Asmus (2003: xx).
2 Maria Wagrowski, 'Incantations and Realities: Do Europe and America Need Each Other Even Less in Security Issues?', *Rzeczpospolita*, 29 March 2005, p. A8.
3 Judy Dempsey, 'Newly Confident Germany Defends its Interests', *International Herald Tribune*, 24 February 2005, p. 5.
4 Chancellor Angela Merkel, 'Germany's Foreign and Security Policy in the Face of Global Challenges', Munich Conference on Security Policy, 4 February 2006: *http://www.securityconference.de/konferenzen/rede.php?menu_konferenzen=&menu_2006=&menu_konfer&sprache=en&id=170&*.
5 Karl-Heinz Kamp, 'An "Honest Germany"', *Wall Street Journal*, 22 July 2005.
6 Anatol Lieven, 'The West's Ukraine Illusion', *International Herald Tribune*, 8 January 2006.
7 Freedman (2005–06: 24).
8 Aysha (2005).
9 Carl Bildt, 'Europe Must Keep its Soft Power', *Financial Times*, 1 June 2004.
10 Judy Dempsey, 'In Europe, Divisions among Old and New', *International Herald Tribune*, 3 June 2005.
11 Murray (2005).
12 Cornish and Edwards (2005).
13 Meiers (2005).
14 de Wijk (2003–4).
15 Judy Dempsey, 'NATO Agrees to Lend its Help in Darfur', *International Herald Tribune*, 9 June 2005.
16 The International Crisis Group (2005).
17 Record (2003).
18 Biddle (2005).
19 Dana Milbank and Claudia Deane, 'Poll Finds Dimmer View of Iraq War', *Washington Post*, 8 June 2005, p. A01.
20 Sidney Blumenthal, 'Happy Talk', *The Guardian*, 14 January 2005, p. 25 and Zbigniew Brzezinski, 'George W. Bush's Suicidal Statecraft', *International Herald Tribune*, 13 October 2005, *http://www.iht.com/articles/2005/10/13/opinion/edzbig.php*.
21 'The Republican Rift', *The New Yorker* Online, 23 October 2005, *http://www.newyorker.com/online/content/articles/051031on_onlineonly01*.
22 Lawrence B. Wilkerson, 'The White House Cabal', *Los Angeles Times*, 25 October 2005.
23 Bacevich (2004) and Stephen J. Hedges, 'Critics: Pentagon in Blinders', *Chicago*

Tribune, 6 June 2005.

24 Kurtz (2003).

25 Welt (2005).

26 US NSS (2006).

27 Fergusson (2004).

28 Guy Dinmore, 'US Sees Coalitions of the Willing as Best Ally', *Financial Times*, 4 January 2006.

29 Kaplan and Kristol (2003).

30 *http://www.sgpproject.org/events/Black per cent20Dawn per cent20Final per cent20Report.pdf.*

31 'Lugar Speech for CSIS Conference on Transatlantic Efforts for Peace and Security on Norway's Centennial Anniversary', States News Service, 9 March 2005.

32 'Diplomacy – Bush's European Tour', *Financial Times Information*, 6 March 2005.

33 R. Nicholas Burns, 'An Alliance Renewed: NATO', *International Herald Tribune*, 16 March 2005, p. 9.

34 James Dobbins, 'America Is Punishing Germany for its Iraq Opposition', *Financial Times*, 13 July 2005.

35 IISS (2005) and Flanigan (2005: 1).

36 Michel (2005).

37 Guillaume Parmentiers, 'A Transatlantic Task Force Fight for Freedom', *Financial Times*, 10 March 2005, p. 19.

38 President Discusses American and European Alliance in Belgium, *http://www.whitehouse.gov/news/releases/2005/02/20050221.html.*

39 *http://www.peacenews.info/issues/2403/pn240303.htm.*

Bibliography

Abramovich, Morton and Heather Hurbunt (2002), 'Can the EU Hack the Balkans? A Proving Ground for Brussels', *Comment*, Council on Foreign Relations, September–October.

Ackermann, Alice (2003), 'The Changing Transatlantic Relationship: A Socio-Cultural Approach', *International Politics*, Vol. 40, pp. 121–36.

Albright, Madeleine et al. (2003), 'Joint Declaration: Renewing the Transatlantic Partnership' (Washington, DC: Center for Strategic and International Studies), 14 May.

Allin, Dana (2004), 'The Atlantic Crisis of Confidence', *International Affairs*, Vol. 80, No. 4, pp. 649–63.

Andersson, Jan Joel (2001), 'Terrorn och svensk säkerhetspolitik' [Terror and Swedish Security Policy], *Internationella Studier*, No. 4, pp. 22–6.

Andrews, David M. (ed.) (2005), *The Atlantic Alliance Under Stress. US-European Relations after Iraq* (Cambridge: Cambridge University Press).

Andreyev, Andrei (2003), 'How Do Russians View Cooperation with Europe?', *Russia in Global Affairs*, Vol. 1, No. 2, pp. 90–102.

Antonenko, Oksana (1999–2000), 'Russia, NATO and European Security after Kosovo', *Survival*, Vol. 41, No. 4, pp. 124–44.

Antonenko, Oksana (2004), 'The NATO–Russia Council: Challenges and Opportunities', paper presented at the Conference on 'Dual Enlargement and the Baltic States: Security Policy Implications', Tallinn, 11–13 February.

Arbatova, Nadia (2000), 'Russia–NATO Relations after the Kosovo Crisis', in Yuri Fedorov and Bertil Nygren (eds), *Russia and NATO* (Stockholm: Försvarshögskolan ACTA B14 Strategiska Institutionen), pp. 43-74.

Arter, David (1996), 'Finland – from Neutrality to NATO?' *European Security*, Vol. 5, No. 4, pp. 614–32.

Asmus, Ronald (2003), 'Rebuilding the Atlantic Alliance', *Foreign Affairs*, Vol. 82, No. 5 (September–October), pp. 20–32.

Asmus, Ronald and Kenneth Pollack (2002), 'The New Transatlantic Project', *Policy Review*, No. 115 (October–November), pp. 3–19.

Asmus, Ronald D., Anthony J. Blinken and Philip H. Gordon (2005), 'Nothing to Fear', *Foreign Affairs*, Vol. 84, No. 1 (January–February), pp. 174–8.

Aysha, Emad El-Din (2005), 'September 11 and the Middle East Failure of US "Soft

Power": Globalisation contra Americanisation in the "New" US Century', *International Relations*, Vol. 19, No. 2, pp. 193–210.

Bacevich, Andrew (2004), *The New American Militarism: How Americans Are Seduced by War* (Oxford: Oxford University Press).

Baev, Pavel (2003), 'Putin's Western Choice: Too Good to Be True?', *European Security*, Vol. 12, No. 1, pp. 1–16.

Baev, Pavel K. (2004), 'The Evolution of Putin's Regime: Inner Circles and Outer Walls', *Problems of Post-Communism*, Vol. 51, No. 6 (November–December), pp. 3–14.

Bagajski, Janusz and Ilona Teleki (2005), 'Washington's New European Allies: Durable or Conditional Partners?', *The Washington Quarterly*, Vol. 28, No. 2 (Spring), pp. 95–107.

Baker III, James A. (1995), *The Politics of Diplomacy* (New York: Putnam).

Baker, Mark (2003), 'U.S.: Rumsfeld's "Old" and "New" Europe Touches on Uneasy Divide', *RFE/RF News*, 24 January, *http://www.rferl.org/nca/features/2003/01/24 012003172118.asp*.

Baluyevskiy, Yu. N. (2003), 'Russia and NATO: Principles of Interrelations, Prospects for Cooperation', *Military Thought*, No. 2, pp. 27–33.

Baranovsky, Vladimir (2001), 'Russia: A Part of Europe or Apart from Europe', in Archie Brown (ed.), *Contemporary Russian Politics: A Reader* (Oxford: Oxford University Press), pp. 429–42.

Bassin, Mark (1991), 'Russia Between Europe and Asia', *Slavic Review*, Vol. 50, No. 1, pp. 1–17.

Batt, Judy and Dov Lynch, Antonio Missiroli, Martin Ortega and Dimitrios Triantaphyllou (2003), 'Partners and neighbours: a CFSP for a wider Europe', *Chaillot Papers*, No. 64, September.

Batt, Judy (2005), 'The Question of Serbia', *Chaillot Papers*, No. 81, August.

Becher, Klaus (2004), 'German Forces in International Military Operations', *Orbis*, Vol. 48, No. 3, pp. 397–408.

Berendse, Gerrit-Jan (2003), 'German Anti-Americanism in Context', *Journal of European Studies*, Vol. 33, No. 3–4, pp. 333–50.

Berman, Russell (2004), *Anti-Americanism in Europe: A Cultural Problem* (Stanford: Hoover Institution).

Bertram, Christoph (2003), 'The Weakness of Power: A Response to Robert Kagan', *The European Policy Centre*, 16 May, *http://www.theepc.be/en/default.asp?TYP=SE ARCH&LV=279&see=y&PG=CE/EN/directa&AI=295&l=*

Biddle, Stephen D. (2005), *American Grand Strategy After 9/11: An Assessment* (Carlisle: US Army War College), pp. 1–44.

Bjereld, Ulf (2004), 'Svenskarna, Nato och Irak–kriget' [The Swedes, NATO and the Iraq War], in Sören Holmberg and Lennart Weibull (eds), Ju mer vi är tillsammans [The More We Are Together] (Göteborg: SOM-Institute, Göteborg University), pp. 165–70.

Black, J. L. (1999), 'Russia and NATO Expansion Eastward: Red-Lining the Baltic States', *International Journal*, Vol. 54, No. 2, pp. 249–66.

Blinken, Anthony (2001), 'The False Crisis over the Atlantic', *Foreign Affairs*, Vol. 80, No. 3, pp. 16–34.

Bogdanor, Vernon (2005), 'Footfalls Echoing in the Memory. Britain and Europe: The Historical Perspective', *International Affairs*, Vol. 81, No. 4, pp. 689–701.

Boot, Max (2002), *The Savage Wars of Peace: Small Wars and the Rise of American Power* (New York: Basic Books).

Bordachev, Timofei (2001), 'The Russian Challenge for the European Union: Direct Neighbourhood and Security Crises, in Iris Kempe (ed.), *Beyond EU Enlargement, Vol. I: The Agenda of Direct Neighbourhood for Eastern Europe* (Gütersloh: Bertelsmann), pp. 47–64.

Bosworth, Kara (2002), 'The Effect of 11 September on Russia–NATO Relations', *Perspectives on European Politics and Society*, Vol. 3, No. 3, pp. 361–87.

Braithwaite, Roderic (2003), 'End of the Affair', *Prospect*, No. 86 (May), pp. 20–23.

Brovkin, Vladimir (1999), 'Discourse on NATO in Russia During the Kosovo War', NATO–EAPC Research Fellowship, Final Report, *http://www.nato.int/acad/fellow/97-99/brovkin.pdf*.

Brzezinski, Ian J. (2003), Deputy Assistant Secretary, Bureau of Europe and Eurasian Affairs, US Department of State, Hearing of the European Sub-Committee of the House of Representatives International Relations Committee, 29 April, *http://wwwc.house.gov/international_relations/107/80289.pdf*, pp. 23–31.

Bukvoll, Tor (2003), 'Putin's Strategic Partnership with the West: The Domestic Politics of Russian Foreign Policy', *Comparative Strategy*, Vol. 22, No. 2, pp. 223–42.

Burwell, F. and Ivo Daalder (1999), *The United States and Europe in the Global Arena* (London: Macmillan).

Calleo, David P. (2004), 'The Broken West', *Survival*, Vol. 46, No. 3 (Autumn), pp. 29–38.

Capell, Kerry (2003), 'Can Blair Repair the US–Europe Rift', *Business Week*, No. 3827, 7 April, p. 38.

Carr, Fergus and Paul Flenley (1999), 'Nato and the Russian Federation in the New Europe: The Founding Act of Mutual Relations', *Journal of Communist Studies and Transition Politics*, Vol. 15, No. 2, pp. 88–110.

Ceaser, James W. (2003), 'A Genealogy of Anti-Americanism', *The Public Interest*, No. 152 (Summer), pp. 3–19.

Chalmers, Malcolm (2001), 'The Atlantic Burden-Sharing Debate – Widening or Fragmenting?', *International Affairs*, Vol. 77, No. 3, pp. 569–85.

Chandler, William (2003), 'Foreign and European Policy Issues in the 2002 Bundestag Elections', *German Politics and Society*, Vol. 21, No. 1, pp. 161–77.

Chicago Council on Foreign Relations and German Marshall Fund (2002), 'Worldviews 2002: American and European Public Opinion and Foreign Policy', *http://www.worldviews.org/detailreports/compreport/html/summary.html*.

Cimbalo, Jeffrey L. (2004), 'Saving NATO from Europe', *Foreign Affairs*, Vol. 83, No. 6 (November–December), pp. 111–21.

Clark, Wesley K. (2001), *Waging Modern War* (New York: Public Affairs).

Commission on Neutrality Policy (1994), 'Commission on Neutrality Policy, *Had There Been a War...: Preparations for the Reception of Military Assistance, 1949–1969* (Stockholm: Fritzes).

'A Common Strategy on Russia' (1999), 'A Common Strategy of the European

Union of 4 June 1999 on Russia', *Official Journal of the European Communities*, L 157/1, 24 June.

Cooper, Robert (2003), *The Breaking of Nations: Order and Chaos in the Twenty-First Century* (London: Atlantic Books).

Cordesman, Anthony H. (2005), 'Rethinking NATO's Force Transformation', *NATO Review*, Spring, *http://www.nato.int/docu/review/2005/issue1/english/art4.html*.

Corn, David (2004), 'Al Qaeda Disconnect', *The Nation*, Vol. 279, Issue 1 (7 May), pp. 4–6.

Cornish, Paul (2004), 'NATO: The Practice and Politics of Transformation', *International Affairs*, Vol. 80, No. 1, pp. 63–74.

Cornish, Paul and Geoffrey Edwards (2005), 'The Strategic Culture of the European Union: A Progress Report', *International Affairs*, Vol. 81, No. 4, pp. 801–20.

Cox, Michael (2003), 'Martians and Venutians in the New World Order', *International Affairs*, Vol. 79, No. 2, pp. 523–32.

Cox, Michael (2005), 'Beyond the West: Terrors in Transatlantia', *European Journal of International Relations*, Vol. 11, No. 2, pp. 203–34.

Crowe, Brian (2003), 'A Common European Foreign Policy after Iraq?' *International Affairs*, Vol. 79, No. 3, pp. 533–46.

Daalder, Ivo H. (2003), 'The End of Atlanticism', *Survival*, Vol. 45, No. 2 (Summer), pp. 147–66.

Danchev, Alex (2005), 'How Strong Are Shared Values in the Transatlantic Relationship?' *British Journal of Politics and International Relations*, Vol. 7, pp. 429–36.

Danilov, Dmitry (2005), 'Russia and European Security', in Dov Lynch (ed.), 'What Russia Sees', *Chaillot Papers*, No. 74, January (Paris: European Union Institute of Strategic Studies), pp. 79–98.

Deutsch, Karl (1957), *Political Community in the North Atlantic Area: International Organization in the Light of Historical Experience* (Princeton, NJ: Princeton University Press).

de Wijk, Rob (2003–4), 'European Military Reform for a Global Partnership', *Washington Quarterly*, Vol. 27, No. 1 (Winter), pp. 197–210.

Diamond, Larry (2005), *Squandered Victory: The American Occupation and the Bungled Effort to Bring Democracy to Iraq* (New York: Times Books).

Diner, Dan (2002), *Feindbild Amerika: Über die Beständigkeit eines Ressentiments* [Enemy Image of America: On the Durability of a Resentment] (Berlin: Propyläen).

Dockrill, Saki (2000), 'Forging the Anglo-American Global Defence Partnership: Harold Wilson, Lyndon Johnson and the Washington Summit, December 1964', *The Journal of Strategic Studies*, Vol. 23, No. 4 (December), pp. 107–30.

Donnelly, Thomas (2003), 'Statement of Thomas Donnelly, Resident Fellow, American Enterprise Institute, before 108th Congress House Armed Services Committee, 26 February.

Downing Street Memos (2002), Excerpts from material in secret Downing Street memos written in 2002, *http://news.yahoo.com/s/ap/memos_excerpts*. The information, authenticated by a senior British government official, was transcribed from the original documents.

Dunne, Tim (2004), 'When the Shooting Starts: Atlanticism in British Foreign Policy', *International Affairs*, Vol. 80, No. 5, pp. 893–909.

'Effective Multilateralism to Build a Better World' (2004), Joint Statement by President George W. Bush and Prime Minister Tony Blair, Public Papers of the President, 24 November, *http://www.whitehouse.gov/news/releases/2003/11/2 0031120.html*.

Ervasti, Pekka (2004), *Irakgate: Pääministerin nousu ja ero* [Iraq-Gate: The Rise and Resignation of the Prime Minister] (Helsinki: Gummerrus).

Etherington, Mark (2005), *Revolt on the Tigris: The Al-Sadr Uprising and the Governing of Iraq* (Cornell: Cornell University Press).

Fallows, James (2004), 'Blind into Baghdad', *The Atlantic Online*, January–February, *http://www.theatlantic.com/issues/2004/01/fallows.htm*.

Fergusson, Niall (2004), *Colossus: The Price of American Empire* (New York: Penguin Press).

Finnish Security and Defence Policy 2004, Government Report 6/2004 (Helsinki: Prime Minister's Office), *http://www.defmin.fi/index.phtml/page_id/326/topmenu_id/7/ menu_id/326/this_topmenu/7/lang/3/fs/12*.

Fischer, Joschka (1994), 'Les Certitudes Allemandes: Grundkonstanten bundesdeutscher Aussenpolitik' [German Certainties: The Main Constants of German Foreign Policy], *Blätter für Deutsche und Internationale Politik*, Vol. 39, No. 10, pp. 1082–90.

Flanigan, Stephen J. (2005), 'Sustaining U.S.-European Global Security Cooperation', *Strategic Forum*, Institute for National Strategic Studies, National Defense University, No. 217, September, pp. 1–6, *http://www.ndu.edu/inss/strforum/SF217/ SF_217_817_finalweb.pdf*.

Forsberg, Tuomas (2001), 'One Foreign Policy or Two? The New Constitution and the European Policies of Tarja Halonen and Paavo Lipponen', *Northern Dimensions: Yearbook of Finnish Foreign Policy 2001* (Helsinki: Finnish Institute of International Affairs), pp. 3–12.

Forsberg, Tuomas (2004), 'The Security Partnership Between the EU and Russia: Why the Opportunity was Missed', *European Foreign Affairs Review*, Vol. 9, No. 2, pp. 247–67.

Forsberg, Tuomas (2005), 'Russia's Relationship with NATO: A Qualitative Change or Old Wine in New Bottles?', *Journal of Communist Studies and Transition Politics*, Vol. 21, No. 3, pp. 332–53.

Forsberg, Tuomas and Graeme P. Herd (2005), 'The EU, Human Rights and the Russo-Chechen Conflict', *Political Science Quarterly*, Vol. 120, No. 3, Fall, pp. 1–24.

Forsberg, Tuomas and Tapani Vaahtoranta (2001), 'Inside the EU, Outside NATO: Paradoxes of Finland and Sweden's Post-neutrality', *European Security*, Vol. 10, No. 1 (Spring), pp. 68–94.

'Founding Act on Mutual Relations, Cooperation and Security between NATO and the Russian Federation' (1997), Paris, 27 May, *http://www.nato.int/docu/basictxt/ fndact-a.htm*.

Freedman, Lawrence (2005-06), 'The Transatlantic Agenda: Vision and Counter-Vision', *Survival*, Vol. 47, No. 4, pp. 19–38.

Friborg, Anders Tang (2004–5), *Afghanistan, Lessons learned from a Post-War Situation*, Danish Institute for International Studies (DIIS) Working Paper No. 2004/5, pp. 1–46, *http://www.diis.dk/graphics/Publications/WP2004/afr_afghanistan.pdf.*

Frum, David and Richard Perle (2003), *An End to Evil: How to Win the War on Terror* (New York: Random House).

Fukuyama, Francis (1989), 'The End of History?', *National Interest*, No. 16, pp. 3–18.

Gaddis, John Lewis (2004), *Surprise, Security, and the American Experience* (Cambridge, MA and London: Harvard University Press).

Gardiner, Nile and John Hulsman (2003), 'The President's State Visit to Britain: Advancing Anglo-US Special Relationship', *Heritage Foundation Reports*, Backgrounder No. 1707, 14 November.

Garton Ash, Timothy (2003a), 'The Great Divide', *Prospect*, No. 83, March, pp. 24–6.

Garton Ash, Timothy (2003b), 'Anti-Europeanism in America', *New York Review of Books*, Vol. 50, No. 2 (13 February), pp. 32–4.

Garton Ash, Timothy (2004), *Free World: Why a Crisis of the West Reveals the Opportunity of Our Time* (London: Allen Lane).

Gordon, Philip (2001), 'Bush, Missile Defence and the Atlantic Alliance', *Survival*, Vol. 43, No. 1, pp. 17–36.

Gordon, Philip (2003), 'Bridging the Atlantic Divide', *Foreign Affairs*, Vol. 82, No. 1, pp. 70–83.

Gordon, Philip H. and Jeremy Shapiro (2004), *Allies at War: America, Europe, and the Crisis over Iraq* (New York: McGraw Hill).

Gnesotto, Nicole (2005), 'Preface', in Dov Lynch (ed.), 'What Russia Sees', *Chaillot Papers*, No. 74, January (Paris: European Union Institute of Strategic Studies).

Grabbe, Heather (2004), *The Constellations of Europe: How Enlargement Will Transform the EU* (London: Centre for European Reform).

Granholm, Niklas (2003), 'Sverige och Irakkriget: Ett svenskt dilemma' [Sweden and the Iraq War: A Swedish Dilemma], in Bo Ljung (ed.), *Irakkriget 2003: En preliminär analys* [Iraq War: A Preliminary Analysis] FOI Rapport 0852, Stockholm, April.

Grant, Charles (2003), *Transatlantic Rift: How to Bring the Two Sides Together* (London: Centre for European Reform).

Gray, John (2003), 'American culture is animated by a heresy: That human nature is not inherently flawed but essentially good', *New Statesman*, Vol. 16, No. 740 (20 January), pp. 21–4.

Gray, John (2004), 'Blair's Project in Retrospect', *International Affairs*, Vol. 80, No. 1 (January), pp. 39–48.

Grushko, Alexandr (2002) 'On the New Quality of Russia–NATO Relations', *International Affairs* (Moscow), Vol. 48, No. 5, pp. 23–30.

Gunter, Michael M. (2005), 'The U.S.–Turkish Alliance is in Disarray', *World Affairs*, Vol. 167, No. 3 (Winter), pp. 113–23.

Guzzini, Stefano (1998), *Realism in International Relations and International Political Economy: The Continuing Story of Death Foretold* (London: Routledge).

Guzzini, Stefano (2004), 'The Enduring Dilemmas of Realism in International Relations', *European Journal of International Relations*, Vol. 10, No. 4, pp. 533–68.

Habermas, Jürgen and Jacques Derrida (2005), 'February 15, or What Binds Europeans Together. A Plea for a Common Foreign Policy, Beginning in Core Europe', in Daniel Levy, Max Pensky and John Torpey (eds), *Old Europe, New Europe, Core Europe: Transatlantic Relations after the Iraq War* (London: Verso), pp. 3–13.

Hacke, Christian (2003), 'Deutschland, Europa und der Irakkonflikt', *Aus Politik und Zeitgeschichte*, B24–25, 10 June, pp. 8–16.

Hague Conventions (1907), 'The Hague Conventions, 18 October 1907: Rights and Duties of Neutral Powers and Persons in Case of War on Land (Hague V)' and 'War at Sea (Hague XIII)'.

Hamilton, Daniel S. (2004), 'What is Transformation and What Does it Mean for NATO?', in Daniel S. Hamilton (ed.), *Transatlantic Transformation: Equipping NATO for the 21st Century* (Washington, DC: Center for Transatlantic Relations), pp. 3–24.

Harnisch, Sebastian (2004), 'German Non-Proliferation Policy and the Iraq Conflict', *German Politics*, Vol. 13, No. 1, pp. 1–34.

Harris, Owen (1993), 'Collapse of "the West"', *Foreign Affairs*, Vol. 72, No. 4, pp. 41–53.

Harvey, Robert (2003), *Global Disorder: America and the Threat of World Conflict* (London: Constable).

Haukkala, Hiski (2000), 'The Making of the European Union's Common Strategy on Russia', *Working Paper No. 28* (Helsinki: The Finnish Institute of International Affairs).

Haukkala, Hiski (2003), 'What Went Right with the EU's Common Strategy on Russia', in Arkady Moshes (ed.), *Rethinking the Respective Strategies of Russia and the European Union* (Helsinki/Moscow: Finnish Institute of International Affairs/Carnegie Moscow Center), pp. 62–96.

Heisbourg, François (2002–3), 'How the West Could Be Won', *Survival*, Vol. 44, No. 4 (Winter), pp. 145–56.

Heisbourg, François (2004), 'US-European Relations: From Lapsed Alliance to New Partnership', *International Politics*, Vol. 41, pp. 119–26.

Hellenberg, Timo and Christer Pursiainen (2004), 'Finnish Crisis Decision-Making: The Case of 9/11', *The Finnish Yearbook of International Affairs 2004* (Helsinki: Finnish Institute of International Affairs), pp. 79–96.

Hellmann, Gunther and Sebastian Enskat (2004), 'Umfragedaten zu deutscher Außenpolitik und Deutschlands Rolle in der Welt seit 1990. Eine Dokumentation' [Opinion Poll Data on German Foreign Policy and Germany's Role in the World since 1990. Documentary Report] (Frankfurt am Main: University of Frankfurt).

Hellmann, Gunther, Rainer Baumann, Monika Bösche, Benjamin Herborth and Wolfgang Wagner (2005), 'De-Europeanization by Default? Germany's EU Policy in Defense and Asylum', *Foreign Policy Analysis*, Issue 1, pp. 143–64.

Herd, Graeme P. (2004), 'Out of Area, Out of Business', *The World Today*, Vol. 60, No. 8–9 (August–September), pp. 4–6.

Herd, Graeme P. (2005a), 'Colourful Revolutions and the CIS: "Manufactured" versus "Managed" Democracy?', *Problems of Post-Communism*, Vol. 52, No. 2 (March–April), pp. 3–17.

Herd, Graeme P. (2005b), 'Moldova and the Dniestr region: Contested Past, Frozen Present, Speculative Futures?', Central and Eastern Europe Series, Conflict Studies Research Centre, 05/07, Defence Academy, UK, February, pp. 1–17, *http://www.da.mod.uk/CSRC/documents/CEE/05%2807%29–GPH.pdf.*

Herd, Graeme P. and Ella Akerman (2002), 'Russian Strategic Realignment and the Post-Post-Cold War Era', *Security Dialogue*, Vol. 33, No. 3, pp. 357–72.

Herd, Graeme P. and Tom Tracy (2005), 'Democratic Civil–Military Relations in Bosnia Herzegovina: A New Paradigm for Protectorates', *Armed Forces & Society*, Vol. 32, No. 1 (Winter), pp. 1–17.

Herd, Graeme P. and Martin Weber (2001), 'Forging World Order Paradigms: "Good Civilisation" versus "Global Terror"', *Security Dialogue*, Vol. 32, No. 4 (December), pp. 119–21.

Hill, Christopher (2004), 'Renationalizing or Regrouping? EU Foreign Policy Since 11 September 2001', *Journal of Common Market Studies*, Vol. 42, No. 1, pp. 143–63.

Hoffman, Stanley (2000), 'Towards a Common European Foreign and Security Policy', *Journal of Common Market Studies*, Vol. 38, No. 2, pp. 189–98.

Hoffman, Stanley (2003), 'US–European Relations: Past and Future', *International Affairs*, Vol. 79, No. 5, pp. 1029–36.

Hollander, Paul (2004), *Understanding Anti-Americanism: Its Origins and Impact at Home and Abroad* (Chicago, IL: Ivan R. Dee).

Hulsman, John (2003), 'Cherry-Picking: Preventing the Emergence of a Permanent Franco-German-Russian Alliance', *Backgrounder* No. 1682, Heritage Foundation, 18 August.

Hunter, Robert (2003), 'NATO–Russia Relations after 11 September', *Journal of Southeast European and Black Sea Studies*, Vol. 3, No. 3, pp. 28–54.

Hunter, Robert A. (2004), 'A Forward-Looking Partnership', *Foreign Affairs*, Vol. 83, Issue 5 (September–October), pp. 14–18.

Hunter, Robert and Sergey Rogov (2004), *Engaging Russia as Partner and Participant: The Next Stage of NATO–Russia Relations* (Santa Monica, CA: Rand).

Huntington, Samuel (1993), 'The Clash of Civilizations', *Foreign Affairs*, Vol. 72, No. 3, pp. 22–49.

Huntington, Samuel (1996), *The Clash of Civilizations and the Remaking of World Order* (New York: Simon and Schuster).

Ikenberry, John (2002), 'Introduction', in John Ikenberry (ed.), *America Unrivaled: The Future of the Balance of Power* (Ithaca, NY: Cornell University Press), pp. 1–28.

Inglehart, Ronald and Wayne E. Baker (2000), 'Modernization, Cultural Change and the Persistence of Traditional Values', *American Sociological Review*, Vol. 65, No. 1, pp. 19–51, *http://wvs.isr.umich.edu/papers/19–51_in.pdf.*

International Commission on the Balkans (2005), 'The Balkans in Europe's Future', April, pp. 7–28.

'International Crisis', *Flash Eurobarometer*, No. 114, December 2001 [Question No. 4], *http://europa.eu.int/comm/public_opinion/flash/fl114_en.pdf.*

International Crisis Group (2005), 'The EU/AU Partnership in Darfur: Not Yet a Winning Combination', *Africa Report*, No. 99, 25 October, *http://www.crisis-group.org/home/index.cfm?l=1andid=3766*.

International Institute for Strategic Studies (IISS) (2005), 'Transatlantic Relations: Persistent Predicaments', *Strategic Comments*, Vol. 11, Issue 7 (September).

Ivanov, Sergei (2004), 'International Security in the Context of the Russia–NATO Relationship', speech at the 40th Munich Conference on Security Policy, Munich, 7 February.

Ivanov, Sergei (2005), 'Maturing Partnership', *NATO Review*, Winter: *http://www.nato.int/docu/review/2005/issue4/english/special.html*.

Jakobson, Max (1998), *Finland in the New Europe* (Westport, CT: Praeger).

Janes, Jackson and Eberhard Sandschneider (2004), 'A US-German Agenda for Bush II', *Internationale Politik* (transatlantic edition), Vol. 5, Issue 4, pp. 3–9.

Jervis, Robert (2005), *American Foreign Policy in a New Era* (New York: Routledge).

Joffe, Josef (1984), 'Europe's American Pacifier', *Foreign Affairs*, No. 54, pp. 64–82.

Joffe, Josef (2003), 'Continental Divides', *National Interest*, Issue 71, Spring, pp. 157–61.

Johnson, Paul (2003), 'Anti-Americanism is Racist Envy', *Forbes*, 21 July, *http://www.forbes.com/global/2003/0721/017.html*.

Johnston, Alistair Iain (1995), 'Thinking About Strategic Culture', *International Security*, Vol. 19, Issue 4 (Spring), pp. 32–64.

Jones, Erik (2004), 'Debating the Transatlantic Relationship: Rhetoric and Reality', *International Affairs*, Vol. 80, No. 4, pp. 595–612.

Jones, James L. (2004), 'NATO Transformation: Institutional Change Through the Four Pillars of Transformation', lecture at the George C. Marshall European Center for Security Studies, Garmisch-Partenkirchen, Germany, 3 November.

JSP 777 (2005), Joint Service Publication 777, Ministry of Defence, UK, 5 February: *http://www.mod.uk/linked_files/issues/nec/nec_jsp777.pdf* (accessed 5 January 2006).

Judt, Tony (2005), 'Europe vs. America', *New York Review of Books*, Vol. 52, No. 2 (10 February), *http://www.nybooks.com/articles/17726*.

Kaase, Max and Andrew Kohut (1996), *Estranged Friends? The Transatlantic Consequences of Societal Change* (New York: Council on Foreign Relations).

Kagan, Robert (2002), 'Power and Weakness', *Policy Review*, No. 113, June–July, *http://www.policyreview.org/JUN02/kagan.html*, pp. 3–29.

Kagan, Robert (2002–2003), 'Symposium: One Year After: A Grand Strategy for the West?', *Survival*, Vol. 44, No. 4 (Winter), pp. 134–9.

Kagan, Robert (2003), *Of Paradise and Power: America and Europe in the New World Order* (New York: Alfred A. Knopf).

Kampfner, John (2005), 'Operation Bush Dance', *New Statesman*, Vol. 18, No. 844 (31 January), p. 8.

Kaplan, Lawrence F. and William Kristol (2003), *The War over Iraq: Saddam's Tyranny and America's Mission* (San Francisco: Encounter Books).

Karaganov, Sergei (2005), 'Russia and the International Order', in Dov Lynch (ed.), 'What Russia Sees', *Chaillot Papers*, No. 74, January.

Karp, Regina (2005-06), 'The New German Foreign Policy Consensus', *The Washington Quarterly*, Vol. 29, No. 1, pp. 61-82.

Katzenstein, Peter (2002), 'Same War, Different Views: Germany, Japan and the War on Terrorism', *Current History*, Vol. 101, No. 659, pp. 427–35.

Kay, Sean (2003), 'Putting NATO Back Together Again', *Current History*, Vol. 102. No. 662 (March), pp. 106–112.

Kazantsev, Boris (1999), 'NATO: Obvious Bias to the Use of Force', *International Affairs* (Moscow), Vol. 45. No. 3, pp. 38–42.

Keohane, Robert O. (1989), *International Institutions and State Power: Essays in International Relations Theory* (Boulder, CO: Westview Press).

Keohane, Robert (2005), *After Hegemony: Cooperation and Discord in the World Political Economy* (Princeton, NJ: Princeton University Press, 2nd edn).

Khudoley, Konstantin (2003), 'Russia and the European Union: New Opportunities, New Challenges', in Arkady Moshes (ed.), *Rethinking the Respective Strategies of Russia and the European Union* (Moscow/Helsinki: Carnegie Moscow Center/ Finnish Institute of International Affairs), pp. 8–30.

Kissinger, Henry and Lawrence Summers, co-chairs; Charles Kupchan, project director (2004), *Renewing the Atlantic Partnership: Report of an Independent Task Force* (New York: The Council on Foreign Relations).

Kohut, Andrew (2003), 'Anti-Americanism: Causes and Characteristics', Pew Research Center for the People and the Press, 10 December: *http://people-press. org/commentary/display.php3?AnalysisID=77.*

Kosals, Leonid (2001), 'Russia's Elite Attitudes to the NATO Enlargement: Sociological Analysis', Final Report, NATO–EAPC Research Fellowship, Moscow, *http://www.nato.int/acad/fellow/99–01/kosals.pdf.*

Kozyrev, Andrei (1993), 'The New Russia and the Atlantic Alliance', *NATO Review*, Vol. 41, No. 1, pp. 3–6.

Krastev, Ivan (2004), 'The Anti-American Century', *Journal of Democracy*, Vol. 15, No. 3, pp. 5–16.

Kriendler, John (2005), 'NATO Headquarters Transformation: Getting Ahead of the Power Curve', Conflict Studies Research Center, Special Series 05/29, June, pp. 1–30, *http://www.da.mod.uk/CSRC/Home.*

Kronvall, Olof and Magnus Petersson (2005), *Svensk säkerhetspolitik i supermakternas skugga 1945–1991* [Swedish Security Policy in the Shadow of the Superpowers 1945–1991] (Stockholm: Santérus).

Kupchan, Charles A. (2002), 'The End of the West', *Atlantic Monthly*, Vol. 290, No. 4 (November), pp. 42–5.

Kurtz, Stanley (2003), 'Democratic Imperialism: A Blueprint', *Policy Review*, No. 118, April–May, *http://www.policyreview.org/apr03/.*

Lamers, Karl and Wolfgang Schäuble (1994), 'Reflections on European Policy', in Brent Nelsen and Alexander Stubb (eds), *The European Union: Readings on the Theory and Practice of European Integration* (London: Palgrave Macmillan, 3rd edn). Original: 'Überlegungen zur europäischen Politik', *http://www.wolfgang- schaeuble.de/positionspapiere/schaeublelamers94.pdf.*

Lang, Kai-Olaf (2004), 'Störenfriede oder Ideengeber? Die Neuen in der GASP' [Troublemakers or Sources of Ideas? The New Members and CFSP], *Osteuropa*, Vol. 54, No. 5–6, pp. 443–58.

Layne, Christopher (1993), 'The Unipolar Illusion: Why New Great Powers Will Rise', *International Security*, Vol. 17, No. 4 (Spring), pp. 5–51.

Layne, Christopher (2003), 'America as European Hegemon', *National Interest*, No. 72, Summer, pp. 17–30.

Leffler, Melvyn (2005), '9/11 and American Foreign Policy', *Diplomatic History*, Vol. 29, No. 3 (June), pp. 395–413.

Light, Margot (1996), 'Foreign Policy Thinking', in Neil Malcolm, Alex Pravda, Roy Allison and Margot Light, *Internal Factors in Russian Foreign Policy* (Oxford: Oxford University Press/Royal Institute of International Affairs), pp. 33–100.

Linden, Ronald H. (2004), 'Twin Peaks: Romania and Bulgaria Between the EU and the United States', *Problems of Post-Communism*, Vol. 51, No. 5 (September–October), pp. 45–55.

Lindley-French, Julian (2002), 'In the Shade of Locarno? Why European Defence is Failing', *International Affairs*, Vol. 78, No. 4, pp. 789–811.

Lipponen, Paavo (2003), Speech at the Finnish Institute of International Affairs, Helsinki, 10 December, *http://www.paavolipponen.org/cgi–bin/puheet.php?key=65.*

Ludlow, Peter (2002), 'EU–US Relations: For Better or for Worse', *EuroComments*, Briefing Note No. 4, 4 June.

Luif, Paul (2003), 'EU cohesion in the UN General Assembly', Occasional Paper No. 49, European Union Institute for Security Studies, Paris, *http://aei.pitt.edu/archive/00001613/01/occ49.pdf.*

Lundestad, Geir (1998), *'Empire' by Invitation: The United States and European Integration, 1945–1997* (Oxford: Oxford University Press).

Mahncke, Dieter (2001), 'Russia's Attitude to the European Security and Defence Policy', *European Foreign Affairs Review*, Vol. 6, No. 4, pp. 427–36.

Mahncke, Dieter, Wyn Rees and Wayne C. Thompson (2004), *Redefining Transatlantic Security Relations* (Manchester: Manchester University Press).

Markovits, Andrei (2004), 'European Anti-Americanisms (and Anti-Semitism): Ever Present Though Always Denied', Working Paper Series No. 108, Center for European Studies, Harvard University, *http://www.ces.fas.harvard.edu/publications/Markovits.pdf.*

Marshall Center (2005), 'The Baltic Region and South Caucasus: Strategies for Cooperation and Patterns of Reform', Conference Report, Vilnius, Lithuania, 8–10 February 2005, *http://www.marshallcenter.org/site–graphic/lang–en/page–pubs–conf–1/cat/xdocs/conf/conf–reports.htm.*

Mastny, Vojtech (2002), 'The New History of Cold War Alliances', *Journal of Cold War Studies*, Vol. 4, No. 2 (Spring 2002), pp. 55–84.

Matser, Willem (2001), 'Towards a New Strategic Partnership', *NATO Review*, Vol. 49, No. 4, pp. 19–21.

McCallum, John (2003), 'NATO in Afghanistan: A Litmus Test for the Alliance', *Canadian-American Strategic Review*, 3 December: *http://www.sfu.ca/casr/ft-mccallum3.htm.*

Mead, Walter Russell (2004), *Power, Terror, Peace and War: America's Grand Strategy in a World at Risk* (New York: Alfred A. Knopf).

Mearsheimer, John (1990), 'Back to the Future: Instability in Europe after the Cold War', *International Security*, Vol. 15, No. 1, pp. 5–56.

Meiers, Franz-Josef (2005), 'Germany's Defence Choices', *Survival*, Vol. 47, No. 1 (Spring), pp. 153–66.

Menon, Anand (2004), 'From Crisis to Catharsis: ESDP after Iraq', *International Affairs*, Vol. 80, No. 4, pp. 631–48.

Mertes, Michael (2004), 'Schein und Sein. Das Schlagwort vom deutschen Antiamerikanismus' [Appearance and Reality: The Slogan of German Anti-Americanism], *Internationale Politik*, Vol. 59, No. 2, pp. 78–84.

Metz, Steven (2003–4), 'Insurgency and Counter-Insurgency in Iraq', *Washington Quarterly*, Vol. 27, No. 1 (Winter), pp. 25–36.

Meyer, Christopher (2005), *DC Confidential* (London: Weidenfeld and Nicolson).

Michel, Leo G. (2003), 'NATO Decisionmaking: Au Revoir to the Consensus Rule?', *Strategic Forum*, No. 202, Institute for National Security Studies, National Defense University, Washington DC, August.

Michel, Leo (2005), 'Transatlantic Ricochet: How U.S. Reassessments Will (or Will Not) Transform Europe', *EuroFuture*, Autumn, pp. 12–17.

Mihalka, Michael (2005), 'Values and Interests: European Support for the Interventions in Afghanistan and Iraq', in Tom Lansford and Blagovest Tashev (eds), *Old Europe, New Europe and the US: Renegotiating Transatlantic Security in post 9/11 Era* (Aldershot: Ashgate), pp. 281–303.

Miller, John J. and Mark Molesky (2004), *The Oldest Enemy: A History of America's Disastrous Relationship with France* (New York: Doubleday).

Missiroli, Antonio (2003), 'EU Enlargement and CFSP/ESDP', *European Integration*, Vol. 25, No. 1, pp. 1–16.

Missiroli, Antonio (2004), 'CFSP and ESDP after Enlargement', Conference Memorandum, 14–15 May, *http://www.iss-eu.org/activ/content/rep04-07.pdf*.

Missiroli, Antonio (2004–5), 'Central Europe Between the EU and NATO', *Survival*, Vol. 46, No. 4 (Winter), pp. 121–36.

Moïsi, Dominique (2003), 'Reinventing the West', *Foreign Affairs*, Vol. 82, No. 6 (November–December), pp. 67–74.

Moravcsik, Andrew (2005), 'An Ocean Apart', *The American Prospect*, March, pp. 30–7.

Morgenthau, Hans (1948), *Politics Among Nations* (New York: Alfred Knopf).

Mowle, Thomas A. (2004), *Allies at Odds? The United States and the European Union* (New York: Palgrave Macmillan).

Müller-Braneck-Bocquet, Gisela (2002), 'The New CFSP and ESDP Decision-Making System of the European Union', *European Foreign Affairs Review*, Vol. 7, pp. 257–82.

Murray, Alasdair (2005), 'When the Dust Settles', *Centre for European Reform Bulletin*, Issue 42.

Natapoff, Sam (2004), 'A More Perfect Union?', *The American Prospect*, Vol. 15, No. 9 (September), *http://www.prospect.org/web/page.ww?section=rootandname=View PrintandarticleId=8341*.

Nelson, Dan (2003), 'Transatlantic Transmutations', *Washington Quarterly*, Vol. 25, No. 4 (July), pp. 51–67.

Neumann, Iver (1996), *Russia and Europe* (London: Routledge).

Neumann, Iver (1999), *Uses of the Other: 'The East' in European Identity Construction* (Minneapolis, MN: University of Minnesota Press).

Neumann, Iver B. and Henrikki Heikka (2005), 'Grand Strategy, Strategic Culture,

Practice: The Social Roots of Nordic Defence', *Cooperation and Conflict*, Vol. 40, No. 1, pp. 5–23.

Nikolaidis, Kalypso (2005), 'The Power of the Superpowerless', in Tod Lindberg (ed.), *Beyond Paradise and Power: Europe, America and the Future of a Troubled Partnership* (New York: Routledge), pp. 93–120.

Nilsson, Ann-Sofie (1991), *Den moraliska stormakten: En studie av socialdemokratins internationalla activism* [The Moral Great Power: A Study of Social Democratic International Activism] (Stockholm: Timbro).

9/11 Commission Report: Final Report of the National Commission on Terrorist Attacks upon the United States, 22 July 2004, *http://www.cbsnews.com/htdocs/pdf/fullreport911.pdf*.

Nolan, Mary (2004), 'Anti-Americanism in Germany', in Andrew Ross and Kristin Ross (eds), *Anti-Americanism* (New York: New York University Press), pp. 125–43.

Nye, Joseph (2000), 'The US and Europe: A Continental Drift', *International Affairs*, Vol. 76, No. 1, pp. 51–9.

Ojanen, Hanna, Gunilla Herolf and Rutger Lindahl (2000), *Non-Alignment and European Security Policy: Ambiguity at Work* (Helsinki: Finnish Institute of International Affairs).

Ojanen, Hanna (ed.) (2004), *Neutrality and Non-Alignment in Europe Today* (Helsinki: Finnish Institute of International Affairs).

O'Loughlin, John, Gearóid Ó Tuathail and Vladimir Kolossov (2004), 'A "Risky Westward Turn"? Putin's 9-11 Script and Ordinary Russians', *Europe–Asia Studies*, Vol. 56, No. 1, pp. 3–34.

Otte, Max with Jürgen Greve (2000), *A Rising Middle Power? German Foreign Policy in Transformation, 1989–1999* (New York: St Martin's Press).

Packer, George (2005), *The Assassins' Gate* (New York: Farrar, Straus and Giroux).

Papp, Daniel (2002), 'Conclusion: The United States and Europe in a Globalizing World', in Howard Hensel (ed.), *The United States and Europe: Policy Imperatives in a Globalizing World* (Aldershot: Ashgate), pp. 231–48.

Pei, Minxin (2003), 'The Paradoxes of American Nationalism', *Foreign Policy*, Issue 136, May, pp. 30–7.

Pew (2003), 'Views of a Changing World 2003' (Washington, DC: Pew Research Center for the People and the Press).

Philippart, Eric and Pascaline Winand (2001), 'Ever Closer Partnership? Taking Stock of US–EU Relations', in Eric Philippart and Pascaline Winand (eds), *Ever Closer Partnership: Policy-Making in US–EU Relations* (Brussels: Lang), pp. 387–430.

Pond, Elizabeth (2004), *Friendly Fire: The Near-Death of the Transatlantic Alliance* (Washington, DC: Brookings Institution Press).

Primakov, Yevgeni (1999), *Vospominanyja: Gody v bol'shoi politike [Recollections: Years in Great Politics]* (Moscow: Sovershenno Sekretno).

Putin, Vladimir (2005), 'Speech at the meeting of the Security Council', Moscow, 28 January, available at *http://www.ln.mid.ru/brp_4.nsf/e78a48070f128a7b43256999005 bcbb3/854cb2ebb38d7704c3256f970049179f?OpenDocument* (2 February 2005).

Rabkin, Jeremy (2004), *The Case for Sovereignty: Why the World Should Welcome American Independence* (Washington, DC: AEI Press).

Radu, Michael (2003), 'Old Europe vs. New', Foreign Policy Research Institute, e-notes, 12 March.

Record, Jeffrey (2003), 'Bounding the Global War on Terrorism', Strategic Studies Institute, the US Army War College, Carlisle, PA, December, *http://www. carlisle.army.mil/ssi/pdffiles/00200.pdf.*

Redwood, John (2001), *Stars and Strife: The Coming Conflicts between the USA and the European Union* (Basingstoke: Palgrave).

Regelsberger, Elfriede (2004), 'Are There Problems Arising from Enlargement and the Draft Treaty Leading to Paralysis instead of Synergy?', paper presented at the FORNET Meeting, Brussels, 23 April.

Revel, Jean-François (2003), *L'Obsession anti-americaine: Son fonctionnement, ses causes, ses inconséquences* (Paris: Plon).

Rhodes, Matthew (2004), 'Central Europe and Iraq: Balance, Bandwagon, or Bridge?', *Orbis*, Vol. 48, No. 3 (Summer), pp. 423–36.

Rice, Condoleezza (2000), 'Promoting the National Interest', *Foreign Affairs*, Vol. 79, No 1 (March), pp. 45–62.

Riddell, Peter (2003), *Hug Them Close: Blair, Clinton, Bush and the 'Special Relationship'* (London: Politico's).

Ries, Tomas (2002), 'The Atlantic Link – A View from Finland', in Bo Huldt, Sven Rudberg and Elisabeth Davidson (eds), *The Transatlantic Link. Strategic Yearbook 2002* (Stockholm: Swedish National Defence College).

Risse, Thomas (2002), 'The Atlantic Link – A View from Finland', in Bo Huldt, Sven Rudberg and Elisabeth Davidson (eds), *The Transatlantic Link. Strategic Yearbook 2002* (Stockholm: Swedish National Defence College).

Risse, Thomas (2004), 'Kontinuität durch Wandel: Eine neue deutsche Außenpolitik?' (Continuity Through Change: A New German Foreign Policy?), *Aus Politik und Zeitgeschichte*, B11, 8 March, pp. 24–31.

Robertson, George (2003), 'Time to Deliver', *The World Today*, Vol. 59, No. 6 (June), p. 12.

Robertson, George (2004), 'Transforming NATO to Meet the Challenges of the 21st Century', in Daniel S. Hamilton (ed.), *Transatlantic Transformation: Equipping NATO for the 21st Century* (Washington, DC: Center for Transatlantic Relations), pp. 25–36.

Rodman, Peter W. (1999), 'Drifting Apart? Trends in U.S.-European Relations' (Washington, DC: Nixon Center).

Rontoyanni, Clelia (2002), 'So Far, So Good? Russia and the ESDP', *International Affairs*, Vol. 78, No. 4, pp. 813–30.

Ross, Andrew and Kristin Ross (eds) (2004), *Anti-Americanism* (New York: New York University Press).

Rubin, James P. (2003), 'Stumbling into War', *Foreign Affairs*, Vol. 82, No. 5 (September–October), pp. 46–67.

Rudberg, Sven, Stefan Ring and Tommy Jeppsson (2002), 'The Transatlantic Link: Relations Between the United States and Sweden', in Bo Huldt, Sven Rudberg and Elisabeth Davidson (eds), *The Transatlantic Link. Strategic Yearbook 2002* (Stockholm: Swedish National Defence College).

Rudolf, Peter (2005), 'The Myth of the "German Way": German Foreign Policy and Transatlantic Relations', *Survival*, Vol. 47, No. 1 (Spring), pp. 133–52.

Rumsfeld, Donald H. H. (2002), 'Transforming the Military', *Foreign Affairs*, Vol. 81, No 3, pp. 20–32.

Rumsfeld, Donald (2003), 'Address to 10th Anniversary Celebration', George C. Marshall European Center for Security Studies, Garmisch-Partenkirchen, Germany, 11 June.

Schmitt, Carl (1996), *Der Begriff der Politischen* [The Concept of the Political] (Berlin: Duncker and Humbolt [1932]).

Schröder, Gerhard (1999), 'Außenpolitische Verantwortung Deutschlands in der Welt' [Germany's Foreign Policy Responsibility in the World], *Internationale Politik*, Vol. 54, No. 10, pp. 67–72.

Schwarz, Hans-Peter (2005), 'For German National Interest: It's High Time to Restore Our Lost Foreign-policy Compass', *Internationale Politik* (Transatlantic Edition), Vol. 1, Issue 1, pp. 89–93.

Schwok, René (2001), 'Drifting Apart? Dissociative and Associative Approaches', in Eric Philippart and Pascaline Winand (eds), *Ever Closer Partnership: Policy-Making in US–EU Relations* (Brussels: Lang, 2001), pp. 363–85.

Šedivý, Jiří (2005), 'Unprepared? Germany in a Globalizing World', conference organized on the occasion of the 50th anniversary of the German Council on Foreign Relations, Berlin, 11–12 March (unpublished conference paper).

Šedivý, Jiří and Marcin Zaborowski (2004), 'Old Europe, New Europe and Trans-atlantic Relations', *European Security*, Vol. 13, No. 3, pp. 187–213.

Select Committee on Intelligence, United States Senate (2004), 'Report on the U.S. Intelligence Community's Pre-war Intelligence Assessments on Iraq', 7 July, *http://intelligence.senate.gov/iraqreport2.pdf*.

Sergounin, Alexander (1997), 'Russian Domestic Debate on NATO Enlargement: From Phobia to Damage Limitation', *European Security*, Vol. 6, No. 4, pp. 55–71.

Short, Claire (2004), 'Shoulder to Shoulder; Hug Them Close: Blair, Clinton, Bush and the "Special Relationship", Peter Riddell, Politico's', *The New Statesman*, *http://www.epolitix.com/EN/MPWebsites/Clare+Short/2917964e–72c7–4cb1–8177–48cfd941f34f.htm*.

Simon, Jeff (2003), 'Prepared Statement for Committee on Foreign Relations, United States Senate, Hearing on NATO Enlargement', 3 April.

Skidelsky, Robert (2003), 'The American Contract', *Prospect*, July, pp. 30–35.

Smith, Julie (2005), 'A Missed Opportunity? New Labour's European Policy, 1997–2005', *International Affairs*, Vol. 81, No. 4, pp. 703–21.

Smith, Michael (2004), 'Between Two Worlds? The European Union, the United States and World Order', *International Politics*, Vol. 41, No. 1, pp. 95–117.

Smith, Michael E. (2004), 'Institutionalization, Policy Adaptation and European Foreign Policy Cooperation', *European Journal of International Relations*, Vol. 10, No. 1, pp. 95–136.

Spence, Jack and John C. Hulsman (2003), 'Restructuring America's European Base Structure for the New Era', *Heritage Foundation Reports*, 25 April, *http://www.heritage.org/Research/Europe/bg1648.cfm*.

Stent, Angela (2002), 'American Views on Russian Security Policy and EU-Russian Relations', prepared for the IISS–CEPS European Security Forum, Brussels, 14 January, *http://www.eusec.org/stent.htm*.

Szabo, Stephen (2004), *Parting Ways: The Crisis in German-American Relations* (Washington, DC: Brookings Institution Press).

Szamuely, Helen (2003), 'The Myth of a Single European View: Old Europe and New', The Bruges Group, comments, *http://www.brugesgroup.com/mediacentre/comment.live?article=145.*

Talbott, Strobe (2003), 'War in Iraq, Revolution in America', *International Affairs*, Vol. 79, No. 5, pp. 1037–43.

Tardy, Thierry (2006), '"Prevention" *versus* "Pre-emption": Where Does the EU Stand?', in Giovanna Bono (ed.), *European Foreign and Security Policy after September 2001 and the 'New War on Terror': Reconstructing Global Order?* (Brussels: Institute for European Studies, Vrije Universiteit Brussel, forthcoming).

Tewes, Henning (2002), *Germany, Civilian Power and the New Europe: Enlarging NATO and the European Union* (Basingstoke: Palgrave).

Trachtenberg, Marc (ed.) (2003), *Between Empire and Alliance: America and Europe During the Cold War* (Lanham, MD: Rowman and Littlefield).

Transatlantic Trends 2003 (Washington and Turin: German Marshall Fund and Compagnia di San Paolo, 2004), *http://www.transatlantictrends.org/.*

Triantaphyllou, Dmitrios (2002), 'The EU and Russia: A Security Partnership', seminar memo, Paris, European Union Institute for Security Studies, 25 March.

Urquhart, Brian (2005), 'Extreme Makeover', *The New York Review of Books*, Vol. 42, No. 3, (24 February), *http://www.nybooks.com/articles/17750.*

US NSS (2006), The US National Security Strategy, 16 March, *http://www.whitehouse.gov/nsc/nss/2006/.*

van Ham, Peter (2001), 'Security and Culture, or Why NATO Will Not Last', *Security Dialogue*, Vol. 32, No. 4, pp. 393–406.

Védrine, Hubert (2003), *Face à l'hyperpuissance: Textes et discours, 1995–2003* [Confronting the Hyperpower: Texts and Speeches, 1995–2003] (Paris: Fayard).

Wagar, Warren (1992), *A Short History of Future* (Chicago, IL: University of Chicago Press).

Wallace, William (2005), 'The Collapse of Britain's Foreign Policy', *International Affairs*, Vol. 81, No. 1, pp. 53–68.

Wallander, Celeste (2000), 'Institutional Assets and Adaptability: NATO after the Cold War', *International Organization*, Vol. 54, No. 4, pp. 705–35.

Walt, Stephen (1998–9), 'The Ties that Fray: Why Europe and America are Drifting Apart', *The National Interest*, No. 54, pp. 3–11.

Walt, Stephen (2004), 'Additional View', in Henry Kissinger and Lawrence Summers, co-chairs; Charles Kupchan, project director, *Renewing the Atlantic Partnership: Report of an Independent Task Force* (New York: The Council on Foreign Relations), pp. 29–30.

Waltz, Kenneth (1979), *Theory of International Politics* (Reading, MA: Addison-Wesley).

Waltz, Kenneth (1993), 'The Emerging Structure of International Politics', *International Security*, Vol. 18, No. 2, pp. 44–79.

Weidenfeld, Werner, Caio Koch-Weser, C. Fred Bergsten, Walther Stützle and John Hamre (eds) (2004), *From Alliance to Coalitions – The Future of Transatlantic Relations* (Gütersloh: Bertelsmann Foundation).

Wendt, Alexander (1999), *Social Theory of International Politics* (Cambridge: Cambridge University Press).

Welt, Cory (2005), 'Uzbekistan: The Risks and Responsibilities of Democracy Promotion', *PONARS Policy Memo 365*, June, *http://www.csis.org/ruseura/ponars/policymemos/pm_index.cfm*.

Williams, Michael (2005), 'What is the National Interest? The Neoconservative Challenge in IR Theory', *European Journal of International Relations*, Vol. 11, No. 3, pp. 307–37.

Williams, Paul (2004), 'Who's Making UK Foreign Policy?', *International Affairs*, Vol. 80, No. 5, pp. 909–29.

Wither, James (2005), '"Uniquely Close"?: The Anglo-American Special Security Relationship', George C. Marshall European Center for Security Studies, April (unpublished manuscript).

World Values Survey (2003), *http://www.worldvaluessurvey.org/*.

Wörner, Manfred (1990), 'A Common Europe – Partners in Stability', speech to Members of the Supreme Soviet of the USSR, 16 July, *http://www.nato.int/docu/speech/1990/s900716a_e.htm*.

Yost, David (1998), *NATO Transformed* (Washington, DC: United States Institute of Peace).

Zaborowski, Marcin and Kerry Longhurst (2003), 'America's Protégé in the East? The Emergence of Poland as a Regional Leader', *International Affairs*, Vol. 79, No. 5, pp. 1009–28.

Zevelev, Igor (2002), 'Russian and American National Identity, Foreign Policy, and Bilateral Relations', *International Politics*, Vol. 39, No. 4 (December), pp. 447–65.

Zhurkin, Valery (project leader) (2001), *Between The Past and the Future: Russia in the Transatlantic Context* (Moscow: Russian Academy of Sciences).

Zielonka, Jan (2004), 'Challenges of EU Enlargement', *Journal of Democracy*, Vol. 15, No. 1, pp. 22–35.

Zinni, Gen. Anthony (2004), 'Remarks at the Center for Defense Information Board of Directors Dinner', 12 May, *http://www.cdi.org/program/document.cfm?DocumentID=2208andfrom_page=../index.cfm*.

Zoellick, Robert B. (2001), 'A Republican Foreign Policy', *Foreign Affairs*, Vol. 79, No 1 (March), pp. 63–78.

Zwack, Peter B. (2004), 'A NATO–Russia Contingency Command', *Parameters*, Vol. 19, No. 1, pp. 89–103.

NEWS AGENCIES

Agence France Presse
Associated Press (AP)
Interfax News Agency
ITAR–TASS News Agency
Mediamax News Agency

Reuters
RIA Novosti
STA News Agency
States News Service
UPI

NEWSPAPERS

Aftonbladet
Argumenty i Fakty
Berlin Direkt
Die Bild-Zeitung
Boston Globe
Chicago Tribune
Christian Science Monitor
Dagens Nyheter
The Daily Telegraph
Diplomatichesky Vestnik
The Economist
The Financial Times
The Financial Times Deutschland
Fond Obshestvennoe Mnenie
Frankfurter Allgemeine Zeitung
Frankfurt/Main Frankfurter Allgemeine
Göteborgs-Posten
The Guardian
Handelsblatt
Helsinki Hufvudstadsbladet
Helsingin Sanomat
The Independent
International Herald Tribune
The Irish Independent
The Irish Times
Itogi
Kaleva
Krasnaya Zvezda
Los Angeles Times
Le Monde
Moscow Gudok
Moskovskiy Komsomolets
The New York Times
The New Yorker
Nezavisimaya Gazeta
Nezavisimoye Voyennoye Obozreniye
The Observer
Rossiiskaya Gazeta
Seura
Der Spiegel
Der Standard
Der Stern
Svenska Dagbladet
Sydsvenskan
Tageszeitung
US Department of Defense News Briefing
Wall Street Journal

Index

Chatham House Papers

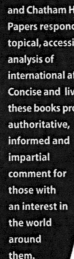

Global events move fast and Chatham House Papers respond with topical, accessible analysis of international affairs. Concise and lively, these books provide authoritative, informed and impartial comment for those with an interest in the world around them.

THE NEW ATLANTICIST
Poland's Foreign and Security Priorities

KERRY LONGHURST & MARCIN ZABOROWSKI
University of Birmingham; European Union Institute for Security Studies

This book is an authoritative account of Poland's emerging foreign and security policies and will contribute to an understanding of the foreign policy preferences of an enlarged EU.

Sept 2006 / 128 pages / 1-4051-2645-0 pb / 1-4051-2646-9 hb

EXIT THE DRAGON?
Privatization and State Control in China

Editors: STEPHEN GREEN & GUY S. LIU
Standard Chartered Bank, Shanghai; Brunel University

"A lucid and comprehensive guide to China's privatisation puzzle. This book is a must-read for anyone trying to understand the big patterns or the devilish details of state-owned enterprise reform in China."

Arthur Kroeber, Managing Editor, China Economic Quarterly

Drawing on the research of ten scholars from around the world, this volume evaluates China's privatization experience by investigating the efficiency and fairness of the sale process and the credibility of the government's ambition to create world-class state-owned conglomerates.

Feb 2005 / 256 pages / 1-4051-2643-4 pb / 1-4051-2644-2 hb

PUTIN'S RUSSIA AND THE ENLARGED EUROPE

ROY ALLISON, MARGOT LIGHT & STEPHEN WHITE
London School of Economics; London School of Economics; University of Glasgow

This authoritative work examines recent changes in Russia's relations with the European Union, NATO and other international actors, and explores the patterns of support for these various orientations among the Russian public.

Aug 2006 / 256 pages / 1-4051-2647-7 pb / 1-4051-2648-5 hb

BRITAIN AND THE MIDDLE EAST
The Contemporary Policy Agenda

ROSEMARY HOLLIS
Chatham House

This authoritative book examines contemporary British policy in the Middle East, focusing on Iraq, the Arab-Israeli conflict, the Barcelona Process and bridge-building to Washington as contrasting illustrations of the British approach.

Sept 2006 / 176 pages / 1-4051-0298-5 pb /1-4051-0297-7 hb

Also available in the series:

Vladimir Putin and the Evolution of Russian Foreign Policy
BOBO LO

Through the Paper Curtain
Insiders and Outsiders in the New Europe
Editors JULIE SMITH
& CHARLES JENKINS

European Migration Policies in Flux
Changing patterns of Inclusion and Exclusion
CHRISTINA BOSWELL

World Trade Governance and Developing Countries
The GATT/WTO Code Committee System
KOFI OTENG KUFUOR

Blackwell Publishing